D1135287

A MOTHER'S BETRAYAL

www.penguin.co.uk

A MOTHER'S BETRAYAL

Emma Hornby

BANTAM PRESS

TRANSWORLD PUBLISHERS
Penguin Random House, One Embassy Gardens,
8 Viaduct Gardens, London SW11 7BW
www.penguin.co.uk

Transworld is part of the Penguin Random House group of companies
whose addresses can be found at global.penguinrandomhouse.com

First published in Great Britain in 2022 by Bantam Press
an imprint of Transworld Publishers

A CIP catalogue record for this book
is available from the British Library.

ISBN 9781787634695

Typeset in 11.55/15.22pt ITC New Baskerville by Jouve (UK), Milton Keynes.
Printed and bound in Great Britain by Clays Ltd, Elcograf S.p.A.

The authorized representative in the EEA is Penguin Random House Ireland,
Morrison Chambers, 32 Nassau Street, Dublin D02 YH68.

Penguin Random House is committed to a sustainable future
for our business, our readers and our planet. This book is made
from Forest Stewardship Council® certified paper.

For Pam, a lovely lady much missed.
And my ABC, always x

I must be cruel only to be kind:
This bad begins and worse remains behind . . .

– Hamlet

Chapter 1

1867

BOBBING HER CHIN towards the blush-coloured teacup with its pretty gold rim that was standing in the centre of the table, a weary sigh fell from Mara's lips. 'That's it, Aggie. My last piece, so it is. Sure, I want to cry.'

Her friend and neighbour pursed her mouth in disgust. 'As would I, lass, in your position. Ale-sodden, good-for-nowt wastrels they are, the lot!'

Mara rested her cheek in her palm and heaved another long breath. To think that the gorgeous crockery set, a gift to her grandmother for faithful service from her wealthy employees at the turn of the century, had survived the passing years unscathed. Later, when it was handed down to Mara's mother, it had miraculously avoided becoming lost to the pawnshop when times were lean – and this they certainly had been, more often than not. Eventually, upon Mara herself inheriting it, and besides numerous additional upheavals in between, it had even endured the voyage across the choppy Irish Sea when she'd braved the crossing to England a decade before.

And for why? she asked of the Holy Mother in her mind. Only for it to be smashed to dust little by little at the shovel-like hands of her own menfolk? The truth made her chest ache with a familiar hopelessness and sorrow. Was nothing sacred – safe – beneath this roof?

'You ought to give him a good kicking, lass, whilst you have the opportunity,' Aggie suggested, motioning to the prone man sprawled across the bare flagstones before the fire snoring loud enough to raise the dead from their graves. 'Go on, Mara. Do it, girl. It'll make you feel better! Ram your clog right between his ribs – and to hell with Seamus O'Hara!'

Following the other woman's gaze and in spite of her upset, Mara felt a giggle bubble up in her throat at the mere prospect. 'Sure, he'd break my face for me were he to waken and catch me in the act. Mind you, I am tempted, so,' she added, smothering a snort with her hand.

'Right, well. I'll get revenge on him in your place, then. Watch this.' Mouth set purposefully, Aggie hitched up her mammoth bosom, rose from her chair and stalked across the floor.

Halting by Seamus, she lifted her foot – frozen with disbelief, Mara could only watch on in horror. Yet if she'd really expected her friend to deliver the promised kicking, she was soon proven wrong. Instead, Aggie positioned her feet either side of the man's head. With an impish grin stretching her features, she shot Mara a wink. Then she squatted over his face and released a blast of wind so long and so loud that it seemed to shake the house's very brickwork.

Mara was both disgusted and overcome with hilarity in

equal measures. Wiping away tears of mirth, she shook her head at the chuckling woman, who had now resumed her seat, and said, 'Mother of God, Aggie! Oh, if only he knew!'

'Huh. He don't fricken me.'

'You're a braver woman than I am, love, that's for sure.'

Mara's earlier remark regarding the punishment her husband would have doled out had been no joke – he would as well, she knew. Seamus had one holy terror of a temper on him when stone-cold sober – in the grip of drink, he was the devil himself and capable of anything.

His sons were little better.

Least of all the eldest O'Hara offspring, Conrad.

This last thought had her eyes creeping towards the door, and an involuntary shiver ran the length of her spine.

As though she possessed the power to see into Mara's mind, Aggie raised an eyebrow and asked, 'Where's the rest of them at, then?'

'Eamon and Eugene are away upstairs sleeping off the ale. And Conrad's out, glory be to God.'

'So what set off the ruckus this time?'

Mara let her shoulders rise and fall. 'Oh, the usual. The four of them arrived back from the Brewers Arms in foul moods, having lost more than one hand at their gambling. They were quarrelsome the minute they stepped through the door – I just knew there was going to be trouble. Their backbiting and blaming one another as to whose fault it was that they'd lost their money grew, and the next thing you know fists were flying. Seamus there bore the brunt of it. The lads set on him and knocked him down before parting ways, leaving me to clear up the damage they'd caused – as always.'

The other woman flicked her eyes around the small and dreary room that was completely devoid of beauty or comfort; besides the lone teacup, any cheap trinket or ornament or nice material the family might have managed to acquire over the years had been destroyed long ago during the regular skirmishes. She clicked her tongue. 'Well, it's glad I am you were harmed none. I thought it best to call in and check on thee once the commotion had died down.'

Mara nodded her gratitude. More than once over the years she'd become caught in the crossfire and it had been left to her neighbour to bathe better her wounds and soothe away her pain. 'Thank you, Aggie.'

'Eeh. I don't know how you put up with it, lass.'

'Sure, I've no choice in the matter, have I? They don't listen to me no matter how hard I might plead or beg – and they're only getting worse. The battles are a daily thing of late.'

'I know that well enough, don't I?'

Mara bit her lip. 'Aye, you must. These walls are as thin as dust, after all . . . I bet you rue the day we moved in next door to you. I am sorry, Aggie.'

'Now then, we'll have less of that,' Aggie chided softly in response, patting her friend's hand. 'To be honest, I've grown used to the noise by now,' she lied – it was clear she was merely trying to lessen Mara's contrition. 'Besides, 'tain't your doing, is it? Nay, it ain't your shame. It's these swines you're stuck with, Lord help you.'

Mara shot her husband another glance. If she screwed

up her eyes and concentrated very hard, she could almost see him as he used to be when they first met. Six foot and stocky, possessing a thatch of thick black hair and a smile on him that could stop your heartbeat in its tracks, he'd snared her attentions the moment she'd laid her sight on him. Hardly able to believe her fortune when it appeared his interest matched her own, she'd readily accepted his offer of walking her home from the cotton works each day at the end of her shift. And that, she knew, had been the biggest mistake of her life.

If only she could have been given a vision of what that one decision would lead to, she'd have kept her head down and told Seamus O'Hara to take a running jump into nearby Ashton Canal. Oh, she would. But well, you couldn't turn back the hands of time, could you? *More's the pity.*

'I thought I'd struck gold, you know, Aggie, in the beginning,' she murmured, her stare still on the sleeping man. 'I couldn't believe he wanted to pursue me; I reckoned I was the luckiest girl in all of Manchester.'

'Eh?' Her friend's face was a picture of incredulity. 'Are we talking about the same Seamus?'

'Oh, he was different back then. Or at least that's what he had me believe. I was employed at Wharf Street Mill at the time, aye, and he at the nearby dye works. We caught one another's eye one day on the walk home, and that was that. I'd only been in your country a handful of months – my cousin and me were just beginning to settle in, so we were. Then Seamus there crashed into my life and everything changed.'

'Cousin? I didn't know you had family here, lass. In the

few years we've dwelled side by side here at Heyrod Street, you've never afore made mention of it.'

No, you're right, I haven't, for it hurts too much. Mara's smile was tinged with pain. 'Our Rebecca. We ain't seen each other in such a long . . . a long time . . .' She pressed her fingers to lips now dangerously aquiver. 'Oh, but I miss her so.'

'What occurred, lass?'

'*He* did.' She threw Seamus yet another look. 'Rebecca had his card marked from the off, sensed somehow that he wasn't all he seemed. Me, being the *amadán* that I am, I wouldn't listen. Even when I discovered soon after that Seamus was widowed and had three young lads at home, sure, didn't I refuse to believe Rebecca's warning? She knew it was merely an unpaid skivvy and ma to his kids he was hunting for, that any woman would have done. But you see, I was smitten, and his flattery kept me hooked. She couldn't bear to stand by and watch me be made a fool of – she gave me an ultimatum: Seamus O'Hara or her.'

'And you chose him.'

Mara's voice was a whisper. 'I did.'

'Eeh, lass.'

'After the wedding, Rebecca and me grew further and further apart until, eventually, we lost touch altogether. By the time I came to realise that what she'd suspected had come true, it was too late. I was chained to him and, embarrassed by my own blindness and misjudgement, I didn't feel able to seek her out – her "I told you so" was the last thing I needed to hear.'

Seamus shifted position on a grunting snort, and the women paused in their conversation to glance across, Mara

6

holding her breath lest her husband had overheard her lamentations. Her cousin wasn't ever mentioned beneath this roof; he'd forbidden even so much as the utterance of her name long ago.

'So you don't even know where the lass is, then, or how she's faring?' asked Aggie when the man's snores had settled into a steady, rhythmic pattern once more.

'No. The last I knew she was still at the lodging house we stayed at when we first arrived in England. But that was such a long time ago – so many years have passed, she could be anywhere by now. As for how she is . . . Oh, Aggie, I hope she's good and well!'

'Ay, that's bloody rotten for you, lass. Couldn't you have a search about, see if you can't find owt out? It's worth a try, and you never know—'

'No, I couldn't,' Mara cut in, her head swinging from side to side in sheer horror at the idea. 'Sure, Seamus would never allow it.'

Aggie left to return to her own brood next door shortly afterwards, and with a sigh Mara rose to begin preparing the evening meal. Then, remembering the precious last link to her past, she paused and lifted the pink cup.

Cradling it tenderly, she flicked her eyes about the room in search of somewhere new that might afford this item at least a chance of survival. Only recently, after yet another drunken skirmish, she'd opted to secrete it and its matching saucer on the back shelf behind the teapot, confident they would be safe there, that the others wouldn't happen across them – the males of this household would never dream of lowering themselves in making a pot of tea, it being to their minds women's work, after all. Today's fight, however, had dashed her hopes to nothing.

Limbs had been flailing, and a flying clog – whose, she couldn't say, not that it mattered – had suddenly whizzed past her head and landed, *bang*, on the aforementioned shelf, knocking the teapot to the ground and sending her cup and saucer spinning. The cup had toppled on to its side and mercifully stayed there, but the saucer had followed the teapot on the southward journey to shatter into a dozen pieces.

She had to save this last item, *must*. But where? In the end, she shrugged her shoulders in defeat and placed the cup in her apron pocket. Incurring the men's wrath should they have to wait for their meal was something she'd rather not risk; she'd try to think of a better hiding place for the cup later.

Her attentions now on her usual duties, she crossed to the fire. Stepping over her husband without missing a beat, as though a slumbering body in the middle of the kitchen floor was the most natural thing in the world – which of course in this house, it oftentimes was – she set the large pan of water waiting nearby over the flames to heat.

Recent talk of her dear cousin, however, still dominated her thoughts and as she went about her task she did so with only half her mind on the here and now. Therefore, she failed to hear the door opening sometime later, didn't realise there was someone else present until she felt the dig to her ribs.

She turned with a gasp – then emitted another sharp breath to see Conrad standing in front of her.

They stared at one another in silence. At nineteen, he was tall and broad-shouldered with a good head of dark brown curls – the copy of his father in years gone by. But it was Conrad's eyes that set the men apart – and had the power to turn Mara's spine to wax. Two crystal jet pools that seemed to cut right through you like a blade; she gave an involuntary shudder. Even as a child he'd unnerved her with his wolf-like stare. There was something behind it, something she couldn't pin down but was there all the same. Like a predator almost, sizing up its prey. How she dreaded being in close proximity to this person she was meant to love as a son.

'Well?'

Snapped from her reverie by his low bark, her brows drew together in confusion. 'Well what?'

Conrad jerked his chin to the pan she was holding. 'Are you for dishing up or what?'

'Oh. Aye. Aye, soon. It shan't take more than a few minutes.'

He pulled out a chair at the table and sat down. Leaning back, thick arms folded, he regarded her for several minutes whilst she flitted about. Yet he made no attempt to engage her in further conversation, and she was only too willing to follow suit.

Small talk was a thing she and this stepson didn't indulge in, and never really had. Oh, she'd tried in the beginning; he couldn't deny her that much at least. But it had been like trying to extract blood from a stone – all her attempts at even acquaintanceship, let alone friendship, had fallen flat. The brooding nine-year-old that he'd been when she'd first joined the O'Hara home had refused point blank to give an inch and, over time, she'd given up trying to coax him into doing so.

The younger Eamon and Eugene, all snot and scabby knees, had proven marginally easier. In need and somewhat more desirous of a female presence in their lives, given perhaps their tenderer years, they had grudgingly come around to accepting her after some months. She'd done the best that an inexperienced seventeen-year-old knew to mother them – so far as they would allow her, at any rate. Not so with Conrad. He'd snubbed her tentative attempts at every turn.

Today, their relationship, such as it was, was wrought with an ever-increasing tension that left her chilled. Troubled, too. And aye, scared in her own home, it was true. The other lads, by no means what you might call innocents themselves, looked up to their older brother with a mix of awe and fear, as though he were some mode of God. Even big, tough fellow Seamus appeared wary these days of his unpredictable firstborn. And things were only getting worse . . .

'Bread.' Pulling Mara from her fretful musings as she placed his meal before him, Conrad nodded across to the small brown loaf and she hastened to fulfil his order. Without a word of thanks, not that she would have expected any, he tore off a chunk with his large hands, adding, 'And what does a bloke have to do to get a brew in this house?'

'Not break our only teapot,' she retorted, her earlier anger reigniting with the memory of her broken crockery. 'You'll just have to go thirsty, won't you? 'Tis your own fault, so. If you lot didn't keep coming home roaring drunk and creating merry hell—'

'Enough, woman.'

'And youse broke yet another piece of my beloved service,' she went on, too heartsore with grief, now, to hold back. 'Sure, I can't have nothing, can I? One measly cup, that's all you've left me with, thanks to your stupid, drink-addled antics—'

'I said *enough* – else I'll really give thee summat to whinge about,' he finished as an aside, his slit-like stare flashing malice as it fell to the bulge in her pocket and guessed what was there. 'Happen I should smash the last damn item, aye. Happen that would finally shut you up and we'd all get some perishing peace!'

His threat held her tongue. Meek now and hating herself for it, but too afraid to fight on, Mara's hand snaked to her throat. She swallowed hard. 'Please don't. *Buachaill go maith*,' she murmured, hoping her use of the endearing term from her motherland would halt his mood.

He gave her a withering look, then smirked and continued eating. Mara hid a sigh of relief that disaster had been averted and continued dishing out food for the others.

After crossing to the foot of the stairs to call down Eamon and Eugene, she busied herself with washing up a few pots so as not to have to look at Conrad. One part of her couldn't wait until he'd finished and was out of the house again, which was his usual routine; yet another part wished to God he wouldn't, for the outcome was inevitable. Causing mayhem in the town, drinking himself into a stupor and rolling home to waken her up with his bawdy singing – or worse, his temper. And of course, as was the norm now, he would rope his father and brothers into his activities . . . She was bone weary of it, she was really. She just prayed that, for one night at least, he'd curb his behaviour – and if he didn't that the other men wouldn't follow his lead.

Yawning and scratching their broad bare chests, the younger O'Hara lads appeared in the kitchen. Their eyes were bleary and their dark red hair, by coincidence the exact shade as Mara's own, was sticking up in all directions. Taking a seat either side of their brother, they mumbled acknowledgement for the meal and began to eat.

'You're welcome, lads, tuck in,' she responded with a half-smile to the barely passable expression of thanks – but it was better than nothing at all. 'Mind you, there'll be no tea to wash it down with. The pot got smashed.'

Eugene clicked his tongue. 'But I'm parched.'

'Tough. You shouldn't go around fighting, then, should you?'

For the first time, the males threw a glance towards their father, still sprawled out fast asleep on the flagstones across the room. They shared a grin.

'Daft owd bastard,' said Conrad, whilst his brothers nodded agreement. 'He deserved that thumping, any-road. Supped too much too soon, didn't he, and his pickled brain couldn't keep track of the game. We lost close to twelve shillings because of him.'

'Twelve . . . twelve shillings?' Mara was aghast. 'Mother of God, that's three weeks' rent! How will we manage?'

'Fret not, Ma.' Spearing a carrot, Eamon puffed out his chest confidently. 'There's another game planned tonight – Conrad set it up.'

Why wasn't she surprised? It was always Conrad's doing. The

12

clear instigator of the family, from him she'd have expected noth-
ing else.

'It's a good purse at stake,' Eamon added, 'and we're going to win it.'

'By hook – or by crook,' piped in Eugene with a wink at the double meaning, and the others released gurgles of laughter at his quip.

With a long sigh, Mara turned her back on them and returned to washing the dishes. Drinking to excess and fighting, gambling and conning and stealing ... Was there any low left to which this family wouldn't sink? She was so very tired of feeling worried and fearful, was brain-numbingly sick of it all. Not that they cared one iota for that or would ever be willing to change their ways. Just where had it all gone wrong? *More to the point, where would it end?*

When her stepsons had left home for the evening and she'd cleared the table, Mara eased herself into a chair. The soft ticking of the clock and her husband's crackly breaths were the only sounds, and she closed her eyes. In her mind, hazy shapes cleared slowly into familiar images and a small gasp left her. She saw the squat, one-roomed cottage of her childhood, her ma and da and half a dozen siblings – all buried beneath the Irish clay in eternal sleep long ago ... Tears burned behind her lids, and these she blinked away, along with the painful remembrance. How she missed it all and her sweet green isle.

She'd pined for Ireland for many months when first embarking on the monumental step to emigrate and, even now, despite her feet having been on English soil for many years, would occasionally recall home with a pang, knew that would never leave her whatever age she might reach. Of course, back then she'd had her cousin. Mara doubted she'd have coped else. Rebecca had made the bewildering transition bearable. Rebecca had *always* made everything seem conquerable. How she yearned for her now, more than ever before . . .

Seamus suddenly rolled on to his side and opened his eyes. He lay for a moment, beetle brows creased in puzzlement, before raising himself on an elbow. Catching sight of Mara, he asked, 'What's the time at?'

'Just gone six,' she told him.

'In the morn?'

'No, the evening.'

He stumbled up and stretched to his full height. Lifting his arms above his head, he yawned loudly. 'Where's the lads at?'

'Gone out.' She too rose and nodded to where his share of the food sat warming by the hearth. 'Will you eat now?'

'What is it?'

'Stew.'

'Aye, go on.'

She ladled the gravied mutton and root vegetables into a tin dish and after collecting a spoon set them in front of him with the last of the loaf. Returning to her chair, she watched him for several minutes as he ate before asking tentatively, 'You and the boys . . . couldn't you maybe take things a wee bit easier tonight, Seamus?'

'What d'you mean?'

'Well . . . The ale-glugging and other things.'

Though his frown had returned, he didn't look up. 'What other things?'

14

'Seamus, please, you *know* what—'

'And who the divil d'you think you are to think to dictate to me?'

The atmosphere thickened ominously, his bulbous drinker's nose glowing a deeper mauve, as it was wont to when he was close to losing his rag. She banked down a ragged breath. 'I – I'm sorry, Seamus, I didn't mean . . . I'm just weary of it, I am,' she blurted on a cry of desperation, her endurance spent. ''Tis every single day of late: tossing away money as if we're millionaires, bashing one another about, destroying the house . . . And that's only the stuff I'm aware of! God alone knows what else youse get up to when you leave through that door—'

'You shut your trap.' His tone was low with menace. 'Else the back of my hand shall do it for thee.'

'But husband—'

'I'm *warning* you.'

Silenced, Mara dipped her head subserviently, though inside she could have wept with crushing defeat. But had she expected him – any of them – to heed her pleas, really? Nevertheless, she'd had to at least try.

'Don't I keep you in luxury?' Seamus was saying now. 'Provide you with all you could need?'

Her gaze sweeping the space, she raised her eyebrows incredulously. Though she didn't dare speak them aloud, the words screamed through her head: Luxury? Just what part of this – any aspect of her existence for that matter – could possibly be classed as such? That it was neat and clean, thanks solely to her diligence and girlhood teachings, was about all that their dwelling had going for it. Had alcohol finally turned his brain entirely? Must have done!

15

'Ungrateful, aye, that's what you are.'

'Ungrateful?' Now, her tongue could not be held – she whispered her response on a harsh laugh. 'That you could have the gall to accuse me so . . . I've given up my *life* to you and your children, and for what? What have I ever got back in return? Disrespect and abuse – in all its forms – that's what!'

The slap to her cheek sent her spinning in her seat. Gasping, she righted herself and held a hand to the stinging spot, but the fire in her eyes couldn't be stemmed.

'I warned you, don't say I never. You had that coming,' he stated calmly before resuming his meal.

Mara glared at his bowed head in all-consuming hatred. *How I wish to God I'd never met you*, she told him wordlessly, her eyes and throat filling with tears. *You're nothing but a brute and a pig – and the same goes for those offspring of yours. One of these days, Seamus O'Hara, one of these days . . .*

'Now, I'm off out.' On a loud belch, her husband wiped food from his bushy beard with his sleeve and rose to his feet. He stood waiting whilst she dragged herself over to the nail in the wall to collect for him his rough jacket and cap, as was expected of her. 'And 'ere, I might be wanting of a play of this later, so you be sure to keep it warm for my return, eh?' he informed her as she made to turn, shooting out a hand to grab between her legs.

Standing passive – it was the best way, she'd learned this over the years, so as not to provoke his anger and make matters worse for herself – she held her breath and prayed he would leave her. Thankfully, her equanimity paid off. Seamus delivered a last painful squeeze and released her. The next moment, he was gone.

16

Through a blur of tears, Mara continued staring at the door long after he'd disappeared. In the solitude of her kitchen, she finally allowed her emotions free rein. Gripping the table's edge for support, she buried her face in her arms and wept bitterly.

'If this be life for evermore, I'd sooner meet death!' she cried in her anguish to the heavens; then, instantly ashamed, she shook her head. 'Oh, forgive me, dear Lord. I didn't mean it. I'm just miserable, so. I went to see Father Kelly for advice, you know, Lord,' she continued on a sniff, her gaze scouring the damp-mottled ceiling as though her saviour might by some miracle appear. 'Aye, some months past, it was. I'd reached my tether's end and I sought him out, desperate for a solution. I revealed to him everything, how my husband and his sons treated me, what home life was like. D'you know what he said? He said it was your will, Lord. He said I was to give thanks for all I did have and that I wasn't to question your design.

'Truth is, I'm struggling, Lord. Oh, I am. How could you want this for me – for anyone? A neighbour on this same road, she suffered a hateful marriage like mine, and one day she too had finally had enough. She upped sticks in the dead of night and fled back to her parents. When her brothers learned of what she'd been suffering, they visited her husband, and they thumped him black and blue. He leaves her alone now, and by all accounts she's happy and well these days, safe again in the bosom of her family.

'I know you don't condone such behaviour, that the wedding vows are meant to be followed for eternity, but Lord . . . can it be possible that maybe, just maybe, you

17

sometimes get it wrong? I only ask for enduring this path which you deem some of us must walk . . . Oh, it's so *hard!* I don't even have the option of leaving, do I – to go where and to who? I haven't a soul to run to, no.'

As the truth was given life, the familiar hopelessness once more settled around Mara's heart, leaving her numb. Pulling herself together, she scrubbed the tears from her cheeks and nodded.

There was no way out of this for her, none, so where was the point in any of it at all?

'Thank you for listening, Lord,' she murmured dully. 'Forgive me for speaking wicked thoughts. Please lend me strength to bear this life you've chosen for me and, in return, I'll do my best to accept it, I promise.'

But would she?

The question tapped inside her head accusingly, but she forced it away – along with the ready answer that had accompanied it.

She'd surely tested God's patience enough this night without provoking his wrath further.

It was the early hours of the morning when Seamus and his sons finally rolled in.

Dragged from her uneasy slumber by the crashing and banging and raucous laughter, Mara curled tighter into a ball and pulled the bedclothes over her head. *Leave me be, please* . . .

No such luck.

'Wench!' boomed her husband from the foot of the stairs.

'Go to hell,' she mouthed to the door.

'Oi! D'you hear me? Shift your idle arse and get down here!'

Knowing it was pointless feigning sleep – it wouldn't make the slightest difference; he'd simply seek her out and drag her to the kitchen by brute force – she banked down her misery and hastened to do his bidding.

'See here, look.'

Juddering to a halt in the centre of the room, Mara's gaze moved back to Eamon's grinning face before returning to the haul he had indicated with a sweep of his hand.

'Didn't I say we'd win, Ma?'

'I can't – can't believe . . .' She inched closer to the mound of shiny coins spilling across the table, eyes wide as saucers. 'Where . . . ? *How?*' she rasped.

'The game, you daft bitch,' Conrad shot across to her from where he sat sprawled in the fireside chair before his brother had a chance of responding. 'Remember?'

'I remember,' she whispered. A knot had formed in her guts and a sickly sensation was rising. This didn't bode well, it didn't, not for any of them.

'And you thought we couldn't do it. You did, didn't you? Admit it.'

'But, Conrad . . . Surely the fellows who lost against youse weren't happy? *Look* at it all; there's a fortune here!'

'Our biggest win yet – and nay, they weren't best pleased,' guffawed Eugene. 'Bloody raging would be closer to the mark, if you must know.'

'Saints preserve us . . .' This wouldn't end here. The rough and dangerous company her family chose to keep surely wouldn't take such a defeat lying down – particularly if the victory had been had dishonestly, as she highly suspected. There would be repercussions from this, she just knew it, Lord help her. 'What will we do?'

'Spend, spend, spend – that's what,' Seamus told her, grasping her around the waist with a harsh hand and bringing his mouth to her neck in a clammy, slobbering kiss, whilst his sons looked on with stupid grins.

Mara shrank from him, cheeks blazing. 'Husband, please—'

'It's bedtime for thee,' he cut in, pulling her nearer to fondle her full bust. Then, throwing a wink deep with meaning to the others, much to their amusement, he added, 'Aye, and suppertime for me . . .'

Her skin crawled with repulsion as he led her towards the stairs, though she did her utmost not to let it show. As she'd learned to her cost over the years, it would only prove worse for her if she did.

Mercifully, as usual the copulation was over in seconds – and Seamus was soon snoring beside her.

Careful so as not to disturb him, she shuffled as close to the edge of the bed away from him as she was able. Though she closed her eyes, she knew sleep wouldn't claim her, not now. The image of that money downstairs terrorising her mind wouldn't allow that.

Just what fresh troubles would befall them all following this? She shuddered to wonder.

Sighing, she settled down to wait out the night and begin the nightmare that was her existence all over again in the morning.

Chapter 2

MARA'S ONE FLICKERING beacon in her otherwise haphazard and worrisome world was her job.

It had become clear early on that what her husband was prepared to hand over to her for the housekeeping would never stretch far enough to support them, and she'd been forced to head out herself and attempt to scrape a living on Manchester's streets. Surprisingly, it had proven a blessing in disguise, and she hadn't looked back. Hawking flowers to mourners outside the local cemetery wouldn't have been everyone's cup of tea, she knew – toiling long hours in all weathers required a hardy constitution – but she enjoyed it. She loved the freedom that it afforded and meeting new people. More importantly, it got her out of the prison she called home for a precious time, and you couldn't put a price on that. Truth be told, she'd have done it for nothing.

Mornings were her favourite time of day; now, in spite of the previous night's occurrences, she went about her routine with a hum and a smile.

Seamus and the lads had left home at the break of dawn for Smithfield Market. That they were not in formal employ as traders or even porters didn't seem to pose a problem; still, they arrived back at the day's end with their pockets jingling with coins. How they earned their spoils, Mara could only surmise. Dealing in stolen goods was her guess, though she didn't trouble herself to probe too deeply. She'd been met in the past with snarls and warnings to 'keep her snout out' if she dared broach the subject and didn't much press the matter any more. Besides, to her mind, the least she knew about their nefarious activities the better.

Standing before the cracked mirror, she reached towards the mantel for the family's only comb, bent and missing numerous teeth and which put her in mind of a gummy old hag. Then gritting her own teeth against the discomfort to come – she'd been hair sore since childhood and hadn't grown out of it, a fact that Seamus and his sons took full advantage of when the mood to subjugate her struck – she teased out the tangles from her curls.

With each stroke, the thick russet mass bounced about her shoulders as if it had a life of its own and, as she did often, she drank in her image with an almost hungry desire, for it wasn't only herself she saw staring back from the mottled surface but Rebecca, too. Cousins they might have been, but you would have been forgiven for mistaking them as sisters – twins even, come to that. From the hair and the small, round face with its fine dusting of freckles to the dark green eyes, height and petite figure, they could easily have hailed from the selfsame womb. It was only their personalities in which they differed, the strong-willed Rebecca possessing a far more forthright manner than she.

22

And common sense. We differ in that regard, too, all right, Mara reminded herself with a familiar stab of regret. *Mavourneen, oh why didn't I heed your warning?*

Shaking the recriminations from her mind – where, after all, was the point in self-reproach? What was done was done – she scooped the locks into a tight bun and secured it with a length of twine.

There stood a widely held belief that all Irish people were ne'er-do-wells, feckless and dirty in habit, and this city was no exception. Immediately Mara opened her mouth she was at a disadvantage – not that she'd have falsified her accent even if she'd been able; she was fiercely proud of her origins and refused to pretend otherwise. Thus instead, not only due to an affronted determination to prove the critics wrong but also to give her job the best chance of success, she took pains with the one thing she both could and was resolute to uphold, and that was her image.

No one would choose to deal with someone of slovenly – or, horror of horrors, lousy – appearance, and she couldn't say that she blamed them. She therefore ensured that she was as tidy as she could make herself before setting out for work.

True, there was only so much a body could do without money aplenty. She wasn't always able to afford soap, and her clothes, to which forever clung a slight whiff of damp owing to the conditions of their dilapidated house that refused to budge however hard she scrubbed, were little better than rags. Nonetheless, they were *clean* rags. Her heavy brown cotton skirts, although more patches than original material, were vigorously shaken out daily and were stain free, and the muck of the slum was regularly scoured from her dark wooden clogs. No one could accuse her of not trying, at least.

A last check of her reflection and Mara nodded and went to collect her woollen shawl. This she donned loosely around her shoulders before lifting the large wicker basket from the floor by the door and leaving the house.

The grey streets swarmed with young and old alike. Men out of work lounged on the corners wearing disillusioned frowns, women chatted whilst enjoying a cup of tea by their front steps, and grubby urchins bounded hither and thither about their cobbled world, screeching in high jinks at their play. Her own footsteps adding to the chaotic chorus, Mara continued through the balmy, early July breeze on her walk to the outskirts of the city.

She much preferred to pick her blooms each morning rather than every few days to be stored somewhere cool and dark at home, as some flower-sellers chose to operate. You stood a better chance of selling more if your wares showed not a trace of wilting, she knew, and so the daily trek for fresh stock was vital. Not that she complained, far from it. This was her favourite aspect of the job.

Industry had swallowed up great swathes of the country over the past century, and Manchester was one of the worst affected areas of the lot. The grey of brick now replaced jade grasses as endless rows of identical, badly constructed dwellings, hastily thrown up to house the ever-increasing toiling masses, claimed the land. Add to this the towering cotton mills, factories, warehouses and manufacturing works which choked the skyline and whose chimneys vomited a

24

constant stream of smoke, cloaking everything in depressing gloom, and it was evident that 'advancement' had come at a hefty price.

The face of the landscape was changed for ever. Only place names such as Angel Meadow, Blossom Street and Sycamore Street remained as a reminder of the abundance in bygone times of gardens and fields, fruit trees and flowers.

It was a far cry from Mara's upbringing among the rich and enchanting views, fertile valleys, silver-topped hills and distant mountains, and it had taken her a long time to get accustomed to her bleak new world. An opportunity to escape the cramped and smoggy confines, therefore, was a welcome one, and she picked up her pace with familiar relish.

Open spaces were few and far between but there were still rare pockets of natural beauty as yet untouched by development tucked alongside the ugliness if you knew where to look, and it wasn't unusual for her to journey out miles to neighbouring areas in her search of flowering plants – Chorlton, Withington and Didsbury, to name but a few; she regularly trawled them all. Today was no different and, strolling along a rutted footpath shaded by a chain of fine willows sometime afterwards, she knew her efforts hadn't been in vain.

The main part of the city let off a terrible stink in the warm air of the summer months, but here on the flat, low fields and hilly rises, a clear, sweet fragrance of sun-brushed grass and newly opened blooms encompassed everything and was a balm to the senses. Mara breathed it all in hungrily. Alone out here, she felt free; tranquil, contented. She always endeavoured to make the most of this time, for reality would return all too soon and she'd be forced back to her cheerless, pewter-coloured existence, damn it. What she wouldn't give to remain in such a place as this for ever.

Folk were drawn to these rural settings during occasional holidays granted by their masters, but today, with the city away at its toil, it was empty of people. Mara cut along a stretch of tall grassland, passed several pleasant streams bordered by hedges of hawthorn, blackthorn and may, and made onwards for the ancient woods in the far distance.

In the ray-dappled shadows, the air alive with a mosaic of wildlife, she removed her footwear and revelled in the feel on her skin of the dead leaves carpeting the ground. Accustomed to country life, the Irish were blamed for bringing to foreign shores the habit of going barefoot – returning to her roots and the wonder of nature in moments like this, she could understand why. Could there possibly be a purer, more glorious sensation?

Her clogs and basket swinging loosely in her hands, she emerged a little later into an open field clothed in vibrant foliage and small blooms in a plethora of hues. Butter-shaded wildflowers of kingcup and long-stalked creeping tormentil vied with the white dazzle of star-shaped common chickweed and mouse-ear. There were even bright blue patches dotted here and there of four-lobed germander speedwell, one of her favourites. With a satisfied sigh, she hurried to gather her finds.

After collecting what she required, she sat cross-legged in the soft turf and took her time arranging the flowers

26

into pretty, colour-complementing piles. Once happy with her work, she bunched them with care into small, neat posies, which she secured with lengths of plaited twine from her basket. Sometimes, if she was really flush, she would head out to the market and splash out on a few pennies' worth of offcuts of silky ribbon, which her customers seemed to appreciate more. Nevertheless, she knew these offerings would sell well.

A warm rain began to fall as she was making her way back towards the city centre, but Mara didn't mind this; she was mightily pleased with today's efforts. Manchester's first municipal cemetery – the newly opened Philips Park – came into view and, after pausing to check that her skirts were free of grass and that no stray curls had escaped the knot at her nape, she nodded and set off once more to take up position by the iron gates.

As she'd suspected, her full basket was quick to grow light and within an hour she'd completely sold out. Smiling at the welcome sound of coins jingling in her pocket – the rent would be paid on time this week, at least – she turned in the direction of home.

'Good afternoon to ye, Mara!'

Halting to look over her shoulder, she shielded her eyes from the sunlight. Then, catching sight of the familiar figure, she grinned. 'Oh, hello, Willie.'

'By but it's a fine day, to be sure.'

''Tis,' she agreed, heading across to where he stood by the roadside with his small barrow.

William Keogh – Willie to his friends – was a short, squat, prematurely balding Irishman around her own age, and a hawker like herself. His and Mara's paths crossed daily whilst out selling their wares, and they had gradually got to know one another. The passage of the years had seen their acquaintance develop and, today, the two were firm friends. With his laughing eyes and easy manner, it was difficult not to take to him – Mara certainly hadn't had any trouble and her life was all the richer for knowing him.

'You've done well today?'

Seeing him glance to her basket, she nodded. 'I have, thank the Lord. And you, Willie?'

Now, it was his turn to follow Mara's gaze; he thrust a thumb towards the half-dozen bundles of kindling that remained on his barrow. 'Aye, can't complain.'

'And your wife and children?' she asked, as she did each day. From the way he spoke of them, it was evident that he was inordinately proud of the family he held dear to him, which warmed her heart to know. Not all men were bad to the bone; Willie here was proof of that. 'They're well?'

'Grand, so. How about youself, Mara?' he added after some moments, and his tone had softened. 'You're coping all right?'

She swallowed a sigh. Willie knew well enough her personal circumstances – it was impossible for him not to, given the cut lips and bruised cheeks she was frequently forced to sport. Not that she'd ever uttered the truth aloud: that she came by her injuries at the hands of the husband and stepsons, who led her a dog's life. However, Willie was no eejit – he'd guessed long ago how she suffered. Though of course it wasn't within his power to do anything, simply knowing she had him as an ally meant

28

the world to her. Just what a life void of him and Aggie Roper would be like, she shuddered to imagine.

'Oh, you know. Same old, same old,' she finally answered with a shrug. 'Actually . . . speaking of my lot, there was something I wanted to ask you.' Her hand travelled to her apron pocket and she flashed a hopeful smile. 'I wondered whether you might be able to help me.'

'Sure, if I can, Mara, I will. You know that.'

Lifting out her pink cup whence it had lain since yesterday, she held it aloft. ''Tis this, Willie. It made up part of a set belonging to my mother, and hers before her. Sure, isn't it the last link to my past and precious to me?' Tears were creeping in. She lowered her eyes with a sniff. ''Tis only a matter of time before it too gets destroyed. I did think to ask my neighbour Aggie to keep it for me, only she has a huddle of little ones who are into everything – sure, it'd come to an accidental end at her home, I worry. And so . . . so I was thinking . . .'

'You want me to hold it for you, Mara?' he finished for her with a smile.

'I do. There's no one else, you see. You wouldn't mind none?'

'None at all.'

Relief escaped her in a drawn-out breath. 'Oh, thank you, Willie. I truly appreciate it.'

He took the cup from her and eased it into the pocket of his tattered waistcoat. 'It'll be safe with me, Mara, have no fear.'

They parted ways soon after and, as she walked the remainder of the way home, Mara's heart was lighter than she'd known it to be in many a long year. It felt almost like a victory. *That's one in the eye to Seamus and the lads!* she crowed in her mind, and a fresh spark of strength lent her height; she entered her house feeling just a little taller than usual.

Yet this new-found confidence proved short-lived: it quickly melted at the scene she was met with.

Juddering to a halt on the threshold, she gawped around open-mouthed whilst her gladness of the day slowly fizzled and died.

The table and chairs were upturned and several of their legs were splinted and snapped. Tin pots and pans were strewn over the floor and twisted all out of shape as though they had been viciously stamped on. The thread-bare curtains that had hung at the small window had been yanked from the rail and torn to shreds. The havoc-wreakers had even gone so far as to destroy their scant foodstuffs, had trodden everything into the flagstones, and the milk jug was smashed in the hearth. And Holy Mother in heaven above, was that a globule of phlegm sitting atop the freshly baked loaf?

This was worse than anything she'd encountered yet, even by her family's standards; her heart dropped to her guts. Damn those O'Hara men!

After a last, hate-filled look around the carnage, Mara removed her shawl and hung it up. Then, gritting her teeth to hold at bay the ball of emotion clogging her throat, she rolled up her sleeves and got to work clearing up.

The best part of an hour, lots of elbow grease and much cursing beneath her breath later, she'd tackled the worst of the mess. The furniture, however, she was powerless to restore to its former state, battered as it was. She simply swept around the now-useless mounds of wood, then, inwardly seething, went to sit on the bottom stair to await the men's return.

Conrad was the first to enter after what seemed like hours – his brothers and father were not far behind. Rising slowly to her feet, Mara braced herself for the scene to come. Yet, unbelievably, the men didn't appear to remember the skirmish; at least, that is, they made no mention of what had taken place.

'What's to eat?' asked Eamon, dragging off his jacket, 'I'm fair clemmed.'

'What's to—' Mara was nonplussed. 'Sure, is that all you've got to say?'

It was then that, for the first time, one of them noticed the heap that was once their table and chairs – staggering on the spot, Seamus pointed a finger with a frown. 'What the divil have you gone and done that for?' he bellowed at her on an ale-laden hiccup.

'*Me?* 'Tis not of my making! Didn't I arrive back to find the house destroyed entirely? This is yours and the lads' doing, as per usual, Seamus O'Hara!'

'Eh? What are you clacking your gums about, you daft bloody bitch? We've only this second walked through yon door.'

It was genuine confusion now rather than drunken amnesia that clouded the face of every man – Mara shook her head. 'But . . . the place was tipped upside down. It *had* to have been youse.'

'McLoughlin and his mob . . .' Conrad's voice was a low growl. 'Them dirty bastards, I'll kill the lot!'

'McLoughlin? Who's McLough—'

'Shift your arse – move it!' he snapped suddenly, cutting her off, his face paling, and sent her careering into the wall as he barged past her towards the bedroom he shared with his brothers. 'I swear to bleedin' God . . . If they've found it . . . I'll slice them apart from cock to throat!'

Thumps and bangs as Conrad ransacked the room above dominated the kitchen for several moments as the rest of them stood blinking at the ceiling in charged silence. Finally, Mara tugged at her husband's sleeve.

'What did he mean, Seamus?' she whispered, at the same time dreading a response. 'Just what's going on?'

'The haul,' Eugene offered through the side of his mouth when his father remained stony quiet. 'Our big win at the game last night. It looks like this McLoughlin who we cheated has took his revenge.'

For pity's sake. She couldn't take much more of their antics – this life. 'You mean to say this fellow broke in and created the wreckage that was waiting for me? That a stranger was prowling around our home?' Thank God she'd been out! Who knew what this dangerous madman might have done to her had she been present!

'Aye. And Conrad shall open wide hell itself if that brass ain't where he left it. Let's just pray for all our sakes that it is.'

'Well?' asked Seamus with definite nervousness when, eventually, his eldest son appeared on the stairs, and Mara held her breath. 'Did they sniff the loot out, lad?'

Conrad glanced from one man to the other. Slowly, a grin spread across his face. He shook his head. 'Nay. Nay, it's still here.'

The air rang with their whoops and halloos, but Mara didn't share in their delight; how could she? If this McLoughlin one was as determined as he appeared, who was to say he wouldn't be back with perhaps next time something more serious in mind?

'Right, you, take yourself along to the Brewers Arms and get us summat to drink – whisky, I reckon, aye,' Seamus demanded, sending her on her way to the street with a shove. 'We're celebrating. And oi, seeing as it don't look like you've gorra meal on t' go here, idle sow that you are, be sure to fetch us back some penny pies and pig trotters to go with it. Well, go on then, gormless. Skedaddle!'

Too wary of reprisal to argue the slur – not to mention bone-tired with it all – she turned without a word and left the house. She was midway to her destination when she realised her husband hadn't given her any money; with a sigh, she dipped into her day's earnings. The rent man would have to wait this week, after all. The thought made her stomach tighten in dread. They were a fortnight behind with payments as it was – please God that, this time, he wouldn't decide to put them out on the road.

'If you please, Seamus, I'll be needing a few shillings off you,' she forced herself to inform him later when the men had eaten and were sipping the spirit by the warmth of the fire, worry of eviction outweighing her fear of his temper. 'The rent's due and we're in arrears as it is.'

'And what have you done with the brass made from flogging your flowers?'

She waved an arm towards the door. 'Sure, almost all of what I fetched in today is now sitting in the beerhouse keeper's pocket. There's the question of furniture, too,

Seamus. What with everything we had having been smashed to smithereens . . . There's not even a dish or pot that hasn't been rendered useless – and we'll need a new milk jug, too. Then there's the curtains. And we haven't even replaced the teapot yet—'

'You think I'm made of money, do you?' he roared, thumping the mantel top with his fist.

Taking an automatic step back away from him, Mara licked her lips. 'No, 'course not. It's just . . . well, what are we meant to sit on, eat from, brew tea in?'

'All right, all bloody right.' With an exasperated grunt, her husband silenced her with a flap of his hand. 'That God-awful whining gob of yours – cuts right through my skull, it does,' he went on. However, though his words were tinged with anger, Mara saw it wasn't the rage he was capable of – he was weakening and, mercifully, she'd get her own way on this. 'Leave it with me – owt for a quiet life.'

'Thank you, Seamus,' she was quick to murmur before he could change his mind. 'I shan't spend a farthing more than I have to, will purchase what's needed just as cheap as I possibly can.'

'You'd better,' snarled Conrad.

Each head swivelled towards him, but he had eyes only for Mara. The whisky had turned his face florid, and his normally piercing eyes were glassy like those of a dead fish. Nonetheless, his clipped tone had held no drink slur – his warning had been crystal clear. Holding his stare, she nodded. Then:

'In fact,' he continued, 'I reckon I'll join you, just to be on t' safe side.'

34

Again, all heads moved in tandem, only now it was to glance at one another in surprise at this unexpected – and unusual – suggestion.

Their Conrad, accompany a woman on a shopping trip? None would ever have believed it, had they not just heard such a thing with their own two ears!

'Aye?' Mara eventually managed to say. 'You and me . . . You're sure, lad?'

'I said so, didn't I?'

'You did, but . . .' The prospect of spending any amount of time in his company alone threatened to fetch her out in a cold sweat. If there was any way at all to avoid it, she must try. 'You know, there is no need, really. I vowed that I shan't fritter a penny, and I meant it.' *She wouldn't dare.* 'You can trust me.'

'All the same . . .' He broke off to take another glug of whisky then nodded once. 'I've made my decision; take it or leave it.'

A quick look to Seamus, who wore an equally puzzled expression but nonetheless inclined his head to her that she should agree, and Mara shrugged. Conrad had spoken, after all – as usual, his word was final. If this be the only option, then she had to go along with it.

'Right so, Conrad. If you think it best—'

'Monday,' he interjected. 'Be ready to leave when I return at noon.'

She gave him her promise. Then, mumbling a good-night, she made for the stairs and bed.

Her husband demanded his conjugal rights that night, as she knew he would. Stumbling into the room some-time later, he shoved her awake and, following the routine of old, she shook the sleep fog from her brain and hauled herself up to kneel on the bare floorboards in front of him and yank off his boots. His rough fustian trousers and jacket followed, then he rolled into bed and, reluctantly, she joined him. This night, however, the copulation itself was far from her mind.

Lying passive, she stared at the ceiling with a small frown, her thoughts in disarray – and Conrad still dominated them when at some point Seamus climbed off her, his lust spent. Nor would her musings allow her peace throughout the remainder of the night.

Just what was the man's motive? For surely, he must have one – she was convinced of it now. But *what?* It didn't make sense.

By the time fatigue finally claimed her, she was still no closer to working out the mystery. She allowed sleep to carry her off with a resigned yet troubled sigh.

Time would soon tell.

Chapter 3

TRUE TO HIS word, on Monday Conrad arrived home at the appointed time.

He'd been out since early with the other men, and Mara had half expected him not to show after all. But he had, and now she must go through with his wishes.

Not a word passed between them as she checked her hair in the mirror, which had miraculously survived the recent onslaught, and donned her shawl, whilst he stood waiting with folded arms by the door. Then she made her way towards him and he turned and led the way into the street.

'There's a second-hand furniture shop on Rochdale Road – Deakin's, it's called – and their prices seem all right,' she remarked as they headed into Great Ancoats Street. 'From what I've seen of the pieces they have on display outside when passing on the hunt for my flowers, it all looks like good quality, too.' And at Conrad's shrug: 'Come on then, this way.'

The place was teeming with those out looking for a bargain, but Conrad's elbows made short work of them; rubbing sore spots and shooting the newcomer black frowns, the crowd parted to let him pass. Scurrying close behind him, Mara made a beeline for the opposite end of the long room and the items she'd spied from the doorway.

'Sure, this seems sound enough,' she said, running a hand along the scuffed surface of a dark wood table complete with matching chairs. The legs were pitted with dents and two of the chairs were a bit rickety, but that mattered not – the asking price was reasonable and the furniture overall was sturdy enough. 'It's a hardy set; there's a few good years of life in it yet. What d'you reckon?'

Conrad threw it a cursory glance and nodded. Then, scouring the space for the shop owner, he beckoned him across.

'Afternoon, sir.' The rotund, cherry-faced dealer shook Conrad's hand with a wide smile. 'All good-quality stuff here, as you can see. You've found summat that's took your interest, have you?' he asked.

'I have: the table and chairs. A fair figure you're wanting for them, an' all.'

The man puffed out his chest with pleasure. 'Oh aye, best prices around at Deakin's.'

'I can see that for myself, sure enough.'

'You're for buying the items, then, sir?'

'That I am. And 'ere, I'll be sure to recommend yon shop to all my friends and family, that I will . . .'

Conrad's praises petered out as the man, arm about his shoulders, led him to a nearby desk to complete the deal – Mara gazed after them in stunned stupor. Never in all the years she'd known her stepson had she witnessed him so amiable as he was now; she was utterly thrown. Her astonishment only intensified as she continued to watch the exchange.

The two were chattering away like old friends and, throughout, Conrad's face was stretched in an unfamiliar smile. At one point he even threw back his head and guffawed heartily at something the dealer said – a sound which Mara could count on one hand the number of times she'd heard it. *Conrad never laughs!* It was rare enough to drag a smile from him! What on earth had got into him?

With Conrad's particulars written down in a small book and the money having changed hands, the transaction was over; the men made their way back across to her. Mara gave her stepson a quizzical look, but he didn't seem to notice.

'Well, thank you kindly, Mr Deakin,' he gushed, shaking the man's hand yet again.

'And thank you, lad. As I said, the furniture will be delivered to your dwelling this evening. It's been a pleasure doing business with thee.'

'And you. Goodbye for now.'

On a last smile, they parted ways; in a daze, Mara followed Conrad back outside.

'That's that, then. Where next?'

'Where . . . ?' Coming to a halt by the roadside, she shook her head. 'Lad, are you feeling all right?'

'Me?' He blinked at her in unadulterated innocence. 'Aye, why?'

'I don't know, you just seem . . .' Cocking her head, she shrugged. 'Different.'

39

'Do I?'

'Aye, you do.'

Mirroring her action, he let his shoulders rise and fall. 'I don't know what you mean. Anyroad,' he added, turning about once more and setting off at a smart pace, 'come on. We'd best be making tracks if we're to get all we need before everywhere closes.'

Not knowing what else to say or do, Mara had no choice but to do as he bid her.

Their next stop differed only in the fact that his high mood and jocularity increased – even the sour-faced pawnbroker wasn't immune to his charm. Mara selected curtains in pale red and a rag rug, along with a milk jug, several mismatched dishes and, most importantly to her mind, a replacement teapot, cream in colour and with hardly any chips at all. Without being prompted the man offered to knock a few pence off the total amount, for which Conrad thanked him with much warmness and back-slapping – she was growing more confused by the minute.

'Here, what d'you think to this?' Conrad asked her suddenly as they were leaving the shop. He reached for something on a broad shelf and held it aloft. 'Pretty, eh?'

Running her eyes over the terracotta vase engraved with birds in flight, she nodded. 'Oh aye. 'Tis grand, so it is.'

'Well . . .' Conrad hesitated for a brief moment; then, to Mara's astonishment: 'Go on, you can have it if you want.'

'Eh?'

'Aye.'

40

'But why?'

He shuffled on the spot for a few seconds as though trying to find the right words, then raised his stare to meet hers. 'Why not? Can't a fella treat his ma, now, nay? A crime, is it?'

Ma. Never before had he referred to her as so. Despite everything, tears pricked behind her eyes. All that had passed between them, and yet now . . . Whatever the reason for the sudden change of heart, she couldn't say. But she was glad of it, she realised. And she intended to hold on to it for however long it lasted.

She could only gaze after him as he retraced his steps back towards the counter to pay. Once outside, however, she could hold back no longer; she drew him to a standstill. The gift had cost a whole shilling and he hadn't even wavered, had handed the silver coin over with nothing but a smile. Had all this today actually happened? He'd been so uncharacteristically nice that it was difficult to believe. 'Lad . . .'

'Aye?'

'I just wanted to . . . to say . . . Thank you. I've seen another side of you today – a better side, and . . . Well, I'm glad you insisted on coming,' she told him earnestly. He answered with a shrug and a grunt, and she smiled down at the lovely vase tucked safely beneath her arm. How long it would survive in her household was anyone's guess, but in this moment she was delighted all the same. 'I think we're done; shall we start heading back home?'

'Try out the new teapot, aye?' he asked, lifting the packages he held.

Her smile returning, she nodded. 'Aye, lad.'

She couldn't recall the last time she'd known such contentment.

That it was down to Conrad of all people . . . Eeh, but it was a strange old world at times!

'So?'

Busy spooning out potatoes into the new bowls, Mara paused to glance at her husband. 'So what, Seamus?'

'What occurred the day?'

Her mouth piqued at the corners in memory. 'We managed to get all we needed, and it was . . .'

'It was what?'

'Well, it was all right.'

'Aye?'

She nodded. Then: 'Sure, I'd go so far as to say enjoyable.'

The furniture had been delivered as promised; now, Seamus leaned back in the chair he'd claimed as his own – the sturdiest one, naturally – and, scratching his head, blew out air slowly. 'There were no bother then?'

'None at all. Conrad, he was pleasant.'

'Pleasant?' he echoed in surprise.

'Kind, in fact, you could say.'

'Kind?' Seamus burst out. 'To thee?'

She couldn't help but chuckle. 'Aye, I know! Fair flummoxed me, it did, too.'

'What's his game, then?'

'I thought that to begin with but I can't see now that there was one. He just . . . well, he looks to have had a change of heart, is all. It's been a long time in the coming, it's true, but I shan't knock it. It's a relief, to be honest, aye. Happen we might rub along a bit better from now on. What says you, husband?'

Though he didn't seem convinced by this, he kept his counsel nonetheless. He held out his hands. 'I'm buggered if I know. Anyroad, enough of the chatter; leave me be and let me eat in peace, won't you, for Christ's sake?'

This she did and went to return the remaining food to the fire to keep warm. The three lads were out and would be back who knew when; however, they would still expect a hot meal – and God help her if there wasn't one waiting for them when they did deem to show up, as she'd learned to her cost in the past.

She stood for a time afterwards and peered about in heady satisfaction. The new curtains were hung, the rag rug placed before the hearth, and the teapot stood proudly in the middle of the freshly scrubbed table. Centre stage, though, was the vase, sitting pride of place on the mantel. Bursts of golden shadow created by the fire's flames picked out the terracotta design, enhancing further its beauty, and Mara found that her lips were twitching yet again – she couldn't remember the last time she'd smiled so much as she had this day.

Her pink cup would look lovely alongside this latest addition. The thought drifted in, then disappeared just as fast. No – she wouldn't risk it. Best that it remained where it was in the safety of Willie Keogh's home, for now at least.

With the latest ruckus still in mind, she glanced to her husband. He'd finished eating and was filling his clay pipe with tobacco; satisfied that she wouldn't be disturbing him, she asked, 'Seamus? Is the feud with that McLoughlin fellow ongoing still?'

43

'How should I know?'

'Well, will he return here, do you think?'

'I can't predict what that mad bugger will do, can I?'

'But it's possible, aye?' she pressed quietly.

'Owt's possible, woman. Fret not, our Conrad shall sort the mob out. So no more talk of it, d'you hear?'

She would have liked to have spoken on it some more, to ask him how much worse things might get, prepare herself. It would do her no favours, though, now his temper had sparked, and so instead she nodded and let the matter drop. She would have her answers in time, no doubt, heaven help them.

'I'm off out.'

Her spirits rose once more at this announcement and she hurried to collect Seamus's outdoor wear. She'd been hoping all evening to have the house to herself so she could invite her neighbour in and show off her lovely new buys. Her family didn't much care for Aggie Roper, thought her nosey and too outspoken, which it had to be said she was – however, Mara liked her and refused to give up their friendship. Nonetheless, it was best that the woman didn't drop by when the men were present, they had both agreed long ago. It was Mara who would get it in the neck after all, and the added hassle just wasn't worth it.

When her husband had gone, she cleared the table and put a kettle of fresh water on the fire. Then she raised her arm and knocked three times on the chimney breast. The answering thump made her smile; crossing to the door, she lifted the latch in readiness and went to empty the dregs from the teapot.

'Evening, lass.'

'Evening, Aggie. Come on in.'

The woman halted in the centre of the kitchen to gaze around. Hands on ample hips, she released a low whistle. 'Eeh, what's all this then?'

'New furniture, Aggie. And here, see the gorgeous vase?' she said, sweeping the air with her arm. 'Sure, does it not brighten the place up no end?'

'That it does, lass. What's the story?'

Mara went on to explain what had transpired since they last met, adding, 'Didn't you hear the commotion at all? Sure, the destruction caused on Saturday must have created enough noise to waken Lucifer in his lair.'

'Nay, lass, I weren't in. I'd gone paying a visit to my brother, Big Red, up Salford way, and were gone for most of the day.'

'Och, that would explain it.'

'They smashed the room to bits, then, you say?'

'That they did. So, you see, we had nothing, needed all new. Whoever this fiend McLoughlin is, he did a right number on the place.'

'Ay, what a to-do – what next with them buggers of yourn, I wonder?'

She shuddered at the prospect. 'I dread to think. Look around you, though, love. Lo and behold, it was Conrad, of all people, who came through for me.'

'He coughed up for all this then, aye?'

'That's right.'

'Mind you, from what you've just told me, it's nowt less than he ought to have done,' her neighbour was quick to point out, her tone hardening once more. 'The house

45

wouldn't have got ransacked in t' first place but for him and his scheming ways, would it?'

Having turned her attentions to mashing the tea, Mara glanced up to nod. 'Sure, I know that right enough.'

'It's still a fair shock, though, him offering to do the decent thing, I will admit.'

Again, Mara bobbed her head in agreement. 'He did so with a bloomin' great smile on his face, too, so he did!'

'That one, smiling? Well!'

Mara couldn't contain a grin. 'I still can't believe it, neither.'

As with her husband shortly before, now it was Aggie's turn to crease up her face in scepticism. Unlike Seamus, however, the woman wasn't backwards in speaking her mind: 'I don't know . . . Sounds a bit iffy to me, all this.'

'I understand why you'd think it, but I can't see what Conrad would gain from his act today. He even . . .'

'He even what?'

'He called me Ma,' Mara murmured, and knew a quiet pride that she couldn't contain. 'Now, I know it ain't much after all that's passed between us, but oh . . . Sure, didn't it bring a tear to my eye? I couldn't help it. Could we have turned a corner at long last, do you reckon?'

'Lass . . .'

'I know that look, Aggie Roper. You think me an eejit, don't you?'

Features softening, her neighbour shook her head. 'Nay, nay. 'Course I don't. Only it's a bit out of the ordinary, him showing a kindness, wouldn't you say? Take this morning, for instance: there were no sign of this decent

46

side you've mentioned when *I* encountered him, that's for certain!'

'I don't understand. This morning . . . ?'

'Aye. I were unlucky enough to cross paths with him whilst out running an errand. A right stinking mood he had on him, an' all. Alls I did was ask what it was he was carrying, what he was about and where he was headed – just to be polite, you understand – and he nearly chewed my head off. Told me to mind my business he did, all snarly, like.'

Busying herself with the tea, Mara hid a smile. *Polite, my eye* . . . By, but her friend was a law unto herself at times, she was, really. It was little wonder she'd received the response she had; others would have undoubtedly taken the same stance as Conrad had they been on the receiving end of such interrogations. Of course, his rudeness was uncalled for, but still . . . There could be no denying that Aggie had a knack of rubbing folk up the wrong way with her nebbing, God love her.

'Nasty young viper, he's nowt else,' Aggie huffed on. 'Fair put the wind up me, he did – not that I let it show, of course. I'd not give him the satisfaction of that, nay.'

'Take no notice, love,' Mara soothed. 'You know how he can be when the mood strikes.' Then when part of Aggie's speech returned to her mind: 'You said he was carrying something?' she asked.

'That's right: a package of some sort wrapped in blue cloth. What it contained, mind, I can't tell thee, but he were acting somewhat shifty, if you ask me.'

Conrad hadn't had anything when he arrived to accompany her into town, she recalled. Nor had she seen something like that in the house. Whatever he'd been holding when he'd encountered Aggie must have come into his possession after he'd left here in the early morning, and he'd then deposited it somewhere else before returning home. But why, and what could it have been? Whatever it was, she knew instinctively it was illegal – had to be. Stolen goods, more likely than not, damn it. Why, *why*, must he act so? Couldn't he see how foolhardy these activities were, what trouble he was placing not only himself but the rest of them in by treading these dangerous paths? First McLoughlin, now this; just when would he ever learn?

''Ere, what about your lovely cup?' Aggie said suddenly, looking around, dragging Mara from her worries and back to the here and now. 'Did it survive, lass?'

'I think the men believe it to be smashed – if the thing has entered their minds at all, that is – but no, 'tis safe, thanks be to God. Willie Keogh's looking after it for me.'

'Him what flogs kindling around the streets by the cemetery?'

'The one and only. It will be all right under his care, he assured me of it.'

'He likes you.'

'Well, of course he does, and the feeling is mutual. That's why we're friends.'

'Nay, I mean he *likes* you likes you. Fancies you, you know,' her neighbour said slowly with an exaggerated wink.

'Tsk! No.'

'Oh aye, he does. I've seen the way he looks at thee.'

'Aggie, Willie has a wife – and a very happy marriage they enjoy, too, by all accounts. Besides . . .'

48

'Besides what, lass?'

'Even if circumstances were different,' she murmured, guilt creeping in to be speaking so of such a kind and thoughtful man, 'he's not . . . well, he's not really my cup of tea.'

Aggie erupted into a cackling fit. Slapping her thigh, she nodded. 'He's an ugly bugger, that's what you mean. Well, he is!' she persisted when a blushing Mara clicked her tongue. 'There's no denying it, lass. You'd not look at him twice, and that's the truth. By gum, even I'd have to think about it!' she finished on a snort.

Despite shaking her head, Mara could hold back no longer; she burst out laughing. 'Oh love, you're terrible, that's what.'

'Aye, but honest!'

'Ay no, we shouldn't say such things He's as fine natured as they come, you know, Aggie. He is, really. I've never known a kinder soul, in fact.'

Whatever response the other woman had, she never got to utter it. In the same second that she opened her mouth the door swung inwards suddenly and in walked Seamus.

To say Mara was perplexed was putting it mildly. 'Husband? Sure, you're soon back.'

It was as though he hadn't heard her. Without a word or glance to either of them, he crossed to his fireside chair and sat down to stare into space as though lost in a world all his own.

Shooting one another a look, Mara and Aggie frowned. 'I'll be away home.'

'All right, love,' Mara mouthed back to her friend.

'You just bang on t' wall should you need owt.'

'I will. See you tomorrow, Aggie.'

When her neighbour had slipped out Mara stood chewing her lip for several moments, unsure what to do. Then, taking a deep breath, she made her way across to Seamus.

Crouching down to his level, she spoke quietly. 'What is it? What's happened?'

Though he shook his head, he offered no reply. Clearly, it was something terrible; his shock was tangible. Never had Mara seen him in such a state as this. Her dread mounted.

'You're scaring me. Talk to me. What's wrong?'

'I . . . He . . .'

'Seamus?'

Finally, he lifted his eyes to meet hers. Terror and anguish screamed from their dark depths. 'McLoughlin and his mob. They've been done for murder.'

'Murder?'

'It occurred this afternoon during a house-breaking. They thought to rob some rich cotton baron of his money and silver, but it didn't go to plan. They'd believed him to be home alone, but he weren't. He fought back and got a bullet in his guts for his troubles.'

'Oh!'

'The menservants managed to apprehend them until the law arrived. It's the talk of the town.'

'I knew they were dangerous, but Mother of God . . . That they were capable of *that*? And to think I believed we'd got a raw deal having the kitchen turned over! It could have easily been us on the receiving end of their evil – any one of us! Thank the Lord they're locked away and we're safe from them!'

'Daft bloody woman. You don't know what you're talking about.' Seamus dropped his head in his hands.

'But this is a good thing, surely? Not for the poor fellow who's dead, obviously, but for us . . . We're free of it, now. Seamus?' she pressed when he answered with a ragged sigh. 'We are, ain't we?'

'I've not told thee the worst of it.'

His tone turned the blood in her veins to ice. 'What? What else?'

'Conrad supplied McLoughlin with the pistol used in the shooting.'

'Oh my . . .'

'The mob have squealed. My lad's been arrested in connection.'

Rising slowly to go and drop into the chair opposite her husband's, Mara shook her head. 'How do you know all this? You witnessed him being taken away?'

'Nay, not me: Eamon and Eugene. The three of them were enjoying a drink when the police stormed the place and carted Conrad off. The beerhouse keeper's just informed me of what went on.'

'Eamon and Eugene weren't able to tell you themselves?'

'They weren't there. They left shortly after their brother were took.'

'Well, where have they gone?'

'I don't know, do I? According to the keeper, they were raging mad and stalked from the premises without saying a word.'

She closed her eyes. 'Pray they didn't do anything foolish and make matters worse. Oh, but how could Conrad have been so downright stupid!' she exclaimed in the next breath. 'No, Seamus, I'll speak my mind,' she insisted when he shot her a warning look. 'Sure, that lad's been nothing but trouble of late. This, this is just the icing on the cake; what in the world possessed him?'

'You mind your tongue. He'd have had his reasons.'

'And you defend him still! Open your eyes, husband.'

Seamus half rose from his chair and stabbed a finger in her direction. 'One more word, woman, just one more word!'

'Oh my . . .' Sudden realisation making her mindless of his growing temper, she cut off his tirade with a gasp. 'The blue cloth. Of *course*.'

'Eh?' He blinked back at her in confusion. 'What you going on about?'

'Aggie Roper next door said she saw Conrad this morning. He carried a package of sorts wrapped in blue cloth – it was the pistol, had to have been. He must have been on his way to deliver it to McLoughlin.'

Her husband stretched to his full height with a low growl. 'That interfering owd . . . She'll keep her trap shut about this if she knows what's good for her!'

'She will, worry not,' Mara hastened to assure him. The last thing she wanted was for her friend to become embroiled in this mess. 'I'll talk with her.'

'You better had, for both your sakes. At the end of the day, it's Conrad's word against McLoughlin's. So far as we know, the law has no proof whatsoever that my lad was involved – and it best stay that way. Do you hear me? Well, do you?'

52

Glancing to his bunched fists, she nodded.

'If we all sit tight and say nowt, they'll have to let him go. Conrad will soon be back home.'

And that would be a good thing? her mind whispered of its own free will.

She lowered her head quickly lest her husband saw the workings of her thoughts reflected in her eyes, and kept her mouth clamped shut. For the answer to her inner question had sprung forth right away, and despite her best efforts to silence it, it would remain with her throughout the night:

Conrad out of the picture might just be the answer to all their prayers . . .

Chapter 4

SOMETIMES, IF MARA was lucky enough and up to the journey, a search along the meadows leading down to the River Irwell would throw up some beautiful spoils. Today they had done just that, and now the contents of her basket dazzled the senses with scent and colour. Corncockle, with their deep mauve petals bearing thin black lines, cuddled with blue violets and primroses in the carefully arranged posies, which she'd bulked up with sprigs of fern and the occasional daisy.

The cream of the collection, however, was the scarlet poppies sitting proudly atop the rest. She'd spotted the lone cluster growing behind a thatch of tall grass quite by chance on her way back, much to her delight, and had darted to collect them. They would fetch in an extra penny than the others for certain.

Now, as she waited patiently by the cemetery gates for the arrival of the first mourners, her thoughts inevitably drifted to home, and the calmness of the morning dissipated, leaving only fretfulness in its wake.

This afternoon, she must pay a visit to the stationhouse.

Not that she'd have chosen to, had the decision been

of her control; no, no. However, Seamus had insisted and so she couldn't refuse, knew better than to try.

Eamon and Eugene had eventually arrived home last night around midnight, blind drunk and half mad with fury. They revealed to their father that they had been scouring the town and McLoughlin's haunts in search of acquaintances, from whom they had hoped to garner more information, but without success. What they *had* managed to find out was that their brother was being held at the police station on nearby Livesey Street for questioning – a plan to get word about Conrad had been hatched right away. And as Mara had feared, it was decided she would be the one to implement it.

The men couldn't very well saunter into the station, couldn't risk that; on this they were steadfast. After all, they might be wanted themselves, for God alone knew what, for all they knew. Anything was possible, owing to their less than legal dealings of late. No. She instead must go in their place. It was the only way – and by Christ she would do it, they had insisted. Their murderous expressions had left no room for doubt as to what would happen should she attempt refusal.

The matter was still on her mind an hour later when Willie Keogh passed by on his usual route – grinning, he called across a cheery greeting and she could offer but a lacklustre response in return.

'Mara?' Frowning, he made his way across. 'Something's happened, so it has. Am I right?'

She attempted to brush off his concern, but without much success. 'It's nothing, really.'

'Aye, and your face says otherwise.'

The ghost of a smile stroked her lips. 'Sure, there's no hoodwinking you, Willie.'

'Tell me,' he urged.

Needing desperately to unburden herself, she made to do just that, but something stopped her. Perhaps it was shame at her family's behaviour, or it could have been reluctance to haul her friend into the mayhem of her life – either way, she kept her tongue. Instead, she said, 'It'll sort itself out with time, I'm sure. I would like to ask ye one thing, though, Willie, if I might?'

'Go ahead.'

'Would it . . .' She paused to glance away, colour now staining her cheeks. 'Would it be a sin to wish bad on someone you have a lawful duty to care about?'

'Bad? How so?'

'Like . . . Like wishing they could be sent away for a while to make life better for others around them.'

He scratched his bald pate and thought for a moment. 'It depends. Does this person practise good living?'

'No, he's a deviant.'

'He's strayed from the righteous path?'

'Oh, long ago.'

'And these people around him that you mentioned – does he treat them badly?'

'He does and, worse still, they've begun following his lead. Soon, they shall be just as rotten and all will be lost.'

Willie nodded. 'Then no, Mara. No, it wouldn't be a sin. 'Tis not wickedness but desperation to make things better for others that drives this, and that's different. Is this man you're speaking of your husband?' he added, giving her shoulder a comforting squeeze.

'No, not Seamus. Someone else. So, what you're say-ing,' she pressed on quietly, craving justification, 'is that were it possible for this harmful influence to . . . let's say be removed for a time – for the greater good, you understand – then it mightn't prove a bad thing?'

'Sure, I can't rightly answer that. Either way, whatever it is that's going on here . . . you'll be careful, Mara. Prom-ise me.'

'Aye, I will. I promise.'

'If you need me for anything, anything at all.'

Smiling, she touched his hand. 'I know. Thank you, Willie. You're a good friend.'

Before leaving her, he reached over and plucked a saucer-shaped bloom from one of the remaining nose-gays. Holding it up, he sniffed deeply. Then he lifted it towards her and tucked the stem behind her ear. 'Pretty, just like yourself,' he announced, making Mara chuckle, before walking away.

By the time she passed through the dull streets for home to drop off her basket, however, her laughter had long since deserted her. Her mind was a host of somer-saulting emotions. She could hardly believe she'd given life to her secret musing about Conrad. Entertaining the notion at all was enough, but to have uttered it aloud . . . Not that her concerns regarded Willie; he wouldn't repeat to a soul what she'd admitted to, she could be sure of that. No, it was the subject matter itself that left her torn in two – and yet at the same time strangely excited. Speak-ing it had made it a whole lot more real. *Possible*. Oh, what was to be done?

'Remember, you're to do whatever it takes to see him,

d'you hear?' her husband threatened a short time later as she was leaving for the dreaded visit. 'Lay it on thick, squeeze some tears out – use whatever bleedin' excuse you must, but do it and speak to the lad. We've *got* to know what's going on.'

'Aye,' she assured him, her insides all a-tumble. 'Sure, I'll do my best.'

'And take that daft poppy out of your hair; what d'you think you look like, anyroad?'

'Pretty,' she murmured on her way to the door. Seamus's scathing 'Huh! It'll take more than a soddin' flower to make thee that!' followed her out.

Mara's district of Ancoats, poverty stricken and crime-riddled as it was, ensured that the station was located at no great distance. Cutting through the backstreets, she shot the smoggy sky continual glances and prayed for strength. She reached the perimeter wall sooner than she would have liked; dragging her feet, she continued forward. Before she knew it, she found herself standing facing the dull and ugly facade.

The four rectangular windows along with the larger, arch-shaped window above the entranceway swam into one jumbled mass in front of her eyes, forcing her to pause and catch her breath. However, this did little to stem her nerves.

Finally, reasoning that the sooner she got this over with, the better, she pushed on and approached the double doors.

Minutes later, and much to her great dismay – she'd half hoped that the station officer would refuse her request; but no such luck, him being an amiable sort – she was being led down a corridor towards the holding cell containing Conrad.

He lifted his bowed head slowly as the door creaked open – and in that moment her earlier chat with Willie had guilt swooping in like an iced tide. Her stepson looked terrible.

'Mara?' Clear relief had swept over his face. He appeared genuinely pleased to see her.

'Hello, Conrad.'

'What's tha doing here?'

She waited until the officer had left them before explaining: 'Your da and the lads . . . they asked me to come. How are you?'

'How d'you think?'

Nodding, she laid a tentative hand on his shoulder. To her surprise, he made no attempt to shrug it off. 'The others, they've been that worried.'

'And you?' he asked on a gurgling laugh.

'Oh aye,' she hastened to say. 'And me.'

'Aye, all right then.'

She glanced away. Then, throwing a look in the direction of the corridor and satisfied she wouldn't be overheard, she whispered, 'The business with the pistol . . . why did you do it, Conrad?'

'It were meant as a peace token. Them buggers wouldn't have left me be, else. They wanted their brass back from that game we set up, come hell or high water – and my blood along with it. I'd caught wind of their plan to burgle that rich bloke and so I offered to get them a weapon to frighten the liver out of him; I reckoned he would back down right away when he found himself staring down a barrel. McLoughlin believed the same and agreed it were a sound idea.'

'Except that's not what panned out, is it? The poor fellow's dead.'

'Well, I know that now, don't I! Daft bloody bastard. He ought to have just kept his trap shut and handed over the spoils and none of this would have happened.'

'So McLoughlin and his gang, they were willing to let bygones be bygones once you'd got them the pistol?'

'Aye – at least that's what they said.'

'So just what have the police been asking? Your da said I was to find out as much as I'm able—'

'This ain't only about supplying them with the pistol, not any more,' he cut in. 'McLoughlin and the others, they're saying I went with them to the house where the murder took place.'

'What?'

'Aye. I just *knew* they'd try summat like this, the dogs.'

'But why?' she asked, shaking her head; it made no sense to her.

Conrad spread his hands wide. 'I reckon they think I tipped the police off – I didn't, but by God I wish I had, now! – and so they're intent on dragging me down along with them.'

'But the menservants,' she pressed on, 'surely they'll testify to you not being there?'

'Oh, McLoughlin thought of that. He's saying I accompanied them as their look-out and so managed to scarper afore the law arrived on t' scene. Acting as an accomplice and not actually firing the shot would likely fetch a lesser charge – a year or two, if that – but it's a charge all the same. The double-crossing scum would deem owt better than nowt.'

'But it's not true. How can it be? You were with me purchasing stuff for the home when the shooting occurred.' She took a deep breath, then: 'And I'll tell them so.' How could she not? It was the right thing to do, after all.

For someone facing such serious allegations, Conrad didn't appear in the slightest bit fazed. In fact, he seemed thoroughly cool and collected. 'That's right,' he said, and a smug grin lit his face, transforming it into one she knew so well. 'The store owners we bought from will tell the law the same thing, an' all. There's no trouble there, nay none. That pawnbroker especially will have remembered – that vase I bought from him will have stuck in his memory well enough. Aye, besides owt else, the way I played up to them all, they're not about to forget me in a hurry, are they?'

Mara's eyes widened slowly, and the recent tide of contrition at wishing him gone ebbed, leaving her cold with devastation. His demeanour yesterday, how kind he'd been to her and the way he'd made her feel . . . It had all been one big ruse. He'd made a great show of having himself noticed by the traders so as to secure himself an alibi should the need arise. He'd used them for his own gain. More to the point, he'd used her, too, in the cruellest way possible. She'd wanted to believe his words and actions to be genuine. She'd believed they might finally be bonding. When all the time . . .

'The police are for speaking to the furniture shop owner and pawnbroker later on today,' Conrad was saying now, though Mara barely heard the words, so consumed was she with the pain-filled truth. 'They'll tell them what

61

they need to hear, and that shall be that. McLoughlin will be proven to be the filthy liar that he is and the authorities will have to let me go. Simple.'

Not trusting herself to speak, she nodded and backed towards the door.

'You just make sure to tell the others I'm well and good and that I'll be home before they know it. You hear?'

'I hear,' she murmured. 'Goodbye, Conrad.'

It wasn't until she emerged into the cool air of the afternoon that she allowed herself to breathe properly – gasping, she leaned against the station wall for support. Tears stung behind her lids; she squeezed her eyes shut tightly and shook her head.

Regular bouts of shame had tormented her since her talk with her husband the night before. She'd found her mind torn between wanting Conrad out of the picture and disliking herself for the uncharitable thoughts. Just for a time, that's all she'd wanted him gone for, for all their sakes. It would offer him the chance of seeing the error of his ways, surely, and with any luck he'd return a reformed character. In the meantime, the rest of them would know some modicum of peace from his behaviour. Then his smiling face when handing her the lovely vase would push through accusingly, his easy tone and pleasant words and the fact he'd called her Ma making her cringe with self-reproach, and she'd be overcome with regret. But now . . .

Now, she knew only one emotion: pure and unadulterated disappointment. And a simmering build of anger wasn't far behind.

She arrived home to find Seamus, Eamon and Eugene waiting for her on tenterhooks. Reining in her feelings, she told them all she'd learned then left the furious trio to discuss the matter among themselves whilst she got started on preparing the evening meal.

Much too consumed with themselves to notice Mara's discombobulation, they suspected nothing. Therefore, when they headed out soon afterwards to drown their sorrows, it was without a single idea of what she had planned.

First, she flitted to the door that her family had just left through and peered both ways along the street. Then, satisfied they had gone, she returned to the kitchen, closing the door quietly behind her. Her palms grew clammy at the prospect of what she must do next, but she pushed herself on. It had to be done. Her mind was made up; nothing would dissuade her now.

Having mounted the stairs, Mara crept along the small landing. Outside the lads' bedroom, she paused to take some deep breaths. Then, heart hammering, she turned the doorknob and slipped inside.

The smell of stale socks and bed sweat that hit her full around the face was almost too much to bear; grimacing, she held a hand to her nose. At her stepsons' instruction, the room had been off limits to her for as long as she could remember, but by God she hadn't realised it might be as foul as this. Besides the stench, rubbish and empty beer bottles littered the floor and, as she picked her way through the debris, she was reminded not for the first time just what filthy hogs these O'Hara lot were, damn them.

'Where could it be . . . *Think*,' she said to herself, staring about through narrowed eyes.

A half-opened drawer in the small chest by the window

snared her attention; biting her lip, she made her way across to investigate. To her relief, when she pushed aside the few woollen garments inside and felt towards the back, just as she'd hoped, her fingers brushed cold metal – *thank you, Lord.* Scooping out the booty, she stuffed handfuls into her apron pocket. Then, making sure to put everything back as she'd found it, she turned on her heel and hurried back down to the kitchen.

Here, she scrutinised the clock tick-ticking quietly on the mantel, and her anxiety intensified.

She must be quick if she was to reach the shops before the police did.

Grabbing her shawl, she threw it around her shoulders and ran from the house.

The furniture store owner was busy serving when she arrived, red-faced and out of puff, having sprinted most of the way.

Hopping from foot to foot in her impatience to speak with him, Mara kept her gaze firmly locked on the large window and the people passing by outside. All the while, she repeated the silent plea: 'Don't let the law arrive just yet. Please, please . . .'

'Yes, madam.' Finally, after waving off his customer, the man turned to bestow upon Mara his beaming smile. 'Can I help you?'

'Sure, I do hope so, Mr Deakin sir.'

Seeing the tears now swimming in her eyes, his brow furrowed. He took her elbow and led her to a quiet corner, where he said to her kindly, 'All right, lass, don't take on so. Surely things can't be all that bad?'

'Oh, if only that were true!' Her frayed nerves were dangerously close to snapping, and she'd begun to tremble. 'I can't believe I'm here doing this . . . And yet, there's nothing else for it – sure, hasn't something just *got* to be done?'

'What, lass?' Curiosity and concern had clouded his features. 'What is it?'

'Do you remember me? I called in here yesterday with my stepson. Large fellow, dark curly hair. We bought from you a table and chairs . . .'

His eyes creased as he thought for a second, then his smile returned and he nodded. 'Ah. Aye, 'course I do now. A sound sort, he were. Promised to recommend my business to his friends. Am I right?'

'Well, yes and no.'

'Yes and—'

'Please, it's hard to explain , , , You see, sir, Conrad ain't the man he pretended to be to ye – by God he's not! That merry act, it was nothing but a circus show. He's wicked and . . . I need your help, sir. Please. Please help me.'

The man listened to her stuttered explanation of recent events, and the role he would now inadvertently play in it, in silence. She revealed all that had been happening of late – Conrad's influence over the household, his criminal activities and how it was affecting her family. When eventually she paused for air, he shook his head slowly, his face grave. 'Things are really so bad at home?'

'Oh, they are, sir. My stepson's antics, sure they make life a living nightmare.'

'So what is it that you reckon I can do?'

'Keep quiet about seeing him here yesterday,' she whispered, heart banging.

'Lie to the police, you mean?'

'I . . . I . . .' She looked away, her cheeks blazing with colour. Had she really expected this to work? Just what had she been thinking? 'Forgive me,' she began, turning to leave, 'I shouldn't have come—'

'Hold on, lass.' His tone had softened and the expression in his gaze now was one of pity. He glanced around as though to be sure no one would overhear, then: 'I didn't say I wouldn't, did I?' he murmured.

Mara was dumbstruck. 'You mean . . . You'll really help me, sir? I have money,' she added suddenly, remembering, and pulled back her pocket to show him the mound of coins as proof. 'If you really are willing . . .'

'God above, lass!' His face was one of horror. 'Put that lot away afore you're robbed blind,' he hissed. 'There's folk round here what would slit your throat for the sake of a few pennies, and that's the truth. Nay, 'tain't your brass what interests me.'

'Then what?' she forced herself to ask, her hand travelling up involuntarily to shield her chest. If she'd got him all wrong and he wasn't the kindly fellow he'd portrayed himself to be . . . If he thought to reward himself with something else she had to offer – well, he was very much mistaken. She'd never sink so low as to do *that*; never, no matter her desperation!

'I went through summat similar with my own son, if you must know,' he revealed on a sigh, slicing through her racing thoughts and making Mara instantly ashamed for her knee-jerk assumption.

'You did?'

'Aye. He too strayed in the wrong direction forra while – and tough love brought him back to us.'

'He went to prison? It reformed him?'

'Aye on both counts. It weren't nowt wrought by my hands, mind you. I didn't shop him in or the like. Nay, he were caught red-handed and so was dead to rights. Nonetheless, it did the trick. So aye, I understand what you're about here the day.'

Her throat had thickened. It felt so very reassuring to know someone understood – and that her plan wasn't an altogether monstrous one after all, that it just might have the power for change. 'I simply want things to get better at home, sir.'

'I know, I see it. And so . . . aye. All right, then. I'll do as you say.'

'Ye will?'

On another deep breath, he nodded. 'Should the law show up here asking if I remember seeing your stepson in my shop, I'll say nay.'

'Oh, thank you. *Thank* you.'

She headed back outside as though on cushioned feet – her relief was unequivocal. *It had been so easy.* She could barely believe it. God bless that man back there and others like him! There really were more decent folk surviving among the rotten in this world than she'd thought.

Whether she'd have such luck at her next port of call, however, remained to be seen.

Squaring her shoulders with a pretence of courage – it was the one thing she most certainly didn't feel – she set forth for the pawnbroker's.

'What?' Having reached the premises then plucking up the bravery to approach the door, Mara was stumped to find it locked. She tried again with the same results then stepped back into the road to peer up at the windows, at a loss what to do. This was the last thing she'd expected.

'The place is shut up, lass.'

Turning, Mara lifted a quizzical eyebrow at the elderly man who had called across to her. 'So I see. Please, have you any idea why?'

'I do that. The owner dropped down dead this morning.'

Her mouth fell open to form a perfect O. 'He . . . *Dead*?'

'Reet sudden, like, it were. I'd put my brass on it being his heart, aye.'

'Oh, thank God. Thank God!'

The man gazed at her as though she were mad, but Mara couldn't hold back; gasping and laughing, she lifted her face to the sky and closed her eyes.

''Ere, that's a bit much, lass, in't it? Owd Tom weren't the nicest bloke, I grant thee, but still.'

'I'm sorry.' Damping down her feelings, she shook her head apologetically. 'It's terrible news, really it is . . . Please, take no notice of me, I . . . I'm not feeling myself right now, that's all.'

Without giving him a chance to respond further, she mumbled a farewell. Then she picked up her skirts and, as though her clogs had spouted wings, set off back in the direction of Heyrod Street.

All was as it should be when Seamus, Eamon and Eugene returned home. The money was returned to the drawer, two cups of strong tea had sufficiently calmed Mara, and the evening meal sat ready and waiting to be dished up. Perfectly normal, just as she'd endeavoured. *They suspected nothing.*

'I can't fathom why the law ain't let the lad go yet. Surely they've spoke to them witnesses by now.'

Keeping her eyes fixed firmly on her food, Mara did her utmost not to react to her husband's questions.

'That lot, they don't know their arses from their elbows, do they?' offered Eamon scathingly.

'Aye, or they're likely making Conrad sweat in the hope he'll offer up a confession. Bastards, they are, the lot.'

A heavy silence followed until Seamus, his eyes creasing thoughtfully, prodded his spoon in Mara's direction: 'So you definitely never left the house again after returning from the station?' he barked.

'No, husband,' she lied with all the conviction that she could muster. 'I've been here all day.'

'You're sure? I'd have thought the police would have been round to see thee by now. They'll be wanting your word that Conrad was in your company when the murder occurred, won't they?'

'I suppose so.'

'Only they might have been earlier but missed thee if you were off galivanting—'

'They didn't,' she assured him soothingly. 'Fret not, I'll put them straight when they do decide to see me. Everything will work itself out, you'll see.'

Placated, Seamus resumed his meal with a grunt, and Mara hid a sigh of blessed relief. The matter was done with, for now at least.

Her husband was surely right, though, she pondered as she nibbled on a hunk of bread without tasting it. The law would want her version of events, wouldn't they? Was Seamus right? Had the police paid her a visit whilst she was away pleading allegiance from the furniture shop owner? It was possible – thank goodness she'd missed them, if so. The state she'd been in upon her return, she'd have never found the words to fool them and secure Conrad's fate.

At least now she had some time to prepare.

And get her story right she would. She'd come too far to ruin it all now.

Chapter 5

'WHAT WE SPOKE of . . . there's been some development, then, Mara?' asked Willie the following day after taking one look at her face.

His friendly concern and soft tone were like a balm to her tortured mind – her facade melted. It felt so good to lower her guard and discuss the matter openly. 'There has, and I'm the one to have made it happen. Oh, Willie, I'm so very afraid,' she whispered, clutching at his sleeve in desperation of his support. 'Sure, have I done the right thing?'

He let his shoulders rise and fall in an honest shrug. 'What's done is done, now. There's no use in berating yourself, so. I wish there was more I could do.'

'Oh no, you've done enough, honest you have,' she hastened to reassure him. 'Just having you to talk through my troubles with is worth its weight in gold.'

'I'll pray for ye, Mara, that everything turns out as you hope. It's all I can do.'

She nodded her thanks. Aggie had said much the same thing when Mara had hinted to her this morning what she'd done. Needing the money, she'd had to cut short the conversation to head off to collect her flowers, but had promised to fill her neighbour in properly this after-noon on all that had happened. She knew that at this very moment Aggie would be by her window awaiting her return, as giddy as a kitten – and who could blame her? News such as this didn't occur every day. Nor did folk turn against the O'Hara men and live to tell the tale. *May God help her.*

Sure enough: 'Eeh, come on in,' Aggie trilled a little later, shepherding Mara indoors with a smile of barely suppressed excitement. 'Tea's on t' go. Go on, lass, sit yourself down.'

Mara eased herself into a seat with a long and weary sigh. The stuffy kitchen was festooned with drying laundry, which hung from a wooden rack above the mantelpiece as well as over the backs of every available chair, Mara's included, and the whiff of damp wool and cotton clung to the air like a shroud. Shooting a glance across the room, she frowned. No fire burned in the grate; how her neigh-bour expected to get all this lot dried any time soon was anyone's guess.

'Ran out of coal, didn't I?' Aggie revealed, as though reading her friend's thoughts. 'I know the weather's mild out there and would do the job faster, but I daren't take the risk, what with the scores of thieving buggers running amok.'

'Here, love.' Mara extracted some coins from her apron pocket and pushed them across the table. 'You're all right, pay me back when you can,' she insisted when the woman made to protest. 'Sure, you can't go without a fire, can ye? Besides,' she added, turning her smile on to the cluster of children of varying ages dotted about the floor immersed in their games, her gaze coming to rest on the younger ones, 'won't the babies need their napkins?'

Aggie hooted with mirth. 'Fret not about that, lass. None of mine ever have the worry of going around with bare backsides – look.'

Watching as her friend whipped up her blouse without an ounce of shame, revealing a thick square of material sitting snuggly beneath each huge breast, Mara laughed out loud at her ingenuity. 'My God, Aggie!'

'Well, we've gorra do what we've gorra do! There's no warmer place than under these beauties, let me tell thee. These napkins will be bone dry in no time at all.'

'You're a tonic, you, love, you are really,' Mara told her with feeling.

It was true. She'd been beside herself on the walk here, despite Willie's reassurance, but Aggie had managed to soothe her anxiety somewhat as only she knew how. It had always been the same; her friend simply had a knack of bringing back her smile and making everything seem like it was going to be all right after all.

How Aggie – widowed and working herself into the ground, juggling several low cleaning jobs in order to support herself and her offspring – managed to remain so chirpy in the face of her own worries and woes with never a word of complaint was anyone's guess. But she did, and now Mara felt abashed. Dumping her troubles on to this fine woman had become a habit she hadn't realised she'd developed; always, it was Aggie she ran to whenever a problem arose, and her friend had never failed her yet, was unwavering with her sympathy and support. On impulse, Mara reached across the table and pressed her hand.

'How are ye for other things, Aggie, love? You're all right for food, are you?'

'Oh aye,' she answered with as much pragmatism as ever, patting Mara's hand in return. 'We'll make do for today, at least. I've a broth on t' go and, though it'll be a miracle to spot any meat in the thing, it's packed with veg nonetheless so will fill the kiddies up nicely. How about thee? You're all right for grub, are yer?'

'I am. Oh, Aggie, what would I do without you, hm?'

'What! By, the thought don't bear thinking about. It'd be a very sad and very boring life for you, lass, that's for certain!'

Chuckling along with her friend, Mara shook her head. 'Sure, you're right, though. And I do appreciate you always being here with a listening ear.'

At this, Aggie's face lit up. She nodded eagerly. 'That's right – and in this instant more than ever afore after what you said this morning. So, lass . . . Are you for telling me all what's occurred?'

'Aye . . .' Though not wishing to insult her friend, Mara knew Aggie's ways of old and so she had to be sure. 'I can trust you to keep it to yourself, can't I, love? The last thing I need is for this to be the talk of the district.'

'Cross my heart and hope to die,' the woman was quick to agree. 'Now come on, out with it, afore I burst with curiosity.'

Mindful of 'little pigs with big ears', as her ma used to refer to youngsters potentially eavesdropping nearby, Mara dropped her tone to a murmur. Yet if she'd expected

Aggie to offer understanding, she was in for a sharp shock. Her friend was horrified at her news.

'When you made mention earlier before hurrying off that tha had summat important to tell me involving Conrad, I never would have expected ...' She shook her head. 'Eeh, Mara, lass, what were you thinking?'

'I ... I wasn't, not really ... Sure, didn't I make my decision out of desperation?' Tears were threatening; she gripped the other woman's fingers tighter. 'Aggie, I thought you of all people would share my reasoning! Willie, *he* agrees—'

'Willie Keogh would swear that dogs have two heads and that the sky was green with orange spots if he thought that's what you wanted to hear, besotted with thee as he is!' Aggie cut in with a click of her tongue.

'But you've borne witness yourself many times how things had got at home, what I've suffered. I had no choice ... Please say I have your support on this!'

'I'm sorry, but I can't do it. Just what the divil will you do should Seamus and the lads discover your treachery – for that's what this is, Mara, when all's said and done.'

'Oh, Aggie!'

'These ain't my words, lass, but them which your menfolk are sure to spout,' her friend hastened to make clear.

'The men, they shan't learn of it.' Mara was adamant. 'I'll do all in my power to make sure of it.'

'Ay, come on now, don't take on so,' the older woman soothed, walking around the table to put an arm about Mara's shoulders as she began to weep quietly. ''Course you have my support, you dafty; you should know that without having to ask. I'm worried for thee is all that it is, lass.'

'But you do understand why I've been driven to do it, Aggie, don't you? Life with Conrad . . . it's unbearable!'

'I know, lass, I know. Look, if you reckon this is the answer to your problems, then I'll not speak another word against it. Just promise me, love, promise me you'll be careful. Them buggers of yourn ain't the sort of fellas to mess with – and that's nowt to what Conrad hisself shall do to thee should he ever find out.'

With a sniff and wipe of her nose, Mara nodded. Her heart was doing somersaults and her limbs felt like lumps of melted wax; she'd never known terror quite like it. Of course, she'd known the risks, what detection could mean, had thought of nothing else, however Aggie's words now had brought the dangers home to her far more and with sickening clarity – *just what was she going to do?*

'Mind you . . .'

'What is it, love?'

As though over the initial shock, Aggie wore now a wicked twinkle in her eye. It was evident she was beginning to revel in Conrad's imminent downfall. 'Oh, but to be a fly on t' wall when he learns his alibi has fell flat!' she crowed. 'By, I'd pay good brass were I able to see that smirk wiped off his phizzog!'

Nervous laughter leaked from Mara's mouth in a series of squeaks. 'Mother of God, he'll have a blue fit for certain . . . Oh, love, I'm that scared!'

Before Aggie could respond, movement from the street caught her attention. Hurrying across to the window, she peered outside. When she turned back to face Mara, her smile had vanished. She released a juddering sigh. 'It's the police. They're knocking at your house.'

'Oh Lord . . .'

'Now's your last chance to change your mind, lass. There'll be no going back after this.'

'Sure, I can't do that, Aggie. I can't. Conrad *has* to be made to change his ways!'

'Right, well. Then you must be calm. Deep breaths. You just try to be as convincing as tha can and the law shan't have reason to suspect otherwise.'

Nevertheless, despite her own insistence, blind panic was beginning to swamp Mara. She swung her head from side to side. 'No, I don't think I can do this, I don't, I—'

'You must if you're to make this work how you want it to. Go on, lass, get it over with. You've come this far.'

The short walk to her own front door felt like the longest of her life – how she made it without her knocking knees buckling beneath her was a sheer miracle. She nodded a greeting to the two men and in a voice that trembled with dread, murmured, 'Afternoon, Officers.'

'Mrs O'Hara?'

'Aye.'

'Mrs *Mara* O'Hara?'

''Tis me, so.'

'We wish to speak with you on a serious matter concerning your stepson.'

She inclined her head. Then, doing her best to control her shaking hands, she opened her door and led the way inside to her kitchen.

'Will ye sit down, sirs?'

They did, and Mara slid into a seat facing them. With

bated breath, she waited for them to begin speaking again. All the while but one thought beat a rhythm inside her head: *Please don't let me slip up and say something I shouldn't, please* . . .

Whether because she was a slum-dweller, Irish, or that he simply assumed her to be the lawless type in general, one of the officers looked to have taken an instant dislike to her – which naturally did nothing to soothe her nerves. He was staring at her with undisguised distaste; she squirmed under his scrutiny. Then he addressed her and her discomfort quickly turned to indignation.

'Don't I know you?' he asked, head cocked.

'No, sir. I don't think so.'

He continued peering at her through narrowed eyes for a moment; then his brow cleared suddenly. He nodded. 'Ah yes. I remember now. I cautioned you for whoring in the city a few nights past, didn't I?'

'What? Certainly not!'

'Come, now. I never forget a face.'

Her cheeks had bloomed with hot colour and her chin lifted defiantly. 'Well, you must, sir, for I've never plied *that* on those streets out there – nor anywhere else, for that matter! Sure, 'tis flowers I offer for sale in my job of work, nothing more.'

Though it was evident he didn't believe a word of it, he shrugged nonetheless and returned to the matter in hand. 'As I'm sure you're aware, an allegation has been brought against Mr Conrad O'Hara regarding his involvement in the extremely serious matter of murder on the afternoon of Monday the eighth day of July.'

Mara swallowed hard. 'Aye.'

'Mr O'Hara, however, vehemently denies any such claim and insists he was in your company purchasing furniture when the crime took place.'

This was it. What answer she gave now would affect them all for the rest of their lives. And would these men take her word as truth anyway? After all, though wholly unjust, they had surely formed a negative opinion of her character already, due to the earlier mistaken identity – would they deem her untrustworthy into the bargain? Again, she gulped down a ragged breath.

What would Rebecca do?

The sudden question – and just as speedy answer – flashed through her mind, and she nodded. Then her mouth was moving and she heard the words burst through the air between them:

'That is a lie. Conrad didn't accompany me. I never saw him all of that day.'

The room seemed to take a gasp; or perhaps the sound was the rushing of blood in her ears, Mara couldn't be sure. One thing she could be certain of, however, was the officers' expressions. They were extremely pleased with her response; it was plain to see.

'The furniture shop owner we have questioned already attests to the same thing, Mrs O'Hara.'

'Right, so.' It was the only reply she could lay her tongue to. Inside, she hid a thankful sigh – this knowledge had lent her strength. There could be no denying that she'd fretted whether Mr Deakin might renege on his promise after all, but no. *Thank God.*

'Well, we have everything we need for now and shan't take up any more of your time. Good day.'

In a state of shock, she rose with them from the table. That was it? Was she mistaken or had it really been that simple?

'So what happens now?' she forced herself to ask.

'Your stepson will be formally charged and held in custody to appear before the magistrate.

'Right, so.' Again, it was all she could manage. 'Well . . . goodbye.'

For a good twenty minutes after they had gone, Mara stood exactly where they had left her, staring into space. It was only a tapping on the window that brought her to her senses – and with it the sheer cold reality of what she had done. Before Aggie was over the threshold, Mara had fallen, heaving with sobs, into her arms.

'Hey now. Come on, come on. Sit thee down, lass. Going by the state of you, I guess I don't need to ask how it went?'

'Without a hitch.'

'Aye?' Her friend's eyes were wide as saucers.

'They swallowed every word.'

'Well, that's good, in't it? So then what—'

'Oh, Aggie. I don't know whether . . . Have I done the right thing?'

'You're a bit behind to be asking yourself that now, lass. What's done is done.'

'Sure, you're right of course, it's just . . .' Shaking her head, Mara dropped her face in her hands. 'I'm all confused.'

Leaving her to put the kettle on the heat for a calming cup of tea, Aggie kept up the conversation over her shoulder. 'A year or two from home shall do Conrad the power of good, lass, as you said. Anyroad, he don't deserve your guilt – just think of the things he's done to thee in the past, what he's put you through.

'Remember the time your husband's dog got loose and it went and got itself run over by the coal cart? That were Conrad's doing; but what happened? He said it were your fault, didn't he, that it was you what left the door open. Seamus didn't half give you a belting over that. And what about when Conrad threw all of his brothers' clothes on the fire in a fit of rage after a daft argument – and who got the blame? You did, aye. He claimed you'd left them too close to the flames when drying the laundry and that's why they went up in smoke. Eamon and Eugene made your life hell, took from you every penny you earned from selling your flowers for months. Then there was the time—'

'But this isn't about tit for tat, love,' Mara interjected with a shake of her head. 'I'm not doing this out of revenge; no, it's not about that, not at all. I couldn't be so petty. I just really do want the lad to see the error of his ways, that's all – for his sake as much as the rest of us. I pray a short stint away will make him grow up a bit, aye, for he's becoming worse by the day.'

'I'm sure it will. Mind you, it's thee I'm more concerned about.'

'I told you, Aggie, I've thought about what I'll say to Seamus and the lads. Sure, they'll not suspect a thing, God willing.'

The woman seemed less than convinced. 'You're sure on that?'

'I am. Haven't I gone over the story in my mind that I

plan to feed to them a thousand times? I wouldn't leave anything to chance – too much depends upon it.'

'Aye, your bloody life for one,' Aggie, blunt as ever, had no qualms in pointing out.

Mara let the subject drop. However, as she busied herself with the teapot, she found that her hands were trembling violently once more.

'The police called to speak with me today.'

Seamus and his sons, having just stepped foot inside, juddered to a halt. 'Aye?' they said in unison.

Wanting to get the ordeal over with as soon as possible, Mara had been unable to wait until the men were fed and settled, had blurted the words on a squeak. 'That's right. This afternoon.'

'And?' Dragging off his flat cap, her husband lowered himself into the chair facing her, his eyes boring into her own. 'You told them everything, the truth of things?'

Holy Mother, give me strength. 'Aye.'

After a moment or two of silence, the three of them released a simultaneous breath. Then they were laughing in relief and patting one another on the back, whilst Mara watched on with a gnawing of her lip.

'Well, that's it then, ain't it?' Eamon bobbed his head in a cocksure nod. 'They'll have to let Conrad go for certain.'

A grinning Eugene was quick to agree. 'How much are you betting he'll be sauntering through that door within the hour?'

'Right, you,' an ecstatic-looking Seamus piped in, giving Mara a harsh shove on the shoulder. He reached inside his trouser pocket and deposited a handful of coins on to the table. 'I want a slap-up meal preparing the night in honour of my lad's return. Well, go on then, jump to it, for Christ's sake. As our Eugene here's just pointed out: Conrad might be home any minute, so we've no time to waste. He's to have a welcome fit forra king.'

Mara offered no resistance. How could she, without evoking suspicion? She did as she'd been bid, quickly donning her shawl to hurry to the nearby shops for provisions, and upon her return got started on the feast she'd been instructed to cook, pointless as she knew the task to be. Conrad wouldn't get to sample a morsel of it, that much was evident to her at least, but for her sake it was best to let the men go on thinking there was a chance. How they would react when they learned the terrible truth was anyone's guess but, for now, their ignorance offered her a modicum of peace – the calm before the storm, for sure. She just prayed she'd have the fortitude to weather the raging maelstrom with the turning of the tide.

The hours trickled by and the men's enthusiasm began to wane, their patience with it. The thick pork chops, boiled potatoes, and carrots and turnips swimming in rich gravy that Mara had prepared went uneaten, and in the place of sustenance several bottles of brandy were brought out of the sideboard. Finally, as the time was nearing nine thirty, Seamus jumped to his feet, his face etched in white fury.

'He's not coming, is he?'

Crushed with shared disappointment, Eamon and Eugene lowered their heads – and Mara did likewise, her heart beginning to drum.

'Them dirty 'orrible bastards down at that station are up to summat, must be,' Seamus bellowed, pacing the room like a caged lion. 'What, though, that's what I'd like to know.'

Mara knew it was time. She must give life to the tale she'd concocted, and it had to be now. Sick with fright, she forced her voice to obey and murmured, 'Husband?'

'What?'

'I . . .'

'What, what is it?' Seamus had halted before her. Arms folded, he stared down at her frowningly. 'Well? Speak up, woman!'

'I . . . don't think . . .' The last word gurgled in her throat as he grasped her by the scruff of her neck and shook her hard, sending her teeth rattling. 'Husband, please! You're hurting me!'

'Tell me, then! Come on, out with it!'

'I don't think the police were interested in what I had to tell them,' she gabbled. 'They knew I told the truth, but from what I could see, they seemed not to want to hear it.'

Seamus released her and dropped into a chair. Rubbing at the stubble on his chin, his voice was a rasp. 'You mean to say . . . they want for Conrad to be guilty? They *want* him to go down for this, regardless?'

'I'm not sure, I . . . possibly, aye.'

'They're for dismissing your version of events?'

'I don't know, husband. Only they seemed not best pleased with my answers. It was like . . . like they had hoped I'd say he weren't with me that day at all.'

'They don't want him to have an alibi.' Eamon was dumbfounded with grief.

84

'They want to think he's lying, that he were with McLoughlin after all,' Eugene added on a croak.

Seamus was incensed. 'They'll not get away with this. They *can't*, I shan't let them!'

'But what will we do, Father? How can we do owt?'

'I don't know, Eamon, do I? But by gum, we've got to try. They ain't for pinning some false accusation on my lad, oh no, not whilst I have a breath left in me. I'll get our Conrad freed, you just see if I don't!'

For the remainder of the long and emotionally fraught night, Mara sat on, offering nods and murmurs in all the right places as the men thrashed out the matter by the light of the guttering candle.

Only when she felt able to escape to her bed did she allow the pent-up tears to fall and wonder just what on earth she had gone and done.

Chapter 6

THE NEXT FEW days were a dizzying mash of legal jargon, half-truths and hearsay, which stabbed at Mara's ears wherever she went until her brain felt like it would explode and she worried she might go mad.

Neither she nor her menfolk could read but, nevertheless, there was no hiding from the case and its progression. On every street corner, newspapers and halfpenny broadsheets screamed the terrible event in gory, illustrated accounts, and the subject seemed to be on everyone's lips. She caught the gossip, overheard snippets of information: the coroner's inquest, the stipendiary magistrate and committal, the imminent trial and the fact that the assizes were due on – it was relentless.

Naturally, Seamus and his sons hadn't escaped the talk and knew for certain now how matters lay. Yet the news of Conrad having been formally charged had had an unexpected effect. The fight appeared to have deserted the men. They were listless, silent, resigned almost, to his fate. More surprising still – and a heavenly blessing so far as Mara was concerned – home life had settled down remarkably. Without Conrad's influence, their visits to the pub had dropped significantly, which meant fewer drunken arguments, subsequent violence and trouble in general. She couldn't recall when she'd last known such calmness. Already her stepson's absence was having an impact, and for the better.

Then came the day Mara had been dreading: she received her summons to bear witness against Conrad at the Liverpool Assizes.

'You're certain you can get yourself out of this, lass?' asked Aggie sceptically when Mara informed her of developments. Mara had had the policeman who served the subpoena read it out to her, and afterwards she'd rushed straight round here to her friend's house, where now she sat anxiously biting her thumb, a bundle of nerves. 'I mean to say,' went on Aggie, 'what if the next part of your plan don't bear fruit? The doctor mightn't agree to it '

'He has to. Sure, there's nothing else for it.'

'Aye well, we'll soon see, eh? When's the trial to take place again? I forget.'

There was no chance of it slipping Mara's mind, that was for sure. The fateful date was seared in her mind both now and for ever: 'Tuesday, Aggie. Three days' time.'

'So when will we send for the medical man?'

She contemplated for a moment then nodded. 'Tomorrow, I think. Sure, ain't Seamus and the lads always away all day on the Lord's Day? Don't ask me where, mind, but you can bet it's up to no good they are, God forgive them. Aye, tomorrow,' she repeated. 'With luck, the doctor will have been and gone and the matter dealt with by the time the men return.'

Mara's mention of the summons to her family that

evening seemed to lend their veins the fire of old. The spark of hope returned to their eyes and their speech was more animated than she'd heard it in days. Surely it was only a matter of time, now, until Conrad was back in the fold where he belonged? Mara's account would do the trick, would show those corrupt police officers who were dead set on sending down an innocent man to be the liars they were, it *had* to . . . And on, and on.

Mara almost started to feel pity towards them.

The improved mood of the men was still evident on Sunday morning; she heard them from her bed leave the house in high spirits, whistling in triad a merry tune. She remained where she was for what felt like an age, had to be sure they were not about to return for whatever reason. When at last she was satisfied that they were indeed gone for the day and that her plan could go ahead, she rose, dressed quickly and hurried next door to alert Aggie.

Her friend was ready and waiting for Mara's signal with clogs and shawl already donned. Telling her eldest child to keep an eye to the younger ones, she hastened out into the street with Mara.

'Sorry to be dragging you from your hearth, Aggie,' Mara told her, shooting the drizzling rain a rueful look. 'My thanks to ye for your help with this.'

'Tsk, no need for all that; anyroad, what are friends for? Now, you go on home and get everything prepared. I'll not be long gone.'

Mara did as she'd been bid and minutes later was tucked up in her bed, practising her pained face. All the while, an army of thoughts marched inside her brain incessantly. Predominating was but one terrifying truth:

88

the doctor was the only person who could help her now. She had to make him believe her, *must* get this right. The alternative was far too terrible to contemplate.

That Seamus, Eamon and Eugene reckoned a corrupt police force had wrought these circumstances was a great relief to her – and something she couldn't risk jeopardising. They were adamant that, so far as the law was concerned, it was a matter of 'the more the merrier'; that Conrad being convicted along with McLoughlin and the rest of the gang would equate to a more favourable justice having seemingly been served for both the victim's family and the public.

Whether Conrad was of the same mind as his father and brothers, or whether he knew her to be at blame, Mara couldn't say. Either way, there could be no chance now of him influencing the others' thinking. He'd been transferred to Kirkdale Gaol, located some two miles from the centre of Liverpool, to await the next assizes, before there could be further opportunity for any of them to see him.

Therefore, of course, she couldn't appear in court. To spout publicly her testimony of lies would change everything. Everyone would know it was her fault, and her life would be over. She must uphold the pretence, must get out of it. And in her desperate state, she had been able to think of but one way of making that happen: convincing the doctor she wasn't well enough to travel for the trial. *Please God it would work.*

'Mara, lass, it's Aggie. I have the medical man here with me.'

At the sudden bawling of her friend from the kitchen,

89

Mara's panic returned tenfold. She gripped the bed-clothes with both hands and mouthed to the ceiling, 'Holy Mother, lend me strength!'

'Is tha decent for us to come upstairs?'

Reminding herself that she had to do this and why, Mara breathed deeply. Then, bringing a croak to her voice, she called, 'Aye, love. Come on up.'

'Mrs O'Hara?'

Eyeing the stooped, ancient-looking man who had entered the room behind Aggie, Mara offered him a weak smile. 'That's right, sir.'

'And what is it that is troubling you, young woman? Your neighbour here stated it was problems with your back, that it came on suddenly during your domestic duties?'

'That's right, sir. I was sweeping the floor and my back just went all of a sudden, like,' she lied. 'Oh, 'tis agony!'

He shuffled to the bedside and, with gentle persuasion, manoeuvred her on to her side. During the short examination that followed, Mara concentrated on making 'ooh!'s and 'ahh!'s in all the right places, which seemed to work – the doctor stepped back with a nod.

'Severe lumbago,' he announced.

'Sure, you think so, sir?' asked Mara, struggling to keep the relief from the words.

'Oh, indeed. I've seen it a thousand times before. As a matter of fact, I myself have been a victim of attack from this excruciating malady a number of times. It really is most debilitating; you have my sympathy, Mrs O'Hara.'

'So . . .' She licked her lips. 'What would you suggest, sir?'

'Well, you must give your poor lame back time to heal, it's as simple as that. The severe irritation in the spinal muscles will subside, however the question of when is a difficult one to answer. It could be days or weeks; it could even be months – one never can say with this plague. I'm afraid that complete bed rest is the only cure.'

Mara could have punched the air, so acute was her happiness at the golden words. 'The thing is,' she murmured, adding a disappointed sigh for extra effect, 'I'm wanted in Liverpool in two days' time, sir. It's the assizes, you see; I've been summoned to bear witness in a trial and I—'

'Out of the question.'

'Aye?'

'Most definitely.' The doctor was emphatic. 'The jerking motion of the train alone would worsen your condition – and that's without the journeying to and from the station, which in itself would prove most injurious, I'm sure. No, it's an impossibility, I'm afraid.'

'I see.' *Dear God, thank you.*

'I suppose there *are* one or two things we could try if you really are intent on making the trip,' he went on thoughtfully, bringing Mara's euphoria crashing down around her ears.

'Oh?' she forced herself to croak.

'I have heard talk of something which is said to cure all forms of rheumatisms such as lumbago and sciatica – electrobiology, they are calling it. It sounds positively frightful, I know, but it does nonetheless purport to produce marvellous effects. Of course, such a thing is still in its infancy and cannot help with your case.'

91

At this last statement from him, hope sparked in Mara once more. She swallowed hard. 'Sure, that is a shame, sir.'

'Yes. Alas, for now, sulphur ointment seems your only option. Rubbed well on to the affected area, it may help in subduing the pain. Applying linseed-meal poultices could also aid a speedier recovery. Some folk even swear by putting raw potatoes in a patient's pockets to bring about betterment – though how that could possibly be beneficial is beyond me. Other than that . . .' He spread his hands wide. Then: 'Tell me, Mrs O'Hara, this trial . . .'

'Aye, sir?'

'Given the fact that it's to take place at the assizes, am I right in assuming that it is of a most serious nature?'

'It is,' she admitted.

'And would your not being there affect the proceedings greatly?'

'Well . . . There is another witness, too, sir. Mr Deakin. He's a furniture shop owner, a respectable man of business – sure, his standing will be enough on its own, I'm certain.'

The doctor appeared satisfied with this. 'Good, good.'

'So, sir . . . you'll provide me with the necessary certificate to state I'm not fit to travel?'

'I will.'

'Thank you, sir. *Thank* you.'

With instructions that he'd have it ready for her that evening, he bade them good day and took his leave. When they heard the sound of the front door click shut at his back, Aggie flopped on to the bed beside Mara and let out a mammoth sigh.

'By gum, lass.'

'Oh, Aggie! Thank the Lord that's over with. Oh, I was so afraid!'

'And me! Eeh, but you did it, you clever thing, yer. It worked, lass, and you're off the hook.'

Mara smiled through her tears. 'The Holy Mother was by my side just then for sure.'

Of course, both were fully aware that the hardest part of the battle was yet to be won.

How breaking the news to Seamus and the lads would pan out – with or without the Virgin Mary's apparent support – remained to be seen.

'What's all this?'

'Evening, fellas. Sit yourselfs down, grub's almost ready.'

'What the divil are *you* doing in my kitchen? Where's my wife?'

Listening to the raised voice of her husband down below and Aggie's milder tone as she attempted to explain her presence, Mara thought she might be sick from the worry. Then a roar of rage rent the air, followed by footsteps thundering up the stairs, and in the next moment Seamus burst into the bedroom. On a small cry, Mara shrank back into the pillows.

'You tell me that that owd bitch down there is lying.'

'Hu—husband—'

'Tell me!' he bellowed, lunging forward to grab a handful of her hair in his meaty fist.

She cried out in agony. 'No! Please! You're hurting me!'

'You are fit to travel to Liverpool. You are!'

'I'm not, I'm not! I mustn't, not under any circumstances, shift from this bed. The doctor says so. I've been stuck here all the day through – I even missed church.'

His eyes widened ever so slightly at this last statement, and Mara was glad of it. She'd known that to some degree it would aid her in fetching him around. She never missed church, after all. For her to do so would have only been for a very good reason, and he knew it.

'Christ's *sake*.' He released his hold and swung away from her with a growl.

'I, I'm sorry—'

'You've planned this, I'll bet. You have; this is all some ruse to ruin our Conrad's chances.'

His closeness to the truth of things brought on shock so acute that instant guilty heat flooded her cheeks. She pulled the bedclothes up to her nose to conceal it, however there was no masking the quaver in her words: 'Husband; no, no,' she wheedled softly. 'Conrad's trial . . . it's as much of a blow to me as it is to you that I'll not be able to attend. Honest, it is—'

'Lies. All lies.'

''Tis not, Seamus, I swear it. My back . . . it's agony to even move an inch. I shan't bear the journey, and the doctor agrees. He gave me a certificate to prove it; Aggie's daughter collected it for me but a handful of minutes past. It's on top of the drawers there, see for yourself.'

He made no attempt to glance in the direction she'd indicated, instead kept his eyes fixed firmly on his wife. For a full minute, he peered at her silently. When finally he spoke, his tone was eerily quiet. 'So. That's that, then.'

'I'm sorry. So sorry.'

'Aye. Me an' all.'

To her perplexity, Seamus gave her a last lingering look and left the room. Alone, she listened for further conflict from downstairs, but none came. All remained calm, the faint clinking of cutlery on bowls as her menfolk ate their meal the only sound.

'Lass?'

It was Aggie standing in the doorway, holding a plate of food. Snapped back to the present, Mara beckoned her inside gladly. 'Seamus, the lads?'

'Having their grub. You're all right?' she added, coming into the room and closing the door behind her. 'I overheard that nasty sod having a go at thee.'

'I'm fine, so. They've said nothing more, Aggie?'

The older woman passed the plate to Mara then sat down on the edge of the bed. 'Not a peep. They're taking it well, I must say.'

'Hm, and isn't that what concerns me? It's not natural. I worried that Seamus would tear me limb from limb, but no. He just . . . he looks to have accepted it.'

'He does?'

Chewing on her lip, she nodded. 'He said, "So. That's that, then."'

'And he left it at that?'

'Aye.'

A surprised Aggie blew out air slowly. 'He didn't put up a fight when I told him I'd be calling in here of a day to see to the meals and tidy around the place whilst you recover, neither. Accepted it with a shrug, he did.'

By now, Mara was beginning to allow herself to dare to

hope . . . Could it be true? Had she really got away with this? It surely seemed so. And yet . . .

'Right, well, I'd best get home to the kiddies,' announced Aggie, getting to her feet. 'I'll be back the morrow, lass. In t' meantime, you just bang on t' wall should you need me for owt.'

'Oh, love.' Holding out her arms, Mara clasped her friend to her with tears in her eyes. 'What would I do without ye, eh? I'll make it up to you, you know. I will; somehow, someday.'

Aggie kissed her cheek. 'Get some rest. I'll see thee in t' morn.'

Alone, Mara allowed her mind to wander over the day's developments, desperate to make sense of it all. She was still mulling over events when, how much later she couldn't say, movement reached her from the stairway. *Seamus retiring for the night.*

Mara went rigid. The door eased open and there he was. She held her breath.

'I thought I'd get my head down in the lads' room.'

'Wha—' She was dumbstruck. This was the last thing she'd expected.

'Aye, in our Conrad's bed,' her husband went on. 'That way, you'll be able to get a decent kip, won't have me bumping into thee during the night and making your pain worse. All right?'

'I . . . Aye. Aye, Seamus.' Her mouth was hanging wide. 'That's ever so thoughtful of you, thank ye.'

He nodded once then turned and left, leaving her gazing after him at the door.

Chapter 7

MONDAY CAME AND went without incident – Mara could barely believe it. Seamus and his sons made no further mention of her 'injury' or Conrad and Liverpool, nor anything in between; in fact, they left her alone completely, showed their faces to her not once.

As planned, Aggie saw to the household duties so not to arouse suspicion, and Mara was left to her own devices upstairs. The peace and inactivity were altogether new to her and, freer of mind now she was sure that the men had accepted the situation, she revelled in it, intended to enjoy this period of ease, however fleeting it may be, for all she was worth.

To her surprise, that night sleep claimed her without effort. She'd anticipated lying awake the long night through, her brain consumed with the what-ifs of the following afternoon's trial, but no. Her eyelids had grown leaden without resistance and she'd allowed unconsciousness to carry her off with an easy and much-relieved sigh.

When the outlines of the hulking figures filling the bedroom doorway swam into focus, at first Mara thought she was dreaming. For several moments she could but squint at them in hazy confusion. She knew not who they might be or what they could want. Nor could she grasp what time it was, or what had alerted her to their presence in the first place.

'Ma? Wake *up*, will thee.'

Was that . . . ? But . . . what on earth?

'Ma!'

Slowly, the slumber fog began lifting, and now she remembered. It was her stepsons she was facing, and it was their insistent calls that had disturbed her. She twisted her neck to glance at the naked window – the inky sky hugging a pearly half-moon showed her it was a while off dawn. Now, only one thing remained unclear; her words tripped over themselves in her haste to discover the answer: 'Eugene? Eamon? What, in the name of Jaysus, is it? What's going on?'

'You need to come. You need to come quick!'

'Come?'

'Aye, downstairs.'

'Down—' Befuddled, she shook her head. 'But why? For what?'

'It's your cousin, Ma. Your cousin's here.'

Her lungs seemed to turn to marble; she found it impossible to snatch in a breath. The incredible statement screamed through her ears over and over – she slapped her hands to them whilst her head shook wildly from side to side as though it had taken on a life of its own.

'Did you hear me?' Eugene pressed. 'Say summat.'

'Rebecca?' The name left her lips on a wheeze. 'My Rebecca . . . here?'

'Aye. Only Father don't want her anywhere near, is for sending her away.'

'No . . . No, please!'

'Come and stop him, Ma. Quick afore she disappears from your life again for good.'

Insensible to all other thought and feeling but the overwhelming euphoria – and choking terror of this wondrous opportunity slipping rapidly like sand through her fingers – Mara was on her feet and darting for the door in a heartbeat.

Smiling, her stepsons stepped aside to let her pass.

On legs that felt like melting jelly, she hurtled down the stairs, tripping and stumbling all the way, and burst with a cry into the kitchen.

'Well, well, well.'

Skidding to a halt, panting fit to collapse, Mara threw Seamus a cursory glance then scanned the space for the woman she'd missed more than life. However, of Rebecca there was no sign. Her confusion was absolute. She turned once more to her husband. 'I don't under— Where is she? Where's Rebecca?'

Sitting forward in his chair, Seamus responded with snarling laughter. 'Well, well, well,' he repeated, lower now.

Mara barely registered it. Drowning in her devastation, she was beyond all logical thinking. 'Ye sent her away? You did, didn't you? You spawn of Satan, ye! I'll find her, I will, I—'

'How's the lumbago?'

The three little words acted like invisible chains – Mara's hot pursuit towards the door died; she froze to the spot. *Good God.*

'A fair miracle this is, for sure.'

This can't be happening . . .

'A medical marvel, I'd say,' continued her husband. 'That must be it, aye.'

Just then, her stepsons emerged into the room and she watched through a film of tears as they went to stand either side of their father. Like the older man, they wore a demon's grin. Understanding slammed. Her heart withered inside her breast. 'Rebecca . . .'

All three men sniggered, with Seamus adding, 'I knew you'd not resist a tale like that.'

'No . . . No! How could you trick me so? How could you be so callous? You rotten liar!'

'*I'm* the liar?' Like the flicking of a switch, his temper erupted. Leaping to his feet, he charged at her like a rabid bull. 'I knew – *knew* – you were trying to pull the wool over my eyes. You *did* plan it, were willing to sit back and watch my innocent lad rot in gaol. And you have the gall to call me callous? You sneaky, vindictive young slut, yer!'

Mara thrashed desperately as the hands wrapped around her throat threatened to pulverise her windpipe. She was on the cusp of passing out when suddenly he released her and, ignoring her splutters and whimpers, hauled her by the scruff of her neck back upstairs.

He launched her across the bedroom, sending her sprawling across the bed, and pointed a finger in her face. 'Now get some sleep. You've a busy day ahead of thee the morrow.'

'I can't . . . can't do it, husband.' She was weeping openly now, fear and turmoil suffocating her like a shroud. 'I *can't* take the stand, I shan't, I—'

'Oh tha can and tha shall. You will go to Liverpool, and you will prove Conrad guiltless, even if I have to drag thee kicking and squealing all the way. That's an end to it.'

Mara could only watch as, before leaving her, Seamus snatched up the doctor's certificate from the set of drawers and tore it into a hundred pieces. He threw them in her direction to rain down on her head like some hideous snowstorm, laughed and stomped from the room.

Stunned, defeated and sick to her stomach, she lay gazing unseeing at the ceiling for a long time afterwards. Her fate was sealed. There was no way out. Existence as she knew it was over – once the truth came out, she'd be lucky to escape the next twenty-four hours with her life.

Worse still was the truth that her dear Rebecca was still just as lost to her as she ever was. Mara thought she'd die from the pain of it all.

A bright but windswept morning had followed the nightmarish night when Mara found herself standing on the crowded platform at Manchester's Victoria Station.

Wedged between the unyielding bodies of her stepsons and with Seamus providing added security from the rear, she made no break for escape, didn't for a second even consider attempting it. It was useless, all of it, and so she allowed herself instead to be led to her doom with all the docility of a toddler.

'Get on the bugger,' her husband demanded when the early train puffed and screeched to a standstill. He sent her into the rickety carriage with a shove and she complied without argument.

A stretch of thirty miles separated the two equally

101

bustling and industrious cities – a little over an hour's travelling. However, they found themselves passing through Edge Hill tunnel before emerging into Liverpool's Lime Street Railway Station as though on a blink – at least so far as Mara was concerned, at any rate. She'd paid no heed to the passing landscape, could remember nothing of the journey.

St George's Hall, which held the assizes, was situated opposite the station and at no great distance from the docks. Mara gazed upon it in awe. Surrounded by huge columns, statues and sculptured pediments, it was an intimidating sight.

According to Aggie Roper, Queen Victoria had said during a visit early in the previous decade that the neoclassical, Greco-Roman hall was 'worthy of ancient Athens' – now, Mara pondered on Her Majesty's description. Truth be told, she had no idea where in the world Athens even was, never mind what it looked like, but if the structure before her was anything to go by, she reckoned it must be a gorgeous place. Formidable or no, there was no denying the courthouse was an impressive one.

'Right then.' Seamus, too, was eyeing the building and, like Eamon and Eugene, he appeared now decidedly ill at ease. Unsurprisingly, anything to do with the law in general always had this effect on the O'Hara men. 'You get going inside afore you miss being called. Me and the lads will stop and wait out here.'

'Husband . . .' Despite her best efforts, now that the time had come, tears were dangerously close by and panic was overtaking her. 'Husband, please. Please don't make me do this. I'm afraid.'

To her surprise, Seamus nodded briefly in understanding. Then, more astonishing still, he gave her arm an awkward pat. 'I know you must be. Standing up in court ain't no picnic, nay. That's why you played daft about having a bad back, weren't it?'

He thought her invention of illness had been wrought through nothing more than mere fear of cross-examination . . . Well. She was more than happy to have him believe that. By God she was. She nodded.

'Aye. I see it now. But well, you've no choice. Conrad needs thee. You just go in there and tell the truth, and it'll be over in no time. Go on, Mara. Go on.'

Queerly, his speech and tone bolstered her and she knew that she could – would – see this through to its completion. *Oh, husband, if only you knew . . .*

She bobbed her head once more. Then she took a deep breath and turned in the direction of the wide steps.

In a haze, over the next few hours Mara drifted through the necessary proceedings as though watching a dream through someone else's eyes.

For the most part, once the trial commenced, she was positioned out of sight in the witness room. Several others were present to keep her company: a couple of maids employed by the deceased cotton baron who had been on the scene in the aftermath of the shooting, as well as the handful of menservants who had apprehended and held McLoughlin and his cronies until the authorities arrived. And there was the furniture shop man.

Dear, sweet Mr Deakin. He'd gone above and beyond for her, there was no doubt. Mara knew she'd be indebted to

103

him for life. With a relieved sigh, not only glad he'd shown but feeling a modicum of comfort to see a familiar face, she'd made a beeline for the chair closest to his.

As they sat in tense anticipation to give evidence, the store owner kept Mara informed on what would be taking place in the main body of the court. The indictment would be read out by the clerk, then the customary question put to Conrad: 'How say you: guilty or not guilty?' – to which he'd indubitably answer, 'Not guilty.' Next, details of the crime and the events that ensued would be gone over, then the speech from the leading council for the prosecution. It would then be time to hear the witnesses – first the police and medical men who had worked on the case, followed by those of them gathered in this here room.

Sure enough, after a few hours of waiting, the door finally opened.

One by one, the domestic staff were called to testify. Eventually, only Mara and Mr Deakin remained unquestioned. Then the officer of the court appeared again and said Mara's name.

On unsteady legs, she rose and shadowed him out.

The judge, jurymen, clerks, lawyers and family of the murdered man, along with crowds of others, swam into a smudged mass – the court was packed out with hundreds of people. Mara staggered, would have fallen to her knees if not for the quick-thinking officer taking her arm. She had known this would be a high-profile case but, by God, she hadn't imagined . . . This was too much, too much! Yet there was no chance of backing out now. None. *Grant me strength, Lord Jesus.*

Clinging on to the officer for support, she shuffled into the witness box.

Then she saw him.

Standing at the felon's bar, perfectly erect with shoulders back and chin held high, Conrad looked in full control of the situation. Though his appearance was altered in some ways – he'd evidently lost weight and the prison barber had been let loose on his hair – his eyes had retained the same intensity as ever. They bore into her like hot coals and she squirmed beneath the scrutiny.

Was he still expecting a full acquittal? she wondered. Or did he know by now what she'd done? Had he been informed of her false account to the police, that she'd told them that her stepson hadn't been on that shopping expedition with her after all? Or could it be he was still in the dark and totally expected her to get him off this charge scot-free? Either way, she surmised, it mattered not. He'd be in clear knowledge of all of the facts soon enough.

She was just thankful that Seamus, Eamon and Eugene were not present to witness what was to come. Of course, Conrad would know of her treachery in a matter of minutes, but the others needn't be aware of it right away – and perhaps not ever at all. By the time Conrad returned home, his year or two of reflection would have mellowed and matured him. He'd understand what she'd done and accept the reason why. He could even decide not to inform the other men of what had transpired today, and the five of them could simply get on with the rest of their lives. It was surely possible . . . wasn't it? *Please God.*

'Your name is Mara O'Hara?'

The council had begun the examination. Dragging her stare from Conrad and her mind back to the here and now, she nodded. 'Aye, sir.'

'The stepmother of Conrad O'Hara, accused?'

'Aye, sir.'

Several further questions were put to her, namely concerning the day of the murder – what had she been doing and where? – which she answered honestly and succinctly. Then came the moment she'd been dreading.

'And did your stepson accompany you into the city to purchase the furniture, Mrs O'Hara?'

Though her heart felt as though it might smash through her chest, she refused to be shaken. She couldn't go back, now. She *couldn't*. Nonetheless, her lips refused to form the mistruth. She swallowed hard.

'I would remind you that you are upon your oath,' the wigged man pressed. 'Please answer the question, Mrs O'Hara.'

Another deep swallow. She clutched the rail and turned her gaze on to the prisoner. 'Please understand, Conrad,' she whispered. ''Tis for the best.' Then: 'No,' she told the assembly loud and clear. 'No, my stepson wasn't with me.'

A flurry of murmurs went around the room but were soon lost in Conrad's cry to the judge: 'But it's not true! I ain't guilty, My Lord! I ain't!'

As the stiff-faced judge ordered silence, Mara was led from the box and back to the witness room.

It was finished. She'd done it.

Before leaving, she hazarded a last glance at her stepson. He was slumped against the bar with his face in his hands. Wiping away a tear, she mouthed to his bowed head that she was sorry. Then she turned and walked away.

'Mr Deakin? Did everything go all right? Sure, your questioning took a lot longer than mine did—'

'It's over.'

'It is?' Mara was shocked. 'Ye stayed behind until the end?'

'I figured as I was the last witness to speak that I'd stop on in court and hear the verdict.'

'I see. And?'

The shop owner opened and closed his mouth then shook his head. It was only then that Mara noticed the grey hue to his skin and the haunted expression behind his eyes. Her voice was a whisper. 'Mr Deakin? What happened?'

'Had I known, I'd never have got involved . . . A year, you said!' he burst out before dropping as though dazed into a chair.

She felt light-headed and nausea was rising. 'What was the verdict? Two years? Surely not three?'

'Your stepson . . .'

'Tell me.'

'He . . . He . . .'

'Please, sir!'

'Conrad. Conrad was sentenced to death.'

Chapter 8

'YOU'VE GORRA TRY and eat summat, lass.'

'I'm not hungry, Aggie.'

'You'll be for making yourself ill, you will!'

Despite her neighbour's chiding and click of her tongue, she nonetheless left Mara be, and Mara was glad of it. Eat? The thought alone had sickness swooping. She hadn't been able to keep a morsel down since ... *Holy Mary Mother of God, release me from this nightmare.*

'Seamus and the lads, they'll come through for Conrad. Fret not, lass.'

'And if they don't?' Mara fired back, more sharply than intended. 'I'm sorry, love, I don't mean to snap. It's just, what if this solicitor fellow they've gone to see doesn't agree to take on the case? What if Seamus was wrong and the lad's chances are dashed altogether? What if—'

'Buts and what-nots won't get thee nowhere, lass,' her friend cut in soothingly. 'Have faith, it's all tha can do. Conrad will secure a reprieve somehow; I can feel it in my bones. Just you wait and see.'

Would he?

Hugging herself, Mara closed her eyes.

The past forty-eight hours had been a living hell. What she could recall of it, at any rate. Large chunks were lost to her, maybe for ever – it was her mind's way of coping with it, of keeping her safe, so not to send her stark staring mad, she was convinced of it.

Snippets of that day would replay inside her brain incessantly, but that's all they were: short bursts of flickering images and sounds, each more monstrous than the last.

She remembered collapsing on to the witness room floor, wailing like a banshee. She remembered Mr Deakin picking her up and supporting her out into the dull afternoon. Who informed Seamus, Eamon and Eugene of Conrad's fate remained a mystery to her, but she did remember the looks on their faces and could hear still their yells and howls of devastation.

The journey back to Manchester was a blank. The thing she remembered next was Aggie Roper rocking her in her arms until she wept herself into a coma-like sleep. Then this morning, her family had announced that they were away into the city to speak with a solicitor of excellent repute – a recommendation by the local priest after Seamus had gone to beg from him his advice.

Now, here Mara was, a quivering wreck and her nails chewed down to the quick, awaiting their return. Why, why had she done it?

'Did you hear me?'

Aware that Aggie was talking again, Mara gazed up at her in hazy confusion. 'I didn't, sorry.'

'I said that they're back, lass, your men. Have I to brew a fresh sup of tea?'

Terror had seized her faculties. She could barely form speech. 'Aye . . . yes. Thank ye, Aggie.'

Her husband and stepsons appeared envigoured and their eyes were bright. It was a good sign – Mara slumped in unequivocal relief.

'What did he say, lads?' Aggie was quick to enquire.

'He'll help.'

'Aye?'

Seamus nodded. 'He reckons we've a sound chance of getting the conviction commuted to a lesser charge. If it's suspected a sentence of death might be passed, the jury always give a strong recommendation to mercy on account, if possible, of the prisoner's youth. Conrad, young as he is, fits the bill.'

'Eeh, thank the good Lord for that.' Aggie's words were genuine. A nasty swine she might view Conrad to be; however, like the rest of them she was steadfast in the belief that he didn't deserve hanging. Never, not that; not by a long chalk.

'So what happens now?' Mara whispered.

'We wait. The solicitor will be in touch.'

Wrapping her arms back around herself, Mara fell silent once more.

There was a shimmer of hope on the horizon, then, after all. Thank God Mr Deakin hadn't accepted her money the day she'd gone to him for help in lying to the police. For it was the loot secreted in the lads' bedroom, which they had 'won' in that card game and that had started all this horrible mess, that her husband was using to pay the solicitor's fee.

He'd discussed with his younger sons whether to spend

it on acquiring a good barrister before the trial began, but the three of them had decided it was unwise. Questions would have been asked as to how they, given their social station, had accumulated such a sum. Besides, they had each agreed with confidence: Conrad would surely be proven innocent at any rate.

The notion therefore had been deemed an unnecessary risk, much to Mara's relief at the time – and now, in light of recent events, crippling shame. However, Seamus cared nothing for anything any more but saving Conrad's neck. He'd bundled up the money earlier and hurried to the solicitor's offices without a second's thought – and mercifully, it looked as though it might just have worked. This period of waiting they now faced that her husband spoke of would be agonising.

That night, as with every other now, she found herself locked in a familiar gruesome dream.

She was back in Liverpool and the court, and the jury were retiring to consider the verdict. Yet when they filed back in, they were no longer men but black and disfigured ghouls. They looked across at her and grinned, displaying mouths filled with long, jagged teeth, making her scream, but no one seemed to hear or care. Then the life-altering question was put to them – and was followed by that single word response, tearing through the room like a pistol shot: Guilty.

The judge let out a demonic cackle and, glancing his way, Mara saw he was donning his black cap. She screamed on and on but, again, no one took any notice. And with tears of mirth coursing down his cheeks, he formally passed the sentence of death.

111

'Why, Ma, why?' her stepson cried out over and over as he was led away by the gaoler.

'I'm sorry! I'm sorry!'

'Help me, Ma, please!'

'*Mo buachaill go maith!* No! No!'

'Mrs O'Hara?'

Bleary-eyed through lack of decent sleep, Mara blinked at the well-dressed man on the doorstep in dumb confusion.

'My name is Thomas Heslop—'

'Are you the solicitor, sir, who spoke to my husband last week?' she blurted as realisation hit; there was no one else it could be.

He nodded, smiled. 'I am. Is Mr O'Hara at home?'

'He's not, but sure he ought to be back any minute. Please, come in.'

The man removed his hat and followed her inside. He accepted her invitation to sit but declined a cup of tea and, not knowing what else to do, Mara took the chair opposite him to await Seamus's return.

'I am glad to have this opportunity of speaking with you in private, if I'm honest, Mrs O'Hara.'

His statement – and the serious tone in which he'd delivered it – threw her. She frowned. 'You are, sir?'

'I have been going through the court reports sent on from Liverpool, and . . .' He paused to clear his throat. 'I am assuming that your family are not aware that you testi-fied *against* your stepson?'

Colour assaulted her cheeks; she gasped. *My God.* How had she not realised this would come to light? She'd been so consumed with shame and regret and her mind haunted with what might happen, she'd failed to consider this completely. 'Oh, sir! Sir, I, I . . . !'

'I suspected as much,' he interjected quietly. 'What was your reasoning behind such a decision, Mrs O'Hara?'

Her explanation poured forth on a torrent. She told him of Conrad's behaviour and his influence over his father and brothers, her surreptitious visit to the furniture shop to secure Mr Deakin's alliance. She revealed her hoodwinking of the doctor and how her husband had had her thinking he was accepting of her diagnosis, only for her to discover he'd lulled her into a false sense of security in the cruellest way possible – she left nothing out.

The solicitor sat back and released a long breath. 'That's quite the story, Mrs O'Hara.'

Gulping down a sob, she dabbed at her eyes with her apron. 'Aye, sir.'

'The sentence enforced must have come as a great shock to you.'

'Oh, it did! Sure, didn't Conrad himself tell me he'd be given no longer than a year or two? I'd never have done what I did otherwise, never. Sure, the guilt has crucified me. I couldn't have imagined this would happen; you must believe me.'

'For what it is worth, I do.'

'Thank ye,' Mara told him earnestly. 'D'you know, though, thinking back, I reckon the judge had made up his mind about Conrad from the outset. Sure, I remember glancing across to him and saying to myself: he looks deeply affected by this whole thing – perhaps a touch too

113

much, aye. He stared at my stepson as though he was a bug who ought to be crushed.'

'It is possible that the judge knew the murder victim on a personal level.'

Mara bobbed her chin thoughtfully. 'Aye, mebbe. I never considered that.'

'One thing is clear: he decided to make an example of each one of the accused and saw through with it. The deceased was a very important man of the city, after all; heads had to roll, and roll they shall. McLoughlin and his associates can be placed directly at the scene of the crime and stand no chance of a reprieve – that party of slayers will undoubtably hang. Conrad, on the other hand, given his lesser apparent involvement . . .'

'Oh, why did I *do* it?' she repented on a harsh whisper. Then: 'Mr Heslop, my husband and stepsons cannot find out. They're of the same mind that the court is just as corrupt as the police and that's why Conrad was found guilty, that I'm not to blame but instead tried my best and did everything right. The truth . . . it would create a world of unimaginable trouble. They'd kill me for sure; and likely Mr Deakin, too, into the bargain – oh, and dear Aggie Roper next door, for she knew about the plan as well! Please, sir. You won't tell them, will ye?'

'No, Mrs O'Hara,' he said after some contemplation. 'That is not to say they won't uncover the true facts from some other source.'

'But you'll not reveal it, sir, no? You promise?'

'You have my word.'

Hearing just then the clod of her menfolks' boots approaching the house, she hastened to ask, 'And Conrad, sir? Be honest with me, please: what are his chances of escaping the hangman's noose?'

'Strong. Very strong.'

Forcing back fresh tears, Mara allowed herself a half-smile of optimism. Then her family was entering the kitchen and, after mouthing a final thank you to the solicitor, she left the men to their talk and slipped away upstairs.

Mr Heslop was renowned for not letting the grass grow under his feet – the wheels were set in motion immediately to give effect to the recommendation of mercy. He launched a petition, which to the O'Haras' shock and gratitude received many thousands of signatures, and duly dispatched it for presentation to the Home Secretary in London. Then came the torturous wait that would determine not only whether Conrad would live or die but life as they knew it for the rest of them, too.

Finally, on a bright-skied afternoon at the start of the new month, the solicitor received the all-important reply.

Mara, Seamus, Eamon and Eugene gazed at him across the kitchen table, none daring to breathe. Then Mr Heslop was speaking and, licking their dry lips, they leaned forward as though of one body to hear his news.

'The request of the petitioners has been complied with.'

The family shared an anxious frown with each other before swivelling wide eyes back to the solicitor.

'And what does that mean in plain English?' Seamus asked him.

A smile spread across Mr Heslop's face. 'It means, Mr O'Hara, that your son *will* have his sentence commuted.'

'Mother of God – thank you!' Mara burst into uncontrollable sobs whilst, around her, her menfolk laughed wildly and grabbed one another in tight embraces.

After some moments, Seamus jumped to his feet and reached across to pump the solicitor's hand. 'Thank you, truly. We're forever in your debt, sir.'

'So how long will Conrad have to do instead, then?' Eamon wanted to know, his face still split in two in a huge grin.

To their bewilderment, Mr Heslop's smile slipped. He sighed and shook his head. 'Yes, indeed. That's the part I was getting to.'

'Sir?' Seamus dropped back into his seat slowly. 'Not one of penal servitude for life? It can't be life!'

'No, Mr O'Hara, no. Not that.'

'Thank *God*,' the three men breathed in unison, visibly sagging.

'The sentence . . .' Mr Heslop paused to glance at them in turn. Then, lowering his eyes, he cleared his throat. 'The sentence has been commuted to transportation to a penal colony overseas.'

A stunned silence gripped the very air. It was Mara who was first to regain the power of speech.

'Tran—*transportation*?' she choked, rearing back in her chair. 'But . . . sure, wasn't it abolished several years back?'

'Theoretically, yes. Convicts being sent to New South Wales and Tasmania – or Botany Bay and Van Diemen's Land, as they are more generally known – has indeed ceased. However, owing to a shortage of labour, they are being shipped still to this day to Western Australia.'

'How long?'

'Seven years.'

Lord, no.

'I know this is not what you expected – me neither, for that matter. However, you must take comfort in the fact that Conrad has at least escaped execution. Your son will *live*!'

'Aye, and for how much longer?' Seamus bellowed, thumping the tabletop, his lips tinged white in unadulterated fury. 'Them slave ships are akin to Lucifer's lair – we've all heard the stories. Illness and disease are rife. Countless poor souls perish from the terrible conditions onboard afore they ever have chance to reach their destination!'

'Months and months at sea, chained up like an animal . . . And even if Conrad does survive the passage, what will life be like for him?' Eugene murmured, shaking his head. 'Exile in them barren and scorching-hot far-flung lands . . . it's a holiday in hell.'

'Seven *years* in hell,' croaked Eamon, dropping his head in his hands.

Shooting the company sympathetic glances, Mr Heslop gathered up his legal documents and rose from the table. 'I will take my leave of you now but will be in touch again once I have more details,' he told them quietly. 'When you have all had time to digest the news, you will see that this outcome is the lesser of two evils, I am sure of it . . . Good afternoon.'

The door clicked shut at the solicitor's back, and Seamus closed his eyes.

'Fetch whisky,' he rasped to no one in particular. '*Now,* damn it. And plenty of it.'

*

Conrad was one of almost three hundred other convicts onboard the gaol vessel *Hougoumont* when it departed England from Portsmouth in mid-October. It would become the last ever transportation voyage – precisely eighty years since the landing of the First Fleet.

Newspapers reported in Shipping Intelligence columns that the craft docked in Fremantle, Western Australia, on 10 January the following year – a journey of almost three months, during which time one prisoner died.

The stress proved too great for the heart-torn father.

Days later, Seamus suffered a massive stroke and passed away in his sleep.

Chapter 9

1872

DISTANT BIRDSONG FILTERED through the smog. Mara tilted her face to the sky and closed her eyes.

Her basket sat ready-filled with blooms nearby, her clogs alongside. All around her was peaceful and still, devoid of people and life in general. A sigh whispered from between her lips. She snuggled down deeper in the tall grasses and allowed the soft blades swaying in the gentle breeze to tickle her ears and cheeks.

Five years.

The passage of time had stolen by as though on a heartbeat. Five years to the day since Conrad's arrest, when fate had seen fit to set in motion the chain of events that followed. How was it possible? Would Eamon and Eugene realise the significance of the date?

At the thought of her stepsons, Mara's lids flickered open, fetching her back to reality. She rose and slipped into her footwear, lifted her basket and set off back towards Ancoats.

When she reached Heyrod Street, she cast her sight on

the house in which she'd spent so many years with her family. And as she knew it would, as it always did through sheer habit, her step faltered upon approaching the door. However, as she'd had to train herself to do, she repeated what she did daily: she picked up her feet once more and continued on for the new place she now called home.

'All right, lass?' Aggie acknowledged her return with a warm smile.

'Aye, love. Is there any tea going begging? Sure, I'm parched after that long trek.'

The other woman nodded towards the pot then inclined her chin to the arrangements of flowers. 'Sound pickings, I see.'

'Aye,' agreed Mara, placing the basket by the table and easing herself gratefully into a chair. 'Though I hope they're still fresh-looking and not wilted entirely whenever I can manage to get to the cemetery. This heat dries them out in no time, so it does.'

Tut-tutting, Aggie shot the adjoining wall a dark look. 'Well, you know my stance on that, right enough. I don't know why you still bother with them two swines—'

'I've already told ye why more than once,' Mara cut in quietly.

'Aye, and yet still it makes no sense to me. Leave them to rot, I say. You owe the pair naught, and they deserve nowt less!'

With a shrug, Mara let the matter drop. There was next to no use in arguing the point with her friend – Aggie wouldn't see her reasoning on this. So far as she was concerned, Mara ought to have severed all ties with the remaining O'Haras the minute Seamus was placed in the ground, and that was that. Except it wasn't, not so far as Mara herself was concerned. Nothing was ever that simple, was it? Besides, didn't she owe them? If not for her actions . . . They had no one now but her. She couldn't abandon them, grown as they were. She just couldn't.

'There you go, them's your summons,' announced Aggie as a harsh thump sounded through the chimney breast from next door. 'You'd best not keep their lordships waiting. Hard-faced sods.'

Mara gulped down the rest of her tea, then without a word hurried off for next door.

She found her stepsons nursing aching heads in their chairs by the dead fire. Murmuring a good morning to them, which was met with silence, she gave up on further pleasantries and crossed to the wooden box containing the coal. Soon, flames danced among the black cobs and she put the filled iron kettle on the heat for tea.

In between preparing the breakfast, Mara flitted about the space dusting furniture, wiping down surfaces and washing pots; as usual, the lads hadn't lifted a finger in her absence. By the time she'd placed their food in front of them and donned her shawl once more, she felt like she could do with a good lie-down.

She'd been up with the larks to pick her flowers, and the long walk to the outskirts of the city and back, coupled with running about after her stepsons, had almost worn her out. However, there was work to get to now, then when that was over with she must shop for provisions before returning here to cook the lads' evening meal. Later still, there would be their supper to see to and a last clean-up of the place before she could even think of collapsing exhausted into bed – to begin it all over again tomorrow.

Was Aggie right in what she said? The thought whispered through her mind, despite everything. Eamon and Eugene were fully grown, after all, and more than capable of fulfilling their own needs, should they have to. Besides, they were not born of her own flesh when all was said and done; she had no real obligation towards them. Particularly not these days, not now her husband was gone.

As it was wont to do, yet still in spite of the years, that last truth made her catch her breath. *Widowhood* – it was still a novelty to her, this. Seamus's death had come as a complete and utter shock; she'd never imagined herself to be free of him, not for many years to come. Though she'd known inexplicable relief that he was no more, she'd nevertheless shed a tear for him and all that had passed. The loss of his firstborn son had shoved him headlong into an early grave without a doubt – of this she was acutely aware – and her guilt had almost been her undoing for a while. And that, she supposed, was why she stayed.

The remaining O'Hara men had lost half of their family – their heroes, in a sense – owing to her decisions. She'd done her utmost in those early dark days to keep them from slipping into the black abyss of despair and, somehow, she had. It hadn't been easy. Their raw grief had slithered into every corner and crevice of their home and daily life, and had clung there for many, many months – she'd fretted at times that they would never come through the other side. But eventually they had, bit by bit – with not a little help from the bottle.

Mara had at first tried to ignore how much spirits they

were knocking back, reasoning they needed some form of outlet for their pain. When it became too obvious to pretend to herself any longer that their habit was not growing worse, she'd attempted suggesting gently that they cut back their consumption. Yet she may as well have been talking to the chimney back for all the good it did; her words had fallen on deaf ears, had had no impact whatever.

They began rolling in from the pub later and later, more often than not with noses blooded and eyes swollen from besozzled altercations with other hard drinkers, and still nothing she could say got through to them. Then the fearsome tempers began to show themselves at home, too – not only towards each other, but to her as well.

Soon, snarls worsened to yells, shoves progressed to slaps, and she'd known she was nearing the limit of her endurance, couldn't put up with it for very much longer.

It was almost six months ago now, as she surveyed a fresh split lip in the mirror one morning, which she'd received from Eamon the previous night whilst Eugene watched on with a laugh, that the crux had come; something inside her snapped. Leaving her stepsons snoring in their beds, she'd left the house and gone to beg her neighbour to let her lodge with her. Aggie being Aggie, she'd naturally agreed immediately, and Mara had been dwelling with the Roper clan ever since.

'I'll be away to the cemetery then with my posies,' she told her stepsons now. Engrossed in their meal, they responded with grunts without looking up – rolling her eyes, she secured her shawl around her shoulders and escaped into the street.

123

Having collected her basket of wares from Aggie's, Mara made off for her place of work. Thankfully, her flowers still held life and she did good trade. She'd almost sold up when the sky suddenly dimmed, heralding rain. The sun scuttled from sight as though for cover, and Mara was giving the moody clouds that had gathered a rueful look when a hand on her shoulder had her almost leaping from her skin. She sprung around with a gasp – and only just managed to hold at bay a weary sigh at the newcomer's identity. 'Oh. It's you.'

Willie Keogh bestowed upon her a beaming smile. 'Hello, Mara.'

'Hello,' she offered back with all the enthusiasm she could muster, which wasn't very much. 'You're well?'

'I am. And yourself?'

'Aye, Willie, I'm fine.'

'Grand, grand.'

There followed an awkward silence – at least it was awkward on Mara's part; the Irishman hadn't seemed to have grasped the clear shift in their relationship.

Her living arrangements hadn't been the only change recently. Things had indeed altered between her and Willie, too. His wife had died after a short illness early last summer and Mara had been devastated for the distraught husband. Over the months that followed, she'd tried to be there for him as much as she was able: cooking the odd meal for the family when he was having a particularly down day or helping out where she could with his children, which she knew he'd sincerely appreciated.

Inevitably, their friendship had strengthened and, to begin with, Mara had been glad of it. She'd always had a soft spot for the kind-natured man who had been there for her in her every hour of need; it had been nice to give something back. Yet it had become apparent that Willie's feelings for her had deepened into an altogether different capacity – she was at a total loss what to do.

Unapologetically, unabashed and completely out of the blue, he'd declared the week before that he may have fallen in love with her.

Mara had been incapable of speech; like a grounded fish, she'd simply gawped back open-mouthed. All the while, but one thought had swirled dizzyingly: were these designs on her really new, or had they in fact been there from the beginning, as Aggie had predicted long ago? Whatever the truth, she hadn't the opportunity at the time to ponder on it further – Willie had told her to think on what he'd said and walked away, leaving her staring after him in dumb stupor.

The last few days had been uncomfortable, to say the least. Shocked, confused and more than a little mortified, she'd refrained from revealing what had occurred to anyone, even Aggie, and thus had had no outlet to discuss, make sense of or attempt to find a solution to her dilemma. Nor had she made further mention of it to Willie. Their daily crossing of paths continued as it always did, as had the greetings and exchanging of news. However, their once general chit-chat seemed stilted now, the easy laughter a thing of the past. Mara missed it but knew there could be no going back, now, to how things had been before.

She couldn't unhear those words, just as sure as Willie couldn't take them back – not that he had any desire to, it seemed. So, she'd simply pushed it to one side as if it had never happened; but for how long would that last?

He would bring it up again at some point, was bound to. And what then? What on earth was she going to do, say, when that time came? She didn't share his feelings and never could. Yet hurting him was the last thing she wanted to do. It was all such a mess.

'I'll be seeing ye then, Mara.'

Realising Willie was speaking again, bringing her back to the present with a bump, she nodded without meeting his eye. 'Right, so. Take care, Willie.'

Despite what he'd said, still he went on staring at her – she could feel his desperate gaze boring into her bowed head. Then, as though understanding she wasn't about to utter more, he grasped the handles of his kindling barrow and continued on his round.

From beneath her lashes, Mara watched him go with a bite of her lip. Moments later, the first fat raindrops escaped from the heavens and plop-plopped on to her cheeks to mingle with her tears. Reckoning she'd had enough for one day, she too took her leave; hitching up her basket, she dragged her feet on for home.

A steady downpour enveloped the dull cobbled streets and lanes for the remainder of the day, along with inter- mittent growls of distant thunder. By the time Mara had finished buying foodstuffs and rushed back to begin pre- paring her stepsons' evening meal, she was soaked to the marrow.

Letting herself into her old house with a shudder and click of her tongue, she shook her head to the men. 'Sure, isn't it rotten out there! 'Tis bouncing off the ground that rain, so it is, 'tis coming down that badly—'

'Shurrup, will thee, and look.'

At Eugene's barked interjection, she paused in her task of removing her sodden shawl to glance over her shoulder. Seeing the sheet of paper that he was waving excitedly, her heart plummeted to her toes. 'A letter . . . from Conrad?'

'Aye!'

God help her.

'And today of all days, eh?' added Eamon.

They had remembered the significance of the date after all. 'That's grand, so,' she lied.

'It is that. It's gorra be nigh on eighteen months since last we heard from him – least we know he's well, glory be to God. Here, go and show it to the priest, get him to read it to thee. We're dying to know what it says.'

Eyes downcast, she went to drape her shawl over the back of a chair. 'Sure, it'll have to be tomorrow. 'Tis late; Father Kelly shan't be best pleased if I go disturbing him now. Besides, I've your meal to see to.' Holding out a hand, she flashed a disarming smile. 'Pass it to me and I'll take it along to the priest first thing in the morning.'

Despite their grunts and scowls, the lads did as she bade. Mara placed the letter in her apron pocket then headed to the fire to begin preparing the food.

Just what would this one say? she fretted to herself as she worked. Conrad's previous correspondences . . . She swallowed hard at the memory.

This now was the third time they had had word from him since he'd sailed – Lord forgive her, at times she'd

127

half hoped they had heard the last from him. All manner of things could happen in those far-away countries, after all . . . but no. Conrad was still very much alive. Just what did that mean for her?

I am counting down the hours, Ma dearest, until we are reunited.

Chilling passages from those earlier messages, which she'd done her damnedest to banish from her memory, trickled in to terrorise her.

You have my solemn promise on one thing: it will be a day that neither of us will ever forget.

Glad of the distraction that her chores afforded her, Mara concentrated all of her efforts on them, and yet it was a losing battle; the thinly veiled threats refused to be silenced.

The look on your face when next we meet will be a priceless one, I just know it. It is this thought alone which feeds my blood with strength to survive this hell. Not for anything in this world would I miss that, believe me . . .

Stop it – stop it, she pleaded inwardly with her mind. However, the panic- and nausea-inducing lines churned on regardless and she was glad when the meal was done and she had the excuse to flee back to next door.

'You get round to that priest first thing, d'you hear?' Eamon reminded her as she was leaving. 'We'll be waiting.'

Lying in her bed that night – a lumpy straw palliasse before Aggie's kitchen fire; undeniably uncomfortable but nonetheless preferable in that she wasn't at her old house – Mara's brain was a mush of what-ifs, each more worrisome than the last.

The distance separating her and Conrad meant not a

thing in these moments – still, he had the power to leave her quailing with the possibilities of his imminent revenge. And exact it he would; of this she was in no doubt. Nor, if she was truly honest with herself, could she blame him. Because of her, his life had been torn asunder. He'd had his freedom, his home and his country ripped away from him. His brothers and father also – Seamus permanently. He'd had no opportunity to say a final goodbye to him, would never get to see his father again. Conrad would make her pay, all right. One day, he surely would.

As though sensing her mood and endeavouring to match it, outside the weather had turned fouler still. Rain lashed, thunder cracked like a whip through the heavens, and lightning dazzled the black expanse visible through the small window.

In the shards of flashing light, the letter glared at her from the table. Pulling the thin blanket that covered her up around her chin, she shivered violently. However, she made no attempt to shut her tired eyes.

Sleep wouldn't come, of this she was certain. Nothing could release her from her trials this night.

'Eeh, this awful bloody storm! It's showing no sign of letting up, is it?'

Only half listening, a distracted Mara offered her friend a murmured agreement. But one thought dominated her mind still right now and it had nothing to do with the elements.

'Are you for taking it round to him right now, lass?' Aggie nodded to the letter. 'Stop and have a bit of porridge first, eh, or a sup of tea at least? Norra thing has passed your lips since yesterday.'

The other woman was already lifting the pot, but Mara shook her head. 'I'll not, love, thank ye all the same. I'd rather get this over with, so I would.'

'Well, if you're sure . . .'

'I am. Bye for now.' Before Aggie could waylay her further, Mara beat a retreat.

The rain was falling in sheets – sighing, she drew her shawl up over her head and clutched the ends together tightly beneath her chin. The journey to Father Kelly took but a handful of minutes; nonetheless, by the time she arrived she resembled a drowned rat. He welcomed her with a tut-tut to the murky sky then clasped his hands behind his back.

'Hello, Father.'

'Mrs O'Hara. You're well?'

'Aye, I . . . Aye.' She gave a less than confident nod. Then, taking a deep breath, she reached inside her apron pocket and with great reluctance brought out the note. 'I wondered, Father, if you'd be kind enough to read it? It's from my stepson away in the Australias.'

The priest raised an eyebrow. 'Ah! It's relieved you all must be to hear from him. 'Tis been a while since last you sought me out on such matters.'

'Aye,' Mara whispered, and did her very best to squeeze out a smile, but her efforts fell miserably short. 'It's glad we are to be sure.'

Father Kelly waved her towards a pew and, once they were seated, turned his attentions to the correspondence. Watching his eyes travel over the page and Conrad's dictation written there, Mara's stomach was in ribbons. Then the priest was speaking and she clenched her hands into fists and forced herself to listen.

'Well, you'll be happy to learn this, I'm certain!' he exclaimed.

Her brows drew together in confusion whilst, for reasons she couldn't fathom, her dread mounted. 'Learn what, Father?'

'He writes to say he's no longer at Swan River Colony. He was issued with a ticket of leave some months past.'

It couldn't be. It couldn't be! 'You mean . . . Conrad was released?' She almost choked on a gasp.

'No, no. That's not what it means, I'm afraid.'

Overwhelming relief swamped her. Covering her mouth, she squeezed her eyes shut. *Thank Christ.* 'Then what?'

'A ticket of leave is a *conditional* release. Essentially a "liberation rehearsal" passport, if you will. Convicts earn it by showing exemplary behaviour and productiveness. It permits him to dwell and seek employment outside of the prison, almost like a regular person. I say "almost" as he will have to adhere to certain restrictions. For example, he mustn't stray outside of the district. He will also be required to report monthly to the local resident magistrate.

'It's a means of benefitting both sides: the government ceases having to house and feed the convict and so limits expenditure, and in turn it offers convicts a practice run at reintegration into society by earning their own living and enjoying more freedoms. Of course, the ticket remains valid only on the condition he stays on the right side of the law, you understand.'

131

Mara's head was spinning. She understood enough, all right. Whatever additional details she was hearing mattered not an iota bar one truth: Conrad had been granted enough leeway to stow himself on to a ship. *And come hell or high water, he would grasp any opportunity.* God in heaven, she was done for.

'I feel it only right to warn you, Mrs O'Hara, that things mightn't turn out as you expect in the future,' the priest was saying now – Mara had to force herself to concentrate on his words.

'Father?'

'You must prepare yourself for the fact that he might decide to become a settler out there and not come back to England at all once he's completed his sentence. Many individuals, upon receiving their Certificate of Freedom and becoming a fully free subject again, do choose to forgo their native land in favour of a fresh new start in Australia. Conrad may very well prove to be one of them.'

'Oh, no. He'll be back.' Her tone was flat with acquiescence. 'Make no mistake about that.'

Blind to her inner turmoil, the priest gave a blithe smile. 'Perhaps you're right. After all,' he added, roving his gaze back along the letter, 'as your stepson states here: *Liberty is so near I can almost smell it. Not long now, Ma . . .*'

'Sorry, but I must be getting back,' Mara blurted, rising quickly to her feet and cutting short the hateful lines, which, naturally, the priest took for mere innocent endearments. She'd turn mad in the head entirely should she have to endure a single word more. 'Goodbye, Father. Thank ye kindly for your time.'

Outside, she stood stock still and let the rain beat down

on her bare head for what felt like an age. Each cold drop to her scalp shocked the nerves and halted her racing thoughts – for just a millisecond, at any rate – but that minuscule distraction was better than nothing and indubitably worth the mild pain. One or two folks, themselves having no desire to stand idly and instead eager to reach their destinations and shelter, shot her puzzled looks as they scuttled past, but she paid them no heed. Let them assume about her what they liked, it mattered not; nothing did any more. Soon, Conrad would be here and life as she knew it would cease to exist.

An overpowering urge to flee to her private woodland world on the city's fringes struck her like a physical force. She would sit among the sodden blooms and all verities would rise from her like steam to glide away on the breeze . . .

But it couldn't last – nothing ever did. And then what?

She must confront reality eventually, and it might as well be now.

Eamon and Eugene suspected nothing of her internal sufferings as she relayed to them the contents of the letter – minus, of course, the references to herself, which she was always mindful to omit. The task completed, she took her leave of them and drifted back to Aggie's in a queer kind of daze.

'Lass?' Her friend was on her feet instantly. 'By God, you look terrible! What the divil's happened?'

'Hm?' Mara tried to process the woman's speech, but it floated from her grasp and the room began to spin. 'The furniture, Aggie . . . it's moving. I feel . . .'

'Oh bugger; you're for fainting, lass! Fret not, for I'm here. I've got thee . . .'

Hands closed around Mara's upper arms; on a sigh, she let the darkness carry her off.

'D'you know, you'll be the ruddy death of me, you will.'

'Aggie?'

'Aye, lass, it's me.'

Mara blinked through the dim light. Dull pain throbbed behind her temples and her throat felt scratchy. 'I'm not too good.'

'You're not, nay.' Her friend's voice was soft. She smoothed back curls from Mara's forehead with a tender touch. 'It'll be from getting caught out in that rain. You've a fever coming on, I reckon.'

Remembrance trickled in, bringing with it burning tears. 'Oh, love. I'm done for! The letter ... Conrad's coming home!'

Aggie's gasp was one of horror. 'What? They've let the insane sod loose?'

'In a manner of speaking. He was granted more freedoms months ago for good conduct – one of them being to live outside the gaol walls. If that man can convince or coerce someone into stowing him aboard a ship, then he'll do it. He could be at sea bound for England right now, could be on his way back as we speak!'

'Sshhh, lass.' Aggie soothed away her distress gently. 'Don't take on so, you'll use up your energy.'

'How can I not worry, though? Eeh, I'm that afraid! He's going to kill me, I know it – and who can blame him, really? I took everything away from him. I've ruined his life!'

Her friend put a finger under Mara's chin and brought

her gaze around to meet hers. 'Now you listen to me, lass. That swine brought all this on his own head. Aye, he *did*,' she insisted when Mara made to protest. 'Getting hisself embroiled in gangs and guns and goodness knows what else – him getting locked up were bound to happen sometime, with or without your help. Who knows what future crimes he'd have gone on to commit? What we've to figure out now is how to get thee away from here afore his return. Away somewhere safe, aye, where he'll not find thee.'

Mara knew she spoke sense. Hadn't she had the same thought countless times? Yet the prospect of uprooting her whole life remained still a daunting and frightening one. And besides, where on earth would she go? She had nowhere, no one. 'It's useless, love.'

'Couldn't tha go back to Ireland?'

'No, love. There was nothing for me or Rebecca there all those years ago when we said goodbye to it – sure, it's one of the main reasons we left in the first place. There's even less reason to return today.'

'Was it the famine what did it, lass?'

She nodded. 'I was only around four of five when the first blight struck, but I recall it vividly. Rebecca's ma died when she was a baby, and her da and mine were brothers. My uncle worked the land, which he rented – it was a modest holding in terms of size, but they scratched by relatively well – and my own da toiled for him alongside. And so when the blight hit, it affected both our families.'

Here, Mara paused to cast her friend a wistful smile. 'It was a simple life we led, Aggie. Our cottage was but a single room – we were piled one on top of the other with no space between to swing a mouse and had barely anything in the way of possessions. Yet we had each other, and that was enough. We were happy, you know, and had nothing to complain about. I can picture it all now if I close my eyes, remember to this day the smell of the bog peat that we burned to warm the home in winter, hear still my mother singing as she washed our clothes at the river . . .

'Towards the end of that spring 1845, there came a dry spell the like of which we'd never known before. Weeks and weeks and weeks of glorious sunshine. Rebecca's an only child but she was more like a sibling than a cousin to me and my brothers and sisters; we'd always been inseparable. Throughout those days of constant fine weather, it was no different. We had a grand time playing in the fields and paddling in the streams. It was all fun and games to us, young as we were, never imagining what impact the heatwave could have on the land. Then the rains came, and we saw that the adults were beginning to grow worried about the upcoming harvest . . . Oh, Aggie, it was an awful time.'

Releasing a pained sigh, Mara shook her head. 'As with so many others, all of my uncle's potatoes were reduced to a stinking, black and mushy mess. They were our main food source, and so, when we had none to eat . . . The fear of starvation was a very real one. We didn't know what we were going to do.'

Aggie had tears in her eyes. 'What *did* you do?' she asked in a whisper.

'We caught tiddlers from the river and, if we were lucky, the odd rabbit in the fields – in fact, anything even remotely edible that we could lay our hands on went towards making a meal. But it was just never enough to fill the pot – or our bellies. We were forever wanting.'

'Eeh, lass.'

'Hunger is a horrible thing,' she went on quietly. 'It gnaws at your very bones, so it does, after a time. Having to watch his children growing starving-thin and listen to their cries of hunger was too much for my father: as so many others had been forced to do, he began spending the rent money on food. And just like those other tenants, we found ourselves evicted by the military troops and our home destroyed. Such was life back there under English rule – oh, how I hated your lot then and longed for revolution and a free, independent Ireland!'

Her friend was nodding. 'And no wonder. I can understand that. I can, aye.'

'We were luckier than those homeless folks reduced to sleeping under the stars – my uncle took us in. 'Course, this meant more mouths to feed for us all, and our hardship was greater still. But for my uncle we'd have been doomed. He signed with the Board of Works set up by the British government and got himself a job roadbuilding. The money wasn't great but it was better than nothing at all – and we needed every penny as my father was now unable to earn. Losing our cottage broke something inside of him; he seemed to age twenty years overnight. His spirit was crushed, and his will to live deserted him. Before Christmas rolled around, he'd passed away.'

'Mara, love, that's terrible.'

'How the rest of us ever managed to survive that first winter, I'll never know. But somehow, we did. With nothing left to us but hope, we clung on for the next harvest

137

and prayed for all we were worth that it would be a healthy one.'

'But it weren't,' said Aggie softly.

Closing her eyes, Mara shook her head. 'Watching those little white flowers of the potato plants blossom was a beautiful sight. Didn't we dare believe that the dark days were truly behind us? Then came reality and devastation: the crops turned out to be as putrid as those of the previous year. The blight had struck again. Sickness and starvation were already wiping out whole families – now, things became even worse. Then at the start of the new year, tragedy found our home and changed my life for ever.'

'What occurred, lass?'

Mara had to swallow back sobs before she could continue. 'Half mad from the hunger, my siblings gorged on diseased potatoes – they couldn't help themselves, Aggie, were desperate. They caught the Yellow Fever and were dead within the week.'

'All of them?' Her friend was aghast.

'Aye, all six. My poor mother was shattered, could never have recovered from such a loss.'

'She died an' all?'

'She did, of a broken heart, shortly after. My uncle raised me alongside Rebecca the best he knew how, but it was far from easy – for any of us. When eventually he himself passed away, my cousin and me knew there was nothing left for us in Ireland. Keen for a fresh start, we pooled every penny left to us by my uncle and bought ourselves a passage to England. The rest you know, so you do.'

Aggie blew out air slowly. 'By gum, you ain't half been through the mill, you poor lass.'

138

'Aye.'

'I don't even know what to say.'

Scrubbing away tears, Mara couldn't help but smile. 'Sure, that's got to be a first for you, love, eh?'

'Cheeky bleeder, yer!' the other woman cried. Nonetheless, she was grinning. 'Eeh, well. I guess you fleeing to Ireland *is* out of the question, then, all right.'

''Tis, and there's nowhere else besides, so it's pointless dwelling on it further. Anyway, Aggie, I could never leave you.'

'You could and you must.' Her friend was resolute. 'There's gorra be a way, there just has to be. Conrad alone is bad enough, but you just wait when he tells the others what you did . . . Them stepsons of yourn shan't rest till they've made you pay. I know it and so do you. Lass, you have to leave here. You must go and never come back.'

The friends hugged tightly, both shedding bitter tears. When they drew apart, Mara glanced away with a guilty shake of her head.

'Lass?'

'There's something else I should have told ye but didn't know how to. Willie Keogh . . . he declared his love for me.'

The woman released a low whistle. 'Bloody hell, that's all you need, on top of everything else.'

'Aye.'

'Slippery sod! I knew he had his beady eye on thee. Didn't I say?'

'You did. I don't feel the same for him in that way, and yet I don't want to lose him as a friend, neither. Oh, why is everything such a hideous mess? Aggie, what am I to do?'

'There's but one thing you'll do right now, lass, and that's get some rest.'

'But ... I've Eamon and Eugene's meals to see to and—'

'What? Them pair can look after themselves forra change and lump it!'

Mara smothered a yawn with the back of her hand. 'I *am* exhausted, so . . .'

'Aye, so just you stop right where you are. Sleep is what you're short of. It'll build your strength. And by God,' she added grimly beneath her breath, 'you're going to need as much of that as you can lay your hands on, and no mistake.'

Chapter 10

EVERY BUMP AND creak, each knock at the door and voice in the street left Mara a quailing wreck.

Contrary to Aggie's warning, the dreaded fever hadn't come but, in its place, Mara had developed a nasty head cold. Concerned it might worsen into something more sinister, her friend had insisted she take it easy, and Mara had been confined to the house for three long days. Without the distraction afforded by work, but one thing had dominated her thoughts throughout: Conrad. The prospect of his imminent return had lodged at the forefront of her mind and, despite her best efforts to evict it, refused to leave. Mara oftentimes worried she might go mad.

By Saturday, she'd reached her limit. As soon as the first dawn light appeared over the rooftops, she threw back the blankets and rose with a sense of renewed purpose. Hiding herself away here and wallowing in her own misery wasn't going to change matters. She had to try to get back to some mode of normality – and she must earn. Besides, when and if the time came that she was forced to flee, she'd need funds, wouldn't she? Could hardly get very far without.

Though Aggie, upon listening to Mara's reasoning, gave a reluctant nod of understanding, still she couldn't hold back a frown of displeasure. 'I just think tha ought to stop, put inside in the warmth forra little while longer, lass, that's all. After all, that blasted rain *still* ain't buggered off, has it? Over a week it's been at it for now – and, like yesterday, the storms are worse than ever today!'

'I must get out, even if it's only for an hour or two.' Mara was resolute. 'Sure, aren't these four walls beginning to feel like my prison? I'll be grand, love, honest. Besides, won't Willie be worrying over me? He ain't seen hide nor hair of me for days. I have to put his mind at rest that I'm all right.'

Clicking her tongue, Aggie waved her off to the door. 'Well, on your head be it, lass. Just you mind you don't get struck down by that lightning. Shocking, it's been – I ain't never known the like of it in all my born days!'

Mara couldn't help but smile. 'I'll try, so.'

'Aye. Anyroad, go on then, you get off, if you really must. I'll see thee later.'

The sky was ditchwater in colour and looked as though it had been smudged by a giant, grubby hand – Mara pulled a face at it. A damp curtain hung like a pall over everything; you could almost reach out and touch the air itself. Still the rain continued to fall relentlessly, mixing with the general muck and refuse to gather in foul-smelling rivulets along the tumbledown streets.

She'd picked the bare minimum of flowers required to make up a few bunches – soggy and bedraggled as they were by nature's onslaught – and was heading back towards Ancoats when she discovered that during the few short hours she'd been gone her usual route had altered beyond recognition. Stopping dead, she gazed around open-mouthed.

London Road – a chief thoroughfare and part of the main artery of the city – had disappeared. In its place were sprawling lakes, some a quarter of a mile in length and easily several feet deep, making it seemingly impassable. It was like the world as she knew it had been gobbled up and flipped on its head.

Spotting a stunned-looking man wading through the waters towards her holding a toddler above his head, she cried across: 'You there! What's happened?'

'It's the Medlock,' he called back, tone hollow with incredulousness. 'It's burst its banks.'

'Mother of God!'

'Get yourself to safety, lass, for things will only get worse afore they gets better.'

'I will. Take care!' she added to his retreating back as he hurried as fast as he could manage on his way.

Figuring that whatever direction she tried she'd wind up running into the same problem, and reasoning that if that man could manage whilst encumbered with a child then surely she could, Mara took some calming breaths. Then, holding out her arms to aid her balance, she set off with slow and measured steps through the deluge.

Floods were nothing new to the area. Both Manchester and neighbouring Salford had suffered a number of them throughout the years.

The worst of these, and which locals now referred to as the Great Flood, had occurred during late November of

'66, almost six years ago, when a bloated River Irwell had broken its embankment.

The terrible event had torn families apart and caused thousands of pounds' worth of damage. Scores had fled their homes, and many of those who stayed were left without drinking water or gas. When finally the rains stopped and frost arrived, folk had assumed the situation was over. However, the monumental clean-up that followed was to prove a cruel and pointless task. To their horror, the rains returned. Water that had begun to recede swelled once more, and a second flood swept in.

The loss to life and property during that dark period had been devastating but, somehow, they had got through it. Surely, people had been asking themselves ever since, *surely* they would never experience anything so bad again?

Yet here they were. Mara could have wept.

The water reached to her thighs in places and she was beginning to regret not having attempted a different route after all. Nonetheless, she continued pushing on steadily and, to her great relief, she eventually emerged into adjoining Fairfield Street, exhausted and shivering violently, but mercifully unscathed.

The further on she trudged, the more severe the situation became. Pausing at one point to catch her breath, she clung to a gas lamp for support and peered around through a blur of tears. Everywhere was carnage. The turgid waters had increased in velocity and by now were fast-flowing; it was an effort to remain on your feet. Yet that wasn't the only hazard posed. As the putrid, sewage-sullied river surged along on its devastating mission of subjugation, it dragged with it all in its path.

144

Materials of every description, from goods and machinery carried from surrounding works and factories to drowned dogs and pigs and household furniture, jostled with one another, and avoiding injury from the pitching debris was a near-impossible task. Still, the flood level was climbing, so much so that it threatened to reach the bedroom windows of some dwellings and particularly those of low-lying cottages.

Screams and shouts rent the air from all sides as terrified families scrambled down rickety ladders to be rescued by neighbours below. Others, poverty-stricken as they were and desperate to save what meagre belongings they possessed as they could, staggered under the weight of hastily gathered bundles tied to their backs.

By some miracle, the majority of the fleeing masses managed to haul their way to higher ground and relative safety. Some were not so lucky and were swept off on the currents.

Damping down her panic, Mara had begun to fight her way once more for home when a hand on her shoulder stopped her in her tracks. She craned her neck around – and let out a sob of pure relief: 'Willie!'

'I thought my eyes were playing tricks on me . . . Sweet Jesus, Mara, what are you doing here? Are ye all right?'

'Aye. No. Sure, I don't know . . . Oh, please help me!'

'Come on, this way.'

Clinging on to the Irishman's hand for dear life, Mara allowed herself to be led through the swampy narrow lanes and backstreets.

They turned another corner and another, concentrating all the while on dodging pieces of wood and glass and

145

fallen masonry from ancient buildings unable to sustain the onslaught and that had collapsed into the dark waters. Suddenly, a flash of grey bobbing just below the surface appeared, catching her gaze – she shunted aside to avoid it. Yet, as it passed by, something made her turn back. A cry caught in her throat at the grisly image she was met with.

The 'object' had shifted position, was no longer floating horizontally but vertically. There, jutting through the water, was a hand. It swayed gently with the ripples, as though waving her on her way. Squeezing shut her eyes, Mara released a scream.

'Christ in heaven above!'

Locked in shock, she could only watch on as Willie, having taken in the situation, thrashed his way across. He reached beneath the waters and eased the body to the surface – and now, it was his turn to let out a yawp of horror.

It was like a vision straight from hell.

Mara covered her face with her hands, desperate to blot out the horrific image, but it was branded on her memory and she knew it always would be – just what did it *mean*?

'Willie?'

'I don't know, Mara.'

'But . . . what . . .'

'I don't know,' he repeated, and there were tears on his lashes. 'I can't understand it either.'

The corpse was badly decomposed.

This person wasn't newly deceased, wasn't a victim of the flood. They had been dead for months, easily.

How was this possible? What on earth was going on?

146

In a daze, they continued on their way. However, they had gone no further than a few yards when Willie juddered to a halt. He grasped Mara's arm. 'Oh my . . .'

'Mother of God!' she croaked.

There was another body up ahead.

'Jesus, Mara, don't look,' Willie advised after hurrying across and taking in the condition up close. He held out his arms to shield her from the sight. ''Tis terrible, just terrible . . . This poor soul has been dead years at least!'

'Years?' Her incredulousness was absolute. She felt light-headed with the bewildering uncertainty of it all. 'Just what is *happ*ening?'

'Let's get out of here – come on.'

Mara didn't need telling twice – she took the hand he held out to her and they fled the grim scenes as quickly as the waters would allow them.

When they emerged into the next street and spotted a crowd huddled around something in the road, they shared a look of dread; it didn't take much guesswork to figure out what held their attention captive. With much reluctance, they made their way across.

'There's more back the way we've just come,' Willie informed them hoarsely. 'What the devil can it mean?'

'It means,' murmured a member of the group, 'that the flood has destroyed the cemetery at St Philips. Coffins have been washed clean from their graves, and bodies are scattered all around the city.'

United in their distress, a hush fell on the gathering. And to think they had dared believe that this situation and the day in general was bad enough. This just got worse and worse.

147

'The lass here can only have been buried a matter of days ago, Lord love her,' said someone else, nodding to the corpse at his feet. 'She ain't much ravaged by decay, nay. Mind you, she looks to have took a nasty beating afore death claimed her if her phizzog's owt to go by.'

Mara had refrained from looking; now, she shot the figure in question a quick glance. Then she did a double-take – and another. As if they had taken on a life of their own, her feet moved forward and in the next moment she was pushing through the swell of people.

Willie called out to her, but it was as though he spoke from miles away; the words were too muffled and dis-jointed to reach her or make sense. In a dream-like state, she halted and stared down at the woman fully. The world rotated. Her legs gave way and she fell to her knees on a whimper.

The body was bloated, the discoloured flesh purple-green in hue, the face indeed hideously disfigured. But the hair . . . The hair was as it had always been, as Mara remembered it.

She reached out and smoothed slimy mud and grit from the thick, fiery tresses. Then she forced her eyes downwards – further, further – towards the left wrist and what she knew she'd find there. Sure enough, a string of orange glass hung around it limply. Life left her own heart. She threw herself across the still chest, the chest that would never rise and fall again, and wailed like an injured beast.

'Mara?' It was the Irishman. He touched her shoulder with a hesitant hand. 'Mara, what in God's name . . . You know her?'

'Aye,' she finally managed to choke out.

'Who?'

''Tis my cousin, Willie. 'Tis my Rebecca.'

'Mara's fit for nowt more this day, and that's that.'

'But she said—'

'And *I* said nay, Willie Keogh! I know what's best for the lass.'

The Irishman opened his mouth to argue the point further, but Mara got in before him: 'It's all right, Willie. I know I was adamant earlier, but it was the grief talking. I've had time to think and see now that Aggie's correct in what she says,' she murmured. 'Besides, I'd have no joy even if I were to try, not right now. The city's been turned on its head. Folk have more pressing concerns on their minds than helping me find out what became of Rebecca. No one will have answers for me today.'

'Aye,' piped up Aggie in agreement, directing at Willie a vindicated sniff. 'So let's just drop the notion, shall we?'

'Right, so.' He rose abruptly, face stiff. 'I'll be away, then.'

Mara walked with him to the door. 'Don't take it personally, Willie, it's just Aggie's way,' she told him gently – it was evident that he'd taken umbrage to her friend's manner, and who could blame him? 'She's protective of me, so she is. That's all.'

Though he offered a nod of understanding, his smile was strained. 'Will I call on ye tomorrow? I'd still like to accompany you to the church if you – or anybody else,' he added, throwing Aggie a look over Mara's shoulder, 'have no objections.'

'I . . .' Though she'd have liked to have undertaken such a task on her own, highly personal and emotive as the subject was, she didn't feel able to deny him. He'd been so kind and supportive of her today; she shuddered to wonder what she'd have done without him. 'Aye, all right. Thank ye, Willie.'

When he'd gone, she returned to her chair beside Aggie's at the table and shook her head. 'You were a bit rude to the man, there, love. Sure, I didn't know where to put my face.'

'Well, he gets on my nerves. Don't ask me why, mind, but he does all the same. There's summat about him I just can't warm to.'

'Och, Willie's harmless enough. He's been very good to me, Aggie – and today especially so.'

'It's glad I am that your paths crossed, aye,' the woman was forced to admit. 'God alone knows what could have befallen thee had they not done. Eeh, d'you know, I can hardly believe it all. What a terrible, *terrible* thing to happen again.'

'We must thank the Lord that our own street here weren't much affected, Aggie. So many have been forced from their dwellings, and more besides left with nothing.'

'You're right there, lass.'

After seeing an inconsolable Mara home several hours before, Willie had made his way back to the more severely affected areas to offer what assistance he could. He'd returned in the evening around six thirty, bedraggled and exhausted to the point of collapse, but notwithstanding thankful to report that the flood waters were receding. It was the news they had been hoping for and

150

each had shed a tear of blessed relief that the worst was over.

'So Keogh's for going with thee tomorrow to speak with Father Kelly?' Aggie wanted to know now as she reached for the teapot.

Mara nodded. 'That's right.'

'I thought you said you'd rather go alone?'

'Aye, I would, but . . . Willie was good enough to offer. I didn't like to say no.'

'You don't worry you might be leading him on?' Her friend, never one to withhold her opinions, lifted an eyebrow. 'He's in love with thee, after all, you know it yourself; it's the wrong idea you'll be for giving him if you ain't careful.'

Biting her lip, Mara glanced away. 'I don't mean to, would hate to give him false hope . . .'

'Then you must tell him how you feel, put the matter to bed once and for all. It shan't bode well for either of youse if it's not nipped in the bud, and soon, you mark my words.'

'You're right, I know, only I haven't the energy to even think on all that just now . . . Oh, Aggie, what a day!'

With a sigh, the other woman reached across the table for Mara's hand, and her tone had softened. 'I know, lass.'

'My poor, *poor*, darling Rebecca . . .'

'Eeh, I am sorry.'

Mara buried her face in her arm and let devastated tears, which she'd barely managed to stem for more than a few minutes all day, run freely once again. 'I don't know how I'll ever bear this,' she wept. 'All these years I held on to the one secret hope that I'd find her somehow and we'd be together again. Now, it'll never be. She's gone, Aggie, gone from this life – and I wish I were with her!'

'Lass, lass.' Aggie stroked Mara's fingers comfortingly. 'You mustn't speak like that, nay. She'd not want to hear you saying such things, surely?'

'But how will I go on? How can I accept that the rest of my days must pass without her ever being in them again? You tell me that.'

Aggie shook her head. 'I don't pretend to have all the answers, lass, but there's one thing I do know: you're not to even think about doing owt daft. D'you hear?'

'But I have nothing to live for no more, Aggie! I don't!'

'Listen to me.' The woman had come to crouch beside Mara. She drew her sob-wracked form into her arms. 'I ain't never lied to thee, have I? Well, have I?'

'No.'

'Right then, so tha knows that what I'm about to tell thee is the honest truth. You're not finished on this earth, my lass, not by a long chalk. You'll meet your cousin again someday, but that time ain't yet, and nor would Rebecca want it to be, nay. You're needed here, lass, don't you see? Promise me right now you'll dash any ideas of doing harm to yourself from your mind. Promise me, Mara.'

'I didn't really mean it, I'm just . . .'

'And you'll not ever harbour such dreadful thoughts again?'

'I'll not, love. I promise.'

The women embraced. Then a banging came at the wall from next door, cutting short the moment, and they both sighed.

152

'I'll do for them two buggers one of these days, I will!'
Aggie fumed.

Murmuring that she'd best see to her stepsons' evening
meal, Mara got to her feet, but her friend eased her back
into her seat.

'Don't you even think about it,' she chided, draping
the blanket back around Mara's shoulders. 'You need to
rest and warm up; you ain't budging from yon fire this
night for nowt.'

'But—'

'I'll go.'

'You're sure, Aggie?'

'If it means you stopping put here, then I suppose I'll
have to. Mind you, it ain't grub that I'd like to dish out to
them! A ruddy fat smack would be on the menu instead if
I had my way, let me tell thee! Don't fret, I'm just sound-
ing off, shan't start a ruckus for your sake,' she hastened
to add when Mara bit her lip. 'You'll be all right seeing to
the kiddies upstairs should one of them stir?'

'I will so. And thank ye, love.'

'You just relax. I'll see thee later.'

Aggie left and, moments later, Mara heard her entering
the house next door. Despite her friend's reassurances,
Mara was well aware of how easily Aggie's temper could
flare with enough provocation – and what her volatile
stepsons' reaction to this might well be – and she kept her
ears pricked with bated breath. However, as the minutes
ticked on, all remained still and quiet, much to her relief.
With a sigh, she snuggled deeper into her chair and let
the calming atmosphere of the dim-lit kitchen soothe her
tattered nerves.

153

Rebecca is dead. Those three words just didn't sound right when put into a sentence together, even now.

Was it really true? she asked herself, as she had numerous times over the hours – then quickly pushed the thought away as the gruesome vision of her cousin's corpse assaulted her mind in confirmation.

'What happened to you?' she whispered to the empty air, hugging herself in her desperation for comfort. 'Where have you been throughout the years since last we saw each other, and with who? Oh, love, how have things turned out so badly?'

Even if by some miracle the answers to her burning questions had made themselves known to her, she wouldn't have heard them – a thunderous voice leaked through the wall, cutting off all other sound.

'Why, you blackhearted pair of divils, yer! You ought to be ashamed.'

It was Aggie. Frowning, Mara crossed the room and pressed her ear to the thin bare bricks separating them.

'I inform you of all the lass has been through the day, hoping you might show at least an ounce of sympathy, and still you can think only of yourselfs?' her friend went on. 'Mara could have drowned in them flood waters, aye, but you're not mithered one bit, are youse? And on top of all that, she suffered the horror of finding her dear cousin's body in the bloody street – but again, you care not a jot about that, neither, do youse? Just what is wrong with them brains of yourn, eh? Warped is what youse are – warped!'

Oh, Aggie, there's no point in trying to reason with them. Just let it drop, please, Mara begged silently. Then her stepsons were speaking and she felt the colour drain from her face:

154

'Oh, shut tha trap, you silly owd bitch,' Eamon spat. 'Did you really think we'd care two figs? That Irish slut means nowt to us and never has.'

'Aye,' put in Eugene. 'That bogtrotter you call a friend could drop down dead the morrow and all's we'd be worried about was who we'd find next to cook our meals.'

They laughed like demented donkeys, the sound like daggers in Mara's ear and heart. In that moment, it was like a veil had lifted and the world appeared clear.

She saw finally the true way of things – and she felt a first-rate eejit. The boys – all three – that she'd spent the best part of her life raising felt nothing for her – *nothing* – and never had. She'd wasted so much time and effort, and for what? By Christ, she owed them nothing, not any more. From now on, they were on their own, and to hell with the lot of them!

As the inner vow was made, she knew a sense of finality, peace almost. And she knew without a shadow of doubt that all that had gone before was no more, and that things would never be the same again.

It was time to put herself first, for once. God help anyone who attempted to get in her way.

Chapter 11

THE AFTERMATH OF one of the worst floods to ever visit the city was a sobering sight the following morning as Mara and Willie made their way towards Philips Park. The complete destruction of so many businesses and dwellings alike was unfathomable and had left many questioning whether Manchester could ever recover.

As usual, the poorer class in the more densely populated districts was among the hardest hit, and particularly those living in cellars. Their homes had been left utterly ruined and surely wouldn't be free of damp for many years to come, they were certain.

To add to the devastation, the river had left behind a hideous parting gift: a thick blanket of filth that encompassed everything. Sludgy earth, sand and gravel coated the saturated streets, making travel in all its forms a treacherous affair – Mara made sure to hold tight to Willie's arm for fear of slipping headlong into the gutter.

Despite all this, there was one thing that the people had to be thankful for. Unlike the last great overflow, miraculously, no one was as yet reported to have died this time around.

Collection boxes for the relief of the sufferers had been organised and both Mara and Willie donated a few pence each. However, though empathetic of their plight, Mara didn't dwell on the thought for too long – couldn't. For all too soon, the church was upon them and but one thing dominated every aspect of her existence once more: seeing Father Kelly and getting answers about Rebecca.

They found the priest by the cemetery gates. He had his eyes closed and his face was haggard; he looked as though he hadn't caught a wink of sleep the previous night – which, in all likelihood, given the circumstances, he probably hadn't. Sorry to disturb him but aware nonetheless that wild horses wouldn't have kept her from speaking with him, Mara approached with a soft clearing of her throat.

'Mrs O'Hara.' His tone was void of its usual energy. 'Good morning.'

'Hello, Father. Might I talk with ye?'

He nodded and without another word led the way to the church.

Once inside, Mara got straight to the point: 'The dead who were disturbed from their graves during yesterday's flooding, Father . . .'

He released a long and heavy sigh. 'Aye, indeed. It was the Roman Catholic section that was affected. I've just conducted a more thorough surveyance of the area and regret to say it is in a most shocking state. They say bodies and bones were scattered all across Manchester – and there are many more as yet unaccounted for and still to be recovered. Witnesses reported seeing a number carried

157

off into the Mersey ... unbe*liev*able. I just cannot ...
Terrible business. Truly terrible.'

'My cousin's remains were among those ripped from
their resting place.'

At her emotional outburst, the priest was taken aback.
His countenance fell. 'How do you know that, Mrs
O'Hara?'

'I know, Father, because I came across her myself in the
waters.' Mara was openly weeping. 'Oh, to witness such a
thing!'

He was quite clearly appalled. 'My dear child . . . I can
well imagine.'

'I stayed with her until they removed her body with the
rest to Fairfield Street Station for examination, never left
her side for a moment, honest I didn't!'

'There, there, Mrs O'Hara. Don't take on so, I believe
you.'

Realising that her rising hysteria wasn't helping matters
and wouldn't get her anywhere, she gave a great, shud-
dering breath and forced back her composure. 'Forgive
me, Father.'

'No need for apologies, none whatsoever. Now, take a
moment and, in your own time, tell me why you're here.'

'Well, the thing is, I hadn't seen or spoken to her in ever
such a long time. I recognised her right away, though; it
was the hair, so it was. Then I spotted the bracelet, the one
she'd worn since we were children, and that confirmed it
to me. I'm hoping, Father, if you can tell me more, anything at all you might remember? She hasn't been
deceased long, you see, and so surely there's a chance you
recall her internment? Perhaps you recognised whoever

attended her funeral? If I can find them, then I can start to piece together what Rebecca's been up to all these years. I really have to know. It'll help bring me peace, and sure, don't I need that more than anything? Can you help me, Father? Oh, can you? Please?'

The priest patted her arm, his eyes deep with sympathy. Then: 'Wait here.'

When Father Kelly had left, she shot Willie, hovering nearby, a hopeful look, and he nodded with a smile in response. Moments later, the priest was back. He carried now a large ledger and her heart leapt in expectancy.

'The burial register,' he explained. He flicked through the most recent pages, running his finger down each one as he scanned the names. 'Rebecca . . . Rebecca . . . Ah, and here is her entry.'

Mara craned her neck to see it – pointless, really, given the fact she couldn't read, but she was hungry for anything concerning her cousin, whatever that might be. 'What does it tell you, Father?'

'Not a lot other than she was buried on the seventh of July.'

'That's it?'

'I'm afraid so.'

'And you don't remember her funeral service or who was present?' Mara was growing desperate. 'Try to think, Father, will ye? Please.'

He screwed up his eyes for a moment and looked into the distance as though searching inside his memory, then, sighing, he shook his head. 'I'm sorry, Mrs O'Hara, but I cannot recall. You must understand that in my line of work . . .'

159

She was bitterly disappointed. 'I do,' she forced out. 'Thank you anyway, Father.'

'So what now?' Willie wanted to know when they had taken their leave and were making their way back to Aggie's.

'To be honest with you, Willie, I think I'd prefer to be alone.'

'Oh. Well, if you're sure?'

'I am,' she said thickly, past the lump threatening to choke her. 'I wouldn't be much company, so I wouldn't. 'Tis by myself that I need to be right now.'

He left her with the promise that he'd call to see her again tomorrow – with no fight left within her to attempt to either argue the point or think up a suitable excuse, Mara let him have his way with a shrug.

The gut-wrenching despondency remained with her as she continued on through the lanes for home, and by the time she reached Mitchell Street she felt she could have curled into a ball right there and then and wept for a week.

Where it came from, Mara couldn't say: a vision of a moon-like face framed by a mound of fluffy, iron-coloured hair slammed suddenly into her mind.

The long-forgotten image was as clear to her as if it had appeared through thin air right in front of her – her step faltered and she stumbled. She nodded slowly. Then renewed purpose was once again swelling her breast and she found herself spinning on her heel, turning her back on Pollard Street and the direction of home.

Seconds later, she was making off at speed towards the

heart of Ancoats and her old lodging house on Wood-
ward Street.

Reality returned the instant her knuckles touched the
wood and foolishness swooped in to take hope's place.
Cursing herself, she shook her head.

Fifteen long years had been and gone since two young
and frightened Irish girls first knocked at the door of this
neat establishment. It was a lifetime ago – and an utter
waste of her time coming back. Surely?

'Aye?'

Mara gazed, stunned, at the woman who had answered
her knock. It *was* her, here still, after all this time . . . It
was almost like she'd never been away. 'Belle? Belle, it is
you!'

'Rebecca?' The colour drained from the lined face and
she staggered back. 'But nay, it can't be, it can't, it—'

'No, Belle. It's Mara, her cousin.' She took the elderly
woman's hands in her own. 'You remember me, don't ye?'

'Mara?'

'Aye, 'tis me.'

'Eeh, lass, Mara! Eeh, and where've you been hiding
yourself, then? Ay, but what am I thinking?' she said in the
next breath in her soft, sweet voice that Mara recognised
so well. 'My manners have upped and left me, it seems.
Come on in, lass, come on in.'

When they were seated in Belle's private sitting room
with a cup of piping tea, Mara let her eyes travel around
the familiar prints adorning the walls and smiled. Not a
thing had changed, so far as she could see; it had on her

a restful effect. So much had altered in her life over the passing years – it was a comfort to know that some things at least had remained the same.

'So what's fetched thee here after so long, lass?'

Brought back to the present, Mara's small smile slipped. She placed her cup on a side table to her left and folded her hands in her lap. 'Rebecca. Rebecca's dead.'

'Aye. Awful business, love, awful.'

'You knew already?' And at Belle's nod: 'Do you also know what happened?'

'That I do.'

'Oh, please, won't ye tell me?'

The woman bobbed her head again, albeit this time reluctantly. 'If you really want me to, lass ... It ain't a pretty story.'

Mara's heart was hammering so badly she feared it might smash from her chest. *Good God, just what was she about to unearth here?* However, she had to hear it, would never know peace else. 'Tell me,' she mouthed.

Belle took a deep breath, then: 'It was the syphilis, lass.'

'What?'

'I said—'

'I know what you said, Belle ... but surely ... No, it can't be true! Not her. Not my Rebecca.'

'She weren't your Rebecca, lass – not the one you knew and loved, at any rate – not towards the end,' the woman stated gently. Pity shone from her eyes. 'She were a tortured soul was Rebecca. I did my best for her, but ...' Belle wiped her nose on her apron and shook her head. 'She couldn't be helped.'

162

Rising unsteadily, Mara paced the floor. 'Why? *How?* How could this happen?'

'She fell on hard times is what it was. She said that after struggling to find employment she finished up turning to the oldest profession there is: streetwalking.'

'Oh God, I can't bear this.' Mara put her face in her hands and sobbed.

'When you left here to get wed, Rebecca got herself a job serving in some alehouse or other. The position came with a room on the premises, and she moved out of here not long after. She'd drop in from time to time to visit me and she seemed well; she were content, aye. Then there occurred a spot of bother – her boss tried summat with her one night that he shouldn't. Only his wife took that scoundrel's side, and Rebecca found herself out on her ear.

'She returned here for a while until she gorra new job, then she was off again. And that's how it were for years. She'd be doing all right for a spell, and then some calamity or other would befall her and she'd be back lodging with me.

'After a time, she just couldn't seem to find work, permanent or otherwise. It got to her, that did. I noticed she was inning and outing it at all hours of the day and night, and so I confronted her. She admitted she were selling herself but begged me not to throw her out – 'course, I didn't; though I were far from pleased, as you can imagine. Then, at the opening of this year, she announced she'd found herself a nice little job skivvying in a well-to-do household up in Salford. Glowed with new hope, she did, lass. She changed overnight, packed

163

in all that other stuff she'd been up to. She'd really turned a corner, aye.'

Throughout the speech, Mara had listened, tears coursing unchecked down her cheeks without interruption. Now, as silence filled the room, she turned from where she'd been standing staring unseeing out of the window to face Belle.

The old woman had her eyes closed and was wringing her hands; it was clear she was finding it difficult to hold back her emotions.

Mara's tone was gentle. 'What happened next?'

'I'd not seen nowt of Rebecca forra few months when she turned up one day out of the blue. As I opened the door, she collapsed in my arms. She were bad, lass, and reet so. I couldn't believe the change in her. She were out of it for days with a fever. When eventually she came to and was strong enough to talk, she told me she'd left Salford and her job at Cresslea Manor. She'd had to, you see, for the syphilis sores had started appearing and she couldn't bear them knowing. Eeh, but this world can be wicked at times! Finally, she'd got her life together, found respectable employment and were looking forward to a fresh start, and then that had to go and happen. Such a cruel twist of fate. By, I did feel for the little love.'

Slumping back into her seat, Mara hugged herself tightly. 'You were with her when . . . when she . . .'

'I were, lass; I nursed her right to the end. Eeh, her poor bonny face . . . Mind, she never did lose that glorious hair of hers, as other sufferers normally do, glory be to God. Thankful of that, she were.'

The comment from the man yesterday who had found

164

Rebecca returned to Mara, and she scrunched shut her eyes. He'd assumed she'd taken a nasty beating – they all had. This truth was far more painful to accept. Her cousin's beautiful features had in fact been eaten away by the deadly venereal disease. *My dear, darling girl. I'm so, so sorry . . .*

'You're her mirror image still – more so, lass, as you've got older,' Belle was saying now. 'My heart fair stopped in its tracks, it did, seeing thee on t' doorstep! I really thought for a moment it were Rebecca's spirit come back to visit.'

'Jaysus . . . I understand now,' Mara croaked as a sudden thought came back to her. 'Why didn't I see it sooner?'

'See what, lass?'

The arrogant policeman who had taken her statement about Conrad years before – and his accusation of catching her whoring in the city . . . Given their similarity, he'd mistaken her for her cousin. It was Rebecca he'd been referring to all along.

Her head spun with self-reproach. 'If only I'd *realised.* Sure, wouldn't I have tracked her down there and then, despite what Seamus might have said?'

'You mustn't blame yourself.'

'Of course I should! I could have helped her, I could. She might still be here now but for me.'

'Nay, nay,' Belle tried; however, it fell on deaf ears. Mara could never be consoled, nor would anyone ever convince her otherwise.

'Be honest with me.' She had to know. 'Did Rebecca . . . Did she ever talk about me?'

The old woman's response was tender. 'Every day, lass.'

Mara would have gladly died to escape the agony of it.

Perhaps she had died.

She certainly felt that way inside.

'Here, get that down thee.'

Mara accepted the fresh brew that Aggie held out to her and sipped at it slowly. The day and everything she'd learned had taken something from her, perhaps for ever, she felt. It was like a cloying fog had gathered around her heart and mind and snuffed out all thought and feeling, plunging her very essence into impenetrable darkness. Her soul seemed hollowed out, her grief insurmountable. This was one loss she couldn't endure. She'd never get past this.

'Here we go again,' her friend announced wearily as a hammering on the adjoining wall leaked through to them. 'You can set your bloody watch by that pair – if we had a watch, that is, which we ain't, but you know what I mean.' Then, seeing that her attempt at lightening the mood with humour had fallen flat, she added, more quietly now, 'Have I to tend to them for thee again, lass?'

'No.'

'I don't mind—'

'I said no,' Mara growled. 'Ignore them.'

Aggie's surprise was evident. She nodded slowly. 'Aye, all right, if that's what you want. Lass?' she added after some seconds. 'Are you sure you're . . . well?' She tapped her temple. 'Upstairs, I mean.'

'Who knows? I don't much care, to be honest.'

'Eeh, lass . . .'

166

'Ignore them,' Mara repeated as another thump from next door sounded.

'Now are you sure you don't want me to—'

'I'm sure. I'm done running after those two – and so are you. They can starve for all I care. I've been craven-hearted for far too long, but not any more. It's over with.'

'You heard, didn't you?' said Aggie, nodding. 'Last night – what Eamon and Eugene spouted.'

'Aye.'

'I didn't like to say owt to you on my return, knew it would upset thee.'

'I'm not upset.' Mara's tone was flat. 'I'm not anything.'

Aggie was gnawing her lip. 'You've hardened, lass, and it frickens me. Ain't there nowt I can do to make it better? Owt at all?'

'I abandoned my cousin to marry Seamus. I left her all on her own to die. How can you, or I, or anybody else possibly make that better?'

With a sigh and a shake of her head, the older woman lapsed into silence, leaving Mara alone, as she desired to be, with her savage thoughts.

Chapter 12

SALFORD WAS EQUALLY choked with belching chimneys, narrow lanes and courts, slum dwellings, factories, mills and numerous other works as Manchester – and was just as dingy and grimy as its overshadowing twin. However, it was similar in another aspect too, in that, on the rolling hills of the outlying suburbs, those of importance – wealthy manufacturers or merchants and their ilk – enjoyed a life of opulence far from the filth and smoke of industry.

Kersal was one such spot. Situated some two and a half miles north-west of Manchester city centre, its position on a lofty cliff overlooking the Irwell was a perfect feast for the eyes – another world entirely to what the lower sections of society were accustomed to. And it was here, on a steep easternly rise, where stood Cresslea Manor.

Why she'd come, Mara couldn't say. The draw had been a strong one nonetheless; she'd simply had an overwhelming urge to be close to it.

She supposed it was because this was the last place Rebecca had been happy. Gazing upon it might enable her to soak up her cousin's energy, any last remnants of her presence that remained. Perhaps. She didn't know. She wasn't sure of anything any more.

Sitting cross-legged close by in the grasses, Mara peered out at the picturesque residence for most of the afternoon. Finally, her aching joints and parched throat forced her up and, after shaking out her skirts, she reluctantly made off towards home.

She made a point of taking the opposite route back, which would take her past the side of the property, so as to catch a glimpse of the servants' and tradesmen's entrance. Spotting a few wooden chairs standing beneath a huddle of trees near the open kitchen door, a small smile tugged at her lips. She could well imagine the staff sitting out here enjoying a well-earned break in the breezy shade – had Rebecca been one of them? More than likely. It really did seem a serene and overall pleasant place to work; no wonder Belle had said that her cousin had liked it here so much.

'Leave go! Oh, please!'

The sudden and desperate-sounding cry rang across the open hill. Mara slowed to a standstill. Brow creasing, she gazed about her. However, all remained still. Unable to place whence it had come and from whom, she had no alternative but to continue on her way.

'Eeh, you brute! Nay, don't do that, don't!'

The plaintive yell carried on the air again just as Mara was drawing level with a drystone wall – and whipping about, she realised now it was coming from Cresslea.

Unsure what to do, she bit her lip and glanced around. However, there was nobody here but her; the surrounding land was deserted.

'Leave *go*, I said!' the voice begged yet again.

'Hello?' Mara called out towards the source of the noise. And when no answer was forthcoming: 'Are you in trouble?' she enquired, more loudly this time.

'Aye! He'll not listen! Oh, help somebody!'

'Wait, I'm coming!' With no other thought in mind than helping the woman, who was clearly being attacked by some sex-mad beast, Mara set off on a run. Before she knew what she was doing, she had burst inside the manor-house kitchen – the scene she was met with stopped her dead in her tracks. 'What the . . . ?'

A young woman dressed in a frilly apron, her snowy mob cap askew over her eyes, was on her knees in the centre of the room. Standing facing the maid was the biggest dog Mara had ever seen. It was holding in its solid jaws what appeared to be a large joint of beef – and the maid was gripping the other end with both hands and trying desperately to wrench it free.

Stunned, Mara watched for a moment as they struggled in their battle of claiming ownership, then her senses returned and she sprang into action. Skirting past the grappling duo, she whipped the cloth from the table and crept up behind the hound. Then, quick as a flash, she threw herself forward, wrapping the material around it and hauling it away.

The move proved successful; caught by surprise, the dog dropped the meat and turned its attention instead to freeing itself from its confines. Mara held tight until the maid had scurried to open wide the kitchen door before releasing it, sending it on its way into the courtyard with a swift slap to its backside.

After it had bolted outside, Mara hurried to close the door then turned to face the panting woman. They gazed at one another for several seconds in a dazed stupor then burst out laughing.

'I don't believe what I've just witnessed . . . Sure, when I heard you crying out, I thought some fellow had got a hold of you!'

'That were Cuthbert, the master's dog. It appeared from nowhere when I was lifting the beef from the oven – eeh, it's a swine! I don't know what I'd have done without your help. Ta ever so, love.'

Mara shot the sorry-looking joint clutched under the maid's arm a frown. 'Meant for the family's dinner, was it?'

'What d'you mean, "was"? It still is!' the woman exclaimed, bringing the meat out to assess the damage.

'Tsk! Surely you're not for serving that up now . . . It's filthy, so it is, and it's studded with teethmarks.'

'But there's nowt else! I've been entrusted to run the kitchen; I'll be out of a job before the day's through otherwise! I must give them something!'

'All right, don't take on so,' Mara soothed as the hysterical maid began to wail. 'Mebbe it can be saved after all . . . Pass it to me, let me have a proper look,' she instructed. Then, with more confidence than she felt, she added, 'Fret not, we'll think of something.'

Having laid the meat on the table, the women circled it, scrutinising it through narrowed eyes. Finally, Mara turned to the maid and nodded.

'Get me a damp cloth and a knife – the sharpest you can find. I have an idea.'

171

The maid did as she'd been bade then stood aside, nervously biting her nails whilst Mara got down to it.

First, Mara gave the whole thing a thorough wiping down. Fortunately, the kitchen was scrupulously clean – it was obvious that the floor was kept diligently swept and scrubbed, as barely any dirt or fluff marred the meat from that quarter. Instead, it was the pools of stringy saliva that proved the real crux; Mara had a task continuing through the bouts of nausea that assaulted her as she worked. However, she managed it somehow, and when eventually she stood back to survey her efforts, she was satisfied with the results.

The maid brightened momentarily with hope, then her mouth drooped at the corners again and she sighed. 'What will we do about the chewed parts, though, love? The family will spot them for what they are right away.'

'Let's see if this does the trick,' Mara told her, reaching for the knife. 'It's worth a try, and we've nothing to lose.'

'Go on, then, I trust thee.'

Tilting the blade, Mara carefully shaved the areas rendered jagged by the dog's teeth, smoothing the surface with gentle compressions as she went. However, no matter how hard she tried, it was an impossible ask; it remained an ugly, misshapen lump and she was forced to suggest an alternative.

'We'll have to cut the joint up, I think.'

'But . . . we can't. It's meant to go to the dining room whole for the master to carve!'

'Sure, there's nothing else for it. 'Tis beyond rescuing as it is.'

After a long hesitation, the young woman threw her

hands up in defeat. 'All right, love. Owt's better than nowt. Work your magic and see what tha can do.'

Taking her time, Mara got to work slicing it neatly. The maid provided a platter and she arranged the pieces along the silver surface as attractively as she could, then garnished it with sprigs of parsley. Finally, they stepped back to inspect it. The tension was palpable.

'What do you think?' asked Mara quietly.

'It's all right, aye,' she whispered back. 'I reckon I might just get away with it.'

'Right, then. You get this lot up to them before it's stone cold,' said Mara, indicating the tureens of steamed vegetables and potatoes that were to accompany the beef. 'I'll leave ye to it.'

The maid stopped her with a hand on her arm as she made to turn for the door. Eyes shining with gratitude, she smiled. 'Thank you. Truly. You've saved my skin the day and I'll not forget it. I'm Meg, by the way.'

'I'm Mara,' she responded warmly. 'Well, goodbye and good luck, Meg.'

'Ta-ra, love – and thanks again!'

After slipping from the house, shooting a sulking Cuthbert lying by the trees a wry look as she passed him, Mara set off for home. And much to her surprise, given how the day had started out, she noticed that a smile went along with her.

The following day, Mara found herself retracing her steps to Cresslea Manor.

She stood in the distance for an age, her eyes trained on the chairs outside in the cobbled courtyard. However,

173

though a steady trickle of different servants would appear for short periods then return inside to resume their duties, Meg didn't look to take a break. Or if she did, she had chosen to spend it indoors rather than in the cool outdoors.

Mara was about to give up and continue on her mission of collecting flowers when a figure emerged from the kitchen. The dark, chestnut hair caught the sun, leaving her in no doubt as to who the newcomer was; her heart lifting, she edged her way nearer.

'Hello there, Meg.'

'Mara!' The maid's face stretched in a dazzling smile. She seemed delighted to see her. 'Eeh, I was hoping I'd come across thee again.'

Glancing back to the door, Mara halted, unsure whether to go further, but Meg brushed aside her concerns: 'Don't worry none about the others, love; they're all away at their work.' She patted the seat closest to hers. 'Sit thee down a while.'

'You're sure?'

'Aye, aye. Come on, take the weight off.'

Mara accepted the invitation and folded her hands in her lap. 'No Cuthbert today?' she asked with a wink, spotting that the space beneath the trees was empty.

'Nay, glory be to God! He's out walking with the master.'

'Speaking of him . . .' Mara lowered her tone. 'How did the dinner go?'

'Oh, gradely. Eeh, my heart weren't half banging, love, when I entered that dining room – Lord alone knows how they didn't hear it! I feigned innocence when he raised

174

his eyebrows over the joint having been already cut up, put it down to a lapse in memory. No one questioned it.'

'And the taste?'

'Nope, they made no mention of that, neither. I reckon dog slaver must be an undiscovered delicacy, for they complimented me afterwards on how delicious the meal was. Not that I fancy putting it to test, like; I'll take their word for it. Aye, apparently it was the best beef they'd ever had.'

'Oh, Meg,' Mara squeaked past the hand she'd slapped to her mouth. 'Aw, that's rotten of us, so it is!'

'I know, aye. I felt terrible watching them tucking in, but what choice did I have? Mind you, I were almost tempted to come clean just to see the looks on their faces!'

Meg's impish giggles were infectious; Mara couldn't help chuckling along. ''Tis wicked you are.'

'It's reet nice to have found a friendly face, Mara,' she told her earnestly. 'I ain't been in Manchester long, you see, and don't know a soul outside of this house.'

She'd figured as much. After all, had Meg been here for a good length of time, she'd have surely worked with Rebecca, and the maid hadn't mistaken Mara for her, as others had been wont to do, had she? It was clear she'd never set eyes on her cousin. 'Where is it you hail from then?' she asked.

'Not too far away: Bolton town. I toiled there for the master's mother: Mrs Braithwaite. Her son Luke is a widower, you see, and once his children began flying the nest, Mrs Braithwaite reckoned he ought not to be here alone. And so, when his last daughter wed and moved out last month, Mrs Braithwaite shut up her house in Bolton and took up residence at Cresslea to keep him company. Naturally, her servants went with her, and here I am.'

'It must have been hard leaving all you know behind – sure, don't I understand that myself well enough? And how are you finding Cresslea? The domestics are accepting of you Bolton lot?'

'Aye, they're norra bad bunch – well, them what are left, anyroad. Owd Mrs Braithwaite fired most of them off when we got here. She's a stickler for the rules, you see, and insisted on going through the manor's books. The accounts were in a shocking state, the household expenses much higher than they should have been. Turns out the staff had been pilfering from the master for years. They were out on their ears quick sharp, I can tell thee. She'll not stand for no nonsense will my mistress.'

'Well, good on her, I say.' If there was one thing Mara could not abide it was a thief. 'Sure, that's a terrible way to behave.'

'You're right enough there, love.'

'My cousin was employed here, you know,' Mara revealed. 'She left shortly before you would have arrived. Fear not, mind – no way would she have been involved in the scheming against your master. Rebecca was as straight as an arrow.'

'You've got that right,' a voice said quietly behind her.

Mara turned in surprise to find a tall and thickset man leaning against a tree close by. Arms folded, his flat cap pulled low obscuring most of his face, he nodded. 'Rebecca would never take a farthing of the ill-gotten gains.'

'Sorry, who . . . ?'

'This is Roger, the groom,' Meg informed a confused Mara. 'He's one of Cresslea's original servants, has been employed here years.'

The man stepped forward and Mara thought he'd extend a hand to her in greeting, however he didn't. He simply stared at her intently, his eyes raking over every inch of her as though he couldn't quite believe what he was seeing. Finally, she broke the charged silence.

'You knew my cousin, then, Roger?'

'Aye,' he replied after a long moment. 'Rebecca . . . she was my friend.'

'She was happy here.'

His Adam's apple bobbed in a deep swallow. 'That she was.'

'She . . . She died,' Tears had thickened her throat. 'It happened several weeks ago.'

Though his expression didn't alter, the colour drained from him and a muscle twitched at his stiff jaw. 'How?'

'An illness,' she stammered, not quite meeting his eye. 'An illness took her.'

'I'm sorry.'

'Aye, me too.'

'Well. I'd best get back . . .'

'Of course. Nice meeting ye, Roger.'

'And you.'

The women watched him stride away until he'd disappeared from view then shared a sorry sigh.

'Your news stole the wind from his sails, there, all right. I've never seen him like that afore,' said Meg.

'Aye.'

'Looks like he were reet fond of your cousin.'

'Aye,' Mara murmured again. Clearly, he must have been.

'Sorry, love, but I'd best get back inside, an' all.' Meg got to her feet reluctantly, and Mara was just as sorry to see her go.

'Mebbe I could call and see ye again?'

The maid's face lit up. 'Eeh, would you?'

'Aye, if you'd like me to.'

'Well, 'course I would – ain't we friends, now, after all?'

The query left a warm glow inside Mara; she smiled. 'Aye. Aye, we are.'

'How about the same time tomorrow? Does that suit thee?'

'It does. Goodbye, then.'

Meg waved her away with a grin before hurrying off to the kitchen and, returning the gesture, Mara turned back in the direction of Ancoats.

She was glad to have found a new friend in the pretty young maid. Meg was a likeable sort and sunny-natured with it. She had a way about her, could lighten your mood in an instant – something that Mara certainly craved right now. Already she was looking forward to the following day's meeting.

Aggie picked up on Mara's reposed disposition immediately that she entered the house; her eyebrows lifted in gladness. 'All right, lass?'

'I am, Aggie.'

'Well, I for one am relieved to see it. You look more like your owd self than I've seen thee in days. So come on then, out with it,' she added, eagerly leaning forward in her seat, her interest piqued. 'What's occurred to fetch that bonny smile of yourn back, then?'

'Well, to be honest, love, I haven't been completely straight with ye,' Mara was forced to admit.

'Oh? About what?'

She pulled out a chair then poured herself a cup of tea from the pot. 'In the mornings when I've left the house . . . I ain't been going to work, as you thought I was.'

Aggie stared back in puzzlement. 'Then what *have* you been doing?'

'I've been in Kersal.'

'Kersal? What the divil for?'

'I wanted to see Cresslea. Cresslea Manor,' she explained when her friend shook her head in mounting confusion. 'You remember I told you that Belle from the lodging house said my cousin had been working there before she took ill? Well, I had a yearning to see it for myself. Ay, love, it's a grand place. I can see why Rebecca was happy there.'

'Eeh.' Aggie looked troubled. 'You must be cautious, lass. Them moneyed folk don't take too kindly to the likes of us loitering about their property. They'll have the law on you as quick as you can blink – and shan't take the time to hear your explanation, neither, however innocent it might be.'

Mara patted her hand reassuringly. 'It's all right, really it is. I've met a new friend: Meg. She's a maid there and she's ever so nice. We got chatting, and sure, didn't we just hit it off? She says I'm welcome to visit her again.'

'And will thee?'

'Aye, I think so. Besides, I feel closer to Rebecca there, somehow. It's a comfort, you know?'

Aggie nodded understandingly. 'I can see it would be, lass. Just be careful, though, won't you? Her master shan't be best pleased if he thought you were keeping this Meg girl from her work.'

'I will, don't worry. We're only for talking when she's taking her break, so it's not like we're taking liberties.'

Placated, Aggie nodded. Then: 'Them two next door were round here earlier shouting the odds,' she announced with a roll of her eyes.

'Eamon and Eugene? What about?'

'You not cooking and cleaning for them no more. I told them straight, I said, "Mara ain't being your unpaid skivvy no more; them days are over, so like it or lump it."'

Mara's earlier calm was rapidly diminishing. 'And what did they say to that?'

'What d'you think? They went ruddy ballistic.'

'Oh, love. Oh, I'm sorry to have put you in that position . . . They didn't harm you or nothing, did they?'

'Did they bloody hell, like! I gave them a tongue-lashing right back and threatened to shove the poker up their bone-idle arses – they soon scarpered.'

'Oh, Aggie.' Mara couldn't contain a smile. 'I do love you, you know.'

'Aye, well, the buggers ain't bullying me. They'll not leave it at that, mind,' the older woman pointed out grimly. 'You mark my words, they'll be for haranguing thee until you give in to their demands.'

'I'll not give in.' Mara was adamant. 'I felt I owed them

for what happened with Conrad, but I shan't be treated like a dog no more, refuse to. I deserve better.'

Aggie slapped her thigh with a hoot of laughter. 'That's the spirit, lass! Sod 'em! Eeh, it is nice to see you like this, you know.'

'Like what?'

'Confident. Nay, that's not the right word.' She screwed up her eyes for a moment as she searched inside her brain for a more apt description, then, locating it, clicked her fingers: 'Alive. Aye, that's a better way of putting it. You've gorra bit of fire in your belly, lass, and it shines from thee. Keep it. Don't you lose it, now, d'you hear?'

Bobbing her head, Mara had tears in her eyes. 'I promise.'

'Oh aye, and another thing: that Willie Keogh called here looking for thee again this afternoon.'

Mara's mood plummeted once more. 'Did he?'

'He's persistent, I'll say that for him.'

'Aye. I've been avoiding him, love, if I'm honest.'

'Well, I worked that one out, I'm not daft. When will you just put the sorry sod out of his misery and tell him you ain't interested? It has to be done some time.'

'I know, I know.' Mara heaved a weary sigh. 'Oh, Aggie. Why does everything have to be so complicated?'

Her friend's answer came without hesitation: 'Aye, well. That's life for you, lass.'

Chapter 13

'HELLO, CUTHBERT.' SITTING on her haunches, Mara gave the dog a vigorous stroke. Lapping up the attention, tail wagging furiously, he threw himself at her, knocking her on to her back in the grasses, where he proceeded to lick her face to within an inch of its life – chuckling, she rolled away from him and jumped to her feet. 'Scoundrel, you! Where's Meg, hm? Let's find her, shall we? Come on. Good boy.'

Despite their less than agreeable first encounter, she and Cuthbert had since formed a mutually pleasing bond. He'd await her arrival each day by the trees, and on spotting her would bound across to sprawl at her feet for a belly rub, whilst she waited out Meg's arrival. The routine was something Mara looked forward to the moment she awakened in the mornings; she couldn't imagine her days without Cresslea in them, now.

Today, Meg was already seated outside the kitchen's door and ready to greet Mara with a warm smile. 'All reet, love?'

'Aye, you?'

'Oh, you know, can't complain. Sit thee down,' she instructed, 'and I'll fetch us a sup.'

Mara waited until her friend had returned with two steaming cups of strong tea to ask quietly, 'Meg, lass, are you sure this is right?'

'What?'

'Handing out brews to all and sundry. It's been playing on my mind . . . it feels like stealing, somehow. It's the master's tea, after all.'

Meg's tinkling laughter floated around the courtyard. 'Number one, I don't hand out brews to all and sundry. Only to you, and you're my friend. Two, it's hardly theft. Anyroad, even if it were, the master and his mother ain't likely to miss a few measly tea leaves. And three, this here's from the servants' own supply what the master provides us with for our personal use. So no more fretting, all right?'

'Sure, when you put it like that . . . I suppose so.'

'Good! Now, drink up afore it grows cold,' Meg told her with a wink.

Shaking her head and smiling, Mara did as she'd been bid.

Mellow and melodic birdsong rang on the balmy afternoon air and, as the women sipped their drinks in companiable silence, they tilted their heads skywards to watch the blue and great tits and common blackbirds hopping among the leafy boughs. After some minutes, a figure appeared over the crest of the hill in the distance – Roger.

Having spotted him first through the overhanging branches, Mara's eyes widened and she watched his advance without making mention of it to the other woman.

Why, she couldn't be sure. Perhaps it was that she was aware that Meg would have called hello to him, and that for as long as was possible she wished to delay that. Yes, maybe that was indeed it. Because for reasons she was unable to identify, she knew an odd sense of pleasure in observing him alone in his natural form.

His step broad and sure, back straight and toned arms swinging steadily by his sides, he exuded ease and belonging with the solitary land. Mara recognised it immediately, understood that deep connection with rurality, too. It was almost as if, like her, he'd been born to it. Somehow, he made her feel she was home.

Was it this which had also drawn Rebecca to him? she wondered. The thought was a comforting one.

'Here comes Roger,' Meg announced suddenly, nodding ahead and hauling her friend from her ruminations.

Mara made an act of feigning unawareness. 'The groom?' she managed mildly, praying all the while that her blush wouldn't surface. 'Oh aye, I see him now.'

He was almost abreast with the house when he noticed them. Locking eyes with Mara, a slight frown tugged at his brows and, for the briefest moment, his step faltered. Then Meg was waving him over, and thrusting his hands in his pockets he made his way across.

'All reet, Roger?'

He gave Meg a nod then brought his gaze back to Mara. 'Hello.'

'Hello.'

'Have you the time to spare for a sup?' Meg asked him, swatting away a fly half-heartedly. Then, without waiting for a reply: 'Hang on, I'll fetch thee one.'

However, as she made to rise, he stopped her. 'Nay. I'd best get on.'

In the next moment, he was gone again. Glancing from the corner around which he'd disappeared, Mara couldn't stem a ripple of disappointment.

It was always the same. He would offer her a cursory greeting should their paths happen to cross whenever she visited here, but that was as far as it went. No further words or desire on his part to spend a second longer in her company, not even a smile. She was somewhat baffled by it and couldn't help but feel mildly hurt.

'Take no notice, love, it's just his way.'

'Sorry, what?'

'Roger. His standoffishness: it's how he is. He means no harm by it.'

Realising she must have allowed her emotions to show on her face, Mara attempted a nonchalant shrug to cover her embarrassment. ''Tis all right, so. I'd hardly noticed.'

'He's more at ease with the animals than he is people, I reckon. Well, apart from the master. Holds him in high regard, does Roger – and the sentiment's mutual, aye. He's a firm favourite with Luke Braithwaite; he wouldn't trust no one else but Roger with his horses, nay.'

Mara knew a sense of relief learning this. So it was highly probable that he didn't dislike her after all, as she'd begun to suspect. He was simply a man of few words; some fellows were like that. It wasn't personal, meant not a thing. Besides, he couldn't be so disagreeable, could he, if Rebecca had taken to him? She'd been able to spot a good man – and a bad one, as proven with Seamus – when

185

she saw one. And as Roger had revealed himself, he and her cousin had been friends.

The groom was still on her mind later when Mara arrived home. Entering the house, however, all thoughts died upon being confronted with the very different man seated with Aggie at the table. Taken aback, it was some seconds before she could speak: 'Oh. Willie.'

'Hello, Mara.'

'Aye, hello . . . What are ye doing here?'

'He came to see thee, lass – again,' piped up Aggie before he had a chance to explain. 'He's been worried about thee as he's not clocked hide nor hair of thee for weeks. And well, figuring he'd not be put off and would keep on banging at yon door until he got to talk to thee, I reckoned I might as well invite him in to await your return.'

Catching her friend's 'it had to happen sooner or later so just get it over with and lay your cards on the table' look, Mara nodded defeat. Of course, Aggie was right. She couldn't keep this up – it must end here.

Distracting herself with removing and hanging up her shawl to enable her precious moments to gather her speech, her stomach was in knots. The last thing she wanted was to hurt Willie, who had been nothing but a friend to her – and a good one at that. *Damn it, why did he have to develop feelings for her like this? It could only ever have been doomed to change everything for the worse.* Finally, she forced herself into the chair facing his, knew now was the time. She could run from this no longer.

'I'll take myself out to the street for a breath of air, let youse discuss your business in peace,' Aggie informed them, not unkindly. 'The kiddies are all off playing; you'll not be disturbed.'

Mara and Willie smiled and nodded their thanks; the door clicked shut at the woman's back and they were alone.

Willie was the first to break the silence: 'How've ye been?'

'Aye, well enough. Yourself?'

'Fine.'

'Good, good.'

Awkward silence filled the ensuing seconds, until: 'Mara, what's going on?' Willie blurted out. His tone was almost pained; her heart went out to him.

'I'm so sorry, Willie. I've acted cruelly, so I have, and you don't deserve it.' She heaved a sigh then continued. 'I've been avoiding ye. That's why you've not seen me as usual at work each day; I've been selling my wares at another cemetery.'

'I was worried. I thought something had happened to ye.'

'I'm sorry,' she whispered again.

'Why did you do it, Mara?'

Dipping her head, she closed her eyes. 'I avoided you because I didn't want to cause you hurt . . . I've been too cowardly to say it, but the truth is . . . I don't love you back and I won't marry you.'

He sagged back in his seat. 'But . . . you love my kiddies, don't you?'

'I'm fond of them, Willie, aye, but that's not reason enough to—'

'And me? You *do* love me, Mara. We're both of us

widowed now and there's nothing to stop us. We, we get along so well . . .'

'No, Willie. It's but fondness I hold for you, too. If I've led you to believe otherwise then I can only apologise, but I don't think I have . . . did I?'

'No,' he admitted. 'No, you've never given me false hope.'

'Then sure, I don't know what else I can say other than thank you for the offer, but no thank you.'

He remained unmoving, staring at his clasped hands on the tabletop, for a long moment. Then, without a word, he reached for his flat cap and got slowly to his feet.

'We'll be all right, won't we, lad?' Mara asked him thickly. 'Our friendship means an awful lot to me; I don't want to lose it. Please?' she pressed when he remained silent.

'I'll see you, Mara.'

'Willie, come on now, don't leave it like this,' she tried. However her attempt at reasoning was cut short by the shutting of the door.

'Oh, Meg, it was pure torture. The look in his eyes . . . it's something I'll never forget.'

It was the following afternoon and the women were seated in their usual spot by the trees. Mara had spent a terrible night, had barely managed to snatch more than an hour's sleep due to her fretting, and her head thumped dully from exhaustion.

'I just don't know what I'll do to make it right,' Mara went on. 'Sure, he'll never forgive me, I know it.'

'From what you've said, this Willie bloke is a decent

188

sort,' offered the maid soothingly. 'He'll come round, love, I'll bet.'

'That's Aggie's way of thinking, too, but I'm not so certain. He was crushed.'

Despite her guilt, Mara couldn't nonetheless deny that she was relieved it was over with. The subject had laid heavily on her mind for many weeks and she was glad that the burden had lifted. But Willie's face . . . His devastation haunted her. Yet how in the world could she have handled it any differently – and how now to make it right? The only obvious option was to go back on her word and agree to wed him regardless. That he'd make a sound husband, she had no doubt. But no, she couldn't do it. She'd be living a lie, they both would, and that wouldn't be fair on either of them.

'Give him space. Once he's had time to come to terms with it, all will be well. You'll see, love.'

'Oh, Meg, I do hope you're right . . .' Mara's voice petered out as she spotted Roger making his way towards them. Much to her confusion – and not a little shame – she instantly felt a touch better for seeing him.

'Meg.' He nodded to the maid then repeated the action with Mara. 'Hello.'

'Hello,' she murmured back.

Normally, he would have given his excuses and made a sharp exit. Today, he didn't; instead, he remained where he was. Wearing a frown, he studied Mara's face. 'Has something occurred?'

So stunned was she by this, she was momentarily lost for words. 'I . . .'

'Mara's a bit out of sorts the day is all, but it'll work

189

itself out,' said Meg, realising her friend was struggling to answer. 'Ain't that right, love?'

'Aye. I'm fine, really.'

The groom nodded again and made to leave, however before he could – and much to her own surprise – Mara stopped him:

'Roger?'

He turned to look at her over his shoulder. 'Aye?'

'Thank ye all the same for asking.'

His eyes softened ever so slightly. He inclined his head then continued on his way.

If Meg noticed the tension in the air, she didn't voice it. Smothering a yawn with the back of her hand, she stretched and dragged herself to her feet. 'No rest for the wicked – I'd best get in.'

'All right, lass. I'll see ye tomorrow?'

'You will. Ta-ra for now, love.'

'Bye, Meg. Bye, Cuthbert,' Mara added with a smile, giving the dog slumbering in the shade a last stroke. A final wave to her friend, then she set off with the usual pang of regret to be leaving the peaceful countryside behind for the cramped and dingy slums.

She'd been home just a handful of minutes when harsh knocking came at the door – sharing a frown with Aggie, Mara went to answer it. Much to her puzzlement, she discovered it was the Irishman: 'Willie!' she exclaimed. 'Oh, come in, do.'

'I won't, if it's all the same to you.'

Inwardly cringing at his stony tone and equally stiff countenance, Mara nodded miserably. 'As ye wish.'

'I just came to return this.'

190

'My cup . . . But Willie, you didn't have to—'

'Aye, I do.' He held the delicate pink drinking vessel with its pretty golden rim out to her. 'Take it.'

'Does this mean . . .' Tears stung behind her eyes. 'Won't I see you again?'

He didn't miss a beat: 'Take it,' he repeated.

With great reluctance, Mara obeyed, but before her fingers had a chance to reach it Willie released his hold. As though in slow motion, she watched it drop through the air between them and shatter into pieces at her feet.

The last link to her past and her pride and joy – gone. Her grief was unparalleled.

'Butter fingers.'

Forcing her gaze back up to meet his, a sob caught in her throat. Willie was smiling. *He was smiling*. He'd done it on purpose . . .

Frozen, she gazed after him as, hands in pockets and whistling a merry tune, he sauntered away down the street. And she knew that, this day, she'd gained a fresh enemy.

Chapter 14

'MARA?'

'I . . . I . . .'

'Mara, what's tha doing here? What's wrong?'

'I didn't know where, where else to go, I . . .'

'It's all right. Come with me.'

With a head full of nothing, she allowed Roger to lead her off across the moon-stroked field.

She was vaguely aware of passing towering trees silhouetted black against the navy sky, then the groom was assisting her inside a squat stone cottage and she emerged into an open space that shimmered rose-gold from the glow of a small wood-burning fire.

Roger secured the door behind them, shutting out the whining wind and lashing rain, and crossed to the tiny window, beneath which stood a square pine table. He pulled out one of its two chairs, carried it across the room and positioned it before the crackling flames. Then he returned to where he'd left Mara, took her elbow and guided her towards it, then helped her to sit and draped a blanket around her shoulders.

As the warmth thawed her icy bones and life returned

to her limbs, so too did her senses. Bringing up her hands, she covered her face and burst into silent weeping.

'Drink this.'

It was Roger. He was holding a tin cup from which rose silver-thin threads of steam. Mara accepted it and in between swallowed sobs took several sips of the black, unsweetened brew before passing it back.

'Better?'

Indeed calmer now, she nodded.

'You shouldn't have been out there in t' dark alone.'

'I didn't know where else to go,' she repeated.

'You were hoping to see Meg?'

Again, she bobbed her head. 'I thought I might catch her taking another break and get to speak with her, seek her advice. I waited and waited, but she didn't appear. It grew dark and the rains came, but still I stayed, didn't know what else to do, couldn't go home . . .'

Roger had crouched down in front of her. His deep tone was low. 'Why not?'

'Because Aggie would have seen my distress and would have wanted to know the reason for it, and I couldn't talk to her about it, couldn't tell her, couldn't disappoint her . . . I'd promised her I wouldn't be cowed again, *promised* her I'd not let no one dim my fire, but Willie has. He has, and I'm frightened! Why do so many people hate me so? I'm so downright *tired* of being afraid, of looking over my shoulder. Why, Roger, why? When will it end?'

He didn't speak, simply took her body, wracked once more with fresh sobs, into his arms. He smelled of horses and straw and good clean earth, which she found comforting, and his strong hold made her feel instantly safe from the world and everything in it; Mara clung to him.

'I knew this afternoon that summat had occurred,' Roger said after a while. 'You wore the same look Rebecca used to do whenever she were troubled.'

'Tell me about your friendship. Were you very close?'

He was silent for a few moments, then: 'We were.'

'Did you love her?'

'I were fond of her, aye.'

'And she you?'

'Aye. Least I thought she was. Then one day without warning she announced she was leaving, and that were that.'

Mara was torn. Should she tell him the reason behind Rebecca's decision to return to Belle's lodging house? The prospect felt so very wrong, as though to voice it would be sullying her cousin's character. Besides, could the bare truth of it really make a difference to the groom's feelings?

'Were the two of you ... intimate?' she eventually plucked up the nerve to ask, knowing his response would determine her decision. If his answer was yes, she'd reveal it for certain, couldn't hold something of that magnitude back from him. As she awaited his answer, she realised she was praying for all she was worth that he'd deny it.

'No,' he said finally.

Thank God. Mara sagged, relieved in more ways than one.

'What of your troubles? Do you want to tell me?'

She shook her head. 'Not right now.'

194

'Not right now,' he echoed.

Outside, the weather raged on. It battered the cottage as though intent on crushing it to dust, however it couldn't touch its occupants – nothing could. All else but being here in this moment, together as one, had ceased to exist. Mara felt it and knew he did, too.

'I'm glad you found me,' she murmured against his broad chest.

'Me too,' he whispered.

She pressed closer into him and his arms tightened in response. His heart was beating as fast as her own; she felt it beneath her cheek.

'Roger . . . I don't want to leave you.'

'Then don't. Stay.'

Ever so slowly, she eased back to look into his eyes. The raw hunger reflected there snatched her breath away. With a large hand, he smoothed from her face damp curls that had escaped their confines. Then he dipped his head and brought his lips to hers.

Their kiss was hard and deep, almost desperate. When they drew apart they were gasping, their bodies ablaze, their touch urgent to explore further. It was Mara who acted on it first. She stood and led him to the bed against the far wall.

They undressed one another feverishly, their hands and mouth devouring each new part as it was exposed. When she guided him inside her, the room sang with their simultaneous sighs. It was as though a lifetime of waiting had at last found an end. Never had any one thing felt so wholly and utterly right.

The birth of another day was approaching when, finally,

they rose to dress. Mara made the bed then sat on its edge and watched Roger prepare breakfast for them both at the table. They ate their bread smeared with dripping and drank their tea in easy silence. Then he donned his heavy coat and cap and she her shawl, and hand in hand they left the cottage.

When they reached the edge of a wooded area that would take Mara back towards Ancoats, she drew Roger to a halt. 'I'll be fine from here.'

'You're sure you don't want me to walk thee home?'

'No, no. Besides, you'd best get back or you'll be late for work.'

In the seclusion of the dawn-lit coppice, he circled her waist with his hands and pressed her against a tree. Melting into him, she wrapped her arms around him and closed her eyes.

'I'd begun to think that you didn't like me. Whenever you saw me in the courtyard—'

'Aye! How hard I tried to stop away, knowing you'd be there, but it was impossible. I've struggled to keep thee from my mind for what seems like for ever; I'll never manage it now,' he told her in between dropping feathery kisses across her neck.

She laughed softly. 'Haven't I watched you from afar for weeks, too?'

'How will I get through the day without touching thee, tasting thee?'

His hardness throbbed against her and her own desire peaked once more in response. Arching her back, she sought his mouth for his kiss. 'I'll come to ye. Tonight.'

'You swear it?'

'Aye.' She couldn't keep away now, even if she tried.

They parted ways and Mara felt she could have floated the remainder of the way to Heyrod Street. Never had she known an energy like this or fulfilment on this level before. Put to the test, right now she reckoned she could have conquered the world.

'Lass!' Aggie was out of her seat in a flash the moment Mara entered the kitchen. Tut-tutting, she clasped her to her mountainous breast. 'Christ Almighty, where the hell have you been? I've been beside myself.'

'I'm sorry, really I am. The last thing I meant to do was worry you . . . I'm fine, love, honest.'

'I've been imagining all sorts, thought Conrad might have shown up and got a grip of thee . . . Where were you?'

Unsure how her friend would react but aware she had to be truthful – she owed Aggie that much, at least – Mara broke eye contact to stare at the floor. 'If you must know, I spent the night with a man.'

'Man? What man? Not that Willie bloody Keogh, surely to God!'

'Oh Jaysus, no.' The very notion now made her skin crawl.

'Then who?'

'Roger – the groom at Cresslea.'

Aggie blew out air slowly. 'Well, you kept that one quiet.'

'You don't think bad of me, love, do you?'

'Mara, lass, you're a grown woman. What you choose to do is no one else's business but your own.' A slow smile spread across her face. 'Enjoy yourself, did you?'

'Oh aye. He's wonderful, Aggie.'

'So I can tell! Good for you, anyroad. I'd say tha ruddy well deserves it after bearing that rotten oaf Seamus for as long as you did.'

Mara could settle her mind to nothing throughout the following hours. Even her meeting with Meg did nothing to ease her fizzing emotions – how could it, knowing Roger was nearby? Reasoning that for the time being it was best not to mention to the maid what had transpired between them, Mara kept her counsel. And when the groom made his appearance as they were enjoying their cup of tea, she did her utmost to act as naturally as she always did.

'Meg.' He nodded to her then turned his stare on to Mara. 'Hello,' he said, greeting her in his usual fashion.

'Hello, Roger.'

He left soon after, as he normally did, but not before giving Mara the softest of winks. She flashed him a ghost of a smile in response then returned her attention to an unsuspecting Meg, yet still it took all of her will not to dart after him as he strode away.

Sunset saw her on the same route she'd taken the previous night – only this time, she was heading there of her own accord and at a far greater pace. When she emerged into the clearing, she saw Roger was waiting for her at his cottage door. They shared a smile, then she was running again to fall into his arms and his bed.

'I sickened for thee all day,' he murmured into her hair later as they lay, drowsy with contentment, in each other's arms.

'Oh, me too. How I kept my hands off ye in front of Meg, I will never know.'

'I can't be parted from you. Not now.'

Something in his tone made her study his face closer. She saw that his eyes had deepened with what she could only describe as pain. 'Roger? What is it?'

'Losing Rebecca . . . it hurt, Mara. I couldn't go through that again—'

'Oh, my love, my love,' she cut in gently when he scrunched shut his eyes, wrapping him in her warm embrace once more.

'You've got inside my head. You're a part of me now, you know?'

She did. It matched her sentiments for him entirely. And yet . . . 'Roger?'

'Aye?'

'This. Us. Is it because I remind you of my cousin?' She had to be sure.

His response was immediate: 'Nay, Mara. I'll not deny that the two of youse are similar in looks – how could I? – but this, it goes beyond that. Rebecca was Rebecca, and you are you; you're your own person. I was fond of her, it's true, but with thee . . . I feel you in my heart, my very bones. It's *you* I want, for *you*. You understand?'

Tears wobbled on her lashes. She nodded. 'Aye, Roger. Aye.'

'I think . . . I'm *sure* . . . I love thee.'

For a long moment, she was too choked to speak. 'No man has ever said that to me before.' Seamus certainly hadn't.

'And no woman has ever said it to me.'

'I lo—'

He stopped her by putting a finger to her lips. 'Nay,

lass. Don't say it 'cause you think it's what I want to hear. Not if it ain't true.'

Mara drew his hand away and gazed deep into his eyes. 'I love you,' she said slowly, clearly, and meant it with every beat of her heart.

'Us two, for ever.'

'Always.'

'You're going to wear yourself out, lass, toing and froing as you are all the time. I don't know why you don't just move in that groom fella's cottage and have done with it.'

It was approaching evening and Mara was preparing to set off for Salford to see Roger. After giving her hair a final check in the small mirror, she turned to face her friend and folded her arms. 'Oh, sure, I can see his master being pleased with that!'

'I bet you would, though, given half the chance. You would, wouldn't you!' added Aggie on a chuckle when Mara smiled bashfully. 'Why, you young divil, yer!'

'I'm like a moth to a candle, love: I just can't stop away.'

'And he feels just the same?'

Taking a seat beside Aggie at the table, she nodded. 'Last week . . . he told me he loved me.'

'By gum, that's moving a bit fast, in't it?'

'Any other time, I'd likely be inclined to agree with you. But not with this. I don't know, can't explain it. It's *right*, love. It's almost like, somehow, it's been a long time in the coming, you know?'

Mild concern had clouded the other woman's features. 'Don't get me wrong, I do hold with love at first sighting, reckon it can happen on occasion, aye. I just don't want to see thee get hurt is all it is.'

'I'm not an eejit, Aggie.' Mara knew her friend only had her best interests at heart, and her voice was soft. 'I know the difference between love and lust – I had plenty of practice there as Seamus's wife. It's love with Roger, honest.'

'If you say so, lass.'

'I do. Please be happy for me, Aggie.'

'Ay, now. 'Course I am! Eeh, come here.'

Enveloped in the woman's comforting embrace, Mara closed her eyes and sighed. 'I never dreamed I could know a joy like this. Happiness . . . it's always been a thing meant for other folk, not for me. I can scarcely believe it's happening.'

'Well, do.' Aggie spoke firmly now. 'If anyone deserves it, my lass, then it's thee. Grab it with both hands and hold on to it tight, and to hell with the nay-sayers – me included.'

Mara laughed through her tears. 'Thank ye. What would I do without you, eh?'

'Go on then, get on your way if you're going, afore it gets any later. I don't like the thought of thee tramping them hills alone in t' dark. I'll see thee the morrow, lass.'

Mara needed no further persuading. Planting a swift kiss on Aggie's podgy cheek, she grabbed her shawl and hurried from the house.

The weather was mild and the walk was a pleasant one. Nevertheless, Mara didn't hang around to admire the scenery as she would normally have done. She had but one thing on her mind – the man waiting for her – and it took precedence over everything. She doubted anything else could ever come close again.

So absorbed was she in thoughts of the night to come, she didn't notice Cuthbert snoozing on the cottage step until she was but several feet from the door. Halting, she frowned in confusion. Then she heard it from within – it reached her through the open window: not one male voice, but two – and realisation hit. Roger wasn't alone. And if the presence of the dog was anything to go by, she didn't need to wonder too hard over the identity of his guest. *The master.*

Biting her lip, she turned slowly and had begun to creep away when a loud bark sounded behind her, shattering the silence and jarring her every nerve – damn it, Cuthbert! Swivelling on her heel, she held a finger to her lips, desperation having her hope it might make a difference; of course, it didn't. On the contrary, it only bolstered the dog. Believing it to be some jolly game, he wagged his tail excitedly and barked again, then bounded towards her for a belly rub.

In the next moment, the door opened and, with no time to either move or think, she simply froze to the spot.

Taking in the scene, Luke Braithwaite arched an eyebrow in surprise. He whistled once and Cuthbert instantly let Mara be to go to his master's side.

'Sir, I . . .' she attempted a stuttered explanation. But she had nothing, *nothing.* 'I was, was just . . .'

'Mara. Hello.'

It was Roger. He stepped outside and walked across to her but, unlike her, he seemed not the slightest bit fazed. She tried to convey an apology to him with her eyes for placing them in the situation, and he responded with a 'just follow my lead' look of his own.

'Mara,' he said again, his tone as even as before, 'this is my master, Mr Braithwaite.' Then, turning to the gentleman: 'Sir, this is my friend Mara.'

Luke inclined his head, which she acknowledged with an awkward half-curtsey and a murmured, 'Very pleased to meet ye, sir.'

'I know I asked thee to call by,' Roger went on to Mara, 'but I'm afraid to say you've had a wasted journey. I ain't discussed the matter with the master yet; it went out of my mind completely . . . Sorry, lass.'

Naturally, Mr Braithwaite's interest was piqued. 'What matter is this?'

'Nay, sir, we can worry on this another time,' insisted the groom. 'It's late and I'm sure you're wanting to get back home.'

'It's all right. I'm here now, so you may as well tell me: why was it you wished to speak with me?'

Mara was as curious as Luke – just what was Roger planning? When all was revealed at his next words, it was the last thing she'd been expecting; her mouth fell open in astonishment.

'Well, the thing is, sir, Mara here's seeking employment. I promised to ask thee whether there might be a position for her at the manor.'

'Ah. Yes. Well, I suspect there just might be . . . I don't see any reason why she shouldn't be offered an interview. Of course, the decision will ultimately rest with my mother; she deals with the hiring – and firing,' he added with a definite sigh, 'of staff.'

'That's gradely, thank you, sir.'

'I shall mention it and will give you her answer soon. Good evening.'

'Evening, sir. And thanks again.'

A last nod at Roger, then Luke took his leave, Cuthbert trotting merrily by his side.

'What on earth!'

'Not here,' Roger murmured, cutting short Mara's exclamation. He motioned to the cottage and, still shaking her head with her struggle of making sense of it, she followed him inside.

He secured the door and turned to face her. However, he didn't attempt an explanation. Instead, he closed the space between them, took her face in his hands and kissed her hungrily. Despite the recent scene, Mara was swept away by his furore.

'The master . . . he won't come back, will he?'

'Nay. It were sheer bad luck you ran into him; he hardly ever stops by here. Only one of his horses threw a shoe, you see, and . . . Oh, lass, I must have thee.'

Her own desire at fever pitch, she offered up no resistance. She allowed him to lift her into his thick arms and carry her to the bed.

Afterwards, their passion temporarily spent, she raised herself on an elbow and lifted her eyebrows questioningly. 'So? What did all that mean with the master?'

One arm resting on the pillow above his head, Roger yawned. 'I were thinking on my feet is all. What other reason could I have given him for you being on his land – and at my cottage late evening and alone? Having him believe it were business concerning the manor seemed logical.'

'I suppose so. But sure, what am I to do? What if Mrs Braithwaite *does* want to interview me?'

'I'll just say you were offered another position elsewhere at the last minute, and that'll be that. Don't fret on it.'

Trusting his judgement, she let the subject drop and focused instead on enjoying the precious hours together. *Just the two of them, for nothing else mattered.* He patted his bare chest studded with its dark hairs and she nestled her head back into it with a contented sigh.

Later, in the dead of night, Mara was changing position in bed when something at the window snared her attention. Bleary with sleep, she peered harder through the darkness – then let out a cry. Someone was standing watching them from outside.

'Mara? Lass, what is it?'

She turned to Roger with horrified eyes. 'The window, the window!'

He was awake and on his feet in an instant. He crossed the room and scanned the vicinity through the panes then headed for the door.

'Roger, wait, be careful!' she begged, but already he was making out naked into the pitch-dark field.

The seconds felt like minutes as she awaited his return, trembling with dread. Finally, he was back. He locked the door and came to take her into his arms.

'You didn't see anyone?'

'Nay. It's completely deserted.'

'I did see someone, Roger, really . . . at least I think I did,' she added, biting her lip; she couldn't be sure now.

'Mebbe you were still half dreaming, or it might have been a trick of the moonlight.'

'Perhaps.'

'Come, lie thee down and get some rest.' He drew her back beneath the blankets with him.

Cocooned in his solid hold, she was immediately better. 'I'm sorry. I feel foolish now.'

'You feel gradely to me,' he said, pulling her closer.

Chapter 15

'HONEST, LOVE, I didn't know where to put my face. I thought we'd been rumbled for certain.'

Having been regaled with Mara's encounter with Luke Braithwaite the previous evening, Aggie was cackling with shocked glee.

'Sure, it wasn't funny at the time, let me tell ye!' Mara continued through her own titters. 'Cuthbert, the big bonehead, dropped me right in it.'

'D'you reckon the owd woman *will* call thee to an interview, then?' asked her friend, resurrecting the conversation a little later when they were enjoying a cup of tea. Her laughter had gone now, however, and her eyes were thoughtful.

'I reckon she just might, if her son has anything to do with it. According to Meg, she dismissed most of the servants when she moved in, and so the manor is definitely under-staffed. Apparently, the master's at the end of his tether with it.'

'I'm just thinking, you see; would it be a bad thing if you were to go and work there?'

'What d'you mean, Aggie?'

'Well, consider it: it would mean living in.'

'But I don't want to live at Cresslea. I'm happy where I am.'

'And I love having thee here, but it can't be for much longer, can it? What about when Conrad's released? You and I both know he'll be hot-footing it back to England in a heartbeat – that's if he don't abscond sooner. Lass, when that time comes, you'll be done for.'

She ran a hand over her face with a weary sigh. 'I've forced it to the back of my mind these past weeks, what with finding Rebecca and then Roger coming into my life . . . Aye. I know you're right.'

'Speaking of this fella of yourn, have you told him?'

'About Conrad?' She shook her head. 'I've been putting it off.'

Roger had asked a few times about the night he'd found her stranded in the rain, but reluctant to dredge up her problems – one revelation would undoubtedly lead to another – when everything was sailing smoothly for once in her life, she'd brushed him off each time. He'd respected her decision enough not to probe further until she was ready to discuss it – perhaps now, that time had come.

'Maybe tha should, then,' said the older woman, reinforcing her belief. 'Happen he can advise thee better than me. Talk with him, see what he has to say.'

Mara was feeling nervous when she arrived at the cottage that evening. Her chat with Aggie had made up her mind: Roger had to know. She greeted him with her usual kiss, however, when he began fondling her breasts, and knowing what was inevitably to follow, she stopped him gently. It had to be now, before she cowarded out. The sooner it was in the open, the better for them both.

Puzzled by the rejection, he pulled back to look at her; then, seeing her expression, he searched her face with a frown. 'Mara?'

'I need to tell ye something.'

'Tell me what?'

She led him to the table and indicated that he should sit. Then she took the other chair and folded her hands in her lap. Her heart was thumping.

'The night you came across me looking out for Meg at Cresslea . . .'

Roger nodded. 'Aye.'

'I was upset, upset and frightened, because . . .'

'Because?'

'Because I'd turned down an offer of marriage to a man who later made it plain he was far from happy about it.'

'Willie.'

'Aye. How?'

'You mentioned the name when I brought you back here, said he'd dimmed your fire.'

'I did?' She couldn't recall, so lost had she been in her emotions.

'And what now?' Roger's eyes had creased and his jaw was taut. 'You regret not accepting him?'

'No! Never. How can you ever think that after all we've shared?' She caressed his cheek with the back of her hand and he caught it to drop kisses on to her palm. 'There's not a man on this earth who could match up to you.'

'Then he's been threatening thee? Is that it?'

'Not exactly. It was the way he acted when last I saw

him . . . It was vindictive – cruel. I've never seen him like that, didn't think him capable. Only now, I worry that mightn't be an end to it.'

'Are you saying this Willie might decide to make life difficult for thee?'

She shrugged. 'Possibly. Oh, I don't know. Mebbe I'm worrying over nothing is what it is . . . He wouldn't be the first man to want to ruin me, so aye, why not!'

The groom wiped away with a calloused thumb the tear that had splashed to her cheek. His next words were gentle: 'Tell me.'

Mara did. She revealed her childhood back home in Ireland and the disaster and loss that followed. She spoke of the crossing to England with her cousin, of her meeting Seamus and their terrible marriage. And she told him of Conrad, McLoughlin and his gang, the arrest and trial, her lies and the subsequent transportation to Australia – she left out nothing. Afterwards, she found that she breathed just a little easier. And when Roger walked around the table to take her in his arms, she knew that a total divulgation had been the right choice.

Their lovemaking this night was slow and tender, like a healing of one soul by another. He understood, and he allowed her to experience something that her husband never had or could, and she loved him all the more for it.

Replete and relaxed, they discussed in the early hours over a cup of tea the suggestion of her securing employment at Cresslea. After some consideration, Roger declared he was of the same mind as Aggie, and Mara nodded concession.

'I'll speak to the master the morrow about his mother's decision.'

'Aye.'

'It'll be all right, Mara. The owd bird ain't so bad, if you handle her right.'

'But even if she does agree to an interview, what will I do about a reference? Hawking flowers, I work for myself – I don't have an employer to provide me with a character. Mrs Braithwaite will surely want to see one, and I shan't be able to deliver, so I won't.'

He eased away her concerns with a kiss to her brow. 'Mr Braithwaite trusts me. My recommendation of thee will be good enough, I reckon. You'll see.'

'So you're definitely sure of mind this is the right thing to do?'

'If it means you being some place safe from that bastard Conrad and his brothers where I can keep an eye to thee, then aye.' He paused to sigh and run a hand through his thick black hair. 'It's just . . .'

'Living in at Cresslea,' she finished for him miserably.

'Aye.'

'How would we ever find time to be alone, Roger – properly, I mean? I'd be so busy, there wouldn't be any opportunity to slip to the cottage. And if I should attempt it and get caught, it could mean us both out of a job. Being parted from ye now . . . I don't think I could bear it.'

His tone was so low, she had to lean in to catch the words: 'What if tha didn't have to?'

'Be parted from you, you mean? But how?'

'Marry me.'

211

Mara's mouth fell open. 'Roger?'

'I mean it: marry me. No harm will come to thee as my wife. I'll shield you from this whole world for the rest of your days, I swear it.'

'Aye.'

'You will?'

'I will,' she said fiercely, clasping him to her bosom in a crushing embrace. Tears poured freely down her face. 'Us two, for ever.'

'Always,' he whispered with equal fervour.

The interview was to take place the following morning. Mara was both delighted and terrified in equal measure.

'You're certain Mrs Braithwaite won't expect from me a reference?' she asked Roger yet again. 'Sure, wouldn't I just die if I turn up and she asks me for one? There I'll be, standing in front of her with my mouth flapping like a thirsty fish, without an answer in my head!'

He stemmed her babble with a sound kiss on the lips. 'She'll not, I told thee. The master's explained the situation to her and she's agreed to break with tradition this once. It'll be reet, lass, stop fretting.'

'I'm sorry. It's just so much is riding on this. I can't help but worry I'll do or say something to ruin it.'

'Listen to me,' he murmured, snaking an arm around her waist and pulling her close. 'Nowt shall go wrong, and d'you know why?'

Mara shook her head.

'Because you're clever and beautiful and capable of owt you lay your mind to – I know you'll do just fine. All right?'

'All right,' she agreed, smiling. 'Just what did I do to deserve you, eh?'

'Christ knows, but it must have been summat spectacular.'

Laughing, she swatted him away and went to collect her shawl.

'You're going?' Roger asked as she draped it around her shoulders.

'I am. I can't stop here making love with you till dawn when I've to face Mrs Braithwaite. Sure, I'd be fit for nothing, and that'd never do. I want to be bright-eyed and clear-headed for the interview, so I do, make the best impression that I can.'

'But ... what will I do with myself?' He looked crestfallen – Mara couldn't help but grin.

'You'll just have to have an early night.'

'I'll dream about thee, you know that, don't you?'

She winked. 'Well, I hope for your sake it's a good one.'

'You minx.'

With a squeak, she made to dodge him as he lunged at her, but he was too quick. He swept her up and ran with her to the bed – helpless with giggles, she gave up the half-hearted protests and tilted her head for his kiss.

'See, you know you can't resist me just as much as I can't you.'

'An hour – then I'm definitely away home!'

Reaching out to undo the buttons of her bodice, he smiled. 'If you say so, lass.'

Smothering a yawn with the back of her hand, Mara lifted the teapot. 'I knew I should have gone home!'

Roger grinned through a yawn of his own. 'I'm sorry.'

'So ye should be,' she teased. 'I must look a dreadful sight.'

'Come over here and I'll show thee what I think,' he growled – Mara hooted with laughter.

'Don't you dare. Och, I'm sure I don't know where you get your energy from! Any more of that and I'll be late for Mrs Braithwaite.'

They left the cottage together soon afterwards, Roger to begin his work at the stables and Mara to head to the dreaded interview.

'You'll be fine,' he assured her when the manor came into view and her step faltered.

'Sure, I hope so.'

They shared a lingering goodbye kiss then parted ways. With her heart in her mouth and everything crossed, Mara continued on for Cresslea.

Meg was giddy with excitement when she answered her knock. 'Come on in!'

'Thanks, love.' She flashed her a wobbly smile and followed her into the kitchen.

'I still can't believe this. He's a dark horse, that Roger.'

Guilt stabbed – nodding, Mara lowered her gaze.

Meg had been stunned when she'd informed her yesterday of the impending interview. As casually as she could muster, Mara had spun her a line that she'd got chatting to Roger on her way back to Ancoats one day and had happened to mention she was seeking fresh employment. He'd kindly offered to speak with the master on her behalf, she'd gratefully accepted, and that was that. Of course, the maid hadn't suspected a thing – why would she? However, this hadn't made Mara feel any better; she'd been eaten up with shame ever since.

Lying to her nearest and dearest didn't sit easy with her. For the time being, though, at least, it was the way it must be; she and Roger had both agreed.

If word should get out that they were closer than folk realised, it might hamper her chances at Cresslea. The master would surely guess the real reason behind her visit to Roger's cottage the evening Cuthbert had given her away, and the repercussions could well be serious. And yet, that wasn't the only reason for keeping quiet so far as Mara was concerned. Her main anxiety lay with the possibility of Meg disapproving of her behaviour.

The longer her affair with Roger went on, the harder it had got to come clean. Now, she hadn't a clue how she'd ever pluck up the nerve to tell her. Losing their friendship was a terrible and very real prospect – Mara dreaded the time when she'd be forced to reveal all.

'Imagine it, me and thee working together.'

Pulled from her worrisome thoughts and back to the present, Mara forced a smile. 'Sure, I ain't got the position yet, love.'

'You will, I just know it. Eeh, it'll be gradely.'

'Aye, it will so.'

'Ready?'

Mara sucked in a few deep breaths and nodded. Then, with Meg leading the way, she left the kitchen and made through the house proper for Mrs Braithwaite's drawing room.

Luxury, she'd been expecting, naturally. Taking in her surroundings, however, she was agog; it surpassed anything she'd envisaged. A marble-floored corridor led to another and another, each more beautiful than the one before it. Here was another world, one of exquisite furniture and pictures in thick gold frames, crystal vases and China figurines, solid silver mirrors and candelabra – and a hundred and one other things she hadn't time to take in. Her senses swam with the strange yet wondrous unfamiliarity of it.

'Here we are,' Meg said eventually, coming to halt outside a white door. 'Right, are you ready?'

'No,' admitted Mara.

The maid laughed softly. 'You'll be reet; her bark is worse than her bite. Here, a tip for thee: if you get a bit overwhelmed, just imagine her chomping on that dog-spit-soaked meat and enjoying it – that will ease your nerves no end!'

'Oh Jaysus, Meg, I wish you hadn't brought that up . . . I'll end up laughing for sure, now, I just know it!'

'You'll not, and it shan't be so bad. Anyroad, she's in good spirits this morning so tha should be fine. I wish you luck, love.'

Before she had a chance to respond, Meg knocked at the door then turned the knob. 'Mrs O'Hara to see you, ma'am,' she announced, giving Mara a slight shove on her way.

The door clicked shut behind the maid, and Mara found herself facing the master's mother alone. She stepped forward a few paces. 'Good morning, ma'am.'

Seated behind a high polished desk, dressed in a plum-coloured dress with a large oval brooch at the neck, Mrs Braithwaite was tall, thin and rigid-backed. Her grey-white hair framed a hard face with a long, sharp nose upon which horn-rimmed spectacles balanced precariously – in short, she was the epitome of severity and exactly as Mara had imagined her. She hooked a finger, indicating that Mara should come closer. Licking her lips, she obeyed.

'Your full name is Mara O'Hara?' For her years, her voice was surprisingly high, almost childlike. 'Is that correct?'

'Aye, ma'am.'

'Most odd.'

'Odd, ma'am?'

'Well, yes. It rhymes.'

Mara blinked in bemusement. 'I suppose it does.'

'There is no "suppose" about it. Mara O'Hara – it rhymes, see?'

Doing her best not to frown, she nodded. 'Aye, ma'am.'

'You wish to be considered for employment at Cresslea Manor?'

'I do, ma'am.'

'Are you a thief?'

'A . . . ? No, ma'am, never.'

'Does kitchen work suit you?'

'It does, ma'am.'

'You will receive a wage of twelve pounds per annum, along with an allowance for tea, sugar and beer. You may start on Thursday morning and will work under Meg. She will show you your duties. Good day.'

'Aye, ma'am. Thank ye, ma'am. Good day, ma'am.'

'Well?' wanted to know Meg, who was waiting outside the room, the second that Mara joined her.

Too stunned to process it, Mara leaned against the corridor wall and shook her head. 'I got the job. At least I think I did . . . it all happened so quickly.'

'That's Mrs Braithwaite for you: straight to the point. Did she give you a start date?'

'Aye. Thursday morning.'

'Then you *did* get the job, you daft ha'porth, yer,' said Meg on a chuckle. 'Come on, love, come and have a cup of tea. You look like you could do with it.'

In a daze, Mara followed Meg back to the kitchen.

'You see. I told you you'd be fine.'

'I still can't believe it, Roger. She fired a handful of questions at me then sent me on my way. It was the queerest thing I've ever seen.'

Busy stirring a pot of broth suspended on a hook above the fire, he glanced over his shoulder to smile. 'Tha got the job, that's the main thing.'

'Aye.'

'Meg was pleased, I'll bet.'

An ache of guilt struck her guts once again. 'Aye, she was.'

'What's wrong?'

She shook her head. 'Nothing.'

'Aye, there is.'

'It's just . . . Oh, I feel awful, Roger, lying to people.'

'About us, you mean?'

'Our betrothal is still something known only to us – even Aggie ain't aware of that yet. As for poor Meg, she knows even less.'

'Then tell them. Your position at Cresslea's secured; there's nowt stopping us now.'

'I suppose . . .'

Roger studied her for a moment then crossed the room

to sit beside her on the bed. 'What's really the matter, for there is summat, in't there?'

'I'm afraid,' she admitted, snuggling into him. 'What if Aggie reckons marriage is a bad idea? She's already made mention that we might be moving too fast. And Meg: what if she's hurt that I've kept this from her for so long? What if . . . what if she thinks me a whore?' she finished on a whisper. 'I couldn't bear that.'

'From what you've told me of Aggie, she'll be happy you're happy. As for Meg; well, she would never think that of thee.'

'They're my friends, Roger. I don't want to lose them.'

'And you won't.'

'Aye, but—'

'Mara, Mara . . .' He lifted her chin with his finger and stared deep into her eyes. 'Just for once in your life, be selfish. To *hell* with everyone else. I love thee. You love me. What else matters but that?'

Smiling softly, she brushed her lips across his. 'Nothing. Nothing at all.' And it didn't.

'All will be well, you'll see.'

Chapter 16

A WOMAN ON a mission was how Mara would have described herself the following day. With Roger's strength-lending words running on echo in her mind, she set forth across the Salford hills.

'Hello, love.' Meg greeted her with her usual warmness. Then a grin appeared and she clapped her hands like an excited child. 'Eeh, Thursday's nearly here! Just think, this time the morrow, we'll be working alongside each other beyond that door.' She thumbed towards the kitchen. 'Nervous, are thee?'

'Meg, I need to talk to ye about something.'

The maid stopped to frown. 'This sounds serious.'

''Tis.'

'What is it? Surely it can't be owt that bad,' she began, smiling, yet it died when Mara's expression remained unyielding. She nodded. 'Aye, love. Aye, all right.'

They sat beneath the trees and stared at one another in silence. Mara repeated the words to herself several times more – *All will be well, you'll see* – then began.

'Roger and me: we're to be wed. We . . . I've been seeing him, intimately, for a while and we're very much in love. It was nice at first, it being just our secret, but as time went on . . . Every day, every meeting with you, drinking tea and chatting like nothing was different – it's become torture. I hated lying to you but didn't know how, where, to begin . . . I didn't want you to think badly of me. I'm sorry, Meg.'

'Hm.'

Hm? What did that mean?

Mara awaited more with bated breath. When it came, she jerked back in shock – it was the last thing she could have expected to happen. 'Lass?'

However, the maid was incapable of speech. Hunched double, shoulders jigging, she could barely breathe from laughing.

'What's so funny? Meg, speak to me!'

'Oh, love. Oh, what are you like!' Gasping, she shook her head. 'Your ruddy face; I've never seen a body look so sick with worry! Why?'

'Because I thought you'd think me . . . loose.'

Meg broke into a fresh bout of guffaws. 'Eeh, Mara. Life's for living, love. Besides, I'd forgive thee owt, you're my friend.'

She could have cried. 'You mean it?'

'Aye! I tell you what, you're a lucky bugger. He's a bit of all reet is Roger.'

'Meg!'

'Well, he is. 'Ere, what's he like? *You* know.'

Mara couldn't believe she was hearing this. 'I'm seeing another side to *you* today, never mind you me!'

'I bet he's like a bull beneath the sheets, ain't he? All rampant and masterful. The strong and silent types usually are, so I've been told.'

221

'Lass . . . stop!'

'Ha! I knew it – your blush says it all!'

It was Mara now who was overcome with amusement. She couldn't help herself – throwing her head back, she laughed until her ribs hurt.

'All right?'

They glanced around to find the very man they had been discussing standing behind them. One look at each other and the women collapsed again into a fit of giggles.

Roger stared at them in turn. Then his face cleared and he nodded knowingly. He touched his cap to them both and with the definite hint of a smile sauntered away, and Mara and Meg's laughter went with him.

When finally they had regained their composure and wiped the tears of mirth from their eyes, Mara rose and gave her friend a long and loving hug. Then, buoyed by how this meeting had gone, she set off to complete the next phase and speak with Aggie.

'All right?' asked the older woman, glancing up with a smile from her task of rolling out pastry when Mara entered the house at Heyrod Street. 'It's rabbit pie this evening, lass, if you're for stopping in?'

Without a word, Mara crossed the room and drew her from the table. Then, as she'd done shortly before with Meg, she enveloped her in her arms. If Aggie was surprised, she didn't show it. She simply returned the embrace, stroking Mara's back as would a mother with her child.

'Roger's asked for my hand, love, and I've said aye.'

'Eeh, lass.'

222

'You don't mind?' asked Mara, searching the woman's face for a hint of disapproval.

'And why would I do that? It's not up to me, I'm sure. If it's what tha wants—'

'Oh, it is.'

'Then you bloody well do it and be happy. No one else deserves that more than thee, my lass.'

It had been so simple. Mara was still marvelling over it later as she and the Roper family tucked into their golden pastry and tender meat feast.

To think how much time she'd wasted agonising over speaking with the women, and all for nothing – perhaps she simply was a worry wart after all. Roger, that dear sweet man, had known best all along.

'So,' Aggie said when the plates had been cleared away and they were enjoying a cup of tea in peace, the children out at play, making the most of the lingering summer light. 'Your last evening beneath this roof. Eeh, but I'll miss thee.'

'Don't, love.' Mara pressed her fingers to her trembling lips. 'I can't bear the thought.'

'Aye, you can. It's a new life you're off to grab yourself, lass. Anyroad, it's not like we'll not see each other ever again, is it?' she soothed. Nonetheless, she too was suspiciously bright-eyed.

'Just remember, you stay well away from here after tonight,' she went on. 'Should anyone ask – and particularly them pair next door – it's back home to Ireland I'll tell them you've gone. They'll not suspect owt – why would they? – and neither will there be a thing they can do. They've no reason to loiter about Salford way, have they, so it's highly unlikely they'll just happen to bump into thee up that end. Err on t' side of caution, though, lass, all the same, eh?

'Aye, it's a fresh start you've been given here, so take it and make it work. By the time Conrad gets back, he'll believe thee long gone, and that'll be that – you'll have got him off your back.'

Mara was crying quietly. 'I wish it didn't have to be this way, Aggie.'

'Nay, but it does. You just enjoy that nice job you've bagged yourself and, in a few months' time, wedding the fella you love and living happy ever after. I wish nowt but the best in t' world for thee, my lass.'

Saying their goodbyes in the small hallway shortly afterwards proved an even bigger wrench than either had anticipated. Clutching her paltry bundle of possessions, Mara was inconsolable.

'You'll not forget to visit, Aggie?' she sobbed. 'Remember, I'll be by the statue of Sir Robert Peel in Peel Park at one o'clock every Sunday. I'll wait for an hour before assuming you can't make it, just in case you're running late. All right?'

'All right, lass. I'll do my best.'

A last, tight hug, then they parted company.

Shoulders back and her head held high, Mara turned her back on Heyrod Street for the final time. On she walked, leaving behind her both the good and the bad, tears dripping unchecked down her cheeks, out of Ancoats then Manchester itself; further, further, towards Salford and Kersal and new beginnings.

She was minutes from her destination and had just begun the trek up the hilly rise leading to Cresslea when a voice called her name.

Pausing in surprise, she turned to scan the landscape, but there was no one there. All at once, the atmosphere seemed to thicken. The hairs on the back of her neck stood up.

'Hello?' she called.

Nothing.

Her breathing quickening, she whipped back round and began to run. Moments later, she realised that heavy footsteps were mirroring her own, but before she had a chance to do anything, a hand clamped down on her shoulder.

Screaming, she lashed out blindly. It made no odds – hands thrust forward and imprisoned her wrists, killing any attempt of escape. 'Leave go of me! Leave go!'

'Calm down. *Stop*, Mara.'

She slowed her struggling and peered up into a face she recognised well – the face belonging to the man she'd regarded as one of her closest friends until very recently. 'Willie? What in the name of—'

'I wanted to talk to ye. Only to talk.'

Her voice was a rasp. 'About? What else is there possibly left to say?'

His brows drew together in a frown. 'Sure, there's no need to act dumb. We need to talk about us.'

'Us?'

'Aye. This has gone on long enough, so it has.'

Mara gazed back in utter confusion. For the life of her, she hadn't a single idea what he meant. 'What has? What on earth are you blathering on about, Willie Keogh?'

'You. Me.'

Oh, Lord, no . . .

'It's a mistake you've made,' he went on obstinately. He made to take her hand, but she snatched it back. 'Come on, now. Just admit you were wrong.'

'I wasn't—'

'Sure, there's no shame in it.'

'There's no shame in it because I didn't make a mistake!' Her patience was rapidly waning. 'Look, don't let's dredge up the past. Just get out of my way and we'll forget this conversation ever happened.'

'Let you go, aye? What, back to him?' he snarled.

Mara was taken aback, not only by Willie's comment but by the sudden switch in his demeanour. Spitting steel, his eyes bulged from his twisted face. 'You're mad,' she whispered.

'Oh, am I?'

'Aye. There, there is no man—'

'You're a liar, Mara. I've seen the two of youse with my own eyes.'

Lost for words, she swallowed hard. Had Willie been skulking around the fields and witnessed Roger walking her part of the way home during her early-morning departures?

'I wanted to make an honest woman of you, but you turned me down,' he continued quietly through gritted teeth. 'Yet he gets to mount you without any effort at all?'

'*What?*'

'You give yourself to him just like that. And there was me willing to wed you for the privilege – how much of an eejit am I!'

Her head spun. *How?* 'My God,' she croaked suddenly as realisation slammed. 'The window. I did see someone – you. It *was* you, wasn't it?'

'I saw you heading into Salford one evening and decided to follow you.' Mouth tightening, the Irishman shook his head slowly. 'The things I've watched him do to you . . . And you, you love every minute of it, don't you? Writhing around on that bed like a speared carp—'

'Stop it.'

'The smile on your face when his is buried between your thighs—'

'Stop it! *Stop* it!'

'Panting and begging him for more like a bitch on heat—'

'Enough!'

From where she found the strength and courage, Mara didn't know: drawing back her arm, she slapped him full around the cheek. Willie staggered back and she ran at him with a cry. Grasping the front of his jacket in her fists, she shook him hard.

'You dirty, filthy bastard, ye! I ought to set Roger loose on you and see how you'd like that!'

Whether from her unexpected assault, the prospect of a beating from Roger, or a combination of both, Willie's eyes were wide with horror. 'Mara . . . You wouldn't!'

'No?' Never had she felt so completely violated, and she trembled violently with white-hot rage. 'One word from me and he wouldn't hesitate to take the head from your neck, believe me.'

'I just want you to love *me*. Why him, eh? Why him!'

Mara shook her head. The Irishman cut such a pathetic

figure she found it impossible to sustain her anger. She released him and picked up her bundle from the ground. 'I don't know why, but it will never change. Don't ever come near me again, Willie.'

She walked away from him with as much dignity and control as she could manage. Only when she was over the ridge of the grassy slope did she pick up her skirts and run as fast as her legs would carry her.

'Well, let me hear it.'

'What?'

'Didn't everything work out fine, just like I said it would?'

Bringing a small smile to her lips, Mara nodded. 'You were right, so.'

'A member of the fairer sex admitting they were wrong?' Roger winked teasingly. 'Ah, dulcet tones to warm the heart.'

She tried another smile, but it fell flat; her brain was too filled with other matters to find the energy for it. Namely, Willie Keogh and the horrible episode on the hillside earlier dominated her attention.

For differing reasons, she'd refrained from making mention of it to Roger – the main one being that surely it was over now. Willie wouldn't come near or attempt to accost her again; he'd more than got the message. Moreover – and this she was reluctant to admit, even to herself, but knew it was so nonetheless – she felt sorry for him. She did, even after everything, couldn't help it.

The pain of unrequited love must be the keenest of them all; she'd never set out to cause that intentionally.

Roger inflicting his wrath upon him and adding to the hurt he was undoubtedly suffering already was an unnecessary step too far, so where was the point in it? Besides, she wanted nothing to mar the mood further this night.

Truth was, not only did today mark the final one beneath Aggie's roof, but Roger's too – at least until they were married. Tomorrow she would take up residence at the manor, and this cottage would become out of bounds. Therefore, they must make their final night together here count. That couldn't be possible with the Irishman's actions hanging over them.

'Mara? Has owt occurred?'

Turning now to gaze at Roger, her heart swelled with unadulterated fulfilment. 'No, lad.'

'Only you look as if summat's troubling thee.'

She smothered his probing with a long, slow kiss. Then she led him to the bed.

'You would tell me if it had, wouldn't you?' he asked quietly, and his eyes travelled to the blanket she'd pinned up at the bare window shortly before.

Damping down a stirring of guilt, Mara smiled. 'Aye, Roger. I would,' she lied, hoping Willie would never give her cause to regret it.

Chapter 17

MARA AND ROGER were married at the Roman Catholic cathedral of St John's on a chilly mid-November morning.

With only Aggie and Meg in attendance, it had been a quiet affair. However, Roger and Mara had found it magical nonetheless – in particular the latter, who had cried buckets when they were at last pronounced man and wife.

Luke Braithwaite had been unable to attend the ceremony due to work commitments but had allowed the couple and their guests the use of his carriage. Not wanting any fuss, Mara and Roger would have happily walked, yet the offer was a kind one and of course they had accepted graciously.

Now, as the foursome left Chapel Street and made back towards Cresslea, Mara could have wept anew. Never had she known such elation, hadn't imagined it could exist. Married to the man she loved, *finally*. Mrs Mara Lawson – not a rhyme in sight. The master's mother would certainly approve of that, she was sure! Now all that was left to do was enjoy the rest of their lives together – no hardship on that score.

'Can't we skip this next bit and move straight to our wedding night?' Roger murmured in Mara's ear as the carriage drew nearer to their destination.

Thankful that her friends were deep in conversation on the seat opposite and hadn't overheard, she smothered a giggle with the back of her hand. 'I'm afraid not,' she whispered back. 'Sure, ain't our guests expecting refreshments and to toast our future? Don't worry, the wait will be worth it,' she added with a soft and sultry wink.

Roger pulled a pained face. 'Eeh, lass. Please, don't look at me like that when I'm wearing these tight trousers.'

Mara was still grinning when they drew to a halt outside the cottage.

At the door, she reached for her husband's hand and squeezed. 'We're home, lad. *Home*,' she repeated. After so many months of enforced restraint and making do whenever they could to snatch moments together with stolen clandestine meetings, oh, but it felt wonderful to say.

After the pleasant wedding tea of cold meats and sandwiches, which they enjoyed all sitting together around the table, Mara topped up their ale from the small keg Roger had procured and raised her glass.

'To Aggie and Meg – the bestest friends anyone could wish to have. Thank you both for coming.'

'To the happy couple!' they responded with gusto.

Roger caressed Mara's cheek. 'To you, my lass, for becoming my wife.'

'And finally, to Rebecca,' she said with a quaver in her tone. 'We never would have found each other but for her.'

'Rebecca,' the party said softly in unison.

A short while later, with much embracing and well-wishing, the women took their leave and the couple were at last alone.

'Come here, you.' Roger held out his hand to his wife and she went to him with eyes wet with emotion. In silence, he held her close for an age. Then he took her face in his hands and kissed her tenderly. 'My love.'

'My love,' she repeated back to him.

'I'll make you happy every day, Mara. I swear it.'

As she'd known he would, Roger held true to his word. The two of them floated on life's tide in their own private bubble of contentment.

Seemingly, the seasons passed them by in the blink of an eye and, before they knew it, they were approaching their first wedding anniversary. Mara could barely wait. For several weeks now she'd come to realise something and had chosen to hold off telling her husband until the special day. After all, what better gift to mark the celebration of their union than the news that she was to bear his child?

On the appointed evening, Mara was on tenterhooks. With Meg's reassurance that she'd manage without her, Mara left her duties at the manor a little earlier than usual and rushed home to get everything prepared.

Wanting it all to be perfect, she'd cooked Roger's favourite meal of stew and dumplings and had cleaned and tidied the cottage until it shone. By the time he arrived home from his toil, a good fire burned in the grate and the delicious-smelling food was on the table waiting to be dished up. Mara hurried to welcome him with a kiss.

'Happy anniversary, lad,' she murmured, her heart full with her love for him. 'Come, sit down and eat.'

Later, when they had completed their meal and after much laughter and reminiscing of all they had experienced as a couple up to this point, Roger took her hand and guided her to their bed.

'Roger . . . there's something I must tell ye,' she began, but he hushed her gently and proceeded to undress her.

'Later.'

'But—'

'Later, lass,' he maintained. Eyes darkened with desire, he lifted her up to straddle him. 'I've had a fire a-smouldering in me all day for you; I must have thee.'

'I'm with child.'

The room seemed to hold its breath as they gazed at one another in the thick silence.

'What?' he rasped at last.

'We're to have a baby.' Holding back tears, she grinned. 'Sure, ain't that just the best news in all the world?'

Slowly, he eased her off him and sat up to lean his back against the wall. All vestige of colour had deserted his face and his breaths came in short bursts.

Mara was flummoxed. She laid a hand on his arm, but he didn't react; it was as if he'd slipped into another place, one where her presence hadn't the power to reach him. 'Roger, what is it?'

'You're certain?' he asked after an eternity.

'As I can be, aye. You're happy . . . ain't you, love?'

He met her stare for the first time, held it for a moment then dipped his head.

'Roger—'

'I can't . . . I can't, Mara. I *can't* be a father.'

Dread walked its cold fingers up her spine. 'I don't under— Why?'

'Because I don't know how to. I grew up in an orphanage, you know that. What do I know about raising a child? I don't have the first clue . . . none at all.'

'Oh, lad.' For a terrible moment back there, she'd worried he might grow angry; walk out on their marriage, abandon her and the child, even. Relief trickled through her. 'You just have to love it, Roger. Just love it.'

'It's not only that.'

'Then what?'

'I can't put into words . . . It's me and thee. Us, and no one else. That's how it were meant to be.'

Though she frowned to hear it, she understood. She'd felt that from the very start as well; the intense and all-consuming connection and togetherness that were just theirs alone. Now, though, nature's hand was at play and there had begun a shifting in her, for there must. It didn't have to mean their bond breaking, but simply slackening by some small degree to include another person in their partnership. And neither was it just anyone but a product of their making, of their precious tie – which could only strengthen what they had known before, surely? Roger would grow to see that over time, he would.

Her tone was earnest. 'Sharing each other, our love, with someone else won't change what we have. Never; it couldn't.'

'I'm sorry.'

'Where are you going?' she beseeched him as he climbed from the bed and threw on his clothes.

234

'For a walk. I need to, to think . . .'

'Roger. Roger, please!'

'I'm sorry,' he said again, and disappeared from the house.

She must have cried herself to sleep because the next thing she was aware of was of him picking her up from the mattress to cradle her in his strong arms. He rained kisses on to her hair and she clung to him.

'Forgive me.'

'Always,' Mara murmured.

When he made love to her, it held a sense of urgency, as though he'd lost a part of her already and was desperate to reclaim it. Craving to convince him that all she'd promised was truth, she matched his zeal without limit.

'How will I love it as I love thee?' he whispered later as they lay, limbs entwined, staring into the darkness. And Mara knew in that moment that all would be well. She smiled.

'You will. And by God it'll be the luckiest baby the world's ever seen.'

'He's terrified, Meg, that's what it is.'

Having finished their morning chores, the women were enjoying beneath the trees with Cuthbert for company a well-earned cup of tea.

'It's to be expected. Most fellas get the jitters about becoming a father for the first time, I'll bet.'

Mara nodded agreement. 'It's not just that with Roger, though. It's his past, you see. He ain't ever had anyone to love before I came along, nor a soul to love him back. What we have . . . it's difficult to explain. Right from the start, it's like we stopped being separate people and merged completely into one being, so strong were we struck. It's like an idolisation almost, on both our parts. Us two, for ever and always. We were meant to find one another, without a doubt. We were, I feel it in my very bones, and Roger does too. And that's the problem, so it is: he can't bear the notion of anything possibly coming between that. Nor can he fathom how a level of love such as ours can ever be matched.'

'He reckons he mightn't feel for the child anywhere near what he feels for thee?'

'Aye, to be sure.'

The maid shook her head. 'But of course he will; that's daft.'

'To us, mebbe, but not to him. The idea of his very own child guessing it ain't loved above all else – as Roger himself was not – crucifies him. That, I know, is what he's most frightened of above everything.'

'Eeh, poor bloke. What will tha do?'

'There's but one thing I can do: reassure him till I make him believe it, that he's nothing to fear. That he's going to be *the* best da that ever walked this earth.'

Mara held fast to her vow. And as her stomach grew, so too did her expectations for the future.

Roger had slowly but surely awakened to the situation and the possibilities it held.

He'd observed the changes to his wife's body with an almost childlike fascination, and as the months went on – and with her patient encouragement – he'd gradually grown in confidence to ask questions, bolstering his keen-ness to learn.

The first time he'd felt the child kick, he almost sprang from his skin like a frightened deer. Nevertheless, his smile of wonderment had remained with him for the rest of the afternoon. His next attempt had proved much more successful – these days, he refused to even leave for work in the mornings without first stroking and kissing her bump goodbye.

Now, as spring gave way to summer and the pregnancy neared its end, he was restive with anticipation. Mara was little better. She was mindful, however, to hold her skit-tishness in check. Roger would only feed off her emotions, and the last thing she wanted at this late stage, and after so much careful nurturing to get him to the point he was at, was to send him back into an anxious spiral. But oh, she was fizzing with longing inside. She could barely wait to feast her eyes on the brand-new babe.

Finally, as the first day of July broke over the malachite-coloured moors beyond their dwelling, her pains began.

Eager to keep things as calm as possible for her own sake as well as Roger's – now the moment had come, she found she was a sack of nerves – Mara lay still and quiet for as long as she was able. However, in what seemed like a very short space of time, the waves of mild pain swelled into violent torrents – biting her hand as she saw another spasm off, she knew she couldn't cope alone much longer. It passed and, taking advantage of the temporary respite before the next contraction, she gently shook Roger awake.

'Mara?'

'Now don't panic – it's started.'

His bleary stare instantly cleared. 'You mean . . .'

She nodded.

'Have I to get Mary?'

'Aye, fetch her. Quickly, Roger.'

He was out of the bed and scrambling for his clothes in a trice. After pulling on his boots, he returned to the bed and planted a swift kiss to Mara's brow. He stooped, dropped another on to her stomach, then, flashing a grin, dashed from the cottage.

By the time he returned with the manor's rotund housemaid, who had worked as assistant to a local midwife before going into service and had offered her services in the birthing, Mara was grunting on all fours. Assessing the situation at a glance, Mary ordered Roger to build up the fire and collect water for heating, then made her way over to the bed.

'Stay calm, lass, you're doing well,' she told Mara, kneading her back in an effort to ease somewhat her discomfort. Then, seeing that Roger had completed his tasks, and after ushering him back out into the cool morning with the declaration that the labour room was no place for men, she rolled up her sleeves and got to work.

Just over an hour later, on a final, agonising push, the child emerged into the world, limp and silent. Immediately, it was clear to both women that it was quite dead and had been for some hours.

Without a word, a sombre-faced Mary wrapped the perfect form in a blanket and placed it in its mother's arms. Then she sighed and crossed to the door to inform Roger.

He entered the room trance-like, tears rolling from hollow, haunted eyes. 'Mara . . .'

'Your son,' she said in a monotone, handing him the bundle and turning over to face the wall.

Chapter 18

IMPREGNABLE GRIEF HELD Mara captive for a solid fort-night. She left the bed only when calls of nature deemed it, barely took sustenance, and spoke not a word to a soul.

By the third week, the black mist began to lift and she re-emerged into a reality that was familiar but nonetheless altered indefinitely. Roger was almost insensible with relief.

'We lost him.' Her voice was weak and scratchy from lack of use. 'He's gone.'

'I know, lass. Eeh, I know, and I'm sorry.'

Her husband had sagged to his knees by the bedside to rest his head in her lap, and she stroked his hair slowly. 'Don't blame yourself, Roger, for I know you are.'

'I didn't want . . .'

'Didn't want what?' she asked.

'Him,' he choked, burying his face into her. 'When you first told me, the things I said . . . what if our son heard them? What if that's why he . . . If I'd accepted it from the beginning, mebbe this wouldn't have happened.'

'No. It wouldn't have made a difference. This was how it had to be. It's God's will, so it is, and wasn't for us to decide. Besides, you grew to love your son eventually, and he'll know that.'

'Aye, Mara, but it was too late. It was much too late.'

Roger wept quietly and she shut her eyes and her ears from it and his pain; it was too much to stand.

'Why can't you cry?' he asked her when his emotions had subsided. 'You ain't shed a tear, norra one, and it worries me. 'Tain't natural, Mara.'

She let her shoulders rise and fall. 'I don't know.'

'You'll have to let it out at some point or it'll make thee ill.'

'I can't. My heart . . . it's empty.'

Roger was silent for a moment, then: 'He's buried already, Mara.'

Something struck inside her breast then dulled to nothing. 'When?'

'Last week. We had to, couldn't have left it any longer. I tried talking about it with you more than once but couldn't get through; it's like the words couldn't reach thee.'

'I understand, don't feel bad. It's not your fault.'

'I'm sorry all the same.'

'Was it . . . a nice service?'

'It was, lass. Beautiful.'

Again, that stab deep in her chest. 'He would have had to have a name. You gave him one?'

'Aye.'

'What did you call him?'

'Roger, lass, after me. Is that . . . all right?'

'Perfect,' she whispered.

He nodded. Then he reached over and wrapped Mara in his arms.

They were still holding one another minutes later when a soft knocking came at the door. Roger went to answer, and Meg entered.

'Mara, love . . .'

'Hello, Meg.'

'Eeh, but it's good to see thee up from yon bed.'

Seeing the maid's shiny eyes and wobbling lower lip, Mara opened her arms to her; Meg hurried across to embrace her.

'I'm so very sorry.'

'I know.'

'That poor, bonny young babe.'

'Aye.'

'Aggie Roper sends her love.'

Mara's detachment from the discussion lifted some-what at this; her ears pricked. 'You've spoken to Aggie?'

'I went to meet her at Peel Park last week to let her know what had occurred. I reckoned she'd have been fretting at you not showing, and that you'd have wanted her to know.'

'Thank you, Meg, that was very thoughtful of ye.' Mara's eyes creased in thought for a moment. 'It's Sunday today, ain't it?'

'That's right.'

'Would you walk with me now to the park? I'd like to see Aggie.'

Meg shared an uncertain look with Roger. 'You're sure you're up to it, love?'

'I am. Besides, I could do with the fresh air.'

'Then of course I'll come with thee, aye.'

Her husband followed her as she went to get her shawl.

242

His eyes never leaving her, he watched as she donned the garment then collected her hair into a neat knot at her nape. His mouth curved in the shadow of a smile. 'I'm so proud of thee.'

'I ain't done nothing to warrant it, I'm sure.'

'Aye, you have. You've clawed yourself from the abyss and returned to me. I can't tell thee how glad I am, Mara. I've been going out of my mind . . . I love thee.'

'And I love ye,' she murmured. Then she inclined her head to Meg and the two of them headed off to meet Aggie.

Though the maid cast her regular sidelong glances as they passed through the grey streets, she didn't press her friend over her health or her state of mind, and Mara was glad of it. She wanted no reminders, didn't want to think, not about any of it. The weeks just gone and what led up to them . . . she wanted to forget. Just *forget* – all of it.

They passed through the tall stone archway of Victoria Gates and continued with purpose towards their destination. Made up of over forty acres of former meadowland, the park, with its sprawling green spaces and axial walkways studded with flowers and trees, offered the people of Salford an oasis of peace and beauty in their otherwise cramped and dreary world. Any other time, Mara, too, would have enjoyed the pleasing surroundings at a more leisurely pace. Today, however, nature and beauty were far from her mind; she barely noticed any of it. Picking up speed, she trudged on, Meg struggling to keep up behind.

Upon reaching the eastern terrace, Mara's gaze went straight to the bronze statue of the park's namesake: former prime minister, the late Sir Robert Peel. The figure

243

standing by the circular flowerbed bordering it was unmistakeable – at the sight of her, Mara knew a rush of great relief and comfort. *Aggie will know what to do.* Swallowing down the lump that had formed in her throat, she set off on a run.

'Lass.' Catching sight of her, the woman held out her chubby arms. Mara threw herself into the familiar hold.

'I'm so glad you're here, Aggie,' she uttered hoarsely into her shoulder.

'Oh, Mara. Eeh, my poor girl.'

They drew apart and, linking arms, the three women crossed to a vacant bench nearby.

Tilting her chin to the sky, Mara closed her eyes. 'It's nice to be out of the house, feel the breeze on my skin.'

'How're you bearing up, lass?'

She sighed. 'Oh, you know, Aggie. Muddling through.'

'Meg mentioned last week how you'd . . . well . . .'

'What?'

'You'd slipped into a darkness what no one could reach.'

'It weren't idle gossip, love, honest,' the maid hastened to explain when Mara turned sad eyes on to her. 'It's just, we were worried sick and I hoped Aggie might know what to do, youse two being so close for as long as you have.'

'I did know as well, and I told her so,' Aggie interjected. 'And aye, glory be to God, my advice looks to have worked.'

'What *did* you advise?' whispered Mara.

'Time, lass. Just time, simple as that.'

Mara's eyes creased with doubt. 'Aye?'

'Everybody's built different and we each deal with loss

in our own way. Your body knows what it's doing, what's best for thee. If it reckons you need to shut yourself off awhile and figure things out by yourself, then so be it. Just keep on listening to what it tells thee, lass, and you'll not go far wrong.'

'There are times . . . I worry I'll never figure it out, never.'

Pragmatic as always, the older woman nodded. 'Aye, you will. Be kind on yourself. It'll work itself out in t' end, these things allus do.'

Though the heaviness remained in her chest – that would probably never leave her – she did experience a lifting inside her mind. Her thoughts felt a little bit clearer, brighter; she clung to this crutch for all she was worth.

Sensing her improvement in mentality, Aggie and Mog followed suit; soon the conversation had switched to easier subjects. Aggie spoke of home and her children whilst Meg regaled Mara of goings-on at the manor in her absence – though the maid did so with an undeniably distracted air. Studying her, Mara frowned curiously.

'Has something happened, Meg? You seem different; I can't put my finger on it.'

The maid's cheeks instantly bloomed with colour and a grin that wouldn't be contained stretched her poppy mouth. 'Actually, love, now you mention it . . .'

'What, Meg? What is it?'

'I've gone and got myself a fella.'

'Oh!' Mara exclaimed in surprised delight. 'When did this occur, then?'

'It was last Sunday. I was strolling through the Crescent

245

on my way back to the manor after my visit with Aggie, and I dropped my basket. The next thing I knew, this devilishly handsome man appeared from nowhere and came to my aid. We got chatting and, well . . . we really clicked.'

Mara and Aggie shared a chuckle, the latter asking, 'Does this knight in shining armour have a name?'

'Aye, course he does: Shaun he's called. Eeh, Mara, he is a dream,' she went on breathlessly. 'He did ask if he could see me again on my next day off . . .'

'Which is today.'

'Aye, and I *did* say yes, but . . .'

'But what?' Mara wanted to know. Then understanding hit and she clicked her tongue. 'But I asked ye to accompany me here and you didn't feel able to say no; am I right?'

'Oh, it's all right, love, honest it is!'

'No, it ruddy well ain't.' Mara felt terrible. 'Get yourself off, Meg, and see if you're still in time. If he's that keen, he might still be there.'

Face glowing, eyes agleam, Meg gnawed her lip. 'D'you think? You really wouldn't mind, love?'

''Course not. Now, hurry. Enjoy yourself, you deserve it.'

The maid sprang to her feet and threw her arms around Mara's neck. 'You're an angel, love, that's what.'

'Och. Go on with you before he grows tired of waiting.'

'Aye. Aye, all right. Bye, love. Bye, Aggie. Wish me luck!'

When she'd skittered off, the women looked to each other and smiled.

'She's a nice lass is Meg,' Aggie said.

'Aye, she is. Mind you, I am a bit relieved to have you to

myself,' Mara admitted. 'I wanted to talk to you about something . . . something that's been playing on my mind for a while . . .'

'Conrad,' her friend muttered grimly. 'Am I right?'

She nodded. 'You too?'

'Aye.'

'This month marks seven years – his sentence will soon be up, Aggie. He could be back on these shores before the end of the year.'

'Aye,' said the older woman again.

'Do you really think I'm safe at Cresslea?'

'I do. Least you will be if you just carry on doing exactly as you have been. You've not shown your face back in Ancoats, have you, and that's for the best. They don't know you're even still in the country, never mind so nearby as you are. We just need to keep it that way, aye.'

'Eamon and Eugene . . . they don't ever ask about me?' enquired Mara. Despite all that had passed, she still found herself thinking about them at times.

Aggie shook her head. 'You know what they're like: selfish through and through. They think of no bugger but themselves, them two don't. And well, since that lass they've got shacked up with them came along, her what I was telling thee about last year, they've no need for thee, have they? They gets her to run about for them like a skivvy, now, instead.'

'She's still on the scene, is she? Do you think she and Eamon will bite the bullet and get wed?'

'Well, to be honest with thee, Mara . . .' Looking around to check she wouldn't be overheard, Aggie spoke out of the side of her mouth. 'I said as how she was Eamon's piece, for that's what I assumed after seeing them out in the street together. But now I'm not so sure. It's the walls in them houses, you see; thin as cobwebs, they are. And well, going off the noises I hear of a night from next door . . . it ain't just Eamon she's "friendly" with. Him and Eugene are sharing her, I reckon – a set-up what seems to be agreeable to all three of them. Have you ever known the like? I think it's foul!'

'Good God!' Mara gasped. Then, sighing, she shrugged her shoulders. 'I don't even know why I'm surprised. They're out of control, after all, always have been. What they choose to do is no concern of mine any more, ain't been for a long time.'

'That's right – and 'ere, you make sure to keep it that way. Just do as you have been, stop well away, and carry on with your life.'

She knew her friend spoke sense. Nonetheless, it couldn't stem the bone-numbing terror at the mere prospect of Conrad soon being back on English soil.

Was it possible that the past years had changed him, that he wouldn't be intent still on revenge, on tracking her down?

Her brain offered forth a response without missing a beat: of course it wasn't. Conrad would never let it lie.

What remained to be seen, and the most important thing by far, was whether he'd succeed.

Only time would provide the answer to that.

Roger was awaiting her return at the window when she got back. Spotting him, she paused on the rutted path and they simply stared at one another for a long moment.

248

Then he smiled – a soft and somewhat uncertain smile that she recognised and understood without knowing why – and she returned it. Picking up her feet, she continued on inside.

Over their evening meal, she broached the subject of returning to work. 'It's time. I can't hide away at home any longer.'

'If you're sure you're ready?'

'I am.'

'The master and his mother shan't mind should you need longer, I'm sure,' he pressed on – then held up his hands in defeat when Mara sighed. 'I'm sorry. I don't want you pushing yourself, that's all.'

'Don't apologise. It's me what's in the wrong. You're looking out for me; sure, I do know this. It's just . . . well, we've put on the Braithwaites enough, I'd say. Letting me stop off work with full pay, sending around dinners from their own kitchen when I hadn't the strength to cook for us . . . They've been a great support, so they have. Besides, we must get back to some mode of normality. Life . . . it has to go on.'

'Brushing what's occurred beneath the rug won't make it go away, Mara,' Roger said quietly after some minutes, not quite meeting her eye. 'I mean not to be harsh—'

'Then don't,' she murmured, her own gaze on her food. 'I can't – won't – think about it. What good would it do? Will it bring back our child? No, so there's no point.'

'Mara . . .'

Shaking her head, she scraped back her chair and left the table to distract her attention with tidying the room, and Roger let the matter drop.

249

'Kiss me,' she whispered later when they got into bed. Her husband duly obliged and she allowed herself to relax, feeling a little of the tension that was a constant companion these days rise from her. This was what they always did of a night, after all, and the familiarity was comforting.

Returning to normal life, life as it was before, when there was no loss or heartbreak or pain, was what she yearned for above all else now. Routine was what she needed to survive, surely it was. However, as her hands began to roam, and much to her bewilderment, Roger pulled away.

'No, Mara.'

'But . . . I reckon I'm healed enough from the birth, if that's what troubles you? So long as we're gentle—'

'It's not that. I'm dog-tired.'

'Oh.'

'Sorry.'

Quashing her mild disappointment – never had he foregone lovemaking in all the time she'd known him, and the rejection smarted – she nodded nonetheless. There was, she supposed, a first time for everything. 'You get some rest.'

The following morning, having woken before him, she tried her attempts again. He lay on his back and she brushed her lips along his chest in a series of butterfly kisses. As though on instinct, his arm came around to fondle her buttocks and she brought her mouth up to meet his. He buried his free hand in her hair and drew her closer, his tongue wrapping around her own. Then his eyes opened and it was as though consciousness had flicked a switch – he jerked back with a frown.

'Roger?'

His breathing heavy, he ran a hand through his hair and cleared his throat. 'I'm sorry, I . . .'

'What is it?'

'Nowt. Nowt. It's just, I'm not, not really in the mood . . .'

'No?' Her tone was thick with hurt. 'Then what's that, a figment of my imagination?' she asked, indicating the throbbing evidence of his desire.

He pulled the blankets up to cover his nakedness then made to take her hand, but she dodged him and scrambled from the bed to wriggle into her dress. 'Mara . . .'

'Just forget about it, Roger.'

'Mara, wait—'

'I'm going to work,' she told him. She grabbed her shawl and clogs and dashed barefoot from the house.

Chapter 19

IT WAS OFFICIAL: Meg had fallen heavily and hopelessly in love.

Despite her genuine happiness for her friend, Mara couldn't help feeling a pang of loss to hear the excited chatter.

She recognised only too well those lively eyes, that pink blush and dreamy expression which came with the first flush of romance. After all, it had been hers to know at one time. *One time.* Those heady days seemed like a lifetime ago now.

'Shaun is just so perfect,' the maid gushed.

'So you've said,' Mara told her with a soft smile. It had been several weeks since Meg had made his acquaintance, and these daily outpourings during the friends' usual break beneath the trees was something Mara had come to accept. 'I am pleased you're happy, lass.'

'Eeh, ta, love. He's stolen my heart completely, and I know I have his. In fact, I reckon he might well ask me for my hand in the not too distant future.'

Mara nodded. From what she'd heard from the maid, the budding relationship did indeed seem to be moving along rapidly; it wouldn't surprise her in the least if Meg's assumption proved true. 'So when do we get to meet this heavenly young man?'

'I could ask him here next Sunday, give youse the chance to get to know each other; what d'you think?'

'That sounds nice, aye; I'd like that.'

Meg beamed in delight. 'You'll like him, love, honest you will.'

'If you hold him in such high esteem then, sure, I don't doubt it. It would take a very special fellow to be worthy of ye, so it would.'

'Ay, Mara. You'll have me bawling in a minute,' the maid said with a sniff. 'I am glad you're happy for me.'

'Well, of course I am.'

'There were times . . . well, I often worried that love and marriage might never happen for me, you know? That afternoon you explained to me yours and Roger's feelings for each other, when he was fretting about becoming a father . . . d'you remember? What was it you said: *Us two, for ever and always*? I weren't half jealous, Mara. I cried myself to sleep that night, I did, wished with all my heart I'd one day find someone and get to experience what youse two have. And now it's come true. Eeh, I can't tell thee how thankful I am. I'm the luckiest lass in Manchester, I think.'

Mara couldn't speak past the tears clogging her throat. Yet her emotions were not only for her dear friend, but for herself. She did recall that conversation well enough. How different things had been then, how warm with love and full of hope her heart had been. Then baby Roger had . . . well, he'd had to leave them, hadn't he, and his

253

father had turned from her in a way she never would have believed possible.

Now, they were like strangers who happened to dwell beneath the same roof. Just how had this occurred at all? She couldn't fathom it – was coping with it even less. They had drifted such a distance from one another that clawing back even a semblance of what they once had seemed an impossibility. And it hurt. *God, how it did.*

They were not even communicating, never mind anything else. Since the morning he'd spurned her advances, everything had changed. For whatever reason, he'd withdrawn from her and into himself. And hurt and confused and not knowing what else to do, she'd followed suit. Never had she felt so alone – or as unattractive, not even during her first marriage. As odious as Seamus's hands on her had been and however cruelly he'd used her body, at least he had wanted it, right up until the end. Now, to Roger, she felt utterly invisible.

The uncertainty was crippling. She just didn't know what to do, didn't know for the very first time since meeting him what the future held, and it scared her witless. Just how would this pan out? She wasn't sure whether she even wanted to know the answer any more.

Whereas at one time she'd have prayed the hours away to rush at the day's end back to the cottage and Roger, now she watched the kitchen clock's progress with the hope that the hands would move more slowly. Even work was preferable now to the long evenings filled with only agonising silences at home. Nevertheless, as she knew it must, the time to leave arrived; damping down a sigh, she collected her shawl and, after saying goodbye to Meg, dragged herself out of the manor.

She was half a minute from her destination when the line of thickets to her right suddenly spoke. At least it seemed it was this to whom the voice belonged, for there was no one else around. Which of course was impossible and ridiculous – bushes didn't talk. Then who . . . ?

'Well, well, well. Hello, Ma.'

As though witnessing the scene in a dream, Mara watched open-mouthed the figure who had been crouching out of view stretch to its full height.

She processed the words that had met her ears like hot knives, took in the grin and the piercing stare and the huge, bunched fists with a detached acceptance. Even when it drew nearer and she felt like a physical thing the pure hatred for her oozing from its very being, she didn't react. The shock would never have allowed it, had rendered her senseless; she felt she'd died, and she wished she soon would.

'What? No happy welcome for the hero returned?'

Mara responded with numb nothingness. Still she made not a movement nor a sound when the hands grabbed her by the hair and dragged her into the dense foliage.

Conrad threw her on to her back and dropped to his knees beside her. Gripping her by the jaw in an iron hold, he glared deep into her eyes.

'Say summat,' he hissed.

'I'm sorry.'

Her tone had been eerily calm; his eyebrows twitched

in a momentary frown. Then the murderous fury returned like fire to his eyes and he growled low in his throat. 'Oh, tha will be before I'm done with thee. Make no mistake about that.'

In silent stillness, she waited for the punishment to come. It never did.

Seconds later, Conrad had released her and disappeared into the gathering dusk.

Mara remained exactly where she was. Through the softly swaying twigs, she watched birds flying overhead en route to their nightly shelters. She followed the scudding sky, its tracks of powdery blue deepening to mauve then sapphire, saw the moon's advance on the horizon. Finally, without rhyme or reason, she turned on to her front, crawled into the open and got to her feet. Her legs moved of their own accord; putting one clog in front of the other, she continued on for the cottage.

Roger glanced up as she entered. 'I was just about to come looking for thee – where the devil have you . . . ?' His words petered off as he did a double-take. Slowly, he rose from his chair. 'What is it?'

'I'm tired.' Eyes straight ahead, she walked past him to the bed.

'Mara?'

'Leave me be.'

'Mara, has summat—'

'I *said*, leave me be.'

Albeit with a sigh, he did, and she was free to burrow beneath the blankets with her empty thoughts.

She roused from a semi-doze in the early hours with a feeling akin to a ton weight bearing down on her chest.

An attack of panic or of the heart, she couldn't be sure, but the intensity at last awakened her feelings and then her brain, snapping her fully up. Fear and confusion swamping her, she slipped from the bed and took herself off to the chair by the window.

Conrad was back.

Admitting it acted like a slap to her face and the pressure inside her vanished; she sucked in a long, heavy gasp.

It was true, it was: he was back. He'd been here but had left again – why? The lack of answers made her feel sick to her stomach.

She'd expected torture, degradation at the very least – *something*. However, nothing.

Just what was his game? For this was what this was to him, without question, had to be. He'd had a long time to hone his plan. He knew precisely what he had in store for her, was toying with her, hadn't even started yet. She was the prey and he the hunter. He was playing this slowly, would prowl and stalk until he deemed the time right. All that remained now was to wait for him to strike.

Drawing up her knees and wrapping her arms around them, she stared out unseeing at the star-studded sky. How was it possible he was home? Of course, she'd known his return was inevitable but had believed she had a good few months' grace before that occurred. Had he finally found the opportunity to stow away on a ship back to England, as she'd been expecting? Or perhaps he'd been released early? And *how*, in the name of God, had he found her?

Aggie? Never. Her friend would sooner tear her own tongue out before she'd reveal to Conrad or anyone else her whereabouts, Mara knew. Nor was Aggie aware of his return, for she'd have surely mentioned having seen him next door. Then who?

Another name slammed into her mind, and she nodded slowly. Willie Keogh. Damn it, it had to be. There was no one else it could be. And to think she'd dared believe long ago that she'd seen the last of him. This just got worse and worse. She couldn't handle this, she wouldn't. Why, why did she always seem to meet trouble, no matter how hard she tried to escape and steer clear of it?

Across the room, Roger shifted in his sleep, capturing her attention. She glanced his way with a bite of her lip. How she wished she could run to him, shake him awake and reveal all, beg from him his assurances and support. But she couldn't, could she? Least, she didn't feel able to. She just didn't feel she had him on her side these days. Turning to him when things grew tough just hadn't worked out as it was meant to; hadn't she learned that recently? Already she'd alienated him beyond comprehension. This fresh revelation, such as it was, might tip their already fragile relationship over the brink of no return.

She had to figure this out on her own. But how – *how*?

Her eyes flitted to her shawl and clogs and, of its own accord, her body jerked as though to flee from the chair, the cottage and Salford itself, just keep on going without a word to a soul so there was no one from whom Conrad could ever extract her whereabouts, and never look back. Then in a move that surprised her, her body reacted without her say-so again – only now it was in a display of defiance: her shoulders went up, followed by her chin, and she shook her head.

She wouldn't run, refused to – and why the hell should she? All that she'd caused him, she'd done with the best intentions: for himself as well as others. Of course, were it within her power to turn back the hands of time and do it all differently, then she would, in a heartbeat. But she couldn't, and so she must live with her actions – and the consequences. They both did.

What she would do was try her utmost to avoid being alone. Conrad wouldn't attack in front of an audience, she was fairly confident of that. Thus, so long as she didn't venture out by herself, surely she'd be safe?

Besides the short breaks, which if she did pass outside then she did so in the company of Meg, her days were taken up with work inside the manor. That just left the journeys to and from work.

Until recently, she'd undertaken the former with her husband. Not so any more, owing to how matters between them had soured – Roger seemed to leave the cottage earlier and earlier these days. Well, she'd make it her mission to rectify that first of all, would ensure she walked with him every day from now on. As for her return in the evenings . . . perhaps she could seek Roger out for his company then, too. She'd think of something, God willing, should he become curious of her behaviour. She was determined to figure this out somehow.

Putting her new-found plan to the test that morning proved easier than she'd hoped for. Roger simply nodded when she suggested they set off together and, though they barely passed a word between them on the way, she was nevertheless grateful of his presence. Of Conrad, there had been no sign and, when she reached the safety

259

of Cresslea's kitchen, she found she could breathe a little better once more.

Building up her anxiety by upholding his absence must have been what he was striving for, as there wasn't a trace of him for the remainder of the week – and to her chagrin, it was certainly working.

This was what he wanted; she just knew it. Her looking over her shoulder each second of the day, jumping at every little noise, terrified he'd suddenly appear out of nowhere to wreak vengeance at last, and that would be the end of her. To make matters worse, there wasn't a single thing she could do about it. Blast him to hell, he was her puppet master, in full control of her strings. Just how much more would she take?

By Sunday, she knew she couldn't keep this bottled up inside herself any longer.

Knowing Meg was spending her day off at the manor today as, at her insistence, her beau Shaun was heading out here to make Mara's acquaintance, she knew she must first explain her changed plans to her friend. Meg would likely be disappointed with her, and Mara couldn't say she blamed her – but for her, the maid could have been enjoying her free time with her new fellow somewhere much more exciting than her workplace – but still, it couldn't be helped.

She must see Aggie today, had to inform her of developments and, with any luck, get from her some much-needed advice. The route to the park would be busy enough to ensure her safety, surely? In any case, so desperate had she become that it was a risk she was willing to take.

Mara sprinted the short distance to Cresslea and found Meg drinking a cup of tea at the large kitchen table. Her expression must have said it all; the maid's smile slipped from her face.

'Love? What is it, what's wrong?'

'Meg . . . I'm sorry, but I can't make it this afternoon.'

'Oh! But why?'

'I must check whether Aggie has turned up to meet me today, have to see her. 'Tis important.'

Her friend was crestfallen. 'I was so excited for you to meet Shaun. He was looking forward to it, an' all. Eeh, love, are you sure you can't see Aggie another time?'

She shook her head. 'Sure, I wish I could . . . No, I'm sorry.'

'Nowt's wrong, is there?'

Mara dithered for a long moment. Then, figuring that the woman deserved a proper explanation at least – and really, what harm could telling her do? Perhaps she might even be able to help? – she heaved a sigh and nodded. 'Actually, lass, aye. There is.'

A silent Meg sat dumbstruck through the disclosure. When Mara had exhausted all there was to tell, the maid hurried around the table to throw her arms around her. 'Love, love . . .' There were tears in her voice. 'Oh, why didn't tha let me know all this sooner, eh? Eeh, what a dirty, rotten swine this Conrad sounds! I'd like to give him a piece of my mind, that I would!'

'I'd appreciate ye not mentioning this to Roger.'

'He don't know? But Mara—'

'He can't, Meg. Least not yet. Please, I know what I'm doing.'

'If you say so, love . . .'

'I do. So, you see now, lass, why I must talk with Aggie. She's been a part of this from the beginning – she'll surely have something to say about what I should do.'

Meg was quick now to nod her understanding. ''Course, aye, you must go. 'Ere, I'll tell thee what, happen I can persuade Shaun to stop on here for an extra hour or so? That way, you'll still be able to catch him when you get back from Peel Park. What d'you say?'

Though not really in the mood, today of all days, for making merry with strangers, she didn't feel able to refuse. 'Aye, all right.'

'Eeh, gradely. You'll not regret it, love. He's a reet sunny bloke, will perk you up with his jesting ways without a doubt.'

'Grand, so,' responded Mara, forcing a smile.

'Right, well, you get on with your business and we'll see thee later. Ta-ra, love.'

She bade Meg goodbye. Then, praying she'd reach her destination unscathed – and that Aggie would be there when she did – she set off with fingers tightly crossed.

Her efforts paid off; the older woman had indeed turned up, was awaiting her arrival by the familiar statue with a smile. 'Hello, lass!'

So her assumption had been right – she didn't know, Mara realised. 'Love . . .'

As with Meg shortly before, Aggie noticed her perturbation at once. 'Oh God, what's occurred?' she asked with quiet dread.

'Conrad's back.'

'Bloody hellfire. You've seen him?'

262

'Sure, you could say that. He got a grip of me the other evening when I was on my way home from Cresslea.'

'Eh! And you're still here to tell the tale?'

'My thoughts exactly. I don't know what his game is, but he's up to something, so he is. He said he'd make me sorry for what I did, then, to my great surprise, he let me go.'

'He ain't been back to Heyrod Street – at least I've seen norra peep of him there. Eamon and Eugene ain't mentioned nowt to me neither.'

Mara nodded thoughtfully. 'If they did know Conrad was home, they would also know by now about the part I played in sending him away. They would be on the war path, too, Lord help me.'

'But they're not, so as yet they mustn't know of Conrad's release. Why's he keeping it from them, though, his own brothers?'

'I don't know.' The uncertainty of it all made her head ache. 'I'd like to, mind you. Whatever this scheme of his is that he's concocted ... the not knowing ... it's pure torture, love.'

The gut-churning what-ifs were still on Mara's mind a short while later as she made her cautious way back. Still, despite her ruminations, by the time the manor came into view she was still no nearer to working out what it all meant.

Lost in her own tumultuous world, it wasn't until she spied Meg by the trees that she remembered their arrangement; her heart plummeted. All she could think of doing now was hiding away in bed at the cottage, alone in peace with her thoughts, but of course that was impossible now.

A promise was a promise, and she couldn't let her friend down after giving her word. With a nod and a sigh, she continued on towards the servants' entrance.

'Love! Eeh, you came.'

Her friend was all smiles; Mara couldn't help but be warmed by the welcome. 'I did.'

'Did Aggie show? Was she able to help?'

'She did, and aye, I do feel the better for seeing her. Mind, she could only advise what I'd already suspected she would: I'm to go straight to the police without hesitation if Conrad does show his face again.'

'Aye and she's right, too!'

'So?' Mara asked glancing round, suddenly feeling the desperate need to change the subject. 'Where's this fellow of yours?'

'Shaun's away at the privy, love. He'll not be long. 'Ere, he was less than pleased to hear about your troubles with that ex-stepson of yourn,' she went on. 'Reckons he deserves a good hiding, he does, and I agree—'

'You told him?' Mara was less than pleased to learn that her private business had been discussed with a perfect stranger. 'Sure, I wish you hadn't, Meg.'

'Oh, but Shaun's on your side, love. In fact, I think we should get him and Roger together, aye. They could track the swine down, teach him a lesson.'

Though Mara remained silent to this, she had to admit to herself that Meg's suggestion wasn't an altogether bad one. If only things between her and her husband were better and she felt able to confide in him, Shaun might have indeed proved useful. An added ally – and extra pair of strong fists – could very well have come in handy . . .

'I almost forgot,' trilled the maid, forcing Mara's thoughts back to the present. 'Shaun fetched me a gift, love. Look at this, it's bloomin' beautiful.'

Her joy and excitement were infectious; smiling, Mara watched on with interest as Meg reached behind her chair. Yet when she laid eyes on what her friend had revealed with a flourish, a silent scream caught in her throat. *No* . . .

'In't it the bonniest thing you ever did see?' Meg gushed, oblivious to Mara's horror.

She couldn't speak. Dazed, she dragged her gaze over the terracotta vase engraved with birds in flight. The vase she recognised so well. The vase Conrad had bought for her from the pawnshop to secure himself an alibi all those years ago. *Mother of God, this couldn't be happening.*

Meg was staring at her with her head cocked in mild bemusement; however, Mara was beyond the capabilities of rationality. For one thought was tapping at her brain in contradiction of her belief: Conrad hadn't been back home – on that, Aggie had been adamant. And so, how would he have regained possession of this if that were true? Was it possible that this vase was identical yet altogether different to that she'd owned? More than one existed, surely? There had to be a chance. Or was this merely desperate and wishful thinking on her part?

'Where did Shaun get it from?' she eventually forced herself to ask.

'He said he won it not long since at a travelling fair. Don't you like it?'

'Aye.' And didn't she, after all; always had? 'Really, I do . . .'

'But?' Meg pressed.

'Nothing, lass. Nothing.' Gaze now fixed on the corner of the courtyard in anticipation of the elusive Shaun's appearance, she held her breath. *Lord, do please let it be nothing . . .*

Then there he was.

Mara's shoulders slumped. She closed her eyes in despair.

'Ah, here's Shaun!' The maid sprang to her feet and held out her hand. 'Lad, come and meet my very best friend. This is Mara. Mara, this is Shaun.'

It was as if the very air had caved in on itself; not for anything could she draw in enough to fill her lungs. Light-headedness swooped.

'Shaun, sit thee down with Mara here, and I'll fetch us a sup of tea,' Meg instructed. 'Go on, lad, don't be shy.'

He did and, when the maid had gone, he leaned back and folded his arms. There was a definite self-satisfied smirk hovering at his lips. 'Bet tha weren't expecting that, eh!'

'Shaun?' Mara shook her head slowly in contempt. 'Where did ye pluck that name from?'

'Why?' Conrad asked. 'Don't you reckon it suits me, nay?'

'Just what the hell is your game?'

'I followed that owd bitch Roper from home one day, figured she were up to summat and might well lead me to thee.'

So Willie hadn't had a hand in this, as she'd assumed. Instead, Conrad had been back at Heyrod Street all this time after all. 'Aggie . . . she's not seen hide nor hair of you—'

'Aye, I were careful of that. Eamon and Eugene were under strict instructions not to let on to nobody either.'

'Do they . . . ? Do the lads . . . ?'

'Have I told them what tha did? Is that what you're getting at?'

She nodded.

'Nay.'

'But why?'

'I have my reasons. Anyroad,' he went on in mock brightness, 'as I were saying, Roper didn't meet with thee that day at all, but with Meg instead. I reckoned she might come in useful so I got talking to her. Fell for it hook, line and sinker, she did.'

'That lass has fallen head over heels for you, so she has. And all the time . . . How long did you plan to keep it up?'

'Till she'd served her purpose.'

'It's cruel what you've done to her, *cruel.*'

'She'll get over it.'

He was even worse now than he'd been before, it seemed. 'May the Lord forgive ye, Conrad O'Hara.'

This produced a guttural laugh. 'It's you what should be begging redemption – aye, from me.'

Breaking eye contact, she lowered her head.

'Seeing that vase again gave thee a reet shock, I'll bet,' he went on, clearly pleased with himself. He glanced around to check Meg wasn't approaching then returned his sneering face to Mara. 'It's helped to keep the lass just where I want her, an' all; over the moon with it, she were, so it's worked out sound all round.'

'Just what is it you want, Conrad?'

'To ruin thee.'

The hairs on the back of her neck stood up. She shook her head. 'Lad, please—'

'And I will,' he continued, as though she hadn't spoken. 'A reet nice set-up you've got yourself here. Remarried, into the bargain. Aye, it's all worked out very well for thee, eh? Oh, mind you . . . perhaps not everything.'

'What d'you mean?'

'That day in the park, I overheard Roper and Meg talking about thee. You lost a babby, so I hear? Aw, shame.'

Watching the fresh grin that had appeared light up his face, her stomach lurched in utter disgust. 'That's low even for you. You make me sick, d'you know that?'

'I could say the same about thee, Ma.'

'Don't call me that.' His mocking the death of her child had dulled her fear and, now, anger predominated. Her tone was icy. 'I'm not your ma and never have been, thank God.'

He feigned insult, holding a hand to his heart. 'Oh, that hurts!'

'Stop it. End this now, Conrad. Go on home and leave me be and we'll never have to set eyes on one another ever again. *Please.*'

Whatever his response might have been was hampered by Meg's return. Mara's mouth opened to blurt to her friend Shaun's real identity and just what was going on, however one look at his face and the words died on her lips. The warning glint in his eyes was clear: he'd show no mercy should she even attempt to squeal.

'Here we are, then,' said the maid, handing across their tea. 'So, how're youse getting along, then?'

'Gradely,' Conrad told her with a disarming nod. 'In't that right, Mara?'

Forcing a fake smile, she glanced away.

'Oh, ew . . .' Having taken a sip of his tea, Conrad pulled a face. 'Sugar. I don't take the stuff, lass.'

Meg was mortified. 'Don't you? Eeh, I am sorry.'

'No harm done, it's all right—'

'Nay, it's not. And I so wanted today to go without a hitch . . . Here, pass it to me and I'll brew a fresh pot.'

He gave her a winning look. 'Tha don't mind?'

''Course I don't. Owt for thee, lad, you know that,' she added with a smitten blush before scurrying away.

Conrad had always taken sugar – this was a ploy to get the maid out of the way a little longer . . . With thoughts of what would come next, Mara hid a moan of misery. Clearly, he had something in mind for her. Moments later, watching his expression twist into one of sheer loathing, she knew she'd be proven right.

'End this now?' Picking back up the thread of conversation, his words dripped pure venom. 'Aye, that'd suit thee, wouldn't it? Well, I'm sorry to disappoint thee, *Ma*, but you couldn't be further from what's really going to happen if you tried.'

'Lad—'

'Don't you "lad" me, you evil, lying little whore!' Spittle had formed at the corners of his mouth and his cut-glass stare bulged with barely containable rage – Mara shrank back in her chair. 'Can you imagine for just a single second what I went through? What *you* put me through?

'The voyage . . . that alone near well finished me off. Caged up like some animal in cramped and stifling

269

quarters, rats taking chunks out of you whilst you slept . . .
well, when you did manage to snatch some kip, that is.
There's no peace to be had packed in with so many others,
never, not forra second. The worst of it, though, was the
smell. Hundreds of rank and stinking bodies filling your
nostrils with every manner of stench you can think up.
Shit and sick and sweat, piss and semen – aye, semen,
that's right. You treat a man like a beast and he'll start to
act as one. Months and months of it I had to endure, and
all because of you!

'Then we reached our destination and the real hell
began. You've no idea what it's like in that place. Back-
breaking work, man-eating animals and creatures like
summat from Satan's nightmares, the loneliness . . . Seven
years. *Seven* – and all for a crime I didn't even commit!
You did that! You! By God you'll know what suffering is
afore I'm done with thee!'

Mara had sat mutely throughout the diatribe. Now, she
could think of but one thing in way of a response – it
sounded feeble even to her own ears: 'You were out of
control and growing more reckless still. You said you'd
get one year; two at the most. I never dreamed that transportation was possible . . . I meant not for any of that and
I'm sorry. I'm so sorry, lad.'

He narrowed his gaze and leaned forward in his seat.
'D'you want to know the worst part of all that, out there?'
he asked in a harsh whisper. And at the shake of her head:
'The heat. It seeps right through to the bones. A bit like
this.'

Before Mara had time to react, Conrad struck out and
thwacked the bottom of her cup with his palm, splattering

270

her chest and lap with scalding tea. With a cry of pain, she sprang to her feet.

'Burn, does it? Aye, and even that don't come close to the temperatures I had to deal with, day in day out!' He broke off suddenly as Meg reappeared. Pretending concern, he hastened to Mara's aid. 'Oh dear, are you all right?'

'Fine. I'm fine,' she stammered, close to breaking down.

'You're sure, love?' put in the maid worriedly, taking stock of her steaming clothing.

'Aye, really. The cup . . . it slipped from my hold. I'd better get home, lass, and change.'

Before she could escape, Conrad held out his hand to her. And with Meg watching, she had no alternative but to place hers into it. Smiling, he squeezed until tears pricked behind her eyes.

'It's been nice seeing thee the day, Mara,' he stated cheerfully. Then, leaning in and lowering his tone, he added on a hiss, 'Wait for me by the thickets.'

With a gabbled farewell and trembling from head to toe, she stumbled around and hurried away.

God help her, just when would this ever know an end?

Chapter 20

THE THICKETS APPEARED in the distance and something within her snapped. She'd had enough.

'Enough!' she reiterated on a wail to the barren hills.

Spinning on her heel, she bolted in the opposite direction in search of Roger.

Upon reaching the stable block, she saw he'd opened and cleaned out everything already. All was in good order, swept and washed, but of him there was no sign. Nor had he taken out the horses for their exercise. The animals, she discovered when she went to investigate, were all groomed and present in their stalls, munching on their oats from the mangers.

Looking in the hayloft above proved equally unsuccessful, as did the harness room. Now, with only the coach house to try, she was growing desperate.

Praying she'd find him polishing or oiling the carriage in preparation for the Braithwaites' next outing, she pushed her head around the door.

Empty.

Her disappointment was overwhelming. Us two, for ever and always? Clearly not any more. Mara could have wept.

Accepting that her husband wasn't there for her yet again and couldn't help her, and with no further option left, she nodded in defeat. Then she picked up her feet once more and made her way back towards the thickets.

Conrad was there already. The moment he spotted her his mouth curved in a hard smile. Without saying a word, he gripped her by the scruff of the neck and, in mimicry of before, hauled her into the leafy seclusion.

'Whatever it is you're going to do . . . just get on with it,' she told him, weary now, despite her terror. 'Sure, ain't I lost all strength entirely for further fight?'

'It's glad I am to hear that. Oh aye. D'you know, watching thee snivelling and broken down like this does my heart good—'

'What do you *want* from me?' she interjected desperately.

'Well, you see, I was going to throttle you the first opportunity I got. Now, though, I see it wouldn't be the wisest decision I've ever made. You've gorra good thing going here, a nice position, aye, and I plan to take full advantage of the fact for all it's worth.'

She didn't like the sound of that. 'What do you mean?'

'I don't plan on scratching and scraping forra living, nay. Even scamming and scheming ain't summat I'll have the energy for for ever. It's an easy future I have in mind – and that's where you come in. You've full access to that manor, can pass through it as yer please . . . I want a slice of its spoils.'

'Spoils?'

'Crystal, silver, gold. Whatever you're able to lay your hands on.'

'You mean . . . you want me to pilfer from Cresslea?'

'That's right. And by God, don't even think to refuse.'

Mara was dumbfounded in horror. 'I shan't do it. I shan't!'

The slap that met her mouth rattled the teeth in her head. She held a hand to the stinging spot with a cry. This was why he'd held back thus far from telling his brothers of her part in his downfall, she realised. Eamon and Eugene would be charging up here all guns blazing were they to become aware, and that was something Conrad wished to avoid – at least for now. He didn't want her punishment to be a swift one, no. He had an altogether different – an altogether long-term – plan mapped out instead.

'You've still not grasped just how hopeless your situation is, have you?' he was saying now. 'You don't get to decide what it is you do or don't do. Them days are gone. It's me what decides now, me what holds your future in my hands. I'm your master, and masters must be obeyed.'

Before she had time to blink, Conrad had pushed her to the ground and pulled up her dress. Then he tossed her skirts over her head and wrenched down her undergarments.

'Bitch.' His breathing came in guttural grunts as he fumbled with his trousers. 'I'll teach thee who's in charge.'

Confusion, denial and complete revulsion were drowning her. She was drowning . . . She'd never felt such fear in the whole of her life. 'Conrad, please. *Please*.'

'Shut your trap.'

'No,' she croaked as the tip of his swollen penis tapped

274

against her most intimate spot. *She'd die, wouldn't survive such depravity.* 'You don't want to do this.'

'You're right. I don't.'

What . . . ? For a moment, she thought she'd mis-heard. Then he was speaking again and she realised she hadn't:

'This is my first feel of a woman in seven long years. I've ached for the tight warm hole. And yet, d'you know what? I still wouldn't take your rancid offering even if you begged me.'

Though unequivocal relief had flooded her veins, still his vitriol stung.

She accepted that her thoughts were irrational but still, they refused to be silenced all the same. Not only had her husband rejected her, but now she wasn't even acceptable enough for rape by a madman? How utterly repugnant and worthless must a woman be to warrant such? *Just what was wrong with her?*

'You see, though, here's the thing,' he went on, tap-tapping at her still as he did so. 'I could if I chose to. Just remember that.'

She was weak and he was in full control. Her intimida-tion and humiliation were absolute. She understood how matters stood, all right.

He released her legs with a harsh shove and moved away from her. 'You breathe a word to anyone, and I'll tear out your throat, d'you hear me? Oh, and 'ere, that includes you talking to the law. They've nowt on me, at any rate: I didn't abscond from gaol, was released early for good behaviour. I'm clean as a whistle, aye.'

'Please . . . can I go now?'

He laughed quietly. Finally, he nodded. 'Go on, get out of my sight.'

She was getting to her feet when he stopped her by clamping a hand on her shoulder:

'Wait. Can you hear that?'

Roger! The thought whipped through her brain and hope exploded through her breast. Heart hammering, she listened harder.

'Oh. Never mind – I know what that is,' Conrad stated after some moments.

'What?'

'It's the sound of your life crashing down around your ears.'

Bastard, bastard. Oh, how she loathed him.

With a malicious grin, he winked. 'See thee tomorrow.'

There was one thing Conrad had been incorrect about, and that was his claim that she was free to roam Cresslea at will.

Her position was as kitchen maid and her duties therefore restricted to that one space – how would she manage to slip out undetected and enter other parts of the house? It was impossible.

The dilemma remained with her throughout the morning as she wracked her brains for a means of leaving the room. Then, during the afternoon, the solution presented itself: Conrad turned up on the pretence of seeing Meg.

The maid was delighted at the unexpected visit. She turned to Mara with pleading eyes. 'Love, would you mind . . . ?'

''Course not,' she assured Meg after catching the warning

look from Conrad standing in the courtyard and guessing his intentions. 'You go on and have your break in the fresh air; I'll finish up here.'

Smiling from ear to ear, her friend needed no second telling and trotted off to indulge in a nice cup of tea with 'Shaun' beneath the trees.

Watching her go, Mara had never felt so rotten. Then Conrad was indicating discreetly with a flap of his hand that she should take this opportunity to do his bidding, and with an ache in her heart and her insides tumbling, Mara forced herself towards the baize door.

A glance left and right along the corridor showed her that the rest of the domestics were busy at their assigned duties within the house; not a soul was about. Nevertheless, she dithered, chewing her lip, for an age. Finally, knowing there was no way out of this and that the sooner she got it over and done with the better, she took a deep breath. Then, on legs that felt like jelly, she forced herself on.

Eyes flitting every which way, she stole like a criminal – which was exactly what she was soon to become – through the passageways. Emerging into the main part of the house, the first room she came upon was the master's study. And, judging by the half-open door, it was evident he wasn't within.

Again, she peered around – all remained still. Quick as a flash, she darted inside.

Her heart was beating so heavily she could feel it in her throat as she headed for the huge mahogany desk. She ran her eyes over its surface and the objects there but dismissed them one by one. The last two items followed the same pattern. The inkwell might well be crystal and the letter opener solid silver, but like everything else they were essential, everyday things; Luke Braithwaite would notice their absence immediately. Damping down a sigh, she moved on.

She was sifting through the last drawer of a nearby bureau when she spotted something: a beautiful cigar case ornamented in mother-of-pearl. She reached out and picked it up with shaking hands. In the next instant it was nestled in her apron pocket and she was rushing out of the room.

Mara sped through her chores then brewed a fresh pot of tea. She filled two cups and carried them outside. After passing Meg hers, she turned and handed Conrad his with a brief lift of her brows. Understanding lit his eyes – taking the brew from her, he flicked his chin ever so slightly in the general direction of the thickets. She nodded once and returned to the kitchen.

That evening on her way home from work, she took the detour and headed to their meeting place.

Conrad was waiting, as she'd known he would be. She passed over the cigar case with a feeling of reluctance mixed with relief. On the one hand, she was loath to finalise the 'transaction' and have him get his sweaty paws on the master's possession. And yet at the same time she was more than a little glad to rid herself of the proof of her treachery.

He turned the item over in his hands, scrutinising it with narrowed eyes, and a smile tugged the corners of his mouth. Then he opened it up and, instantly, the pleasure melted from his face. 'You stupid bleedin' *bitch*.'

'What is it, what have I done wrong?'

'Look here.' He thrust the case beneath her nose. 'It's engraved with his bloody initials.'

Mara was puzzled. 'Is that bad?'

'Well, it could be if he reports it missing and then I try and flog the thing.' He released a sigh. 'No bother, I'll figure it out, will have to scratch the letters out or summat . . . Just make sure you don't make this mistake again, d'you hear?'

'Again?' The blood deserted her face in a rapid rush. 'What do you mean? You said it would be just the once!'

'Nay, I didn't. Tha must have just assumed that – and more fool thee. As if I'd be content with this when there's so much more up for grabs.'

'Conrad . . .' Miserable tears threatened. 'I can't take more; they would be missed for sure.'

'And I should be bothered by that because . . . ?'

'Please. I'll lose my position, my good name – *everything* – if I'm found out.' She swallowed hard, adding on a whisper, 'Mebbe even my freedom, too. The Braithwaites would call in the police for certain.'

'Oh, what a hilarious twist of fate it would be should that come about. Come on, you have to admit that would be funny, after everything that's brought us to this point.'

'That case alone will fetch you a few pounds. Don't make me do it again, I beg ye—'

'Mara?' a voice called out suddenly behind them.

Sharing a frown, she and Conrad turned. Roger was making his way towards them.

'Listen up,' Conrad growled through the side of his mouth, and Mara felt something sharp dig into the small of her back. 'A single word to him and, I swear to God, I'll stick this blade in up to the hilt and gut you like a fish. Then he'll get the same. D'you hear me?'

'I do,' she whispered back; not for a second did she deem it an idle threat.

Her husband slowed his pace and halted a short distance away. Face stony, he looked from one to the other. 'All right?'

'Aye. We – we were just . . .'

Coming to Mara's rescue, Conrad held out his hand with an easy smile. 'Shaun. You must be Roger.'

Though Roger glanced to the proffered hand, he made no attempt to shake it. 'That's right.'

'I'm Meg's . . . very good friend,' Conrad persisted, though it was clear he was becoming angered by the other man's standoffishness.

'That's right, and Shaun wants to buy her something nice,' Mara chipped in, wanting now only to bring this conversation to an end and have the men go their separate ways, lest their animosity spilled over. 'He wanted my advice on what he should get her.'

'Is that right?' Her husband sounded less than convinced.

The knife pressed harder into her – Conrad's warning to uphold the lie – and she nodded quickly. 'Aye. 'Tis.'

'Then I'll leave youse to it.'

Watching Roger stalk away, Mara had to fight the urge to scream after him, plead with him to take her home – God dammit, show just an ounce of the fierce and all-encompassing love he'd once held for her. But she couldn't; Conrad would show her no mercy. Instead, she remained the meek and passive prisoner and waited for her captor to deem the time right to let her go.

Finally, with plans laid out as to what she'd steal for Conrad next, and with his repeated promises of the dire consequences should she disobey him ringing in her ears, she was free to head home to the cottage.

She entered to find Roger sitting staring into the dead grate. Not a word passed between them as she built the fire then set to preparing the evening meal. It wasn't until they were halfway through their food that her husband put down his spoon and lifted his head to look at her. Mara did likewise and waited for him to speak.

'Are you sleeping with that man?'

The unexpectedness of the question threw her. 'Of course not!'

'You've never known his touch – intimately?'

The memory of Conrad's member between her legs rushed to her mind and, to her horror, she felt blood flood her face. She shook her head weakly. 'No.'

'I knew it.' Roger was pale and haunted. 'I sensed it the moment I confronted youse that summat had taken place. I see it even clearer right now in your eyes.'

'Roger, please . . .'

'Admit it. Go on.'

'No. It's not what you think.'

'You're my *wife*!'

'Oh, so now you remember!' The words exploded from her. 'By God, you've got some nerve. It's more a stranger I feel to ye these days, ever since . . .'

'Ever since what?' he pushed her when her tirade petered away.

'You know damn well what.'

'Say it. *Say* it, for Christ's sake!'

'Since our child died!' she screamed over him. 'There, that's what you wanted, is it? Happy now, are you?'

Intense relief had softened his features. He reached across and brushed away the tears that were gushing down her cheeks. 'To hear you face up to the loss, see you cry for him at long last . . . Aye, lass. Aye, now I am.'

'Oh, Roger!'

'Mara, Mara, my love.'

She ran to him and he caught her and lifted her off her feet into his much-missed embrace.

'My God, how I've missed thee,' he breathed, showering her mouth in ardent kisses.

'And I've missed you, more than you will ever know!'

His tone was pleading. 'Tell me I'm wrong. Please tell me I didn't push you into another bloke's arms, that he hasn't known your body as only I can.'

'He hasn't, he hasn't, I swear it,' Mara insisted, her hands consuming every inch of him like a fever. 'It's only ever been you.'

'I must have thee.'

She could have wept to have him say it. 'Take me, Roger. Take me.'

Afterwards, it was like she'd been reborn. Stretching languidly, she heaved a full and surfeited sigh. Suddenly, her world didn't seem such a bad place any more.

'I swore the day I took you as my wife to make you happy every day. I've reneged on that, Mara, and I'm so sorry.'

At the pain-filled lines, she turned to look at her

husband. He lay on his back with his arms beneath his head and his eyes squeezed closed. She placed her hand over his heart and knew it beat just for her once again, as it had always done.

'You turned from me.' Her voice was a whisper. 'Why?'

'I didn't mean to . . . It became impossible to reach you again as time went on. It's as though you grew to hate me.'

'I was hurting, Roger. I thought you found me repulsive.'

Rising, he leaned his back against the wall and pulled her into his arms with a groan. 'Eeh, lass. Never. *Never.*'

'Then what? Please, do tell me, because, for the life of me, I can't fathom any of it.'

'Planting my seed in thee – I couldn't risk it. After everything with baby Roger, how his death turned your mind . . . I feared that if you got with child and summat went wrong a second time, I'd lose thee again.'

'My love . . . Oh, my love!' Mara sobbed with sheer joy.

'I love thee with all of my heart. I missed thee with all that I am. I'm sorry.'

'Never must we allow this to happen again.'

'Never,' he vowed in agreement. 'By God, I'm glad to have thee back.'

As was she. Their unity gave them strength; Mara felt it trickle and spread into every corner of her mind.

'Us two, for ever.'

'Always.'

Nothing in this world would tear them asunder ever again. It was impossible – theirs was a love far too powerful for it.

Conrad O'Hara would soon learn that, too.

His evil couldn't touch her now, with Roger back by her side.

'Wakey wakey.'

Her eyelids flickering open, Mara blinked through the darkness.

'Guess who?' the voice breathed again.

Then she saw it.

Illuminated by the moonlight filtering through the window was a figure standing by the bed.

Her lips parted, but the hand was too fast; it clamped down over her mouth and nose, killing her scream in its tracks.

'Try anything and I'll not hesitate,' Conrad said, and now Mara spotted the jagged blade glinting silver at a sleeping Roger's neck.

Seized with disbelief and petrified, she nodded compliance.

'Do you see how easy it'd be,' he told her, inching the weapon ever closer to the tender flesh. 'I could snuff out all you hold dear, should I choose to. Don't you forget that now, will you?'

'No,' she mouthed.

'Just a friendly reminder, that's all. See thee tomorrow.'

In a heartbeat, he'd been swallowed up by the shadows, vanishing like a ghoul into the black night, leaving Mara's plans to end his reign of terror crumbled to dust.

Chapter 21

'ONE MORE KISS,' Roger begged, drawing the shawl from Mara's hands as she made to don it.

Smiling, she obliged, then, as he made to lead her to the bed, she broke away with a chuckle. 'Control yourself, so! I'll be late for work and so will you.'

He relented with a click of his tongue and dipped his head to give her a final peck on the lips. 'See you this evening.'

'See ye later,' she murmured. Then, with a bleakness in her soul of which he hadn't the slightest inkling and never could, she forced herself off to the manor.

Conrad's actions last night had been plain in meaning: he was in full control of her and there wasn't a thing she could do about it. How he'd gained entry to the cottage, she hadn't a clue. And, to be honest, that mattered not, did it? It was the fact that he could come and go as he pleased; he knew that, and so did she. He could have done anything to them whilst they were oblivious in sleep – that was the message he'd wanted to drive home. And, for her part, she'd received it loud and clear.

Compromising the safety of those she loved and cared

about wasn't an option. She had to do as he told her, didn't have a choice. Comply or suffer the consequences was how her life must be determined from now on.

That afternoon, he turned up at Cresslea again, as Mara had known he would. Blind to the pretence that he was there for her alone, Meg could hardly contain her surprise and pleasure. In turn, Mara found it a struggle to hold at bay her sorrow for her besotted friend.

Once more, with the maid safely out of the way in the courtyard with Conrad, Mara saw herself sneaking about the corridors and in and out of the family's rooms in search of something to steal.

This time, and with the warning in mind to avoid items with engravings, she opted for something rather more generic: matching China figurines from the drawing-room display cabinet. They were one pair among half a dozen others of similar style – after carefully spacing out on the glass shelves those that remained, Mara was hopeful that no one would detect the absence.

Nevertheless, as she stole back to the kitchen with her booty, her nerves were in ribbons and a ball of nausea rolled on a continual loop through her guts. Her crimes were detestable to her – for how much longer she'd endure this, she didn't know. Her building shame was becoming impossible to repress.

'Better,' Conrad told her later when she handed over the spoils. 'Aye. Tha did good.'

Mara's heart lifted ever so slightly. 'Oh, then let this be the last time, do. Please, I couldn't stand it again, I couldn't, I—'

'You ain't finished yet, not by a long chalk,' he barked.

'Jewellery next, I reckon. Aye, some nice pieces with big stones – diamonds, if you can manage it.'

Her face fell in devastation. 'I can't do it, Conrad.'

'Tha can and tha will.'

'But ... sure, it'd mean taking from the master's mother.' This felt too great a betrayal – the thought sickened her to the core. She'd given Mara a chance when taking her on as a member of her staff, trusted her now implicitly. Worse still, she was acutely aware that of all the things Mrs Braithwaite couldn't stand, a thief was top of the list. At simply the mere prospect of targeting the old woman personally, the guilt was crippling.

'Tha can and tha will,' Conrad repeated, reaching his arm around her to grab a fistful of her hair. Mara gritted her teeth against the searing pain. 'D'you understand? Well, do yer?'

She nodded on a whimper. 'I'll do it.'

'There you go; wasn't so difficult, was it? You're learning at last.'

'This ain't ever going to stop, is it?' she murmured flatly, and a single tear trickled down her cheek. 'You'll never let me free, will you?'

His reply was low, harsh laughter. 'See thee tomorrow.'

Not this time, spoke her mind of its own accord, making her frown, as she watched him walk away.

The inner vow remained with her throughout the day and into the evening. By the time nightfall drew around, Mara knew what she must do.

How she kept up the act of all being as it should be, she didn't know. However, somehow, she managed it. She tidied around the cottage as was her usual routine at the day's end, then she undressed and got into bed. She made love with her husband, kissed him goodnight and blew out the candle. And then she waited.

When Roger's breathing grew steady in sleep, Mara knew it was time. Turning on to her side, she gazed at him through the darkness for an eternity. Finally, she pressed her fingertips to her lips and brushed them against his. Then she slipped from beneath the blankets and out of the bed.

Never had she known an agony like it as she left the cottage and closed the door softly behind her. However, calling on the last of her strength, she hardened herself to it and, somehow, continued on.

By the full moon's glow, she followed the rough paths through the hills and eventually she reached the centre of Salford. On she walked without pause until she crossed the river into Manchester, and here she allowed herself a brief rest. Then she was off again, taking turn after turn through the dark and dreary streets and lanes until, at last, she arrived at her destination. Throat thick and chest heavy, she knocked at the door.

'Mara? What in the world . . . ?'

'Hello, Belle. I, I didn't know where else . . . can I come in?'

Though a concerned frown tugged at the lodging-house keeper's brows, she nodded all the same and, with tender care, ushered Mara inside. 'Come on, lass. Come on.'

'I'm sorry,' Mara whispered when she was seated by the fire with a cup of tea.

'What's tha apologising for?'

'I shouldn't have come here bothering ye at this hour.'

'Tsk! Bothering, indeed. Talk to me, what's occurred?'

Closing her eyes, she shook her head. 'Where to begin . . . The plain truth of the matter is that it's ruined, Belle. All of it.'

'What is, lass?'

'My life,' she answered simply. 'For the sake of those I love, I can never go back.'

The sear of separation was like an inferno. It consumed every part of her being each and every minute of every day. Only the truth that all at Cresslea were now free from harm kept her going. This, of course, was the most important thing. Her pain paled to nothing in comparison where that was concerned.

Roger's confusion on awakening that first morning and discovering her gone – and later his concern when realising she was missing – was what haunted Mara the most. What he must be thinking, going through, she forced herself not to dwell upon. If there had been any other way . . . But there hadn't been, so far as she could see. Nothing less than her leaving could have got rid of Conrad – and she knew without doubt that this would have happened already, and that those back home had seen the last of him. After all, without her there to do his bidding, what reason had he to hang around? Certainly not Meg, that was for sure.

That poor, sweet girl . . . Thoughts of her heartbroken and pining for her Shaun – a man who had never existed – hurt Mara more than she could express. And yet at the same time, she also knew an undeniable sense of relief for her friend's very lucky escape. Meg might well be suffering now his sudden abandonment but, by God, it was a small price to pay in the long run, even if the woman didn't know it.

The Braithwaites and even dear Cuthbert had also taken root in her thoughts. Had Luke and his mother discovered her deception by now? What must they think of her if they had? They might even believe she'd stolen those things for her own gain and that was why she'd fled. Maybe they had reported her to the police, or at least soon would – and who could blame them? She could well be a wanted woman, for all she knew. Though the notion terrified her, God help her, prison was the least she deserved.

The only aspect of this whole horrible mess that made her feel fractionally better was the knowledge that Conrad's plans were scuppered. Nothing else would pass into his grubby hands that didn't belong to him, no more could his threats or abuse touch her. She was free of his rule; he'd lost and it was over. Never would he get the opportunity again.

Now, as the front door rattled open, heralding Belle's return, Mara abandoned her chore of dusting the small sitting room and dashed out to meet her in the hallway. Today marked five days since her arrival at the lodging house – and the first Sunday – and kindly Belle had agreed to walk to Peel Park with a message from her for Aggie.

'She was there?'

Removing her hat, Belle nodded. 'Aye.'

'You told her exactly what I told you to?'

'I did, lass. Word for word and nowt more.'

'Thank ye, Belle.'

'What's worrying thee?' the lodging-house keeper asked gently when they were seated at the table. 'I never told Mrs Roper where you are, if that's it? Honestly, all's I said was what you wanted me to: I'm a friend of Mara's, she's had to go away, and can you let her husband know she's safe and well. That were it.'

'I believe you. It's not that.'

'Then what, lass?'

'I just wish it didn't have to be this way. I miss my friends and everyone so much. As for Roger . . .' She shook her head, sending hot tears spilling. 'I feel I've lost half of myself. How will I ever bear the parting, Belle?'

'Won't you consider going back at some point? If what you say is true and Cresslea Manor has seen the last of that Conrad, then surely . . .'

'I can't risk it. He'll keep a check on the place some how, you can be sure of that. Should he get wind that I'm back then, sure, he'd simply pick up where he left off. I'd be in the hell of his creation once more – and Lord, would he make me suffer for escaping him. Worse still, though, much worse, I'd have put my husband and my friends in danger again. Conrad wouldn't think naught of harming them to teach me a lesson. What Conrad O'Hara wants, Conrad O'Hara gets, always has. He'd allow nothing to stand in his way.'

'Eeh, Mara. I wish I had the answers on how to make all this better for thee, but I don't. Least everyone will know you're safe, now, eh? That's summat.'

'Aye.'

Just then, footsteps sounded beyond the door and the women cut short their conversation with a shared nod. By the time the young daily maid entered the room it was as though nothing had been amiss; Mara and Belle were ready with a bright welcome and easy smiles.

Daisy's presence never failed to raise Mara's mood, and today was no different. Short and skinny with fawn-coloured hair, cornflower-blue eyes and a smile that lifted the heart, she seemed to bring the sun with her wherever she went. They had hit it off right away. Mara couldn't imagine the lodging house without her; Daisy's arrival was the highlight of her day.

'You're early this afternoon, lass,' said Belle, motioning to the wooden clock on the mantel.

'Aye, I thought it best to. I've them upstairs windows to see to the day and want to make good headway. Filthy, they are. Fret not, mind; by the time I'm finished, you'll be able to eat your dinner off them.'

'Sure, wouldn't the food just slide right off?' asked Mara innocently, her expression po-like.

Daisy released a peal of laughter. 'I didn't really mean . . . Nay, it's just a saying, like. Happen they don't use it back in Ireland? What it means is, you see—' She broke off to spot Mara's shoulders shaking with suppressed amusement. Bunching up her eyes, she cocked her head. 'Hang about, are you pulling my leg?'

'Well, of course I am!' Mara told her, grinning. 'Sure, 'tis fresh air you must think I have between my ears.'

'Now you come to mention it . . .'

'Bold devil, ye!'

They broke into a fit of giggles – watching on with a smile, Belle reached for the empty teapot.

'You've time to spare for a sup with us, Daisy.'

'Aye, if you're sure? Oh but 'ere, let me,' the girl insisted, taking it from her hands. Yet as she made to turn for the kitchen, her eyelids flickered and she staggered. The women were on their feet and at her side in a trice.

'Lass, what is it?' asked Belle in concern.

Taking the girl's arm, Mara guided her into a chair. 'Easy does it. Deep breaths, Daisy.'

'Aye, sorry.'

'You're all right now?'

She nodded. 'Just a touch of dizziness is all. Nowt to worry over.'

'We'll be the judges of that. Now just you stop put whilst I see to that brew,' her employer told her with a wag of her finger. 'A bit of fruitcake wouldn't go amiss, neither, I'm betting.'

Ten minutes later, having consumed a cup of sweet tea and two slices of Belle's baking, Daisy looked infinitely better. The bloom had returned to her cheeks and her eyes were clearer; she smiled somewhat awkwardly.

'Ta to the both of thee. I'm reet, now, honest.'

'All the same, I'll help you with your chores today,' Mara said. Then, when the girl made to protest: 'I insist. Sure, I'd only be sat here otherwise twiddling my thumbs, so I would.'

Daisy relented with a nod and a smile, and the women made for the stairs to give their attention to the afore-mentioned windows.

'How was the lass with her work?' the lodging-house keeper wanted to know later, when Daisy had left for home and she and Mara were seated once more in the private sitting room. 'She didn't suffer another turn?'

'No, she was grand. Tell me, Belle, has something happened like that with Daisy before today?'

Frowning, the old woman bobbed her head. 'Once or twice, aye. I suspected she'd been at the gin at first but, nay, she insists norra drop ever passes her lips. As it did earlier, a sup of tea and bite of summat normally fetches her round.'

'Do you think . . . could it be she ain't eating properly?'

Belle contemplated this. 'She is a bit on t' thin side, eh?'

'It would account for the woozy spells. Or then again . . .'

'What, lass?'

'She couldn't be with child, could she?'

Now, the lodging-house keeper needed no time to consider her answer: 'Oh nay. No way. From what she's let slip to me in the few months she's been under my employ, she don't get chance to even leave the house bar to come here to work. I can't see how she'd find opportunity to get herself caught by a fella, not on her brothers' watch.'

'Brothers?'

'Aye, them's who she dwells with. Their parents must have passed on because, to all intents and purposes, Daisy don't seem to have anyone else bar her siblings. Mind you, I suspect they might at times be heavy-handed with the lass. She'll not admit to it, but I believe they knock her about a bit, you know?'

Mara was horrified. 'Oh no. What makes you say that, Belle?'

'Well, she's come into work sporting a split lip or a bruised cheek on more than one occasion. According to her, she'd fallen over or walked into a wall, but I don't buy it. Nay, summat's not quite right in that household of theirs, I don't reckon.'

'I'm going to keep a closer eye on her from now on,' Mara decided. 'Who else has Daisy to look out for her, if not us?'

'She'll not thank thee for it. I myself once tried to coax her into talking. Got reet defensive, she did – near snapped my head clean off, aye.'

Though Mara thanked Belle for the warning, she nonetheless resolved still to stand by her word. If anyone had experience of living with a volatile family, it was her. The feeling of hopelessness that Daisy was undoubtedly suffering, Mara understood all too well; her chest ached for her predicament. All that remained was to ensure she trod carefully. Surely if she made pains not to push the girl too hard, she'd eventually open up? Either way, Mara was determined to give it her damnedest.

Catching a glimpse of the clock a short while later, Mara's stomach dropped. As it was wont to each day at this time, Roger's image swam into her mind to wash away all other thought. He would be arriving home from work at any minute. *Home to an empty cottage, an empty hearth and an empty bed . . .*

Stop it! she told herself, but as ever, the agonising scenes of her man sitting lost and alone refused to be banished. Just how was he coping without her? That poor, decent man deserved none of this. None!

Suddenly, another face – sunny and bright and stretched in a smile – pushed through the grief cloud and a little of her pain lifted. *Daisy.* Now, she was convinced that helping the girl if she could was what she was indeed meant to do.

Not only did Mara genuinely want to be there for her new friend but, mercifully, it offered a switch in focus, a brief respite from the tumult hounding her brain. By God, she needed all the distraction right now that she could get.

Chapter 22

THE FOLLOWING DAY, Daisy arrived for work at the lodging house looking pale and drawn. Dark circles smudged the skin beneath her eyes, as though she hadn't known sleep the previous night and, unnaturally for her, her mouth was downturned at the corners. Mara invited her to take the seat opposite.

'All right, lass?'

'Aye.'

Cautiously, she stretched a hand across the table and covered one of the girl's. 'You're sure?'

'I said so, didn't I?' Daisy snapped. Then her face creased and she curled her fingers around Mara's. 'Eeh, sorry. I'm bone-tired is all.'

'A late one at home last night, was it?' asked Mara softly.

The girl's eyes widened in surprise. 'Actually, yes, summat like that. There were . . . a bit of trouble, like.'

'With your brothers?'

Daisy blushed to the roots of her hair. 'It were nowt serious, mind,' she added quickly, as though regretting having blurted what little she had. 'It's all done and dusted now, anyroad, so no harm done.'

Nodding, Mara let the matter drop. Tact was her best tool here; pushing the girl would result only in her retreating further into herself. Today had proven breakthrough enough. The most important thing was for Daisy to become comfortable speaking with her. Then, should there be a next time – and, sadly, Mara was almost certain there would be – she'd hopefully feel able to open up a little more.

Realising there would be no further interrogation, the girl relaxed and, over the hours, had reverted to her usual cheerful self. Yet as the end of her shift drew near, and however much Daisy tried to mask it, Mara noticed that her agitation was slowly but surely creeping back at the prospect of returning home. Her heart ached for the poor girl, but what could she do?

She kept a discreet watch over her the next day and the few that followed, but thankfully, Daisy seemed calm and untroubled. Then, on Friday afternoon, she entered the sitting room and Mara saw immediately that she was having difficulty breathing. She hurried across and held her palm to the girl's clammy brow.

'Lass . . . What on earth is wrong?'

'It's nowt, I just—'

'Nowt, my foot,' Mara interjected, escorting her to a chair. ''Tis terrible you look.' She poured her a cup of tea from the pot and placed it into her hands gently. 'Here, drink this. Slowly, now, take your time.'

'Thank you,' Daisy murmured after some minutes.

'You're feeling better?'

'Aye. Lots.'

Mara nodded. The girl certainly appeared to be,

compared to how she'd looked upon her arrival. 'Lass . . .' She paused to sigh. 'If there's anything you'd like to talk about, I'm here to listen. You know that, don't ye?'

Daisy's defensiveness rose to the fore; her shoulders hunched and her eyebrows drew together in a dark frown. However, at Mara's knowing nod, her body slowly relaxed and the anger left her face. She dropped her gaze. Then she rose to her feet and unbuttoned the bodice of her dress.

'Mother of God . . . Oh, lass.'

Shooting a last bitter glance at the livid purple and black bruises streaking her ribs, Daisy readjusted her clothing and resumed her seat.

Mara's lips trembled with emotion. 'Is anything broken, d'you think?'

'Nay. Eeh, it ain't half sore, though.'

'Do you want to tell me what happened?'

She shook her head.

'Did your brothers—'

'I don't want to talk about it!'

'All right, lass, all right,' Mara soothed, kicking herself for her impatience. 'I'm sorry. You don't have to, so ye don't.'

Daisy was silent for a moment, then her face crumpled and she broke into quiet weeping. 'It's just . . . there's no point in the telling. It'll change norra thing.'

'Lass . . . you don't have to stay there, with them. You don't. There's always a way.'

A laugh hollow with resentment leaked from her. 'They'd never let me leave, would kill me first.'

'No one should have to put up with being abused in

their own home, no one, and I should know. Aye,' she went on when the girl looked at her quizzically. 'I understand what it's like, trapped at the mercy of bullying brutes and believing there's no way out. It's soul-destroying – I won't stand by and see it happening to one of my friends. And you such a lovely young thing, too . . . They'll snuff out that fun and happy side of your nature over time, so they will, without you even realising it's happening. A shell of yourself is what you'll be, Daisy, a shell, and they'll have won. Don't let them, lass! Break free before it's too late.'

'Eeh, Mara. I wish I had your bravery.'

Oh, how she felt this girl's helplessness! It was like looking in on herself just a few short years before, sitting so lost and afraid in that God-forsaken house at Heyrod Street. She had a lump in her throat as big as an apple. 'I'm not brave, lass; far from it. One step, that's all it takes. It's what I did, and you can too.'

'But . . . where would I go? It couldn't be here – this is the first place they'd come searching. There's nobody, nowhere, I can run to; it's useless.'

'There *has* to be a way.'

'Well. There is something . . .'

Seeing the spark that had lit up her eyes, Mara leaned in expectantly. 'Go on.'

'I could have them locked away. If I really wanted to, that is.'

'What?'

Daisy nodded. 'They have their sticky fingers in all types of pies. As a matter of fact, there's a few items they've got hidden back home that the law would be very interested in finding, I'm betting. Stolen, you know? Happen if I went to the police station, told them what I know—'

'No!' Mara could barely believe she was hearing this, found it difficult to snatch in a breath, so acute was her confusion and shock. First the abuse, and now this . . . it was like looking in a mirror with this girl. Again, her own history was replaying in front of her eyes – and look how that had turned out. 'Listen to me, lass, you don't want to do that.'

'But—'

'Trust me on this. I did something very similar, so I did. I tell ye now, Daisy, it ripped apart everything, was the worst decision of my life. Still I'm suffering the effects and likely always shall. If I could go back and undo it, I would, in a heartbeat. Don't make the same mistake I did. Don't get the law involved. Please, just don't.'

The fire in Daisy's gaze dimmed then burned out, her last remaining hope with it. She sighed. 'If tha says so.'

'I do. We'll find another way, lass, I promise ye.'

'Happen she could find fresh lodgings?'

Considering Belle's suggestion, Mara rubbed at her tired eyes. She'd spent half the night awake, wracking her brains for an answer to Daisy's predicament, but without success, and in the end she'd been driven by desperation to confide in the older woman.

'A few cheap rooms, aye,' the lodging-house keeper continued. 'We could help her secure some.'

'But how would she support herself if she moved away – for that's what she'd have to do. Remaining in Manchester

301

wouldn't be possible; she'd never know peace, would forever be looking over her shoulder for fear of those rotten brothers of hers stumbling upon her. And well, if she did leave here, then that would mean terminating her employ with you. What if she failed to find herself a new position? How would she pay her rent, feed herself?'

Belle nodded. 'You're right there. 'Course, she could always get work someplace as a domestic. She'd live in, then, wouldn't she, and wouldn't have to fret over accommodation or meals.'

She gazed at the other woman and smiled broadly. By the way she'd delivered it, it was clear that Belle's comment had been a throwaway one; however, it was a sound idea so far as Mara could see. After all, hadn't it worked for herself – admittedly temporarily – in similar circumstances? God willing, things would work out differently for the girl. She would be more fortunate and, for her, it would prove a permanent solution.

'Why didn't I think of it – of course, that's the answer. Belle, you're a genius.'

'Aye?'

'*Aye!* Sure, it makes perfect sense. I'll put the plan to Daisy this afternoon, see what she makes of it.'

'It's a great pity you left Cresslea when you did. You could have put in a word for the lass, got her a job alongside thee.'

Though Mara agreed, her eyes had creased and she drummed the tabletop with her fingers thoughtfully. The manor *was* a maid down now she'd gone. Perhaps it wasn't an impossibility after all . . .

'So what d'you think, lass?' she asked Daisy later, having put the suggestion forward. 'It's surely worth enquiring?'

'And they're all right, are they, at this manor?'

'Oh aye.'

'The master?'

'He's a grand man.'

'And his mother?'

'Firm but fair. 'Ere,' she added as a thought occurred. 'Your names don't rhyme, do they? What's your surname?'

'Drummond.'

'Sure, you'll do just fine then,' she told her with a wistful smile. Then, at Daisy's bemused frown: 'It don't matter, lass, ignore me.'

'What about the other servants, Mara?' the girl wanted to know next. 'Are they agreeable?'

Thoughts of Roger smashed into her mind – as ever, her arms and lips physically ached for him. She swallowed hard. 'Oh, lass, the best.'

'Well, then, if it's such a gradely place to work and live, why did you leave?'

Caught off guard, Mara felt herself flush. She'd had to reveal to the girl her connection with the place, albeit in a diluted capacity. Daisy was aware that she'd been employed there until recently, and that was it. Her marriage to the groom and everything regarding Conrad, Mara wisely kept back, figuring the girl didn't need to be told. In fact, the less she was aware of, the better. What she didn't know about, she couldn't unintentionally slip up about, could she? The last thing Mara wanted was her business discussing and her whereabouts becoming known.

'My leaving had nothing to do with any fault on the part of the Braithwaites or their staff, nothing at all,' she murmured. 'I just . . . it was something I had to do. Take my word for it, Daisy: those folks back there are the best. You'd not find anywhere as grand to work in all the land.'

'And you're certain I'd stand a chance?'

'Och what!' Mara chuckled. 'With a first-rate character reference such as the one Belle will provide you with, sure even Buckingham Palace would snap you up!'

The girl gave a smile. 'I suppose it *could* solve all my problems . . .'

'It could and it shall. Take my word for it.'

'All right. I'll head out to Kersal the morrow and try my luck.'

Mara squeezed her hand encouragingly. 'That's it, lass. You'll not regret it.'

Staring into the fire's hypnotic flames and lost in her own thoughts, Mara jumped when the lodging-house keeper touched her arm. 'Sorry . . . did you say something?'

'I were just telling thee, I'm away to my bed.'

'Oh. Aye. Goodnight, Belle.'

Her friend dithered for a moment; sighing, she resumed her seat. 'Out with it, lass. What's on your mind?'

'Home,' she whispered simply.

'Eeh, love.'

'I wish . . . oh, how I *wish* I was going with Daisy in the morning!'

Belle could offer but a tut-tut in response; what else was there for her to say?

'You don't think Daisy will forget and make mention that I've sent her, do you?' Mara asked worriedly.

'Nay, not her. You said she's not to let on that she knows thee so as to avoid awkward questions, and she won't. Don't fret on it, lass.'

Mara nodded. 'You're right. And please, ignore me my moping; I'm just being selfish. Tomorrow ain't about me but that sweet young girl. This is a fresh chance for her, aye. The sooner she's away from them brothers of hers, the better. She'll be safe, and that's what counts. It's *all* that matters.'

'You've an angel's heart, Mara, lass, that you have. Both me and Daisy are lucky to have thee.'

When Belle had retired and Mara was alone, she let her tears fall. And she did so with a smile in the knowledge that the truth was, with friends like hers, it was she who was the fortunate one.

Switching her attention back to Daisy and the blessed opportunity, she prayed for a positive outcome for all she was worth.

'Mara! Mara!'

The sitting room was dark, the glow from the near-dead fire the only light source. Glancing around in dozy confusion, Mara realised she must have dropped off in the chair. What had woken her she couldn't say – perhaps it was the pain in her neck, she wondered, wincing. She had a terrible crick in it from her awkward sleeping position.

'Mara! Please, it's me!'

The faint cry seeping into her tired brain, Mara stopped mid-stretch to frown. Then, with the realisation that she recognised the voice, her senses returned like a thunderbolt and she was up and dashing for the front door.

'Daisy? What in the world . . . ?'

The girl rushed past her into the house; nonplussed, Mara followed her back inside.

'It's the middle of the night . . . Wait – oh lass,' she soothed, as the only explanation for this hit home. 'It's them brothers of yours, ain't it? Sure, something's happened.'

Panting and out of breath, Daisy nodded. 'I had to – to come, had to talk, talk to thee, didn't know what else to do.'

'What have the swines done?'

'They've been arrested.'

She wasn't sure whether she'd misheard. 'What was that?'

'I did it, Mara. I squealed on them to the law.'

'Oh Jaysus . . .'

'They've been arrested, all of them.'

'Lass, lass . . .' Mara was numb with horror. 'But why? We spoke about it, and you agreed not to take that path. You'd a chance at a clean start tomorrow at Cresslea.'

'Aye, well – I changed my mind! You weren't there today, Mara. You didn't see what they were like, nor the things they were saying . . . I could take it no more. Afore I knew where I was, I'd walked from that hell house to the station, through the doors and up to the desk. Then I opened my gob and it just poured out of me – everything. I told it all.'

'Oh, Daisy.' She took the sobbing, shaking girl into her arms. 'You're all right. Everything's going to be all right.'

'Mara?'

'Aye, lass?'

'I have another confession to make – this time to thee.'

She drew back to stare into the girl's face. 'You do? What is it?'

'The fellas I live with.'

'Aye?'

'They're not my brothers at all. They're my lovers.'

'Your . . . ?'

Daisy nodded miserably. 'All three.'

'Good God.'

'It weren't meant to be that way – and it wasn't, not at first. The fella I fell for . . . I never dreamed he'd turn out how he did. It was just a slave he wanted – in the bedroom as well as the kitchen – I soon learned that.

'One night, he passed me off to his younger brother; sat there and watched, he did, whilst the bastard raped me. From thereon in, it became the normal way of things and I was expected to comply. I hated the situation, I did. *Hated* it. Then, just when I thought things couldn't possibly get worse, their other brother and eldest of the three showed up out of the blue.

'I tell thee, Lucifer's got nowt on him, nowt! He turned that house into a living nightmare. Then, last night . . .' She paused to gulp down a cough. 'Last night, and with my fella's full permission, *he* took me to his bed as well. Oh, the pain, the cruelty . . . It was the final straw. I told the lot of them this evening, I said I ain't putting up with it no more.

'I know it were foolish, know I should have just kept my mouth shut and gone to the manor in the morning, as we'd planned, didn't mean to lose my temper ... I couldn't help it. There they were, laughing and supping their ale, discussing who would have me first that night and what it was they would do – I just saw red. Well, it sent them into a frenzy. I feared for my life, oh did I. I wanted my revenge, and I took it – and by God I'm glad I did. Going to the police . . . it might just be the best thing I've ever done. It is; I'm sure of it now, aye. It's over – *over*.'

Throughout the tear-peppered speech, Mara had stood speechless and rooted to the spot. Aggie's words from the park banged a brutal beat in her skull and the most terrible notion had entered her head. Now, she was almost too afraid to attempt to have it dismissed. *Afraid because the girl here couldn't, would instead only confirm it.*

From where she gathered the strength, she didn't know. Her voice was barely above a whisper. 'Your fellow. Daisy, who is he?'

In the next moment the name was out, and Mara felt her legs buckle:

'Eamon, the sod's called. Eamon O'Hara.'

Chapter 23

'EEH, I CAN'T fathom you out at all. They're locked up and shall be for a very long time, God willing – and that means Conrad, too. It's done with, don't you see? You're free, lass, free.'

Mara's mind was a quagmire of uncertainty – she couldn't dare believe it. 'But should they get off . . .'

'And how can that be?' Belle continued. 'What, they'll try saying that the loot found stashed in their house is their own property and the police will believe them, aye? Come on, lass! That cigar box has the master's initials emblazoned on it, you and Daisy both have said so your-selfs. Besides, in any case, Luke Braithwaite and his mam will confirm that the property belongs to them. Them brothers are banged to rights and there's absolutely no way out for 'em. Accept it, Mara, and bloomin' well go home!'

Daisy smiled agreement. Having been filled in on every-thing, she'd been just as shocked to learn of Mara's identity as her friend had been when finding out who *she* really was. Now, she was of the same mind as Belle and was adamant that Mara should reclaim her life.

'But what if . . .'

The lodging-house keeper threw her hands in the air in exasperation. 'Oh, what's worrying thee now?'

'What if,' Mara repeated and her bottom lip began to tremble – she could barely bring herself to say it: 'What if Roger won't *want* me back after deserting him as I did? I'll never bear it, never . . .'

Belle came to stand in front of her, Daisy joined her, and the two of them took one of her hands each in their own. 'Lass, will you ruddy go home!' they said in unison, and all three women dissolved into tearful laughter.

The cottage appeared on the horizon and Mara was certain that never in the memory of man had there existed a more beautiful sight.

It was still early and she knew her husband wouldn't have yet left for work. He was in there, beyond those grey brick walls, just a few steps away . . . Heart banging fit to burst, she walked on.

When she arrived, she didn't make for the door but instead headed towards the window. Slowly, softly, she peered around the side of the pane.

She saw him right away. He was in his chair at the table facing her, hunched over, pulling on his boots.

Drinking in his image through a film of tears, her lips parted and a moan escaped her. She padded back across the mossy patch towards the rough pathway. Then, praying with all that she was that he wouldn't reject her, she opened the door.

He lifted his head. Their eyes locked and the universe held its breath.

'Hello, Roger.'

'Mara? Oh my God, Mara . . .'

On a raw cry, they threw themselves into each other's arms.

'My darling . . . I'm so very sorry,' she whimpered, burying her face in his neck. 'Oh, lad, forgive me.'

Crushing her to him, his tone was hoarse. 'You left me. How could you *do* it to me?'

'No, no – I did it *for* you, my love! My stepson . . .'

'Conrad.' He nodded when she pulled back with a stunned expression. 'I know he was here.'

'How?'

'Meg. She told me you'd confided in her.'

'So then surely you must see why I had to leave. Oh, it's been hell on earth, the things he made me do!'

'Why didn't you tell me, Mara? You *should* have told me!'

Fat tears were rolling unchecked down her face by now and her chest heaved with emotion. 'I wanted to . . . I couldn't. He threatened to harm ye, so he did, broke into our cottage one night whilst we slept and held a knife to your throat. I was petrified he'd kill you if I didn't go along with what he said. I just didn't know what to do!'

'That stinking bastard – I'll murder him with my bare hands!'

'No, lad. It's over, now. He's gone, been arrested, along with his brothers. None of them can touch us now.'

Roger frowned in surprise. 'How do you know all this?'

She led him back to his seat. 'Come. Sit down and I'll explain everything.'

'Before you begin' – he took her hand and kissed it – 'by Christ, lass, I'm so glad you're back.'

A fresh sob escaped her. She nodded, then began the painful telling.

'It was one evening as I was returning home from work when he waylaid me. He threatened he'd make me pay for what I'd done to him . . . I was sure he was about to kill me right there and then. It was late when I arrived at the cottage – do you remember the night I mean? You sensed something was wrong but I was just so confused, I didn't feel able to confide in you, I . . .'

'The way things were between us back then . . . I'm guessing that didn't help matters, did it?' Roger's regret was tangible. 'We were barely speaking as it was – no wonder you didn't think you could come to me.'

'Aye,' she confessed. 'I kept it to myself, was just in a state of shock that he was back. I almost fled that night – I did, I admit it – but something stopped me; I refused to let him run me out, to leave my life and all I'd built up. Little did I know how bad things would become and that the choice would soon be out of my hands.' She cleared her throat then continued. 'At first, I tried my damnedest not to be alone – it was all I could think of to avoid him. I asked if we could start walking to and back from work again together . . . Aye, that was why,' she added when her husband's face fell. 'With you, I knew I was safe.'

'I should have realised, should have pressed thee for an explanation. I'm so *sorry*—'

'No, please don't,' Mara insisted fiercely. 'I should have found enough courage to tell you. But I couldn't; I was too afraid. That, and stupid. I'm just so *stupid*! Aye, Roger, I am,' she burst out when he made to reassure her. 'It

312

could have saved so much trouble . . . what happened next . . .'

'Tell me.'

'Meg, she was desperate for me to meet her new fella . . .'

'Shaun.'

By the tightening of Roger's mouth, it was clear he was remembering catching them alone – laughing mirthlessly, Mara shook her head. 'Oh, lad, you've really nothing to worry about there, so you ain't. There was no Shaun; he didn't exist. Meg's beau was Conrad.'

'What?'

'Aye. He hoodwinked her, wormed his way into her affections to get close to Cresslea and me. Can you imagine my horror when she introduced us and it was him I found myself looking at?'

'Christ Almighty.'

'I sought you out then. I did, honest. I looked everywhere for you, but you were nowhere to be found.'

'I must have been away in the town purchasing provender for the horses . . . Mara, I'm sorry—'

'It's not your fault.'

'Aye, it is! I should have been *there* for you.'

'You weren't to know, my love.'

'So what then? What did he do?' he asked after some moments, though it was plain he was loath to hear it.

'Conrad told me he was now my master and I had to obey him. He . . .' Hugging herself, Mara flushed with mortification.

'He what? Oh God . . .' In contrast to Mara, Roger turned as white as tripe. 'Please, not that. Please!'

313

'No, he didn't rape me. Just . . . made threats to. I was so scared, Roger. Conrad, he knew then he had me where he wanted me and he, he made me . . . Oh, I'm so ashamed!'

'Tell me what he did. Tell me.'

'He made me steal from the manor. He wanted to set himself up off the proceeds – and I did it. I did, and I'm so sorry. I hate myself for it. The first time it happened . . . later, when I met with him to hand over the spoils . . . that's when you spotted us together. He had a blade to my back the whole time you were there.'

'Bastard!' Her husband sprang to his feet, his face puce with rage. 'Why didn't I *know*? I should have strangled him there and then. I'll never forgive myself for this, never!'

'He'd have used that weapon if pushed – he's unstable in the head, always has been. It was best you didn't know.'

'Even so—'

'No, lad. Don't let it eat you up inside; what's done is done. In a queer sort of way, it turned out for the best.'

'How?'

'Because it was your jealousy at thinking I was having an affair with him that made you see how far the two of us had drifted from one another, how desperate things had got. It brought us back together, really, didn't it? I vowed that first night we made up that I'd tell Conrad his control over me was done with. If he didn't accept it, I'd have told you everything. But I never got the chance, for that was when he broke in here with the knife and threatened to harm you. I knew I couldn't involve you then, that he'd stop at nothing to get what he wanted.

314

'I could see no end to it. I stole for him again, hoping it would be the last time, but it never was; he always wanted more. And something in me just broke. I knew then I couldn't put you at risk any longer, would sooner have died. Nor could I continue mistreating those good people of the manor. I'd had enough of it. Conrad would never stop, let me free. That's when I decided to leave.'

'Where did you go?'

'To the lodging house that me and Rebecca stayed at when we arrived in England. The keeper, Belle, with her heart of gold, agreed to put me up.'

'You didn't see Conrad again?'

'Not a peep, praise be to the Lord.'

'I wish to God *I* had seen him when I called on Heyrod Street.'

'What?' Mara's eyes widened. 'You were at their house?'

Her husband resumed his seat. 'We'd just got back on track – that's what confused me the most, you know, when you went. I had no idea why you'd gone or to where, I just sensed you hadn't left through choice. The not knowing, it near sent me clean out of my mind.

'Meg couldn't shed any light on where you were, but she did say you'd told her that Conrad was back. Aggie was the only person we could think of who you might have turned to, but neither of us knew where she dwelled.

'I didn't know where to turn. Even the police were no help – 'course I had to go to them, could see no other hope,' he added when Mara cringed with guilt. 'They were less than useless, in fact; I shouldn't have bothered. There was little they could do, according to them. To be honest, they didn't take my concerns seriously, I don't reckon. I think they thought you'd left me to take off with another fella or some such – frustrating ain't in it. All I could do at that point were just pray you disappearing had nowt to do with that bastard after all and that you'd return.

'Meg had mentioned that Aggie could be found at Peel Park most Sundays and so I was all set to confront her on the day. However, Aggie got to me first – she turned up here at the cottage. Mine was a relief like no other when she told me you were safe. Mind, she couldn't say where you were either and so I got from her the brothers' address and went to confront them instead.'

Mara spoke in a whisper. 'Why – why would you do that? You could have been beaten, *killed*—'

'Believe me, there was only one person with murder in mind, and it weren't them,' he growled.

'So Conrad wasn't there?'

'Nay. According to his brothers, he hadn't been near the house, lying parasites.'

Her husband was right, of course. Conrad would have been there, all right; Eamon and Eugene would have simply been protecting him. Suddenly, Daisy entered her thoughts and she frowned. 'This was after speaking with Aggie, you say, on Sunday?'

'Aye.'

It had been Monday when Daisy revealed to her there had been trouble at home the previous night. Had the lads been roaring mad at Roger turning up and, later, taken their frustrations out on the girl? Nothing would surprise Mara; she knew that trio of demons better than anyone. They really were beyond deplorable.

316

'I was out of options,' her husband was saying now, and Mara returned to him her full attention. 'After telling Aggie to let me know right away should she see thee or learn owt more, I had no choice but to return to Cresslea.'

Drawing a hand across her wet eyes, she sighed. 'I'll have to get a message to Aggie that I'm well . . . Oh, to put you all through all that! You especially – what I've done to ye . . . Roger, can you ever forgive me?'

'It's me what should be saying them words, Mara, not thee. Never should you have gone through this on your own. You should have had me, my help, support.'

'You're here now. We have each other and nothing will ever come between us again, I swear it. Leaving you was the hardest thing I've ever had to do in my life; it near killed me. Sure, you were never off my mind, morning, noon and night.'

'It's us two, lass, now and for ever.'

'Always.'

They shared an exquisite kiss then held each other tightly.

'About them being arrested,' Mara said, her cheek resting against his chest. 'How long will they get?'

'I'm guessing it's the master's property what they've been done for?'

She nodded. 'Daisy, Belle's maid at the lodging house, well, it was her doing, Lord bless her. We'd grown to be friends whilst I was there, and yet all the time she was seeing Conrad's brother Eamon – I hadn't the slightest idea. Just what are the chances, lad; it's as though it was meant to be, to be sure. Nor did she guess who I might be. The lads only ever referred to me in her presence as . . . well,

317

nothing as civilised as Mara, put it that way. The hell she'd been living in that house, how they'd been treating her . . . Sure, they're rotten to the marrow, so they are. All three, just like their father. Desperate to be set loose from their hold, Daisy went to the police and informed on them about the stolen goods. Hearing they were safely locked up, I felt able to come home.'

'We'll need to discuss this with the master, you know that, don't yer?' her husband told her gently.

'But—'

'It'll be hard for thee, Mara, but it has to be done. He'll see that your part in it weren't by choice.'

'If you're wrong and he does blame me? What then?'

'I'm sure he'll understand.'

'And Meg?' she whispered. 'Will she show understanding, too, that I didn't tell her who Shaun really was?'

At this, Roger hadn't an answer. Donning his jacket, he led the way to the door. 'We'll cross *that* bridge when we reach it, eh?'

The passage of half an hour found the couple seated opposite Luke Braithwaite in his study, tensely awaiting the outcome. Wrongdoings and the motives behind them had been laid bare and every detail gone over – all that remained now was the master's response. Mara's heart was in her mouth.

Finally, Luke lifted his stare from his steepled hands resting on the desktop and looked at his employees in turn. After what seemed an age, his gaze came to rest on Mara. 'You have shown great bravery in coming forward with this information today, Mrs Lawson.'

318

''Tis a relief to tell ye at last, so it is, sir.'

'I can well believe it. You have only ever come across as honest. The guilt must have proved a heavy burden for you to carry.'

Tears pricked her eyes. She bobbed her head. ''Twas, sir, aye.'

'So far as I can ascertain, you, Mrs Lawson, are entirely blameless in this unpleasant affair. So long as I can receive from you your solemn promise that nothing like this will happen again, I don't see why we cannot put this behind us.'

Mara was weak with relief. 'You mean it, sir?'

'I do.'

'Oh! Sure, I don't know what to . . . never expected . . . Happiness has been a long-lost friend to me for more weeks than I care to count; I thought I'd seen the back of it for good. But no. You, sir, have proven to me today that it's still there for the taking. Thank ye,' she added earnestly. 'I shall never, *ever* let you down again, you have my word.'

Luke nodded then rose from his desk. 'I shall travel to the stationhouse this instant and find out how matters stand with regards to those O'Hara men.'

'Sir, should they tell all, reveal my part in taking the stuff from the manor . . .'

He nodded grimly. 'That they may attempt to drag you down with them did cross my mind, too. However, let us be in full charge of the facts before we allow ourselves to assume anything. Whatever happens, I shall do my utmost to ensure you are exculpated.'

Though Mara couldn't say she knew what that last fancy

word he'd used just there meant, it was clear to her it wasn't a bad one to be feared. 'Oh, sir, thank ye.'

'Lawson.' The master had turned to her husband. 'You will prepare the carriage?'

'I will, sir,' Roger confirmed.

'Good, good. I shall see you out there in a few minutes. Oh, one more thing . . .'

'Aye, sir?' asked Mara.

'I believe it would be best if my mother didn't get to hear about what we have discussed today.'

'I understand, sir.' Oh, she did, all right. Given Mrs Braithwaite's stance on stealing, she would surely have Mara dismissed from the manor in a trice, no questions asked. 'Thank ye, sir.'

'Good day.'

This their cue to leave, Mara and her husband bade the master goodbye and exited the room. They waited until they were safely in the corridor before turning to one another and sharing a heartfelt sigh.

'Thank *God.*'

Roger dropped a soft kiss on to her brow. 'Didn't I say it would be all right?'

'You did. I really ought to have more faith in you.'

'Eeh, *finally.*'

She smiled, her husband followed suit, and they retraced their steps to the kitchen.

Upon their arrival here, Meg hadn't been present – much to Mara's relief. With everything else to deal with, she hadn't possessed the strength to face the maid as well. Now, though, as she re-entered the room in front of Roger, she stopped dead in her tracks. Meg was washing dishes at the large stone sink. In the moment that Mara halted, Meg turned, and the two of them locked gazes across the open space.

Reading the situation, Roger tactfully beat a retreat to the stables to prepare the horses, leaving the friends to be alone. In the ensuing silence, the air crackled with tense uncertainty.

Mara was the first to break it. 'Lass . . .'

'Love. Eeh!'

Tears spilling, the friends ran to each other and embraced.

'Meg, I'm so sorry . . .'

'Don't say that. It's me what ought to be apologising. I can't believe I brought him here and back into your life, can't be*lieve* I was blind enough to fall for his lies . . .'

'You mean you know?'

'About Shaun? Or, should I say Conrad.'

'But Roger, he wasn't aware . . .'

'I should have mentioned it to your husband, I know, but I was too embarrassed.'

'Conrad, he told you himself?'

'Oh aye.' She spoke sardonically. 'He told me, all right. Took great pleasure in it, an' all, he did.'

'Oh, lass.'

'I were nowt to him, was I?'

Though it pained Mara to have to do it, she knew she must; she shook her head. 'No, lass.'

Meg shrugged. 'Ay well. Ne'er mind.'

'Listen to me.' Taking her gently by the shoulders, Mara gazed sincerely into her eyes. 'That good-for-nothing gutter slug don't deserve to breathe the same air as ye, never mind anything more. Someday, you'll meet a man who sees you as the rest of us do. He'll fall head over heels for you, and you for him – and aye, he'll think himself the luckiest man in the world for it. 'Twill happen, Meg, I swear it.'

'Eeh, love.'

Her heart ached for the woman. Scrunching up her eyes, she thought for a moment. Then her face cleared and she snapped her fingers. 'D'you know what you need?'

'What?'

'To cleanse that swine and all reminder of him from your mind and your life – go and fetch me that vase.'

Meg returned with it and, without a word, the friends strode out of the kitchen and into the courtyard.

'Do it,' Mara encouraged.

Mouth set in determination, the maid held the terracotta vessel aloft. Then, with a cry, she threw it on to the cobbles, where it landed with a resounding smash. Taking a long, deep breath, Meg brushed off her hands with a sharp nod.

'Better, lass?'

'Better.'

Filled with admiration and pride, Mara crooked her arm. The maid slipped her own through, linking her, and heads held high they walked purposefully back to the house.

Chapter 24

IT WAS APPROACHING nightfall when the master knocked at the cottage. One look at his expression and Mara knew that her optimism had been premature.

'Sir?'

'I've just now returned from the station . . . I'm afraid it's not all good news.'

'Tell us.' Roger's voice was low with dread. 'What's happened?'

'Eamon and Eugene have made full and frank confessions to the theft. They claim it was they alone who took my property, that they broke into the manor and stole the items missing.'

Mara was dumbstruck. 'What?'

'I believe they all guessed that I may defend you and so figured it was pointless mentioning your involvement – that is something we must be thankful for, at least.'

'But to take the blame . . . Why would they do that?'

'It would seem that either through loyalty or coercion they do not wish their brother implicated. They state that he had no involvement in the housebreaking whatever. Inasmuch, Conrad has been released without charge.'

'No . . .'

Roger caught her just in time as she crumpled towards the floor. He was speaking to her, but the blood rushing through her ears was so loud she could barely comprehend it.

'Mara. For God's sake, answer me, are you all right?'

'Aye. I don't . . . No. *No*.'

Murmuring soothing words, he helped her to sit in a chair then turned to his master. 'Just what the hell does this mean? That devil's apprentice gets off with this scot-free – after all he's put my wife through? I won't stand for it!'

For his part, Luke appeared to harbour sufficient anger of his own. 'I'm afraid it does. However, if you can try to look at this rationally,' he added, glancing from him to Mara, 'I think you will see that this does work to your advantage.'

Roger shook his head. 'Sir? How so?'

'Does your wife really have the strength of will for another case, another trial? Think about it, man. From what Mrs Lawson revealed to me earlier, the last time she was drawn into testifying in a crime involving Conrad O'Hara, it almost ruined her. Furthermore, should she be forced to admit to the true events and the part she played, there is a chance in spite of my best efforts that she may well land up facing charges herself. We in this room may accept her reasons for doing so, but will a judge and jury? I for one cannot state for certain that they would.'

'So . . . what? We just keep our tongues and let the others go down for it instead?'

Luke let his shoulders rise and fall. 'It would be two

fewer potential enemies for Mrs Lawson to worry about. Conrad may well have informed his brothers by now of the circumstances surrounding his transportation – to have all three baying for her blood would be a far worse fate.'

'But Conrad must be brought to book. He *can't* just get away with this.'

'Perhaps, in time, justice will be served in some other way. Think about it: the type of person he is, he isn't likely to turn his back on a life of crime. In all probability, his actions will catch up with him at some point.'

'And in the meantime, what? He gets to roam them streets out there a free man? My wife's to just sit here, is she, hoping he don't reshow for a second shot at vengeance? Sir, we can't live our lives like that.'

'The master's right.'

At Mara's words, the men turned for the first time to look at her.

'I cannot face the court, wouldn't endure it a second time. Eamon and Eugene are where they need to be: locked away where they can do no more harm – to Daisy as well as to me. As for Conrad . . .' Her chin lifted in quiet resoluteness. 'Next time, we'll be ready for him.'

The rustling of the leaves blowing in the autumnal breeze sounded unnaturally loud to Mara's heightened senses. Back straight, hands folded tightly in her lap, she concentrated on keeping her breathing steady.

Either side of her were Roger and Meg. They, too, sat tense and alert, their expressions matching Mara's. Even Cuthbert lying with his head on his paws by their feet was uncharacteristically taciturn, as though sensible to the tone.

When the master turned into the courtyard, all four rose as though of one body. Mutely, they gazed at him.

'The trial was brief. Eamon and Eugene were each sentenced to seven years penal servitude.'

That number once again. Mara closed her eyes fleetingly then nodded. 'Where . . . ?'

'They are to serve their time at Manchester's new prison, Strangeways.'

Again, she nodded. 'I must send word to Belle's lodging house, let Daisy know.'

'The morrow,' said Roger.

'And Aggie – Aggie has to be told, too . . .'

'The morrow,' her husband repeated quietly. 'Today, you rest.'

Mara placed her hand in his. Without further discourse, they turned and headed off for the cottage.

When they arrived, he undressed her and helped her into bed. Tucking the blankets around her, he kissed her cheek tenderly. 'Get some sleep.'

'Roger. What we've learned today . . .'

'Shh. It's time to put it from your mind.'

'What we've learned today,' she pressed. ''Tis not the only piece of news. I have some of my own.'

Watching her snake her hand to her stomach, Roger caught his breath.

'Aye, my darling. I'm with child.'

Chapter 25

'BY GUM, LASS. How ain't tha got the hang of it yet?'

Shooting the tiny woollen cap she was holding a wry look, Daisy shook her head. 'I can't fathom it, Aggie. It just won't turn out how I want it to.'

'It favours a ruddy bird's nest!'

At this, Mara, Belle and Meg couldn't help but grin. Nor could the girl contain her amusement; throwing back her head, Daisy hooted with laughter. 'It does a bit, aye!'

'Ne'er mind, no harm done. Pass it here and let's get the monstrosity unpicked, and you can try again.'

Despite the late-spring sunshine caressing the nearby hilltops and the natural heat from the present company, there was still a slight chill in the air in the small cottage; Mara went to put another log on the fire. Before returning to her chair, she cast her gaze outside. Beyond the window, Roger was dangling a branch above Cuthbert's head and the dog was leaping up and down in an attempt to claim it, his tail wagging fifteen to the dozen in the excitement of play – as it always did, a small smile stroked Mara's mouth. With a fuzzy glow of reassurance that they were close by, she returned to her seat.

As Aggie assisted Daisy in her disastrous attempts at knitting, Belle busied herself pouring them all a fresh cup of tea and cutting into slices the fruitcake she'd brought along, and Meg click-clicked away with her needles as she worked on the shawl she was making, Mara allowed herself a contented sigh. These Sunday meetings had become a regular thing. Each week without fail, the trio from Ancoats would trek to Kersal to spend a few enjoyable hours with Mara and Meg. Over tea and cake, or in the colder months hot buttered toast, they would chat and exchange news and generally put the world to rights – and always with plenty of laughter. Mara couldn't imagine life without their gatherings, now.

It had been her husband's idea. Noticing his wife growing more restless and morose as the months rolled on, he'd put to her friends without her knowing the idea of them visiting her here at the cottage. The first afternoon when she'd answered the knock at the door to find the four women standing there with big smiles and ready hugs, a delighted Mara had cried buckets. If she, confined as a necessary precaution at Cresslea under constant supervision lest Conrad returned, couldn't meet her friends in the park or visit them at their homes, then they must come to her, Roger had insisted. How glad Mara was that he had.

At such times, he would take himself outside to enjoy his pipe and a bit of peace or, like today, while away the time entertaining the master's dog, and always without a word of complaint, simply happy in the knowledge that his wife was having a pleasant time. Mara never ceased to be amazed by his thoughtfulness nor remind herself just how fortunate she'd been to meet a man who loved her in the way he did.

Now, as Daisy got started on her third try at the cap, Aggie guiding her closely through casting on the first row of loops on the needle, Mara was filled with gratitude at their efforts over the past weeks. Belle had made the suggestion that they might begin making items for the baby, and it had been met with much enthusiasm. So far, stored in the bottom drawer of the small chest, were two blankets, two gowns, three vests and one cap – this latter item knitted perfectly by Aggie's capable hand; upon seeing it, kind but unskilled Daisy had been prompted into attempting one herself. Add to these the beautiful shawl that Meg had almost completed, and Mara reckoned the child was near enough set for its first months.

For reasons she couldn't explain, she knew that, this time around, all would go well. Her baby would be born fit and healthy – of this, there wasn't a shred of doubt in her mind.

Despite her husband's display of optimism and his obvious desire to spare her unnecessary stress, Mara knew that in the privacy of his own head he harboured concerns all the same. She didn't blame him; after their last loss, it was natural he would be feeling this way. But not she, for their daughter – and Mara was sure that's what this child would be – was a fighter. She was, Mara knew it. And in just over a month's time, when the blessed day that would deliver her to them came, Roger would too.

Her friends left her an hour later – Aggie for home to her children, Belle and Daisy for the lodging house, and Meg for the manor, taking Cuthbert with her – and she welcomed her husband inside the cottage with a hug and a kiss.

'Sit down, lad, and I'll get the evening meal on the go,' she told him. However, as she made to cross to the fire, he caught her wrist gently and stopped her.

'Hang about. I want to talk to thee.'

'Can't it wait? Sure, you must be famished—'

'Nay. It's important, Mara.'

Frowning, her interest piqued now, she sat facing him. 'All right. Go on.'

'I want us to go away.'

'Go . . . Leave Cresslea, you mean?'

He nodded. 'In a few short weeks, our child will be here, and I can't – won't – put him or her at risk.'

'Conrad.'

'Who else?'

Mara reached for his hand. 'Mebbe . . . well, mebbe he shan't ever return. It's been many months, now, Roger. Perhaps he's let the matter lie at last. He might not even be in Manchester, could have moved on from here entirely.'

'He's still around; I'd bet every last farthing I possess on it, in fact. He ain't the sort to live and let live. He's just biding his time, I reckon, just waiting for the right moment to strike. I'll not take that chance, nay. You alone are vulnerable enough. Imagine how much harder it'll be when the baby arrives. If he should . . .' Roger paused to shake his head, and his mouth tightened. 'Should any harm come to our child because I sat idly back hoping for the best, I'll never forgive myself. We must go, Mara. There's no other way.'

She saw the worry etched in his face, the determination in his dark eyes, and she knew now wasn't the time to oppose his decision. Though, inside, she ached to stay more than anything; oh, she did. Leave here, their positions, their employers, their *friends*? The prospect was an unfathomable one – and utterly devastating.

How would they cope with it? She, for one, wouldn't manage the loss. Of course, it went without saying that, as with Roger, her main concern on this earth both now and always was the precious life growing in her womb. And yet . . . *was* such a drastic step necessary by this point? Surely Conrad would have been back by now if he was going to?

Later, when they were in bed and Roger was sufficiently relaxed for her to feel able to, she brought up the subject again. In a tone that was soft and not antagonistic, she laid bare her views. Yet her husband was steadfast:

'We're leaving Cresslea, Mara, and that's an end to it. It's for the best.'

Realising now he wouldn't be swayed in this, she had no choice but to let it drop. Accepting it, however, was another thing entirely.

'I spoke with the master about us going,' Roger announced the following evening as they were eating.

Mara knew that for him to have let the idea be known to Luke Braithwaite meant he was indeed serious about this. Her stomach flipping, she put down her spoon.

'Oh? And what did he have to say?'

'That he'd be sorry to lose us but that he understands our reason. In fact, he went so far as to offer to help.'

'How?'

331

'His mother dwelled in Bolton town afore coming here, did tha know?'

She nodded. 'I did. Meg told me when I first met her.'

'Well, Mrs Braithwaite knows a lot of influential families up there. The master reckons he could persuade her to write to a few, find out whether any of them are in need of staff. It's worth a try. Bolton might only be ten miles or so from here – not far enough for my liking, if I'm honest – but well, it'd suit us for now, eh?'

Doing her best not to let her tears fall – this was all becoming horribly, fearfully real – she murmured an agreement and returned her attention to her meal.

For the remainder of the day and throughout the ones that followed, she prayed to God in her mind that nothing would come of Mrs Braithwaite's enquiries and that Roger's plans, if not dismissed altogether, would at the very least be forced to one side until an alternative presented itself.

Her efforts, however, had no effect.

During Saturday afternoon, her husband came to find her whilst she was on her break in the courtyard to inform her that he'd just had news from the master.

'A family of good standing, and previous neighbours to Mrs Braithwaite, have agreed to an interview. They've been made aware of your delicate condition and understand it wouldn't be wise for thee to travel, and so they've suggested they see me on my own. If they think me satisfactory and I accept the position, they're willing to take you on unconditionally as well.'

'Without seeing or speaking to me first?' She had to admit it was an extremely generous offer.

'They're prepared to trust the word of the Braithwaites, who they hold in high esteem. So what d'you think?'

Mara had to fight the urge to heave a sigh. What she thought was that she didn't want this, didn't want to go to Bolton, to leave here and all they knew and loved. And yet, as her husband, it would ultimately be Roger's decision to make. Women – and wives particularly – didn't get the final say, and especially not in matters of this importance. It was how it was and she accepted it, but oh how she wished they could stay!

'Lass?'

Dragged back to the present, she met his gaze. Then, damping down her own wants and desires, she nodded bravely. 'If you think it the right thing to do . . . aye, let's do it.'

Smiling in relief, Roger stooped to kiss her, 'We'll make it work, Mara. Just you wait and see.'

'When will they interview ye?'

'Tomorrow. I'm to catch the train and be at the house in Chorley New Road by one o'clock.'

Seeing him off the following morning, Mara's mind was a mire of conflicting emotions. In comparison, Roger appeared collected and carried about him an air of quiet confidence; as she'd learned to, she quashed her misgivings and brought to her mouth a smile.

'Good luck, lad.'

'Ta, Mara.' He embraced her, then with a frown cast his stare across the open fields.

Guessing what troubled him, she was quick to offer reassurance. He'd sent word to her four friends yesterday asking them to arrive for their usual Sunday meet-up earlier than they normally would, to save Mara being alone in his absence. 'They'll be here any minute, so they will, don't worry. And look, Cuthbert's here to protect me until they are,' she added, indicating the dog sitting by the cottage door. 'You go on.'

Though he nodded, still he remained where he was, chewing his lip, brows knotted.

'Roger, you'll miss your train.'

'Thank God,' he said suddenly, motioning ahead at the three familiar figures making their way towards them. In the next moment, Meg, too, appeared from the direction of the manor. Satisfied, Roger bade his wife goodbye and took his leave.

Over the next two hours, her friends did their utmost to distract her thinking – and when that failed focused instead on assuring her that all would work out for the best – however, Mara just didn't have the energy to pretend agreement. Drowning her sorrows in yet another cup of tea, she was lamenting for the dozenth time her heartache at the prospect of being parted from them all when, out of nowhere, a torrent of warm water gushed from between her legs.

Locked in shock, for almost half a minute the five women simply gazed at each other open-mouthed. Then they were all gabbling at once.

'It's too early.'

'Nay, Mara, not by much,' Aggie insisted, hurrying across to chafe her hands.

'Mary should be sent for,' she told them, trying her hardest to keep her calm and crossing to the bed to begin preparations. 'The last time . . . it was over fairly quickly. It wouldn't be wise to take any chances, so.'

Meg darted off to collect the maid-cum-midwife from the manor and, in the meantime, Aggie and Belle helped their friend into the bed – Daisy, looking scared stiff, young as she was, remained by the fire, wringing her hands.

By mid-afternoon, Mara's pains were at their pinnacle – sweating and panting, she positioned herself on all fours in readiness for the final crux.

Facing her in a line at the foot of the bed, the four women murmured constant encouragement:

'We're here, my lass, don't you fret,' reassured Aggie.

'Soon be over, Mara,' Belle said.

'Eeh, but you are brave!' breathed Daisy.

'Go on, love, you can do it,' Meg told her.

Mara nodded. Then, closing her eyes, she awaited the next contraction with grim focus.

Standing behind her, poised to assist the crowning, Mary took a deep breath. 'Ready?'

'Ready,' Mara whispered. On a long, low grunt, she bore down with all her might.

'Push, lass!' her friends shouted. 'Push!'

'It's here! You've done it!' announced Mary, catching the bundle in her expert grip.

The following few seconds, as she waited, eyes squeezed shut, not daring to look, seemed to Mara to last a lifetime. Then the most amazing sound she'd ever heard ripped through the stuffy room – the child sucked in one great gasp and released a squawk of such volume it almost brought the roof down.

'You have a fine, healthy girl.'

Laughing, Mara took her daughter into her arms and gazed in awe at the plump and rosy miracle. Then, burying her face into the baby's neck, she burst into tears and cried her joyful heart out.

'He's here.'

The room made for a serene sight. A fire burned in the grate, creating cosiness, its gentle crackles soothing. The bed had been stripped and remade, and a cleaned and changed Mara now lay snug and warm within, the brand-new babe wrapped in her woollen shawl sleeping peacefully in her arms.

Aggie, Belle and Daisy had left for home shortly before and, now, only Meg remained. She'd been awaiting Roger's return by the window – finally, it had come.

'I'll take myself off now, let youse all be alone,' she said as she headed to the door. 'Well done, Mara, and good luck, love. I'm so very happy for thee.'

'Thank you, lass, for everything.'

With a last smile at mother and child, the maid slipped out.

'What's wrong?' Mara heard her husband ask moments later from the pathway. 'I know there's summat – I can see it in your eyes . . . Conrad. Dear God, he's not—'

Meg cut him off with a chuckle. 'Nay, nay. Go on inside and see for yourself.'

'Wha—?' Drinking in the scene, he came to a juddering halt.

Mara cast him a soft and tranquil gaze. 'Roger. Meet your daughter.'

He crossed to them as though in a dream. After pressing his lips to his wife's forehead, he dropped his stare to the child. Eyes gleaming with tears in the candlelight, he brushed a small cheek with his finger and a sigh of wonder whispered from him to encompass the completed family.

'She's . . . ?'

'Absolutely perfect.'

'Are we still in agreement with the name we decided on if it were a girl?'

'Rebecca,' Mara confirmed. There was no other in the world it could be.

'Nothing – *nothing* – will ever come between us three. I'll protect youse with my life until my dying breath, I swear it.'

He'd delivered his vow with total certitude. She knew he'd made it with Conrad in mind. 'The interview?' she forced herself to ask.

'Aye. The positions are ours.'

'Right, so.'

His attention captured by the child once more, Roger failed to notice Mara's frown of despair.

Chapter 26

'WAKEY, WAKEY.'

The words close to Mara's ear had her bolting upright with a gasp.

This time, the room wasn't inky black but lit dimly by the fire, which they had left burning low to keep the baby warm. She was able, therefore, to take in her surroundings. However . . . nothing.

She scanned the space again, peered into every corner just to be certain, but no – Conrad wasn't here. And yet she'd been so sure . . . It *had* been his voice, and he'd uttered that same demand to her as the last time he broke in.

Perhaps – no, not perhaps, she corrected herself, for it was the only explanation – she'd been dreaming. But dear God, it had been so *real* . . .

'Guess who?'

Now, there was no denying the truth; she was wide awake and had heard it clearly – jumping from the bed, she yelled her husband's name. Yet when her eyes came to rest on what should have been him, she saw that the space where he slept was empty. Roger wasn't here.

'What . . . ?' she began, struck frozen with fear and confusion. Then, in the next breath, as the grinning face appeared near her feet: 'No. Lord, no!'

Conrad slithered out on his back from under the bed, where he'd been hiding all along, and got to his feet. 'Long time no see, eh, Ma?'

The look in his eyes was one Mara had never seen before; it chilled her to the very marrow. She took an involuntary step back. 'Where is my husband?' she rasped. 'You get gone from here, d'you hear me? Get out!'

'Not this time. This ends tonight, bitch.'

As if in slow motion, Mara watched him swing around. Though she sensed his intentions instantly, she could do nothing for a split second – by then it was too late. Conrad pounced on the little wooden cradle. Grabbing a fistful of the baby's gown, he snatched her up by the scruff of her neck.

Mara let out a blood-churning scream. She made to launch herself towards him, but his next move had the power to seize her limbs as well as her heart. 'Please, no – please, please, no!'

'I would, you know.' He was holding Rebecca above his head as though to throw her to the hard ground. 'For two pins I'd dash this brat's brains out on these here flagstones without a second's thought.'

'Conrad . . . *Buachaill go maith* . . .' Her breaths came in sharp bursts. She couldn't lose another child, she *couldn't*. 'Give her to me. I beg you, please; she's but a few hours old—'

'Don't you think I know that?' he murmured. 'You reckon me turning up the night is coincidence? Nay. Eeh, nay. I've been watching, waiting, planning this out for months.'

Ever so slowly and with great subtlety, Mara inched forward as he raged on with his manic vitriol.

'I had intended to break into yon cottage and stab you through the heart as you slept. I nearly did, an' all – everything was in place. Then, lo and behold, I find out you're with child. It turned it all on its head, aye, for I knew then there was a better way to make thee pay. Summat worse than owt you could even conjure up in your nightmares; oh, so much worse. Has tha cottoned on yet to what it might be?' he asked in a demonic, sing-song tone.

Moving towards him a little more, Mara shook her head.

'I'll tell thee then, shall I? It's simple, really: tit for tat. You took my family away from me and now I'm going to do the same to you.'

Ice filled her veins as her eyes swivelled back to the empty bed. 'Roger . . .'

'Gone.' Grinning, he wiggled his eyebrows. 'He were the first to meet his Maker.'

'No! No, it can't be, it can't, you're lying!'

'Aye? Then where is he?'

'Roger!' she shrieked at the top of her lungs. 'Roger! Roger!'

'The dead can't hear no more, don't tha know that?'

'No! Roger, Roger!'

'And now . . .' Conrad announced over her hysterics. 'It's time for his daughter to join him.'

'Don't do it, don't do it!'

'Get back!' he barked as she jerked across the floor. Then, thrusting out his arm towards the fire, he dangled the baby over the flames.

Choking on a gasp, she held up her hands in submission.

'Do you want me to toss it? Do you?'

'Please. Please.' She could barely form the words, so all-consuming was her stupefaction. 'I beseech ye.'

By now, Rebecca's distressed cries were renting the air – the agonising sound was like a blade to her mother's heart. Conrad had to shout to be heard over it: 'You think your pleas could ever be enough? You've taken away it all – I lost *everything* because of thee! My freedom, my brothers—'

'Eamon and Eugene – that wasn't my doing! Sure, it won't be for ever, you'll one day have them back.'

'And what of my father? Well?' he thundered when Mara cringed. 'I'll never get to see *him* again *any* day, will I? And why? Because of you, you stinking, filthy Irish whore! I must live with my loss – and now it's your turn.'

'No!' she screamed, diving through the air with outstretched hands as he swung his arm and released his hold on the child. 'My *baby*!'

In the same moment that Mara caught the hem of the gown, halting by some sheer miracle Rebecca's headlong journey into the fire, an ear-splitting bang exploded through the room.

Clasping her child to her chest, she turned to find Conrad gazing at her, his expression one of mild surprise. Moments later, he slumped to his knees. Then he fell forward to land face first on the ground and was still.

341

Taking in the back of his concaved skull oozing thick, dark blood, she blinked. Then she brought her stare up to the figure standing in the doorway.

'Sir . . .'

Luke Braithwaite dropped the smoking shotgun and held out a hand to her. On a cry, she ran to him and he held the two of them tightly.

'Cuthbert drew me here as I was taking him on his last walk of the night. It's like he somehow knew . . . Thank God I listened and returned for my gun.'

'Roger . . . Conrad's killed him. Roger's dead!'

'No, no.'

Her head sprang back on her neck to search the master's face.

'It appears that O'Hara lured him from the cottage with murder in mind and ambushed him. Lawson is lying outside. He's unconscious but alive.'

'Oh!'

Scrambling past him, Mara flew for the door and out into the dark night.

She found her husband spreadeagled on the path, the master's dog sitting protectively beside him. Though blood trickled down his face from a nasty stab wound to his head, Luke had been right: Roger still breathed.

'Darling? Darling, I thought I'd lost ye . . . Husband, speak to me,' she pleaded.

'Mara?'

'My love!'

Eyelids fluttering, he grimaced in pain. 'I heard a noise outside . . . there were no one there. I don't remember owt, owt more . . .'

342

'Sshhh, save your strength. It's going to be all right, so it is. And d'you know why?'

'Tell me.'

Looking from her husband to her daughter, Mara smiled through her tears. 'Because our family is free, free to live and to love, and naught else matters. Nothing can touch us now.'

'Mara?'

'It's over, lad. It's over.'

Epilogue

'LIKE THIS, DARLING. That's it, see how Mammy does it?'

Her cherry lips pursed and green eyes wide with concentration, Rebecca thrust out a chubby, dimple-knuckled hand and plucked a flower from the pile. Under her mother's gentle instruction, she placed it alongside the other bright-coloured blooms.

'There now; sure, who's a clever girl then?' Mara said, gathering them up into a posy and securing the stems together with white ribbon. She placed it alongside the other nosegay in her basket and rose from the warm grasses. 'Come, my darling. Take Mammy's hand, that's it.'

At a leisurely pace, enveloped in nature's song, the two of them set off across the sun-drenched meadow.

The girl's small legs had long since grown tired by the time they reached the cemetery.

Hitching her daughter up in her free arm, Mara nodded ahead. 'Sure, we're here, so we are. Would you like to walk, now?'

Rebecca nodded, and the second her clogged feet touched the ground she was away, toddling off in front towards the gates. Smiling, Mara followed on.

Their first stop was baby Roger's grave. Here, Mara lifted from her basket the wild bluebells and pressed her lips to the petals. She passed the bunch to her daughter and the girl laid them atop the soil covering her brother.

Kneeling side by side and swaying gently, their arms around each other, mother and daughter said a prayer. Then they rose and, after saying a goodbye, crossed the burial ground towards their next destination.

The remaining posy in the basket was one of early daffodils – bringing it out, Mara repeated the same action: she blessed the flowers with a delicate kiss then handed them to Rebecca.

With as much care as before, the youngster placed them down on the resting spot of her namesake. Again, mother and child held one another and said a prayer.

After a murmured goodbye to her cousin, Mara stood. Hand in hand once more, she and her daughter headed back towards the gates.

'Aggie?' Rebecca asked excitedly as the familiar street came into view, and Mara smiled.

'That's right, darling, we're going to see Aunt Aggie. And then, afterwards, we'll pay a visit to Aunt Belle and Aunt Daisy, too. Sure, won't that be grand?'

The girl showed her agreement with a hop and skip of excitement.

Dusk was setting in by the time the pair eventually made their way back to Kersal. However, the gathering shadows creeping in across the solitary hillsides created within Mara not a trace of concern. Not now; these days, nothing could. She felt and was as free as a bird.

Then she saw him.

Her husband, her life, come to meet them. Raising an arm, she waved with a heart full of love.

'Da! Da!'

'Hey!' Roger caught his daughter in his strong arms and twirled her around before holding her little body close. 'My big, bonny lass. Did tha have a good day?'

'Oh, she did,' Mara answered for her with a chuckle. 'She was made a big fuss of, as usual, and sure didn't she love every minute of it? She has everyone wrapped around her finger, so she does.'

'And rightly so, eh, sweetheart? Speaking of which, I do believe Aunt Meg is waiting for thee . . .'

'Cake?'

The besotted father laughed down into Rebecca's grinning face. 'Aye, she's got some freshly baked ready and waiting for thee. Go on and see her – Cuthbert's waiting for thee, an' all.'

Set loose, the girl scampered off in the direction of Cresslea Manor; following on at a slower pace, their arms around each other, her parents watched her go with a smile.

'Have I mentioned yet today how much I love thee?' asked Roger, nuzzling Mara's neck.

She laughed softly. 'Only half a dozen times.'

'Is that all?' He drew her to a halt. Putting his hands around her waist, he lifted her up until her lips were on a level with his own. 'I love you,' he murmured before proving it with a slow and tender kiss.

'And I love ye, lad.' She smoothed a fingertip across the

faded scar by his temple and, as it was wont to, the image of Strangeways prison flashed faintly in her mind. 'Whatever the future holds . . .'

'We'll overcome it,' he told her. 'Us, Mara for ever.'

'Always.'

ABOUT THE AUTHOR

Emma Hornby lives on a tight-knit working-class estate in Bolton and has read sagas all her life. Before pursuing her career as a novelist, she had a variety of jobs, from care assistant for the elderly, to working in a Blackpool rock factory. She was inspired to write after researching her family history; like the characters in her books, many generations of her family eked out life amid the squalor and poverty of Lancashire's slums.

If you loved *A Mother's Betrayal*, pre-order Emma Hornby's brand-new page-turning WWII saga . . .

A Daughter's War
Worktown Girls at War: Book 2

For Renee Rushmore, the arrival of war brings some much-needed freedom. Her father rules the house with an iron fist, and Renee is desperate to escape him.

With men leaving for battle in their droves, she manages to find work on an understaffed farm, where she meets kindly lad Jimmy. She and Jimmy quickly fall in love, but when he is called up to war, and she is thrown off the farm due to a misunderstanding, Renee is forced to go home.

Jimmy's safe return is her only hope of a happy future, but the end of the war is a long way off, and her father is getting worse.

Will she be able to survive the bombs, and her father's cruelty, and find her way back to Jimmy?

AVAILABLE FOR PRE-ORDER NOW

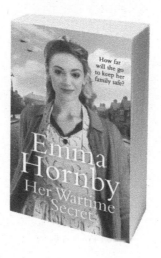

With all the odds stacked against her, can Phoebe find the strength to overcome her past . . .?

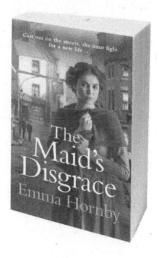

Phoebe Parsons is a liar . . . a shameless harlot
with unscrupulous morals . . .

Phoebe Parsons is destitute, disgraced, and alone. After her mistress tragically dies, Phoebe is forced back on to the poverty-ridden streets of Manchester by her unforgiving new master. Desperately searching for work as a domestic maid, Phoebe soon discovers her reputation is in ruins.

Fearing for her future and haunted by the harshness of her abandonment, Phoebe finds herself living with thieves and drunks in the smog and squalor – until she meets Victor Hayes. An officer removed from his duty and shamed by a cruel lie, Mr Hayes is a kind face among the uncertain threats of living in the alleyways. But Phoebe soon realises the sacrifices she must make to rebuild from the ground up . . .

As their two worlds collide, can they make a new life
from the wreckage? Or will the judgement of
their peers make a pauper of Phoebe?

AVAILABLE NOW

She thought she was finally safe. But a roof over her head comes with a price to pay . . .

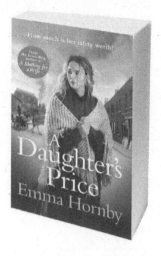

Laura Cannock is on the run. Suspected of killing her bullying husband, his family are on a merciless prowl for revenge. Fleeing from her beloved home of Bolton to Manchester, Laura seeks refuge with her coal merchant uncle. But it soon becomes clear that a roof over her head comes with a price – of the type so unbearable she must escape once more.

Destitute and penniless, a stench-ridden housing court in the back streets of the factories is Laura's only hope of a dwelling – a place where both the filth and the kindness of neighbours overwhelm. Here people stick together through the odds, leading Laura to true friendship, and possibly love.

But with the threat of her past still hanging over her, there's still one battle she must fight – and win – alone . . .

AVAILABLE NOW

JOIN OUR SAGA COMMUNITY

Penny Street

Stories You'll Love to Share

Penny Street is a newsletter and online community bringing you the latest book deals, competitions and new saga series releases.

You can also find extra content, talk to your favourite authors and share your discoveries with other saga fans on Facebook.

Join today by visiting:
www.penguin.co.uk/pennystreet
and follow our Facebook page:
https://www.facebook.com/welcometopennystreet/

Page
TURNERS

Great stories.
Unforgettable characters.
Unbeatable deals.

WELCOME TO PAGE TURNERS.
A PLACE FOR PEOPLE WHO LOVE TO READ.

In bed, in the bath, on your lunch break.
Wherever you are, you love to lose yourself in a brilliant story.

And because we know how that feels, every month we choose
books you'll love, and send you an ebook at an amazingly low price.

From tear-jerkers to love stories, family dramas and gripping
crime, we're here to help you find your next must-read.

Don't miss our book-inspired prizes and sneak peeks into
the most exciting releases.

Sign up to our FREE newsletter at
penguin.co.uk/newsletters/page-turners

SPREAD THE BOOK LOVE AT